MAR 2015

A MEASURE OF LIGHT

A Measure of Light

BETH POWNING

ALFRED A. KNOPF CANADA

PUBLISHED BY ALFRED A. KNOPF CANADA

Copyright © 2015 Powning Designs Ltd.

www.penguinrandomhouse.ca

Knopf Canada and colophon are registered trademarks.

Library and Archives Canada Cataloguing in Publication

Powning, Beth, author
A measure of light / Beth Powning.

Issued in print and electronic formats.

ISBN 978-0-345-80847-9
eBook ISBN 978-0-345-80848-6

1. Dyer, Mary, –1660—Fiction. I. Title.

PS8631.O86M43 2015   C813'.6   C2014-906378-4

Text design by Leah Springate

Cover design by Five Seventeen

Cover image: © John Foley / Arcangel Images
Endpapers image: Courtesy of the Massachusetts Archives,
Mary Dyer's 1659 letter to the General Court, written from the Boston jail

Printed and bound in the United States of America

2 4 6 8 9 7 5 3 1

Penguin
Random House
KNOPF CANADA

To
my mother
Alison Brown Davis
with love

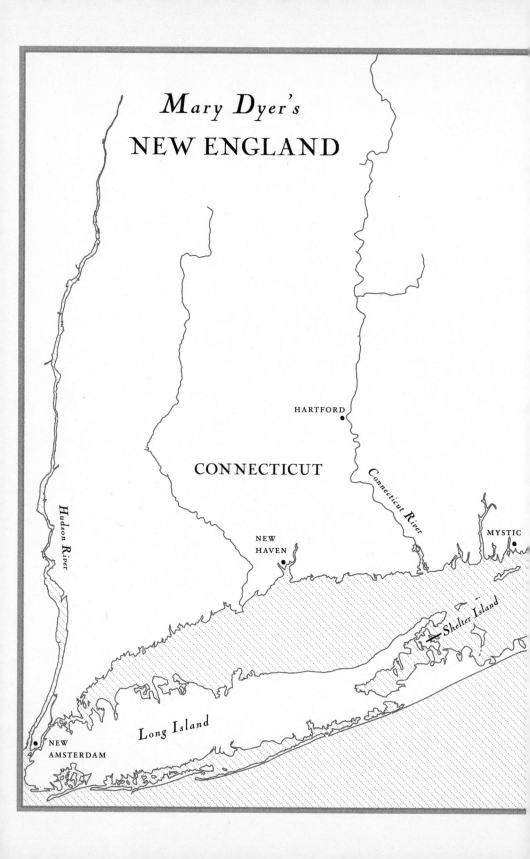

Mary Dyer's
NEW ENGLAND

HARTFORD

CONNECTICUT

Connecticut River

MYSTIC

Hudson River

NEW
HAVEN

Shelter Island

Long Island

NEW
AMSTERDAM

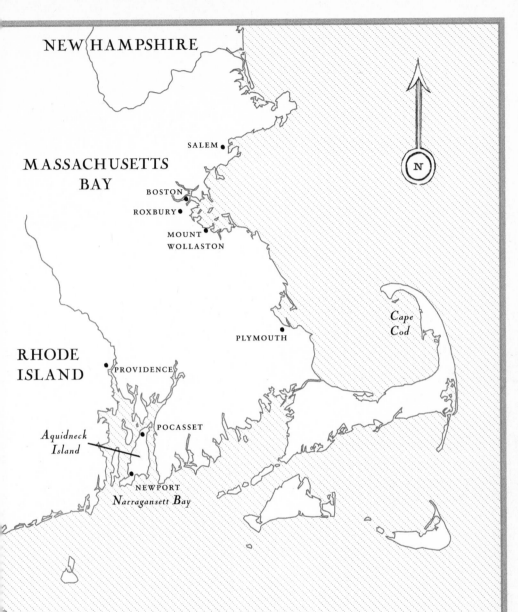

NEW HAMPSHIRE

MASSACHUSETTS
BAY

SALEM

BOSTON
ROXBURY

MOUNT
WOLLASTON

Cape
Cod

PLYMOUTH

RHODE
ISLAND

PROVIDENCE

Aquidneck
Island

POCASSET

NEWPORT
Narragansett Bay

Atlantic Ocean

N

I have laboured carefully, not to mock, lament, or execrate,
but to understand human actions . . .

SPINOZA
Tractatus Theologico-Politicus, 1677

CONTENTS

✳

I.

LONDON

1634

We die and rise the same, and prove
Mysterious by this love.

"The Canonization"
JOHN DONNE

ONE

Martyr's Blood - 1634

SNOWFLAKES BLEW UP THE THAMES on an east wind. Mary picked her way along the narrow streets, heading to the market. It was the day before Christmas. Ropes of holly and ivy sprigged with rosemary looped across wood-and-plaster houses; the air was filled with the yeasty scent of baking, sweetening the stench that rose from gutters. She stepped quickly around a dead dog that lay in half-frozen mud, maggots teeming in its entrails.

Mary heard the screams and shouts of a crowd. The sounds grew louder, rising over London's din of bells, wheels, hammers, shrill-voiced vendors. Like a fish in a weir, she could not resist the press of bodies and was funnelled into a square where people massed before a wooden platform. Three men stood upon it with heads and arms thrust through pillories. Women and children leaned from windows studying the gallants, ladies, merchants, apprentices, beggars, thieves, prostitutes. Breath hung before mouths like the morning webs of spiders.

Mary found herself shoulder to shoulder with a small man. He held a rag to bleeding gum.

"What was their crime?" she shouted, leaning close.

"Puritans," he slurred. Fresh blood seeped into the fabric's weave. "Who did naught but write pamphlets against the king's new . . ." He paused to spit. "Archbishop."

A flash of metal—on the platform, the hangman drew his knife and stepped towards one of the three prisoners. Over the crowd's excitement and protest, a howl rose, broke into a scream. The hangman dropped one of the prisoner's ears into a bucket. Blood spurted from the mutilated scalp. People rushed to the platform holding up bowls, shreds of cloth, sticks.

Martyr's blood. People held such blood in reverence—a purifier of souls, like the waters of baptism.

The hangman stretched out the man's other ear tight as a hen's neck. A fresh roar erupted from the crowd. The knife rose again, sliced down.

Why torment a man so old? Perhaps fifty.

His skin was yellow as spring parsnip; he twisted against his restraints, his mouth a cave. Blood poured down his neck. The hangman pinched one of the prisoner's nostrils, snagged his knife to its edge, made a jagged upward cut.

Mary heard blood rush in her own ears, suffered a drastic dimming of vision. She fought her way from the crowd, stopped against a recessed door in the relative calm of a nearby street.

She had sought nothing more than the ingredients for a Christmas pudding.

Walk, and you will not faint.

Her Aunt Urith's voice came to her, stern, practical, and so Mary took a breath and set forth again. Between the snow and coal smoke, the streets were dark by three in the afternoon; already, people followed link-boys who carried torches, their quivering light reflecting in diamond-shaped windowpanes.

Mary purchased veal, mutton, raisins, nutmeg and cloves. Abstracted, she neither chose nor bargained wisely and then turned southwards, towards home, a small house just down-river from Whitehall, the king's palace.

The walk steadied her. She shifted her bundles, waited for a cart to pass, went down a short street. At its end, she could see the masts of riverboats crossing in the snowy dusk. She pushed open the oak door and set her bundles on the table. Only then, as she removed her scarf and hung her cape, did her hands begin to shake.

Upstairs in the bedchamber her breath steamed on the cold air. She stirred the coals, wound a wolverine fur around her neck and pulled a chair close to the hearth. She took up her Bible but could not read, so pressed it to her breast. Her heart beat fast and light.

The ear, falling through the air like a scrap of meat.

William was a birthright Puritan. She herself was a convert.

The door opened below and she heard her husband's voice. His steps came, eager on the stairs. He burst into the room, smelling of snow and leather, pulling off his gloves. He held a small box.

"I have a gift for—"

"William, I came upon three men in pillories. Puritans. Perhaps they were clergy, I do not know." She hugged the Bible closer, took a long breath. "The hangman did slice off two ears and slit a nostril."

He was not much taller than she, sleek as a ferret. He set the box down, held her face; she smelled the sweetness of jasmine and roses. He was a haberdasher and had a shop in the New Exchange; he washed his hands daily, for he must be gentle with the palms of great ladies, even those of the queen herself, introducing fingers into pearled gloves, delicately tugging gauntlets up plump arms.

"You were not hurt?"

"Nay, William." Her voice held the broadened vowels of Yorkshire.

His lips tightened. His hands fell from her face and he sat, bleak, forgetting the gift. For awhile they did not speak, as if the danger they faced was like shame, whose contemplation was ugly.

"Must be they were clergy," he said. "Archbishop Laud has his spies, now. They sit quietly in churches and report those preachers who refuse the new rules."

"They are required to wear the surplice."

"Aye, and must bow at the name of Christ, and must follow the Book of Common Prayer to the letter and . . ." He spread his hands. "All the rest of it."

Aye, the rest.

"Many are leaving," William continued. "I hear another ship hath sailed for New England. 'Tis rumoured that Archbishop Laud may close the borders."

"Do you think we should go, William?"

He reached for a pamphlet they had been reading aloud to one another. He turned the pages, frowning.

"Boston . . ." he murmured. "Its bay is 'free of cockling seas' with 'high cliffs that shoulder out the boisterous seas.' Every family hath a well of sweet water. 'Those that drink it be as healthful, fresh and lusty as those that drink beer.'"

Mary held out her hand for the pamphlet.

"'Wolves, ravenous rangers, frequent English habitations,'" she read. "'Big-boned, lank-paunched, deep-breasted, prick-eared, dangerous teeth, great bush tails . . . they set up their howlings and call their companies together at night to hunt, at morning to sleep.'" She closed the book, handed it back. "You have your lease, William, your customers."

She crossed her arms to snug the fur closer around her neck. Brown curls, flattened by a linen cap drawn by a string at the base of her neck, framed her forehead; sensing her own doubt, she bit the lips of a mouth so wide, so sensitive, that its tender half-smile, should she catch sight of it in windowglass, bore no relationship to her feelings.

"In Massachusetts, they are free," he said, as if reasoning with himself.

The scene swept over her like a wave of nausea. How delicately the hangman had pinched the nostril between his fingers. How carefully he had positioned the knife.

—

Propped against the bolster, naked, she stared up at the ceiling cloth. Beneath the coverlet, William lay sprawled on his back, one leg thrown over hers. He slept.

As I cannot . . .

She felt herself to be poised between two places of equal, but different, terrors. Here, in England, persecution. There, in New England—wolves, forests, fierce winters.

In either place, however, she would have William.

She had met him at the church of St. Martin-in-the-Fields. Sensing eyes upon her, she had looked across the aisle and seen a young man, narrow face framed by short-cropped hair, green eyes long as willow leaves. He had worked his way through the crowd, afterwards, so they would pass through the door together. In the tumult of the street, she could not move for the intensity of his gaze. He lifted her hand and for the first time she smelled the perfume of his gloves. Then he bowed, spoke: "William Dyer." "Mary Barrett," she answered. They exchanged what information was needful, and he came to her cousin's apartment, where Mary resided, and they went about the city throughout the summer, and married in the fall.

Love for the young man mingled with another joy—the ecstasy of conversion.

A journey.

So the lecturer called it. Some, he warned, would be unwilling to "loose" themselves from all they would leave behind. Yet others, who shed all regrets and desires, might "join the company of saints," a way that was not taken up by the "shell of religion," as he called it, but the "one true way that leadeth unto Life."

She turned on her side, relaxed by memory, and ran a finger along William's collarbone and over the curve of his waist. She felt the stir of his soft prick in her hand, heard his changed breath. He rolled over, tugged at the sheet and tossed it away. Tongues—muscular, agile—while his hand slid to what was no longer hers alone but a shared secret. His fingers, making her mind fly and shatter. *Journey. Join. Loose myself. Loose myself.* Pain as he entered her, and then the conjoining, surprising in its ease. Their mingled cries, the shudder of seed. *Child, make a child.*

On Christmas morning, they made their way through the palace of Whitehall, a vast warren of buildings jumbled on the north bank of the Thames. The scent of roasting meat oiled the air; servants laden with linens and steaming platters choked its alleys. Snowflakes drifted, wide-spaced, wavering, as if threaded on invisible strings.

They entered an apartment overlooking the jousting yard.

"Your coif, Mary, always tipped. There." Mary endured her cousin's possessive touch as Dyota, childless, adjusted the black silk, popping finger to mouth, slicking the curls on Mary's forehead. Cousin Ralf, the king's Master of Robes, appeared in a high-crowned hat, a mustache waxed at the tips, long hair hanging in curls. In the window's cold light, he bent sternly to inspect the yellow leather of William's gloves. The men stood, then, looking out over the quintain and its sandbag, capped with snow.

"Business is good?" Ralf spoke with delicate respect. With two fingertips, he stroked a mole on his cheek.

"The queen hath visited my stall. I have ordered a half-dozen gloves."

"A gift?"

"Nay, for herself. One pair is of white leather, with satin gauntlets." William sketched curves on the air. "Silk arches on the tabs surrounding sea monsters and serpents. And a band of tulips, carnations and lilies."

Only sixteen, I was, Mary thought, handing a Christmas pudding to the serving girl and unhooking her cape, when Urith sent me to

London. "Dyota will find you a husband," Urith had said, with love and regret, placing her hands on Mary's shoulders as if to reassure herself of the girl's strength.

They took their places at a long table. Dyota fussed with her napkin, her lace collars, her garnet necklace.

Hard to believe Urith is her mother.

Urith was not only a midwife but a specialist in the healing of eyes, so skilled that a surgeon in York sent her his difficult cases. Her words were direct and honest; her hands, when not needed, took their rest.

Ralf spoke the prayer. Mary glanced at her young husband. He gave her the shadow of a wry smile before bending his head. They were seated opposite one another, close enough to touch feet. Ralf and Dyota sat far apart at the table's ends, like royalty.

"Amen."

Dyota rang a bronze bell for the serving girl.

Waiting, hands in lap, Mary remembered the day she and her older brother had gone to stay with Aunt Urith. Galfrid, her father, had bent to her, explaining that he had been called away from his surgery to perform an amputation and that he wished to take her mother, Sisley, to see the bluebells. "Only three days," he had said, "and we shall be home." *Bluebells. Fields of them, spreading to the horizon.*

"The king hath brought a European painter to make portraits of the family," Ralf said, lifting his spoon. He took a bite, chewed. His eyebrows lifted with a sorrowful expression, masking pride. "Van Dyck." His long fingers were particular from days spent rubbing gold buttons with a chamois cloth.

"We heard about it at last night's masque." Dyota shaped her mouth busily around the words. "Oh, 'twas brilliant. Inigo Jones did make the set and a man named Ben Jonson wrote the words. The queen herself acted."

Words flew between Dyota and Ralf, spoken rapidly, as if to exclude William and Mary. *Vatican envoys. Spanish diplomats.* Such a frail foundation for a life, Mary thought, eyes on her plate.

"I spoke with the queen's adorable dwarf!" Dyota said. A line of powder crusted the ledge of her double chin. The words of a lecture came to Mary's mind.

"*. . . a dead fly is but a small thing, yet it corrupts the most precious ointment of the apothecary and makes it stink . . .*"

Mary and William glanced at one another again, knowing they served as audience.

"Yesterday, Mary witnessed the mutilation of three Puritan clergymen," William said.

Burnings rose on Ralf's cheeks, his eyes watered.

"Do you know," William continued, holding his spoon with both hands as if to snap it with his thumbs, "'tis said that Archbishop Laud keeps a list of clergymen? He pens an 'O' beside those who are Orthodox. And a 'P' against those who are Puritans."

"I did *not* know," Ralf said, offended. "Where do you hear such things?"

"The Puritans of Lincolnshire have asked me to visit our people thrown in prison. Did you not know that the Tower begins to burst with clergy?"

Mary nudged his foot beneath the table, feeling that he displayed his information like wares on a table.

"You must not," Dyota breathed. "'Twould put Mary in danger. Perhaps even us."

With her vow of obedience, Mary had accepted her place in the hierarchy: the creatures of the earth, plants and animals, the lowliest; then children; then women. Then men. Above them all, God. She bore like a wooden collar knowledge of what was seemly or possible for a wife.

She drew breath, determined to voice her opinion.

"I would go myself, cousin," Mary said. She spoke calmly, cooling William's heat yet buttressing his indignation. "They have done no harm. Some of them were required to answer the Visitation Articles. Nine hundred questions and every one must be answered correctly. Who could manage such a task? No one. Not even those who pose the questions."

Ralf raised a hand, flicking away Mary's words. He leaned towards William.

"I do not know who is in the Tower, or why," he said. His lips quivered. "But keep your nose out of it, William. Those who put them there know the why and wherefore of it, and are better placed than you to have their reasons."

William pushed back his chair. He glared at Ralf. "Gold, silver, lace, stained glass, they would put in our churches. Papistry."

"I heard the queen brought her own confessor," Mary said. "And her Capuchin monks."

"'Tis nothing!" Dyota shrieked, suddenly, slapping the table with both hands. "'Tis her business. Ralf, make them stop this talk."

"Did you not hear?" William said. "Mary saw *clergymen in the stocks*. Having their ears sliced from their heads."

Ralf rose from the table. Love for his king was like a wasting sickness, Mary thought, seeing how shock rendered his skin translucent, like a porcelain glaze.

"'Tis unseemly talk for Christmas, William. You brought this subject to the table and it has spoiled the pudding. You see, your cousin could not finish."

Dyota pressed ringed hand to mouth, tears welling.

Wants me to go to her but I feel no pity . . .

They did not finish their own pudding and Mary did not retrieve the plate on which she had brought it.

—

In March, Mary told William. She had missed two months of her flowers.

When Dyota learned of Mary's pregnancy, she sent a letter of appeasement, with an invitation to visit.

Their time together became a matter of politeness—on Dyota's part, an avid disgorgement of court gossip; on Mary's, of answering questions about her health, which was of great fascination to her cousin.

Mary did not tell her that William went once a week to visit prisoners in the Tower; purchased and brought food, paper, and ink for them; wrote letters to his family in Lincolnshire informing them of what he heard or inferred concerning Archbishop Laud's intentions. She could not tell her of lectures they attended secretly in a Kensington home; or discuss the fact that the countryside was greatly disturbed by Puritans who went to the churches decorated under Laud's edicts— and smashed stained-glass windows, bludgeoned gold candlesticks, burned Books of Common Prayer. Or that Parliament had been shut down by the king, and that many of its members were Puritans.

Dyota bade her servant bring jellies and custards, fussed at Mary, urging her to indulge. Her eyes rested eagerly on her cousin's bosom, which swelled over the lace edging of her dress. Mary tugged at her collar, covering the plump flesh.

"Ah, Ralf and William," Dyota said, beseechingly. "Once the baby arrives they will forget their differences. We are family, after all."

Dyota gossiped with the wife of an earl, who confessed that her husband had brought a beautiful young serving girl from the Shetland Islands and could not keep his eyes from her. Dyota had bade the woman send the servant to Mary. Seeing the girl's sweetness and wondering at her terror, Mary hired her.

Sinnie replied to her mistress in an English filled with peculiar words. She whispered her lilting prayers in Norn, the other language of Shetland. At sixteen, she stood barely taller than a twelve-year-old girl and would not meet William's eyes. Her skin was the colour of cream, peppered with freckles.

On a day of cold rain, Mary and Sinnie sat by the fire in the hall of their little house. Mary picked spine and bones from the flesh of a poached carp. Sinnie pressed a coffin of sweet dough. The large room had but one high window and so by afternoon the soot-blackened walls leaned and shrank in firelight and shadow.

"Memory," Mary said. "*Do you remember the fish?* All I need say to my brother Wyl, and in our minds we will be crossing the bridge through the lilacs' perfume and the scent from the Kettlesing bake houses. And then we stop to watch the trout swimming in the Wharfe. Shadows a-quiver in the green water . . ."

Sinnie had set aside the coffin, was peeling onions. The papery skins fluttered to the floor. She glanced up at her mistress, met her eyes and looked away.

"Do you have brothers, Sinnie?" Mary asked. She was patient with the girl, who seldom spoke and when addressed was seized with fright.

"Aye," she whispered. Slices fell from her knife, circinate hoops juicy on the black wood. She blinked, her eyes filled with onion tears. "Two."

"And would it be as I said? You would speak a word and they would remember, the same as you?"

"Aye," Sinnie repeated. She took a breath, held the knife palm over knuckles, like holding hands with herself for courage. "I could tell of the greit sky over our croft on a spring morning—and if 'twere my brothers present, they would hear the dogs caaing the sheep or see the ponies with their klibbers and meshies and know what I meant if I said 'twas so clear we could see the far holmes and even the beaches of Hildesay."

The girl's longest sentence. She sees we are not so dissimilar.

"My brother died," Mary said. "I did learn of it shortly before you came to us. He went to sea. His ship was lost. Now I have lost mother, father and brother. We were orphans, you see. Our parents drowned together. A flash flood caught their carriage."

At the far end of the hall, a kettle of stew hung from the fire hook, steaming, and three-legged pipkins filled with mussels stood in the coals. Sun had not brightened the room for days. The streets were deep in black mud and the house, sprayed by passing drays, was splattered all the way to the second storey.

Sinnie looked up. Mary saw her eyes lighten with sympathy, and the hint of a sad smile, quickly repressed.

In the ill-lit room, Mary ran fishy hands over her belly. She had dreamed of how she would make for her child goodness and joy such as she had known so briefly, sitting in her mother's walled garden amidst forget-me-not and daffodils.

And now we are in danger. Here, in the place I thought to make a home.

"Soon I will feel the baby kicking," she murmured.

"I am a craft hand with a needle." Sinnie took a breath, lifted the knife. The catch in her voice betrayed how ardently she longed to be setting stitches in a baby's cap rather than weeping over onions. "I can make wee caps and curches and sarks."

The girl bent closer to her work, as if embarrassed by her confession.

Would she come with us?

TWO

Linseed and Lettuce - 1634

✳

WILLIAM AND MARY FOUND THE place, a narrow, tippy house on Blackfriars Street, six storeys high, squeezed by its neighbours like a book on a shelf. William knocked; the door opened a crack and a thin, ginger-haired man peered out. It was Mr. Bartholomew, who, they'd been told, was hiding parishioners from St. Botolph's, William's family's church. Laud had prevented several ships of emigrants from sailing to Massachusetts, so the family had come to London under cover of darkness.

William whispered his connections. The man vanished, reappeared. He opened the door and they slipped inside. The room was crowded. An older woman with wary hazel eyes stood at the hearth, facing the room, baby held over her shoulder, children pressed to her skirts. She watched William and Mary enter, her hand making small circles on the baby's back. Lines of worry marked her forehead, compassion etched creases beside her eyes. She observed them with an intransigence so strong that Mary felt a stab of fear.

"My name is Anne Hutchinson," the woman said. "This is my husband, Will. This is—" One by one, she introduced ten children and four adults: her sister, her brother-in-law, and two spinster cousins.

A servant girl brought a plate of aniseed jumbles. Only one window allowed the lingering, evening light of May; candles had been lit, illuminating pewter plates and varnished oak. The room's ambient rustle of whisper and movement settled.

Anne Hutchinson resumed the tale she had been telling. She recounted how plague had struck their village, Alford, three years earlier, and how they had lost sixteen-year-old Susan and eight-year-old Elizabeth. Devastated, she had withdrawn from friends and neighbours for a twelve-month, seeking solace in religion. Two more babes—her thirteenth and fourteenth—had since followed and she and her husband had made the decision to emigrate. Will had sold business, sheep and the house. They had loaded whatever belongings they would take to America onto carts and made the three-day journey to London.

The baby began to fuss and she settled it to suckle. "'Tis ever my practice to open the Bible at random to see where it pleaseth God to reveal himself. So I closed my eyes and placed my finger upon the page. It fell upon the passage in Isaiah: 'Thy teachers shall not be removed in a corner any more, but thine eyes shall see thy teachers.' Now, before my seclusion, I had been in the custom of holding conventicles at my home to elucidate the sermons of my teacher, the Reverend Cotton, for the women of the village. He had emigrated before. And thus it was revealed to me that we should go thither to the New World."

"The Reverend John Cotton?" said Mr. Bartholomew, amazed.

"Aye. He was forced to flee shortly after his marriage and did not see his wife again until, pregnant, she joined him on the *Griffin*. He is now in Boston and is eager to receive us."

Mary saw Mr. Bartholomew glance at his wife, eyebrows raised; then he cast a second look at Anne almost as if he could not believe his ears. Anne Hutchinson had spoken of the famous minister as if he were an equal, an associate, the way William would speak of his fellow merchants.

"His church was St. Botolph's, in Lincolnshire," Anne explained, as if geography might account for their association, yet Mary heard pride. She watched the woman's large hand stroking the baby's head and felt a small, urgent stirring in her womb.

Talk shifted to the voyage. The men spoke of the tools they had been advised to procure. The words—*frows, spades, axes, augers*—were hard in their mouths, making their chins jut and their eyes narrow. The women moved closer to one another, softer words blending. *Kettles, cradles, skillets, blankets.* Everything they owned was packed away in chests; none of these people belonged, anymore, to London or to England.

Sitting at a small table, William paged through the pamphlet, "New England's Prospect."

Mary, already in bed, put arms around her knees and studied him.

He opened his mouth as if to read aloud, then checked himself. He tossed down the pamphlet, stood, stretched. He undressed and came to bed.

Both sat against the bolster. Mary held the blanket against her chin, gazing at the window's pale square. William leaned his head back into clasped hands.

"They call it the 'New Jerusalem,'" he said.

October.

Mary woke to a violent cramp that seized her breath. Hearing her gasp, William laid a hand on her forehead. She opened her eyes as the pain faded and saw his fear.

"Go for them," she said. "I will pray."

He dressed, stumbling in his haste. He went to the attic door, called for Sinnie, clattered downstairs.

In thee, O Lord, she whispered, *do I seek refuge; let me never be put to shame; in thy righteousness deliver me . . .*

—

They named him William.

He glowed like an apple blossom, wrapped in white lambswool blankets. William wrote the glad news to Aunt Urith and Uncle Colyn.

The baby had long, sly eyes, like his father's. He glanced at Mary as he suckled, a froth of milk in the corners of his lips.

Two days later, his mouth fell slack on Mary's nipple. His limbs were limp, his tiny chest rose high in laboured breath. They sent for a doctor who applied a poultice of linseed and lettuce. By the end of his third day of life, the baby was dead.

William took the swaddling clothes and bade Sinnie pack them deep in a chest. He carried the cradle to a closet beneath the eaves. Mary broke into a fever and the midwife applied hot paper steeped in sage and vinegar to her swollen breasts; the doctor prescribed a paste of herbs to be bound to her wrists. William brought her a pair of gloves. Beige lambskin lined with peach-coloured silk, their gauntlets decorated with ferns of silver thread. He lifted her poulticed wrists, laid the gloves beneath her hands, stroked her knuckles. He wiped her face with a linen cloth.

"Mary, Mary. There will be another child."

God was watching her, holding her baby in his arms. She saw herself standing before him, penitent, weeping, although she lay dry-eyed on the flock-stuffed bolster. *Why?* More light than man, a shattering glory emanating warmth, he turned from her without answering. She felt alone in the dimming light, the last remaining member of her family. She wondered if God assumed her gratitude, since he carried her baby to the field of bluebells, sparing him all earthly sufferings. She stirred her head on the hemp sheet as this vision was replaced with another. *Punishment, not mercy.* She had refused a clear call. She had been meant to encourage William toward the New Jerusalem. For her own selfish ends she had not. She feared the voyage, the wolves, the savage forests. She had wished for a large London house with a garden running down to the Thames.

And God had led her into the presence of Anne Hutchinson. Follow the teachers.

Forgive me.

THREE

Truelove - 1634–1635

ON A NOVEMBER DAY OF bitter cold, Mary and William walked
through driving rain to the house of a Puritan couple. Others joined
them, and they sat grouped around the hearth, drinking bastard or
muscadine. They shared emigrants' letters whose pages were softened
from perusal, their folds worn thin. They took turns reading aloud.

. . . have built a meeting house . . .

*. . . the winter safely passed. Now we do begin our planting.
Cornfields have been impaled. The land is fat on the nearby islands
and hath been brought into good culture . . .*

*Building a mill for the grinding of corn. Large timber, marshland
and meadow doth give a good prospect . . . Beaver pelts, in such
abundance that . . .*

Trade with the Narragansett. Deerskin, baskets.

We do put the heads of wolves on pillars . . .

A woman drew a frightened breath.

"Aye, but we would have muskets," said a young man. "Think,
Margaret! 'Tis the *heads* of wolves they describe. Shot dead. As
some should be here." His voice darkened. "On the past Sabbath, as
we were coming from church, we did see men reeling beneath the
lattices of an alehouse, five of them. They were falling down, faces
red as if parboiled. A woman there was, begging, thin as a starved
dog, children at her skirts. The men did rip at her dress, exposing her
flesh. Two of her boys did protest and one of the men struck out. We

ran forward, but the ruffians ran, too. The woman was left sobbing. Her child's cheek was torn and bleeding."

In silence they contemplated how God's wrath would gather over England for such crime, for frippery and drunkenness, for excesses of wealth and poverty. They could not imagine this punishment but were certain it would come.

The men began to argue about whether they would be abandoning their church if they fled to New England. They would not, some reasoned, for they carried the flame of truth and would keep alive the pure church in the citadel of God's chosen people.

Their words were as cloaks masking the nakedness of obsession. They spread their fingers and then clutched emptiness, betraying a desire to hold firearms, oars, or the handles of ploughs.

Women spoke of more practical matters.

Will we have sheep? Make our own cloth? It seemed from the letters that every woman must be her own tailor, cowherd, malster, baker. They imagined snow falling on the clustered houses of Boston—snow so deep as to buckle paper windows. They dreaded the Narragansett Indians. They wondered if there would be doctors for their infants.

"Nay, Joan," a man said to his wife who had voiced her fears. He was earnest, urging. "Your *preachers* are there. 'Tis a holy enterprise."

Mary had regained her health. Her heart had been smoothed like sand with the waters of other women's assurances—*God took my firstborn; ah, Mary, love, they are angels, gone to Christ; you will have others.* She carried the weight of grief.

"I agree," she said. She held her elbows tight to her sides, folded her hands. Beneath a black coif, her face bore its first, fine perpetual creases—pained curves beside her generous mouth. "I did hear a woman say that her Bible told her to follow her teachers. I believe the Lord wishes us to go."

William spoke. "The Massachusetts Bay Colony hath moved both their charter and their place of meeting from England to the colony. A clever move. Charter, governor and General Court are all in Boston. So they make of themselves a self-governing commonwealth. They have removed themselves from the king's reach."

In September 1635, they waited in Plymouth. The inn's windows drummed with rain. For days, they could catch only glimpses of the small, high-prowed ship, ghostly in the harbour mist.

Early one morning, Mary lay staring at the low plaster ceiling. Pregnant, she had slept poorly. An urgent knocking on their door raised William from the bedstead.

The storm had passed. *Truelove* would sail on the high tide.

"All hands on deck!"

Officers ordered the families below as the sailors began preparations to weigh anchor.

"Do you come, Mary." William's pale face was flushed with the sea light. Beside him were Sinnie and Jurden Cooth. Twenty-two, Jurden was taller and broader than William, prematurely balding, an amused light in his eyes yet thin lips down-turned as if to repress comment. He accompanied them as their indentured servant.

"One minute," Mary said. "You go."

As rowboats hauled the ship out of the harbour, she leaned on the railing, remarking the sudden separation between herself, launched on a voyage of great danger, and the land left behind—stone houses nested below the rocking masts, the sky stippled with birds that wheeled in the autumn sky.

So it may be just before death. Not knowing what lies ahead. Reaching for God's hand.

She felt a pang of regret that the child, six months in her womb, would never know England. Ah, she thought, but it made its own urgent journey.

The deck rose and tipped beneath her feet like a living thing. As they reached the deeper water, the first sail rose, luffed, wavered, then settled itself—gaining familiarity with the sky, gathering the light.

Blankets and quilts hung from post to post along the ship's walls, swaying slightly, marking each family's berth. Below decks, it was dark even in the daytime, and she saw a confusion of details—a child's cap, rounds of cheese, red wool. Unbalanced by her belly, Mary grasped one post and then the next, hearing the whimpers of children and mothers' croons, while sailors' feet pounded close overhead. She found the blankets of their berth drawn back, Sinnie sitting in the far corner. Mary dropped beside her and leaned her head against the planks, listening to the rush of water against the wall.

I wish I could be on deck, watching England slip away.

She sat quietly, thinking that this would be one of many desires that would go unfulfilled.

"Puts me in mind of my home," Sinnie whispered and Mary saw that her face had flushed, as if she were excited. "The croft did feel like this, Mistress, just like this. I did sleep beneath the table with my brothers and sisters, all a-tangle."

A child began a quavery wail. Sinnie wrapped her hands around her knees, buried her head in her lap.

Mary felt the first qualms of seasickness. She lay on the damp straw mattress and brought to mind anything that did not rock, sway, tip, slide. The moors, Aunt Urith's house with its buttery stones, her first child, his gravestone a grey speck in London's reeking din.

They were like the ship's wash, her memories: purling white and crisp, then spreading into the moment.

Dear Lord, we beg of you, be with us now in our peril on the sea, for we do thy bidding.

The wind blew them southwest.

On fine days, families were allowed to gather on deck. The men stood along the railing. The girls lifted strings of cat's cradle from each other's fingers or dressed their Bartholomew dolls; boys flew makeshift kites. The women clustered in the lee of a deckhouse, shoulder to shoulder for warmth—sewing, knitting. Groups of young men—indentured servants—kept to themselves, Jurden Cooth among them.

On all sides was the blue furrowed emptiness.

Mary befriended a young woman from Lincolnshire. Thin, with a stretched, eager smile, she had three children, two girls and a boy. Her husband, a wool merchant, had left a fertile farm and a business built up over generations.

"Our minister was ejected and lost his living," the woman said. "After that we could not bear to go to church. We could not abide by the changes."

She raised her knitting close to her face, needle probing for a dropped stitch.

"We feared the Lord's wrath," she said. "We had a fine big brick house. But my Henry will build again. They say the land is rich."

"We lived in London where my husband had a business," Mary said. "He has brought goods to open a shop in Boston."

Three oak chests sat in the hold. One was filled with gloves, caps, needles, everything needed to start a business. Another held guns, shot and powder and all the farming tools that William had learned would be unattainable. Her own was packed with silver spoons, kettles, dresses. Bolts of linsey-woolsey, skeins of yarn, Irish stockings. Woollen capes, blankets.

The woman put down her knitting.

"I brought the seeds of my hollyhock," she said, wistfully. "Tall, it was, a lovely pink. I'll give you some. It grew beneath my kitchen window."

She looked at the shining waters for a long time.

"Are you frightened?" Mary asked. Her own hands were spread over her belly, receiving the baby's kicks, like a gift.

The woman started. "Aye, but I've told no one. I am ashamed to say so, for 'tis God's will we follow."

"God's commands are fearsome," Mary said. Her lips softened into a sad smile. "We are all frightened, surely."

She be beautiful, Sinnie thought. She curled on a pallet, watching as Mary prepared for bed. She longed to comfort her, for she saw that Mary grieved many things: her family, her tiny son, the people and hills of childhood. Sinnie's own lost world hung in her mind like a locket the size of a fingernail. Sheep, surf and wind splined with the cry of gannets, horsehair fishing lines laid to dry. Brothers and sisters. A mother with gaunt face, eyes drained of pity. *Exhausted, Mother were. She had to send me.* A feeling came, twisted, confused. Father, too, had sent her. Her parents had embraced her. She had ridden away on a pony, at the side of her new master. Sent to a better life. Her neck, jolting as she looked back, watching as they waved; she saw them turn away. Bitter, her heart. And that, too, was bad. They could not have known.

William bent to enter the berth. Sinnie pulled the blanket farther across her face, leaving one eye exposed. *So handsome.* Eyes like almonds, hands of a gentleman. Of a size, they were, William and Mary, when they stood side by side at the railing of the ship.

She with that baby growing big in her . . .

—

On a Sabbath, warmed by winds from the south, one of several ministers aboard took his turn holding worship in the open air. Afterwards, men gathered around the capstan to discuss his sermon. William and Mary stood at the edge of the group.

"He doth say that it killeth souls to be preached to by ordained ministers who are uneducated," a man said. "I agree that we must have men of highest education in our churches."

"Aye," Mary called out. She remembered the words of the Puritan lecturer in London. "But I have heard John Everard say that God is in you 'although you know it not.' That if you are born of the Spirit, you are Spirit. So I cannot see it is of such significance that a man be educated, for he may be educated and yet be hollow within, following rituals without Spirit."

Men turned, in their leather jerkins and hats—startled, eyes narrowed with affront. William's arm slid through hers. She felt a gentle tug.

"Aye, she has a point," a man said, mollifying, forestalling censure. He looked at her belly, exchanged a sympathetic glance with William.

Mary turned away. She bit her lips, felt the heat of blood risen from an agitated heart. William snugged her close as they walked the narrow, canting deck.

"Had you been born a man, Mary," William said, "I believe you would have been a minister. Or a magistrate." He smiled as if picturing the preposterousness of this.

"I have spent years making the same observation." She looked out over the surrounding glitter. Beneath the fierce Atlantic sun, she felt a shift in her feelings. After the death of their parents, Uncle Colyn, a lawyer, had begun teaching her brother, and had allowed her to study alongside. Scripture, logic, mathematics, Greek, Latin, history. *You have a brilliant mind,* he had told her. *Almost like unto a man's.* She had listened, appalled, to her uncle's accounts of injustice, had heard enraged voices coming from behind his study door. Since Aunt Urith was surgeon as well as midwife, Mary had stood at her side and accepted pus-soaked bandages, or bloody bits of amputations—fingers, eyelids. She had helped bathe bodies: women dead in the throes of childbirth; babies; old people. There had been no time for considerations about what a woman could or could not do in the teeming world of her aunt's surgery; or bent over in Uncle Colyn's study, dipping pen in ink, drying the page with cuttlefish powder from her pounce pot.

William was watching her—curious, unsure of her mood.

She did not return his look.

One week, two weeks. Three, four, five, six. Seven.

The king, the queen, the Archbishop of Canterbury, Whitehall, Dyota and Ralf, the tumbling bells, rattle of wheels, heads on pikes, crowd-jaunty hanging days, rats nuzzling entrails, falling ear and gaping wound and blood-soaked hair, *martyr's blood*: it all fell back. Day after day. Fell back. Dream-small and as nonsensical.

Watery soup, bearing maggots. Cheese hard as leather.

Truelove's bow rose, swivelled, fell.

Smiling, a smile not for her. He made a soft tomcat sound. Almost laughing, his eyes fixed upon her. He tugged Sinnie's ribbons. At night, when she closed her eyes for sleep, she saw the salt crusted in the corners of his mouth—his lips, caked with dead skin. Remembered his deliberate stumble, pressing up against her. *Excuse me, Miss.* Dreaded the coming day.

No man, ever. Ever.

—

From the bed, Mary and Sinnie could see the helmsman standing at the whipstaff, squinting up through a shaft of light to watch the sails.

"I will speak to William, Sinnie. He will not bother you again."

"Thank you, Mistress." A whisper. Too upset to talk. Wiping tears with the back of her sleeve. Mary gazed at her. *No wonder. Half the crew yearns to hear the burr of Shetland in her voice.*

"How did you come to leave your home, Sinnie?"

"'Twas what I dreamed. To go into service," Sinnie murmured. Her wet eyelashes were pointed, starry. "'Twas a man visiting the Earl. I was hanging fish in the skeo."

The girl's English was difficult. Mary raised her eyebrows, not wishing to interrupt, for she glimpsed truth like the corner of an envelope slipped beneath a door.

"A wee hut of stone. He asked my name and I did tell him. He said nothing but did ride away up the brae. Later, the Earl asked my father and my father asked me and I said aye. I said aye, I would go with the man to London to be his lady's maid. I was . . . I was . . ."

She bent as if struck with pain in her belly. Then a wail came from her and she snatched up a pillow and buried her face.

Mary sat, gripping her hands, witness to grief's loneliness. But Sinnie cried out only once and then stifled herself—rocking, rocking. The ship rolled and they slid together, pressed close, arms, hair.

"He were at me," she whispered, struggling up. "Agane and agane. I had . . ." Her mouth warped, her eyes touched Mary's belly and sheered away.

"Ah, no, Sinnie."

"Aye. He took me to a woman, rid me of it. Left me on that garret floor bleeding."

Tears brimmed and spilled. Mary eased them away with the back of her hand. Sinnie took Mary's hand, held it tightly.

"I will never marry, Mistress. I will never have babes."

—

A storm raged for two days. Their family bedstead, a slat with belongings tucked beneath, became like a nursery or a schoolroom, as the children flocked to Sinnie. Sinnie moved from berth to berth, holding bowls for vomit, bathing foreheads, feeding babies. Mary's mattress was soaked from wind-lashed water seeping through cracks. She was violently ill. She slept, exhausted; woke to find herself holding a basin of pottage, spoon in her own hand partway to her mouth. The ship rolled, the basin tilted and Sinnie snatched it, wiped her forehead with a cloth, murmured soothing words. Mary grew accustomed to the face so often close to her own, a fairy face whose blonde-lashed eyes bore a merriness notwithstanding their grief dark as the sea's blue.

One of the few literate women, Mary read aloud from the Bible. At first she read to the children and then others came to listen: mothers, aunts, grandmothers and older sisters. They gathered on the mattress, sat on the floor. The women awaited teaching or opinions, and Mary was surprised to find herself voicing them.

"I do wonder about the passage in Matthew 10.34, where Jesus says to his disciples: 'Do not think that I have come to bring peace on earth; I have not come to bring peace, but a sword.' Have you . . ."

She remembered how Uncle Colyn taught by questioning. How he led her into thickets of contradiction, helped her tease solutions.

". . . 'tis difficult, is it not? Down a bit he says, 'He who finds his life will lose it, and he who loses his life for my sake will find it . . .'"

Their eager eyes revealed puzzlement, pondering. Suddenly comprehending, they exclaimed. The men, in their own cluster, heard bursts of laughter, saw the women's heads nested like petals of a chrysanthemum in the Dyers' berth.

"You do us proud, Mary." A grandmother spoke, hoarse-voiced. "A woman with an education."

No, I cannot be minister or magistrate. But there may be other ways to use what I have been taught.

Mary looked down the dark, stable-like space. Some blankets were secured, tied tightly; others billowed as the ship rolled, exposing shoes scattered from neat rows, Bibles fallen from makeshift shelves. She wondered how, in the New World, she would be called upon. She felt the pleasure of a new status, imagined herself starting a dame school, or holding conventicles after sermons, as Anne Hutchinson had done.

Making a better world for the glory of God . . .

William and other men sat on the floor, filling the aisle. The lanterns creaked, swayed. The men bent, low voices augmenting the ship's complaints so that the women could not hear their words.

"What be they doing?"

"Drawing our houses."

Silence fell as the women mused upon this. They heard a man's voice rise as he read from a pamphlet.

"*. . . killed within a stone's throw of our house, above four score Snakes, some of them as big as the small of my leg, black of colour, and three yards long, with sharp horn on the tip of their tail . . .*"

Mary resumed reading, quickly. The two voices merged in a curious poetry.

"*. . . tinsel-winged grasshoppers . . .*"

"*He who receives you receives me . . .*"

"*. . . efts . . .*"

"*What did you go out into the wilderness to behold?*"

"*. . . chopped off with hatchet . . . purple blood . . .*"

William bore a new distraction when he returned to the berth, like a man privy to confidences.

—

Sinnie shook Mary's shoulder.

"They say they can smell land," she whispered.

"What is the hour?"

"Nearly daybreak."

A lantern creaked, regular as a clock, marking the waves. It threw shadows on William's sleeping body. Mary slid her arm over his shoulder, smelled his smoky, oily hair. She moved her lips against his ear.

"Land, William." She felt a sudden exhilaration, almost unbearable. To whisper, when she wanted to empty her lungs on the sound of joy. "Land!"

He woke, instantly. "Can you see it?"

"Nay," Sinnie said. "They can smell it."

The swells grew longer, drawing the bow deep, carrying swash higher on the hull.

One by one, eager faces appeared in the companionway door. Drowsy, tousled, eyes like startled ponies.

Light rimmed the eastern horizon and then the sun rose—the sails steamed and around them the sea sprang into its full palette of greens and blues.

The ship slipped into warmer air. Like relief from pain, it washed over them.

Sinnie pressed against Mary, shivering with excitement. William slid his arm around Mary's waist. Behind them stood Jurden, tall, silent.

All around them, people lifted their chins, flared their nostrils.

"Like new cider."

"Leaves, there be a smell of leaves."

Mary took deep breaths of the delicious scent—a braid of smoke, forest loam, sweet fern, resin.

Small women stood on tiptoe, balancing against their men. "Canst see trees? Canst see trees?"

Trees. They had discussed them, over and over; how, in the New World, trees could be the property of common men, who would not be hanged for felling one. Taller than St. Paul's, Mary pictured them.

Land broke from the sea in a series of blue humps.

One after another, people fell to their knees and bowed their heads, until the sailors, hanging in the rigging, looked down upon an entirely silent ship, with a black-frocked clergyman speaking for all, arms spread.

By nine o'clock, the ship had turned southwards. The blue mounds resolved into hills—indigo, violet, velvety black—and then the passengers could distinguish cliffs and the surf that broke against their rocky feet.

God hath called to us to establish a peaceful kingdom, since his purpose has been destroyed in the old country. In this land, beneath these trees, upon these rocks.

As the land passed, the reasons for their coming clarified in Mary's mind. A simple life, built upon righteousness. Within the churches, nothing but benches and Bibles, rigour of thought and practice. A new society, openly Puritan in all its workings.

The vision filled her, corresponding with the rugged landscape, so clear in the harsh light that mica chips sparked from the cliffs and the wings of birds were as glass shards.

To begin! We shall rise on the Sabbath and go unmolested to our worship.

"What do you think, Sinnie?"

"'Tis bonnie, Mistress," the girl said. Her voice was wondering. "So many trees!" She stood grasping her sleeves, folded arms pulled tight across her chest.

So slight, so sturdy, a repository of remarkable abilities.

"Shall you like it here, do you think?"

"If there are no wolves, Mistress. And if we are not attacked by de'il salvages."

"William has his gun," Mary said. "We shall be within a village."

A plume of smoke rose over the forest, causing an outburst of speculation.

"'Tis as they said. The natives do set fire to the undergrowth."

"Why would they do such a thing?"

"Clear it for hunting."

Mary could make out trees already leafless. From this distance, they were but a grey cloud upon the land, yet here and there were clumps of scarlet, orange or yellow. Blue-black spires pricked through the roil of soft-toned hues.

The smoke thickened and rose higher, unwinding against the sky.

"A settlement! People! Look, look!"

Spyglasses were passed from hand to hand. One reached Mary.

"Salem," a man said.

"Nay, it cannot be. Salem is a city. Must be 'tis some small outpost or other."

A sailor called out. "'Tis Salem!"

Silence.

Mary's glass revealed not houses but rude huts, plastered with mud, thatch-roofed. Trees still bearing their bark lay butt to tip, and behind the makeshift fence a few cows grazed. People clustered, like dabs of paint, watching the ship.

These are their homes?

Murmurs.

"Surely 'twill not be such in Boston!"

The settlement fell aft. The supper hour came but no meal was served. In early evening, *Truelove*'s crew swarmed in the rigging, reefing and furling the sails and the ship began a slow navigation

through islands. The sky turned fiery and the islands became feature-
less, drifting black upon red water. High overhead, gulls flashed in
the remnants of light. The air exuded the smell of cold soil. Rowboats
appeared. Men in loose-sleeved linen shirts wrestled ropes upwards,
the ship was attached, and the little boats inched them forward—
past forested cliffs, past small islands, and into Boston Harbour.

Boston lay jumbled upon a low hill, smoke rising from chimneys,
thatched roofs pale in the October dusk. The harbour was silent,
save for the lap of water against the ship's hull.

Then a solitary cry rose—*"All's well!"*

The mate sent them below.

"Ye'll disembark tomorrow."

Cook prepared a soup made of the last of the salt beef.

The ship rocked, rocked.

They ate sparingly, mindful of tomorrow's fresh provisions,
stunned by the quiet.

In the night, Mary wakened. She lifted her head. Over the chuck
and chatter of water, she heard the howling of wolves.

II.

BOSTON

1634 ~ 1638

I am obnoxious to each carping tongue
Who says my hand a needle better fits . . .

ANNE BRADSTREET
New England poet, 1612–1672

FOUR

Visible Kingdom - 1635

GOLDEN BEADS OF PITCH STUDDED the rungs. Mary's palms were sticky, smelled raw, wild. She took a step onto the pier and staggered from the stillness. William, behind her on the ladder, turned to help Sinnie from the rowboat. Jurden handed up their bundles.

They walked uphill on cobblestones that pressed the thin soles of Mary's shoes, passing into the shade of close-set shops with overhanging gables. Signs creaked in the morning breeze, hung so low that Jurden ducked to pass beneath. Glass windows reflected their passage.

At the top of the street, a shirtless man was collapsed forward in stocks. His head was locked between two boards, his hands hung clamped, arms spread like wings. Two men stood behind him— bent, busy.

Mary reached back, took Sinnie's hand and pulled her close. Sunrise warmed their shoulders; their shadows stretched long and black. The men at the stocks seemed reduced by the clarity of light. One raised a whip, slashed it down. The prisoner's cry mingled with the shriek of sea birds.

God's visible kingdom . . .

She obscured the tide of dismay by quickening her pace, even as William walked faster, too, and placed himself between the women and the scene of punishment.

—

Anne Hutchinson led Mary and Sinnie upstairs to a large chamber at the back of her house. Since their brief meeting in London, two years earlier, Anne's blonde hair had faded. She seemed burdened, her eyes like the needle of a compass, a weighted distinction quickly shifting.

Straw-packed pallets covered in cloth ticking lined the walls. Sweat had browned the casings of misshapen pillows. Bunches of savory, sage, lavender, rue, pennyroyal hung from the rafters—their astringent scent ameliorated the stink of urine.

The women dropped their bundles on the pallets.

"You'll be near your time," Anne declared. She stood with arms folded, examining Mary, half-smiling.

"Aye."

"Settle yourselves and come down," she said. She left swiftly, pausing to nudge an empty chamber pot closer to its pallet.

After she had gone, they looked at each other. Mary shook her head, dazed.

"We be in *America*," Sinnie whispered.

They began to laugh, covering their mouths. Sinnie collapsed on a pallet and buried her face in a goose-feather pillow. They laughed for the voyage, ended, and for the ship not having gone down in the storm; for the sight of the wooden houses, so crude and strangely forbidding; for the man in the stocks; for Anne's self-importance. They laughed for the sleep they had not had the night before—terrified, first, by the quavering wolf song; and then by the day that would dawn.

"Oh, Sinnie." Mary wiped her eyes. "Are we laughing or crying? Hush, now."

They straightened their coifs, brushed down their skirts, and went quietly down the stairs, emerging in a hallway. Through an open door, they found a room in which pallets were stacked beside piles of blankets and pillows. A fire burned on a hearth. Sunlight striped the scratched leather of a Bible.

They heard the high voices of little girls mingled with the murmurs of women and followed the sound into a long, crowded kitchen. Children, elderly women and servants were all industriously engaged. Anne lifted bread on a peel from a beehive oven at the side of a hearth. A tiny girl turned a crisp-skinned goose, hanging on a string before the fire. Bloody gut-smell stung Mary's nose—white hen feathers stippled the floor.

"'Tis the day before Sabbath, you see," Anne explained. She scooped two handfuls of dough from a bowl and began to knead, while her eyes studied Mary as if examining a project she must undertake. "We do no work tomorrow, so all meals must be in readiness by sundown."

Mary met Anne's bold stare, offended by her tone. A silence fell. Anne lifted a wrist to rub her cheek, flour drifting from limp hand.

"We have many ways of living the Lord's commandments," she added.

"I shall have to learn them."

"Indeed you must, Mary, for punishments are severe and are visited upon us all equally, women and men, servants and children. Transgression of any of the Ten Commandments is punishable. In some cases, by death."

Anne spoke equably but Mary heard a quiver beneath the brisk tone.

"We did see a man in the stocks," Mary said, yielding to her curiosity. "Being whipped."

Anne set the kneaded dough onto a cabbage leaf, heeled and palmed it into an oval. "He did not attend church," she said. "He went hunting instead."

Mary glanced at Sinnie, who stood behind her, so compressed by bowed shoulders, folded hands and downcast eyes she was as a reflection.

"I have resumed my meetings, such as I kept in Alford," Anne continued. "My teacher, Reverend Cotton, is here. As you have heard? Yes? I do explicate his sermons for they are too complex for most and I do have much experience in his way of thinking."

I shall not attend, Mary thought, with a sear of resentment.

"You shall be needing me soon," Anne added in a softer tone, coming close, wiping hands on apron and reaching forward. Without asking permission, she took Mary's belly in her hands. "You will send your girl to me as soon as you feel your pains. Do you know what to expect?"

"I have borne a babe," Mary said. "He died, after three days." She felt irritation rising. "I have attended at many births. I worked beside my aunt, in Yorkshire. She was a surgeon and a midwife."

She did not say, "And I did study with my uncle." But she would, if—

Anne's face opened. Respect, surprise. "Ah," she said. And smiled.

After the midday meal, William and Mary, Jurden and Sinnie walked to visit a house that was for sale.

"May it be as described," William said, looking eagerly from side to side.

The roads were broad footpaths snaking out of the town's core, littered with manure, broken crates, rags, bone fragments and the skulls of pigs. Along the way, smoke rose from chimneys, souring the air; and over wooden palisados, steam wisped from middens heaped in gardens.

"Good day, Goody," Mary murmured to passing women, as Anne had advised—*you say Goody to those women you do not know.* They carried buckets, wore cloaks to their ankles, pinned at the collar. White coifs covered their hair; wide-brimmed felt hats were tied beneath their chins. They did not look at the men but slid their eyes at Mary and Sinnie.

They are more subdued than at home. They seem ... cowed. Furtive.

She did not want to voice the thought, which clamoured amongst other realizations. Sinnie clutched Mary's arm.

"Listen."

Together they came to a standstill.

A many-voiced fluting came from the west. The voices soared, higher, higher—then broke, quavered down to silence.

"*Wolves*," Mary breathed. "Far off, I wager."

They stumbled to catch up with William and Jurden.

From Corn Hill Road, which wound through old Indian fields of charred tree stumps, four square miles of the peninsula spread out below, houses like rilled pebbles running to the sea, thatched roofs blending with rocky outcroppings.

"Trimount," William said, stopping to point at three hills. On *Truelove*, he had committed to memory the map of the Shawmut Peninsula. "Down there, Windmill Point. And there, they will build the fort. Does it put you in mind of your island, Sinnie?"

"Aye," Sinnie said. "Only we have nae trees. Not anywhere. And none such as . . . that."

She glanced westwards where forest rolled to the horizon, so vast that the scent of moss and pine resin coiled beneath the colony's odours of smoke and manure. Jurden stood behind William. Carrying nothing, his hands were as ornaments and he stuffed them in his pockets, eyes following Sinnie's gaze.

They came upon the house at a corner, where a new road branched away—Mylne Street, it had been named—on which only a single dwelling stood. The builders had been prosperous enough to put glass in the front windows, although the roof was thatched with marsh grass. The second storey overhung the first, cast a shadow over a rotting wooden bucket. It seemed forlorn to Mary, abandoned.

William pulled open the door. Sunlight lay across a floor of pine timbers, hewn flat, strewn with dead flies. A chimney divided the downstairs into halves with a hearth on each side. William and

Jurden wrestled with a warped door, found that it opened into a slope-roofed shed built onto the back of the house. They went to view the garden and outbuildings.

A ladder leaned through a hole in the ceiling. Mary bade Sinnie climb up.

"There be two big chambers," Sinnie called down. "There is a frame for hanging herbs."

"You can sleep up there, Sinnie. You'll have the risen heat."

The last owners had endured one winter only and left in such haste that they had abandoned many things. A dusty iron kettle hung from a trammel on the charred lug-pole. An earthenware pitcher, its lip broken. Two black leather mugs. Mary pulled a chair from its place at a table and found its seat collapsed, the rushes nibbled away. Through oiled paper in the back windows, Mary could see the shapes of William and Jurden, scooping at the soil with the edges of their boots.

Who were these people. Why did they leave.

"Will we put red felt over the windows?" Sinnie whispered. She had come soundlessly down the ladder.

"Nay, Sinnie, hush!" Mary whirled, put a finger to Sinnie's lips. "Take care. You must not speak of such superstitions here."

She drew a breath. Witch hunters came through Kettlesing in her childhood.

"There is no need. We are . . . we are under the special protection of God. And the Reverend Cotton."

And the watchmen. At that moment, two passed the front windows. They carried muskets and brass-tipped staves. Mary stepped back deeper into the house, thinking that she must hang curtains.

William came around to the street and opened the front door.

"Do you like it, Mary?" He seemed pleased. "I could order our chests to be delivered here tomorrow."

Mary felt the baby make a tremendous heave in her womb. "Yes, 'tis fine."

She ventured to the front window and pressed her face to the glass. As yet, no house had been built across the road and the view was unimpeded—a vista of the marsh, below, and the houses of Boston perched on the hillside above. *Truelove*'s masts rose over their roofs. The ship was being loaded for its voyage home.

The shadows of clouds swept over the marsh, leaving light in their wake. She felt its energy and turned to face the dishevelled room.

Work. Obey. Pray. Remember why we came.

They returned to School Street where they would stay with the Hutchinsons until the house was ready. At bedtime, Mary followed Anne up the stairs. They carried bayberry candles in pewter holders.

Anne stopped, turned to address Mary.

"Tomorrow we do not speak any words that do not pertain to religious matters," Anne said. Her voice held a shade of intimacy. "Do you be sure to tell your servants. Also, you may know the rules but I shall tell you in case you do not. Women are not to speak inside the church. *On any matter.* We do not participate in services, save to sing. We do not vote on church membership."

Anne continued up the stairs, her age apparent only by the measured energy of her steps.

Lying on a pallet beside William, Mary remembered the London nights, when no sound of nature could be heard, only a racket of cartwheels, neighing horses, drunken yells, the shriek, perhaps, of a murdered whore. Here, the wind made a restless tugging, causing mournful whistles; she heard no other sound but the howling of the wolves, an eerie ululation, bearing no relationship to the day just past or the one to come. And despite having found themselves a house of their own, she curled against William, burying her face in his neck, feeling the futility of choice.

—

A spit of morning rain tapped the windowpanes.

At the table, the children stood behind the adults waiting to be handed their bowls. They ate their cold cornmeal porridge standing, and did not speak. Husbands and wives and Anne's two elderly cousins shared maplewood porringers.

Will Hutchinson gave a lengthy Bible reading. He did not read well and Mary noticed how Anne frowned, exasperated. Mary closed her eyes, comforted by the familiar, ancient words.

"As for you, my flock, thus says the Lord . . ."

The servants listened in silence from their table in a pantry off the kitchen.

The entire household set forth at the same time to walk to the meeting house. The rattle of drums, not bells, called them to worship. *Rat-a-tat. Rat-a-tat. Rat-a-tat.*

Men, women, children, servants; all walked clutching Bibles. People stepped from doors, emerged from alleys, a stream of black hats and cloaks, white collars, red stockings.

As they turned into the square, Mary saw Anne reach for the hands of her youngest daughters and followed her gaze toward the stocks and whipping post flanking the meeting house.

A pole had been attached to the stocks so that a rope could dangle from high above, mocking gallows; a young woman stood at the end of the rope, a noose draped around her neck and a sign hung upon her chest.

"A."

Watchmen stood at either side, gripping their staves. Mary dared not lift her head, but passed so close she could have touched the young woman's boots.

The seventh commandment. A capital offence. Will they kill her? Is this but a warning?

The ministers marched through the crowd. They were hunched, as if from excessive study, and wore black skullcaps. Clutching wind-blown papers, cloak billowing, Reverend Cotton led them into the meeting house. Women and girls slipped around to the back of the building, entered through a separate door and filed into square pews with low partition walls, across an aisle from the men.

Mary settled herself as comfortably as she could. Her distended belly strained the small of her back. She kept her eyes on her knees, like the other women, since one glance had shown her all there was to see. Bare plaster walls. No tapestries, no gold chalices, no stained glass. No rood screens, no statues. No chasubles or surplices. No incense. No hymnals.

As it should be.

Elders and deacons faced the congregation.

People stood and began to sing. They sang from memory, with neither accompaniment nor hymnal nor a given starting note.

> *And he shall be like to a tree,*
> *Planted by river-waters,*
> *That in his season yields his fruit,*
> *And in his leaf never withers,*
> *And all he doth shall prosper well,*
> *The wicked are not so—*
> *But they are like unto the chaff,*
> *Which wind drives to and fro.*

Mary closed her eyes. She did not know the music. It rose around her, strange and eerie, in its way.

Then Mr. Wilson, the preacher, rose. He spoke of the Hedge.

Invisible but real, he told them, it stood like a bulwark between them and the wilderness, protecting their godliness, keeping evil at bay. The forces of the anti-Christ dwelt in the forest, he said. Devilish spirits possessed the salvages—unfortunate humans who existed in darkness, most of them having no possibility of redemption or salvation.

He spoke of how, should disorder fall upon the colonists by their own wickedness, God's displeasure would cause the Hedge to burst asunder. Thus, he said, public punishments of those who transgress God's laws.

"*Misbehaviour of one can bring wrath down upon all.*"

Mary strained to understand. It was a new perspective: evil and goodness as communal endeavours. And the Hedge, a strange image to take into her mind, and the reason for the young woman's suffering. Mary wondered if the girl needed to piss, if she were thirsty. If the man with whom she had sinned sat now with the others, unpunished.

Wilson spoke for two hours.

Mary slumped forward against the pain in her back.

The tithing man raised his long stick, one end knobbed with a burl, and whacked the shoulders of a squirming boy. The boy squealed, clapped a hand over his mouth. Mr. Wilson broke off. He glared down at the pews. The tithing man resumed his stately walk.

Straight, sit up straight, or he shall think me asleep . . .

At noon, the congregation rose and went to an adjoining building, the Sabba-day house, with horse stalls at one end and a fire burning on a hearth at the other. No one spoke. They ate brown bread, doughnuts or gingerbread. They waited their turn at the outhouses; then they returned to their pews.

Mr. Cotton began his lesson.

People sat forward on their seats, earnest and expectant. Cotton's face was florid, fleshy; his full lips puckered with dignified sorrow; in his eyes, an expression of suffering benignity. Anne nudged Mary's elbow with her own, slid her eyes at a woman and three children who sat in the pew closest to the pulpit.

His wife and children, Mary guessed.

Cotton preached that the elect are justified, or granted salvation, by God's grace. Then, he said, a person's actions were good. However, good works could not *buy* God's grace. It was freely given, and those to whom it was given were as if one with the Holy Spirit.

He lectured on the sixth chapter of the Song of Solomon.

"'My beloved is gone down into his garden, to the beds of spices, to feed in the gardens, and to gather lilies. I am my beloved's, and my beloved is mine: he feedeth among the lilies.'"

At four o'clock, the congregation was allowed briefly to rise.

At six, Mary suffered pains in her bladder and an intolerable hunger.

The lecture continued until the room was in total darkness save for one candle on the lectern. At eight o'clock, Cotton turned over his last paper. The people rose to their feet with audible sighs.

They sang.

As they left the meeting house, they passed the woman at the mock gallows. They did not look at her.

The next day, when she went to the well with Anne to gather the day's water, Mary was surprised not to hear a single complaint about cold, or hunger, or the length of the sermon. Rather, the women argued about the lecture with heated excitement and Anne told them which parts she would elucidate at her Monday meeting.

Across the square, the mock gallows was gone and the stocks were empty.

"Nay," Anne said, following Mary's glance. "'Twas only a first offence."

On a grey day striated with the first snow, they breakfasted with the Hutchinsons one last time and walked to their new home.

That night, Mary sat up late, absorbing the new space of the little house, turning the pages of her Bible. The baby was due in one week. They wished to baptize it into the church and so they themselves must be accepted into it.

Tomorrow they would stand before the ministers for examination.

She thought of Wilson and Cotton—their bald, uncompromising statements. Of how, here in the New Jerusalem, women had no role in church affairs, and were evidently meant to show humility as befitted their place in the order of creation.

We are above animals, above servants, above children . . .

In the fireplace, a log crumbled in a shower of sparks. William had gone to bed.

"Either I know it or I don't," he had said, bending to press a kiss on her forehead. Unsaid was the fact that he was a merchant, young, strong and clever with a good head for figures. He would be found acceptable.

In the dim light, Mary bent to the Bible, turned the thin paper, felt herself repelling anger. Anne, herself, so clearly one of God's elect— graced with a fertile body and a keen mind—had not been taken into the church without an extra week of examination. *Offensive*, the ministers had called her. *In your words and behaviour.* They had questioned her more keenly than her husband, yet had been unable to find any reason to deny her admission to the church.

Mary looked up from the Bible. Just yesterday they had been slic- ing apples when Anne told her the story of her offence.

"'Twas because on the voyage over I argued vehemently with one of the ministers. People below decks heard our shouts." Anne had flicked a long, curling apple skin onto the floor. "When I objected to his doctrine, he dared to tell me I had no right to ques- tion him." Anne laid her knife on the table and spread her arms. She made her voice pompous, furious. "'For the man is not of the woman, but the woman of the man!' And I said, 'God revealed to me the date of our arrival. Can you predict on what date the ship shall arrive?' He said I could have had no such revelation. 'How dare you say such a thing?' I answered. I advised the women to ignore him for the rest of the voyage. And do you know? The ship arrived on my predicted date."

Mary pictured the night sky as she had seen it minutes ago as she returned from the outhouse. Stars spread in coruscating clouds against the wet-slate blackness. She had heard the distant boom of surf and the rustle of dried blueberry leaves. She had seen the lights of houses. One, here. Far off, another.

Wind moaned in the flue, an updraft so strong that it stretched the flames and wakened the coals.

She picked up the Bible and cradled it against her breast. In such a place, a person's smallest act would be laid bare to God—and thus, she thought, one's existence could become a matter of terror. Or ecstasy.

Three sour-faced men sat at a table, scratching words on linen parchment with turkey feather quills. Their woollen doublets smelled of lard and pancakes.

"And did you see that you were without Christ?"

"Aye."

"And who was it who hath opened thine eyes?"

"I attended to the words of Reverend Everard. 'Twas his sermon on suffering. Romans 8:17. 'If so be that we suffer with him, that we may also be glorified together.'"

"Will you tell us of this sermon and how it gave you new birth?"

"He speaks of self-ends and the dangers therein. He asks us to consider this text: 'Wide is the Gate, and broad is the Way, that leads to Destruction, and many go in thereat: but strait is the Gate, and narrow is the Way, that leadeth to Life, and few there be that find it.'"

"And how thinketh you to find it?"

She bowed her head, knowing she must choose her answer carefully. The child surged in her womb and she could not repress a sigh.

"Sit, Mistress Dyer," said Reverend Cotton. He rose and carried a chair around to the place where she stood.

"How thinketh you to find it?" he repeated, resuming his seat. His voice was not without kindness.

"I will not eschew suffering," she said. "I will heed the words of John. 'He who does what is true comes to the light, that it may be clearly seen that his deeds have been wrought in God.'"

Outside, the gulls mewed as they soared on the winter wind. This morning she had wakened in a room so icy that urine was solid in the chamber pot. She had clung to sleep, drenched in a dream of her mother's garden. Within the garden walls, she might have been bird, bee, zephyr—drifting in essence of summer, the sun-softened petals of blue delphinium or white rose, the pollen-laden sweetness.

She straightened her back, lifted her chin and saw not the men crouched over the table but her dream, its beauty. The awe of it, the wonder. At this moment, Reverend Cotton lifted stern eyes to hers. He seemed startled by her expression, and for a moment they looked at one another and did not move or speak.

William started from his chair. He put an arm around Mary, pulled her back from the hearth.

"Do you send for Anne," she breathed.

It was nearing the shortest day of the year. Although the household had not yet eaten, shadows played on the mud-packed walls. Pain closed down around Mary and took her to where she could not distinguish place or sequence, one minute hearing William calling for Jurden over the groan of the door's hinges, then feeling Sinnie's hands gentle at her waist, the frigid air of the bedchamber, her own voice crying in the distance. And for a blessed moment, the world's return—feather ticking beneath her, Sinnie's yellow sleeve, comfort as the pain ebbed like a broken wave.

Anne swept into the house, talking rapidly.

"More water, Sinnie. Where are the linens? Put these herbs in a pot. Have you hooks? Build up the fire in her chamber . . . 'tis freezing."

She came to the bedside, knelt, took Mary's hands.

"Mary."

Mary twisted with a fresh spiral of pain, crying out for Aunt Urith. She pressed hands to cheeks, panting.

"Open your eyes."

"I will die, Anne. Surely I will die."

"Nonsense. Where are your prayers? Say with me: 'Answer me when I call, O God of my right! Thou hast . . .'"

Anne's eyes were direct and calm.

Other women came—Mrs. Bell, Mrs. Coddington, Jane Hawkins and a nursing mother. Between pains, Mary walked until she no longer had the strength. Then she lay on her side—rocking, moaning. In the breaking light of dawn, she slid to the edge of the bed and lay like a fish in a basket, other women's arms beneath hers, her legs draped in the crook of elbows, a body pressed to her back, voices murmuring in her ears, Sinnie singing softly: and at the moment of Mary's longest wail, a baby slid into the waiting hands of Anne Hutchinson.

"My dear." Her voice was tender. "God hath graced you with a perfect boy."

Mary heard William's voice, light with relief. Hands rolled her, wrapping her in warm cloth. Someone held a mug of hot wine to her lips. Just before the baby was passed for his first milk, to be taken from the breast of the young woman who had come for the purpose, he was lowered into Mary's arms. The baby's veined purple eyelids and wrinkled brow formed an expression of concentration, as if the infant strove to remain in his place of perfection.

FIVE

First Winter - 1636

THEY NAMED HIM SAMUEL.

Two weeks after his birth, a blizzard swept down from the north-east. Fires roared on both hearths, snowflakes were dashed down the flue and hissed in the flames. Mary lay with her back to William; he pulled her close for warmth. She reached a hand into the icy darkness, rocked the high-sided cradle.

William slept deeply, exhausted. The men had begun to build a fort on the point. Every man must work for two weeks—William having closed his shop in the market during the time—for the ministers told them that if they worked as one to obey God, then God would give them prosperity. From sunrise to dusk, he spent the days in a saw pit, or wielding a draw shave, or driving tenon into mortise. He had been made clerk of the enterprise.

The wind retreated, muttered, rose again in hollow whistles.

Along the coast, adrift in the darkness of winter, were other settlements—Salem, Plymouth, Providence. Mary wondered if other English people lay in their beds listening to the storm. If they, like her, felt an occasional, appalled sense of regret at what they had done.

. . . they will not adventure much, they will not sell all, part with all, they will not loose their Hold . . .

She reminded herself of John Everard's sermon that had set her upon her path. Of why they had come. Vanity, excess, the sullied church.

Against the paper window, snow made a crackling spit, like blown sand.

In the austerity of conviction, finally, she slept.

The next morning, they woke to knee-deep snow. Mary stood in the door lifting the baby's hand to wave goodbye to William. The thatched-roofed houses on the hillside above the marsh seemed to her like boulders, grey humps amidst the cresting drifts.

Snow whirled into their faces and Samuel began to cry.

"Hush, my love."

She lowered him into the cradle, tucked the quilt close. The ministers on *Truelove* had lectured that women must produce children continuously in order to populate the New Jerusalem.

She and Sinnie stood gazing down at the baby, whose eyelids thickened as he drifted into sleep.

"Mr. Cotton says that babies are born sprawling in wickedness." Mary spoke as if to herself. "He says they must be led from the evil to which they are naturally prone. He says we must keep them at a distance, nor show too great an affection lest they cease to revere us as they must."

She did not say that she harboured a secret sin, fearing she obeyed Mr. Cotton's second edict by nature rather than by design, for she found herself shielding her heart against its breaking. Every day she woke expecting that Samuel would have died in his sleep; or would be infected with some deadly sickness; or would be killed in an accident by day's end.

"Ah, Mistress. I can see no more wickedness in that child's eyes than I see in a kitten's."

Sinnie dropped to her knees by the cradle, ran the back of her finger over the baby's cheek. She loved to rock him to sleep, whispering of her rocky island, of Finnigirt Dyke, of wild birds' eggs and sheep dogs. Now, beneath her breath, as if to nullify Mr. Cotton's nonsense, she recited the Lord's Prayer in Norn—"*Fy vor or er I Chimeri, Halaght vara nam dit . . .*"

Mary listened, transfixed by the soft rush of words. When the prayer ended, she took a deep breath. "Well, Sinnie. Let's begin."

She watched from the doorstep as Sinnie, bundled in cloak and scarves, trudged away through the snow, buckets swinging from a yoke. On the air, glittering with icy flakes, came the bawling of cows, shouts from the fort. She went back inside, set salt cod to soak, scooped hominy from a basket. The morning's milk steamed—Jurden had set it by the shed door. She heard the chock-chunk of his axe, splitting wood. She paused to consider that everywhere her eyes landed she saw only further work. William's wadmore stockings, their heels worn thin. The lye pot, needing to be emptied. The corn, coming to a boil. Even as she thought this, Samuel's mouth opened in a wet shuddering wail.

At sunset, Mary sat in a low chair by the fire holding the baby to her breast. The room was close from smoke blown back down the flue; messy with wet clothing, sewing baskets, cornmeal spilled on the poplar-wood table. Along the crack under the door, snow lay in a white curve.

William's lantern came swinging through the blue dusk. He entered through the front door, carrying a chunk of knotty pitch pine—candlewood, it was called, since light was cast by burning its resinous splints. A dead duck was flung over one shoulder and his greatcoat was sprinkled with sawdust. He dropped wood and duck on the hearth by her chair. She smiled up at him and felt her mood lift as the oppressive sense of unfinished work was leavened by his presence.

They sat together at the trestle table—William, Mary, Jurden and Sinnie.

Jurden was courting a young woman he had met on the ship. Even so, Sinnie would not raise her eyes to his, kept her elbows pinned to her sides.

William read the prayer and they lifted their spoons.

"Your hand, Miss," Jurden exclaimed, surprised; then he gentled his tone. "What did happen?"

"A burn," Sinnie murmured to her bowl. "I did touch my hand to the brick."

"Sliding this good cornbread from the oven," Mary said. She looked at the two young people, saddened by the formality Sinnie's fear imposed. "You must put more grease on it tonight."

The wind moaned and the clavicle of snow by the doorsill changed shape.

"Roger Williams will not keep quiet," William remarked. "They may send him back to England sooner than spring."

"Who is Roger Williams?"

"A young English minister. A man of strong opinions. He hath been preaching of soul liberty."

Steam from the succotash swirled in the candlelight. Mary repeated the words, to feel them in her mouth.

"'Soul liberty.' What does he mean by it?"

"He feels that every man must form his own opinion on the subject of religion. He hath cried foul to the magistrates for enforcing belief. But that is not the worst of it."

Soul liberty.

"He hath defamed their authority. He says they should not have taken land from the Indians. They say he is entertaining company in his house at Salem and preaching of this."

Their spoons scraped, clattered.

You arrive at a place you have long imagined. And once there, again you look outwards.

Until William was made a freeman by the General Court, he could not vote or buy land. So he must wait, work, keep his counsel. He did not speak about the ministers, the harsh laws.

There is much that I, too, ponder and dare not speak of.

Her breasts were swollen, hot. She saw the drying mush on the wooden trenchers.

Floors to sweep, bowls to scour, the baby to feed.

Her hands ached, her hips and back and legs felt heavy, her eyes were dry. She was so tired as not to be sleepy.

As she poured hot water into the washing-up bucket, William leaned on his elbows, staring into the fire.

Parts of him have vanished, others have grown.

Samuel woke, hungry, and Sinnie was at the cradle, swift as a swallow, soothing the child with Norn words. She handed him to Mary, who tucked herself onto a rush-seated chair and unbuttoned her tunic. The baby's lips found the nipple, began their powerful suck. Mary felt William's gaze and raised her eyes to his.

Undue attachment—not only of parent to child, but of husband to wife—must be guarded against.

Lest ye place the creature before the creator.

This William did not obey. Ambition and worry, like a cloud of sediment, slowly cleared as his eyes rested on her. Were Sinnie and Jurden not in the room, Mary saw, he would come to her, kneel, take her face in his hands. A soft kiss, not to disturb the baby.

"My love," he would say.

Mary wrote to Aunt Urith. The letter would not be sent until the next ship came into harbour and so she kept the paper in a cupboard drawer, taking it out after the day's work was done. It became grease-spattered, redolent of cinnamon and the drawer's pine boards.

January 1636

My beloved Aunt Urith,
I take up my pen in a place so dissimilar from your abode
that words do fail me to put it to a description save to say
that I have heard the howling of wolves only dimmed by an
augmentation of the ever-present and lamenting wind. Baby
Samuel groweth fair and lusty and as for William, the Queen
whose gloves he once chose would now quail before him, so
rugged and rough-skinned hath he become.

She paused. That morning she had passed the whipping post. Blood
and the knotted rope seemed a transference, so quickly did the red
beads leap from the flesh of the man bound to it. He screamed as the
whip fell. Four hours later when she went to Anne Hutchinson's
house, she had seen him again, slumped in the stocks. Dark fluids
oozed from the wounds upon his naked back.

No. She would not write of it.

I am oft worried at myself, for I find my heart closing
against this child. I fear losing him, as I lost the first—and so
I dare not love. Dost thou have knowledge of this in others,
my aunt? God spared thee from childbirth for your skills in
such matters. Sinnie is like a mother to my babe and for this
I am grateful to the good providence of God. Her heart
yearns for children, yet I doubt she will ever have them, so
feared is she of men. The good God hath surely sent her to
me, for she is a treasure beyond compare, and thanks to her
ministerings, Samuel is full-cheeked, perfect in form, and
blesseth us with his childish pratings.
I have begun attending the meetings of Anne Hutchinson.
She hath re-ignited the light of Christ within me that shone

so bright when first I desired to follow the Puritans. Verily I feel a joy to light the darkness that fell upon me at the loss of my dear brother and my first babe. Too, she hath bid me come and learn some of her skills, so that I may help . . .

Mary turned onto Corn Hill Road. She saw other women, veiled by slanting snow, walking singly or in twos. Cowled against the winter wind, they clutched Bibles—capes swirled, skirts kicked by leather boots, the white coifs upon their heads like so many pin-points of brilliance.

The Hutchinson parlour was warmed by a fire on the hearth. The room smelled of feverfew, lemon balm, tansy, hung to dry on hooks. Anne sat at a table; behind her, a window framed the frozen marsh. Her eyes travelled the group, the muscles at the corners of her mouth cording as she listened to questions. Her voice thickened, infused with conviction.

"The Holy Spirit dwells within each of us. We are as we are born, and within ourselves we may apprehend him. We do not need the intervention of ministers," she told them.

The meeting lasted until the sky had darkened. Leaving Anne's house, Mary strode fast, one hand gathering her hood, the other holding a lantern. Dusk wove between the houses, a charcoal density gathering into oblivion roofs, chimneys, upper storeys. Her mind filled with Anne's face, like a canvas stretched tight, corner to corner, beyond which she could see light and warmth.

She cut down an alley. A dim glow of candlelight came from a window, spinning with flakes. She passed a wall, sheltering a midden; heard the sound of pigs—a scuffle, the sound of open-mouthed chewing. Then—silence. A low, evolving growl, joined by a second.

Not pigs.

She quickened her steps, pulled her hood forward, torn by instincts both to run and to freeze. She stopped, turned. Held up her lantern. A broken place in the wall. A snout. She saw the glint of teeth, heard a snarl. A wolf leapt through.

Has not seen me.

A second followed, smaller. She could see grey fur in the candlelight. The animals touched snouts. Then the larger one looked in her direction.

Samuel, William, Sinnie, Urith. God, God, please, O Lord. Her own heart, present in a wild pounding. She pressed fist to chest. Where they would land first, the paws. Then teeth to throat.

I will not die here. I will not.

"Get away!" she screamed. "Get away from me!"

She stepped forward, waving her arms. "BEGONE!"

For an instant they hesitated—and in the next moment, they streaked down the alley, vanished.

A door opened, a man stood silhouetted against the light.

"Who is there?"

Mary ran forward.

"What . . ." he began.

"Wolves," she panted. "In your midden . . ."

He stepped back, pulling her beside him. Crashed the door shut. She collapsed on a chair in the cidery warmth. A woman and two children rose from the table. Mary could not bring herself to say where she had been, or why she had been walking alone at such an hour.

Anne's ideas were openly discussed—at the barber shop, on the Charleston ferry, around tavern tables. Men, now, came to her meeting. So many people crowded her parlour—sixty, then seventy, then eighty—that she added a second.

"Who attends?" William asked Mary, in February. They sat at the trestle table, leaning close, speaking in low voices since Jurden was perched on the settle, elbows on knees in stoic contemplation of the fire, clay pipe in hand. In these coldest months, he no longer slept beneath English wool and deerskin in the back shed, but waited for them to go to their bedchamber so he could spread his pallet on the floor. Sinnie had whispered her Norn prayer to the baby and slipped up the ladder to the icy attic.

"Sir Henry Vane," Mary whispered. "Anne's William, of course. John Coggeshall, William Coddington." These latter three were the colony's most prosperous merchants.

William took up his smoking-tongs, pressed tobacco into the bowl of a white clay pipe. His lips made soft poppings as he sipped at the stem. He looked across into the fire and she saw that he probed a new idea.

"I have noticed a change in you," he said.

He handed the pipe to Mary, who filled her mouth with the sweet smoke. She blew it out through pursed lips and smiled at him. "I have noticed a change in you, as well."

"What are you thinking? About . . ." He made a surreptitious motion with his fingers, indicating their circumstances.

"I find myself questioning," she murmured. "I am not certain about many things."

William's eyes narrowed against the spiralling smoke.

"I will come to her meetings," he said.

She handed the pipe back across the table. He caressed her wrist with the tips of his fingers.

"Good," she whispered, glancing at Jurden. She pressed her own fingers against her lips, smiling, and blew the kiss towards William, like seed from a dandelion.

—

In early winter, the Massachusetts Bay Colony sent militia up the coast to Salem in order to seize Roger Williams, for he had not left the colony, as he had been ordered, nor would recant his strewn, profligate words, nor would be silent.

The captain and his men pounded on the door of Roger Williams's house. It was opened by his wife, who stood holding a newborn baby.

"My husband hath been gone these three days," she said.

She did not know where he was.

The pinnace sailed back to Boston carrying the news that the young minister had vanished into the wilderness.

Sinnie, in her bedchamber, stood on tiptoe to reach down a bunch of savory.

'Tis not as they hoped. They wished for freedom but perhaps 'tis not so different here after all.

They had told her that they wished to go to the New World because their ministers were being tortured, forced to flee, or thrown into the Tower.

They be scunnered. She wanted Mary and William to be as happy as they had been in London, when she had first come to work for them and they had gone out, of an evening, hand in hand.

She listened to their quiet talk below, the floor cracks so wide she could see their heads. They talked of things that would have them terribly punished should anyone hear—how the ministers were wrong in their thinking, and terrified the children, and were cruel, and told the magistrates how to rule.

Sinnie could not understand it, for all that was said in the sermons and lectures was as a language utterly incomprehensible and she longed only for them to be over so she could return to eggs, in a bowl, for flour and her small, quick hands, and the sourdough, and the crust, butter-browned, and the joy of watching their faces.

She glanced at her pallet, considering how sleep came to her easily, for she loved the moment of waking to a life whose tasks were as gifts, whose people were her own.

Crumbs of dried herbs sprinkled down, smelling of summer. Sprigs in hand, she knelt to slip backwards through the trapdoor, one foot on the first rung, thinking of the garret in London where she had dreaded the Earl's nightly visits and how she had splayed herself against a window to glimpse the birds flying northwards.

Oh, I be so lucky. I do wish they could know of it. She thought of her good parents and her brothers and sisters. How she could stand in the doorway of this little house and watch the birds spilling past and have no envy of them.

At Anne's next meeting, Mary sat on a bench beside the fire. Other women perched on low stools or curled on the floor. William and the men stood against the walls, snow-melt dripping from beards and hat brims.

Anne took a sip of cider and passed the cup to a long-haired young man, Sir Henry Vane, who sat beside her at the table.

Sir Henry's father is privy councillor, Mary thought, advisor, and comptroller of the king's household. The young man had refused to crop his blonde curls nor would give up his lace cuffs, although he was so ardent a Puritan that he had convinced his father to send him to New England. There was much that Anne told Mary in confidence. How it was the young aristocrat's presence that had attracted men to her meetings. How Henry Vane planned to run for governor in the spring elections; and if he won, Anne and her followers—so numerous that those opposed to her ideas had coined a phrase, calling them "Hutchinsonians"— would rule the colony.

Mary folded her hands. They were red from a morning spent

washing the hemmed rags she tied around Samuel's bottom—first, walking through the snow to the spring, returning with icy fingers and wet cuffs, buckets swinging and sloshing from a neck yoke. Then: the soaked clouts, the filthed water, wringing, rinsing, hanging the cloths on a wooden rack. As Anne began to speak, Mary closed her eyes and drew a deep calming breath.

"I do not agree with his interpretation of Jeremiah, verses 23 through 33," Anne resumed, arguing her own understanding of the Scriptures, probing the meanings laid upon them by Reverend Wilson. She sliced the air with her hand, pointing, thumb raised.

In time, she closed the Bible; her discourse veered from the sermon.

"The ministers substitute outward form for inward faith. They call themselves 'Visible Saints' and believe themselves sanctified by evidence of their good works. They believe, like Abraham, that obedience not only of oneself but enforced upon others is proof of election. *And thus of salvation.*"

The room stilled with the effort of attention, hand-smoothed coifs and men's hats motionless within the winter light. A fly's frenzy grew loud against the windowpane.

This is the crux of the issue that divides Anne Hutchinson from the Bay clergy.

"This substitution of form for faith and its imposition upon others is the very reason we left England."

A murmur, a growl.

Yes, Mary thought. 'Tis so clear.

"Our salvation will come neither from obedience nor ritual but from *the intuition of grace.* Consider the Apostle Paul, Ephesians 2:8–9; 'For by grace are ye saved, through faith . . .' and '. . . not by works, lest any man should boast.'"

Anne paused, watching the fly's random attack upon the glass. She took breath, resumed.

"As I do understand it, laws, commands, rules and edicts are for those who have not the light which makes plain the pathway. He who has God's grace in his heart cannot go astray."

The room filled with voices.

No need of ministers. As people stood to voice their opinions, Anne sat quietly, watching the uproar, hands flat upon her Bible, an oat straw to mark her page standing upright between two fingers. And Mary saw how Anne Hutchinson caused, controlled, even manipulated the consternation—then evaluated the results keenly, the same way she peered at blood-soaked flesh and the eyes of the dying.

It was dark when they stepped out into the street. The light of William's candle lantern was serrated with driving snow, like finely drawn chalk lines. The governor's house stood directly across from the Hutchinsons' and as they passed beneath its windows she saw Governor Winthrop peering out, hand on drawn curtain, head turned to look down the street. Half-lit, his pointed beard was etched against the room's soft glow. She could not see the expression on his face.

The mother had been labouring for twenty hours and still the baby would not come. The room was close with hips, linens, skirts. Women bent over the fire, frying Johnny-cakes, heating water, ladling cider into mugs. Others sat on a bench beneath the window, whispering, giddy with fatigue; they laughed or uttered little shrieks, hands clapped to mouths.

Mary pressed a cup beneath the nipple of a nursing mother.

"Comes hard at first," the woman breathed, scissoring fingers down her breast. Mary felt a milky mist on her face, watched the level rise. She went to the bed, drew open the curtains. Anne stood at the bedside, her face masked with visualization as she reached beneath the woman's shift.

"Drink," Mary said, holding the milk to the woman's panting mouth. "'twill help." She spoke as if it were an ordinary day and an ordinary cup of milk, not one to accelerate a labour that had gone on far too long.

A scream came that blossomed, passed beyond agony. Gut, blood, a choke.

"'Tis turned," Anne exclaimed. "I have turned the baby! Come, now, come, Mary. Bring me more grease."

The baby slipped into Anne's hands. She cut the cord, wrapped the stump with a belly band and handed the tiny girl to Mary, who lowered the child into a basin of warm wine. A chorus of relieved voices rose; the women came forward to see the infant.

"Ellen? Ellen! Ah, no." Anne's voice. Sudden, furious. "I cannot feel the heartbeat." She pressed her ear to the woman's breast. "No," she panted. "No, no, no."

She palmed her hands and looked fiercely towards the rafters. "Lord, in thy steadfast love, in thy wisdom and grace, spare this servant . . ."

The women joined in prayer, kneeling, crying out. Their cries died away and they prayed silently, hearing, as if for the first time, the blizzard that seized the house, lashing snow in dry specklings against the paper panes, causing the door to rattle on its hinges.

A long, harsh breath came from the bed.

They laid food on the trestle table—Johnny-cakes and the special "groaning" beer prepared for childbirth. They ate by the light of candlewood, a smoky, pitchy flicker; and a candle, guttering on the table. The wind blew like an injured and self-communing beast.

"I wonder," a woman said. She laughed, but glanced and lowered her voice. "How the Lord could have heard over that racket."

Anne set down her mug. Mary saw how fatigue dragged at her cheeks and the corners of her mouth.

"Ah, but he did," she said. She drew a long breath that lifted her striped, blood-stained stomacher.

Mary heard Anne's next words in her own mind before Anne spoke them.

"God hears those he loves . . ."

Occasionally, on winter afternoons, Mary visited the Hutchinsons' home. They sat in Anne's parlour, close to the fire, and talked of the books they had read—discussed the women in Foxe's *Actes and Monuments*, especially sixteen-year-old Lady Jane Grey, Queen of England for nine days, held in the Tower and beheaded.

"Which languages did she speak?" Mary asked, wanting to confirm her memory. She held wool-gauntleted hands to the flames.

"Latin," Anne said, ticking them off on her fingers. "Greek, Spanish, Italian and French. She did believe in justification by faith. She argued with the men, she had no fear."

Mary had been studying the Book of Esther. She imagined the young Jewish woman—perhaps her own age, married to a king who was unaware of her religion—being asked to intercede with him to save her people from slaughter. She opened her Bible, found the passage and read aloud. Finishing, she closed the book, slowly, and gazed into the fire. She felt yearning, a sense of her life stretching before her. Anne, too, was silent.

"The young queen was so brave," Mary offered. "So selfless."

Anne took up the tongs and poked at the logs. "What did you think of my last discourse?"

Mary did not answer the question, forgetting it in the light of the larger question that framed it.

"Do you believe yourself to be in danger?" Mary asked.

Anne bunched her shawl close across her chest, inching her chair back from the revived fire.

"Perhaps," she said. "Perhaps. Yet if so, 'tis not me alone. 'Tis half of Boston and some of the outlying places as well, where people think as I do."

"So many," Mary said. "You have such influence. Surely they will stop you."

Anne glanced at Mary. "Do not tempt me with pride. 'Tis not only me, Mary. 'Tis Reverend Cotton, as well, who shares my views, although he keeps them close; and Henry Vane, and other men, too, who have their own reasons for distaste of those who would make the laws without consent and flay the backs of those they call sinners. Do you know, the children wake at night? They scream in terror after some of Reverend Wilson's sermons." She imitated the minister's nasal intonements. "'These are the sins that terribly provoke the wrath of Almighty God against thee . . .' I tell the children to attend only to the Holy Spirit within themselves, but 'tis a mishmash for them, I fear."

She paused, considering.

"I wish only to awaken people's hearts to the search for grace within themselves, so to maintain the living spirit of our religion. I will argue as does Mr. Cotton, from the truth as given in the Scriptures. For what else did we cross an entire ocean?"

"Yes," Mary said. Still she felt like an acolyte, unsure. "I do agree with you."

Anne slid her eyes at Mary, smiled, slightly.

"Then you, too, may be in danger."

SIX

Whangs and Other Happenings— 1636

✳

MARY RAISED HER FACE TO enjoy the warmth of the sun on her face. She looked out over the bay. Sails came into view, passing the outer islands.

"Sinnie," she cried, rising to her feet. They were kneeling by the front door, sorting beet root. Samuel napped on a bed of wildcat pelts. "The ships! The ships have come!"

The scratch on the windowsill had darkened. Masts and spars rose over the low ridge that rimmed the harbour. By early afternoon, fifteen ships lay at anchor.

Anne Hutchinson's twelve-year-old daughter arrived with a message.

"Mother sends this," the girl said, handing Mary a cloth bag. "'Tis tea brought from London by the Wheelwrights. She bids you come for supper to make their acquaintance."

"Who are they?"

"My uncle, John Wheelwright. He is a minister, married to my father's sister. They have five children. And with them . . ." her voice caught, ". . . is my *grandmother*!"

"Joy for you, indeed," Mary said, infected by the spring light and the girl's excitement. "Surely we will come!"

—

The adults of three families squeezed around one table: Hutchinsons, Wheelwrights and Dyers. Rich, evening light stretched across the floorboards, up the daub wall, onto pussy willows in an earthenware vase.

Anne scooped hasty pudding from an iron pot. Children carried trenchers to the table.

"We shall petition the church that you be co-pastor with Reverend Wilson," Anne said to her brother-in-law, John Wheelwright.

Mary studied the new faces, impatient to hear news of home. Anne snapped spoonfuls of pudding, squinting in the blue-grey swirls of steam, nodding at the places where the trenchers were to be set. The children, Mary saw, were entirely accustomed to their mother's bold pronouncements.

"Wilson is our minister, Cotton is our teacher. Whereas they do both believe in the inevitability of God's will, Reverend Wilson lays undue weight on morality." She paused, glanced at the children. "He believes that by 'works,' a strictly moral life, a person proves that he is saved. There are many who would be glad to set a balance to Reverend Wilson's views. You would be such a one, brother John."

John Wheelwright sat with shoulders held back and chin lifted, accentuating his height, drawing down his eyelids. He wore a silk cap; his cheeks were burnished from the crossing.

"I should be happy to do so." He held one palm upright, his fingertips making minute tremblings. "My views are much like those of Reverend Cotton. Yet I *have* heard talk that he is tainted. Such nonsense. Or is it?" He glanced at Will Hutchinson and William, surprised that the men did not weigh in. "You are as Protestants and Catholics here with your diverging opinions on 'works' and 'grace.' Indeed, it has been well noted in England."

Anne looked steadily at Wheelwright, gauging him. "Aye, there is great controversy. Do not underestimate it. Governor Winthrop would silence me, for he doth believe that my teachings undermine his authority."

"Is it so? Truly?" Wheelwright's voice quickened, startled by her rebuke.

Mary watched steam rising from the trencher set between her and William, a fine column that broke and spun into coils before thinning, vanishing.

We talk as we did in England.

She held Samuel on her lap. He reached for the steaming pudding and she snatched his hand. Spring birdsong was admitted by the half-opened door yet still they wore their unwashed woollens and sat pressed close as if from winter's cold. She becomes angry, Mary thought, watching her friend. She is right, and knows it. The more they try to silence her, the more steely she will become.

Anne circled the spoon around the bottom of the pot. "I say that those graced by the Holy Spirit do apprehend it within themselves. Therefore they *cannot* be preached to by those who do not evidence such grace. I believe some of our preachers are not graced."

Wheelwright's fingers tightened on his spoon. "Indeed."

"Nor do I believe that perfect behaviour evidences sanctification. The governor says that I undermine both the preachers and the laws that do insist upon righteousness."

Will Hutchinson watched his wife, and then slid an appeasing glance at Wheelwright, as if making an offering. "My wife hath set fear in some who need a check on their power. The clergy here have set themselves up like the bishops."

"These are not my motives, Will, and you do know it." Anne spoke quickly, annoyed. "I speak my mind and there are many who show interest."

A large pewter mug of ale was passed around the table, finger-warmed. Each person turned it slightly before drinking. Will Hutchinson drank, then caught William Dyer's eyes as he passed it to him. Mary saw the two men—both merchants, neither with religious passion—share a look. *Will you speak or shall I?* it said, and her William sat forward on his chair and leaned towards the newcomers.

"The issue of works and grace, do you see, is setting a divide between the people, for it becomes a matter of power—whom the people will trust and whom they will follow. There are the ministers and magistrates on the one hand; the merchants on the other. We merchants support Anne Hutchinson. In recent weeks, the General Court hath seen fit to tell us how much we may pay our workers. How much we may charge for our goods. My profits have dwindled overnight."

He wiped his mouth with the back of his hand, passed the mug carefully to the old lady on his right.

"You will find that although there is no clergy on the General Court, *only church members can stand for office.* Do you understand?"

Wheelwright nodded. "Church and state."

"Aye," William said. "When we left, Archbishop Laud and King Charles were hand in hand. Sometimes I do wonder what is the difference here. The General Court doth make its own rules, and they are not the rules of England. If unsure as to what constitutes a crime or how to mete punishment, the court asks advice of the church elders. Or of the ministers."

"And which ministers hold your views, my sister?" Wheelwright asked.

Anne finally took her place at the table. She sat with her hands in her lap looking out the window.

Forty-five years old. And the Lord hath sent her fifteen babies.

The colony's unsoftened light picked out silver hairs wisping from beneath Anne's coif, laid shadows in the spidery lines beside her mouth. Yes, children he had sent, Mary thought—but some he had called home. Susan, Elizabeth, William. Heaven beckoned, heartbreaking in its beauty and its necessity.

"Mr. Cotton," Anne said, her voice suddenly spent. "Mr. Cotton is my teacher and it is his words I seek to elucidate." She sighed, reached for a spoon. "As I did at home. As he has asked me to do here. Will, please to say the grace. Our pudding doth grow cold."

In the late spring dusk, William brought home the news that Henry Vane had been elected governor. They left the front door open to watch the pink light on the water below. The night was alive with clickings and trills—blackbirds, frogs, insects. Mary laughed at William's exuberance.

"Tonight the merchants will set off fireworks in the harbour," he said to baby Samuel, holding him up like a package and tilting him from side to side, making him dance like a marionette.

At bedtime, the throbbing of the peepers were as heat between her legs and she lay naked on the bed, waiting for William. His silhouette paused, in the doorway. She could not read his expression, but heard rustles and clinks as he undressed slowly, facing her. His tongue, circling her navel. Her heels, on the small of his back as he entered her. Afterwards, they lay listening to the sweet chiming of the marsh.

She twirled a piece of his hair, relaxation even in her fingers.

We shall prosper . . .

A week later, William brought more sobering news. The church elders had decided that John Wheelwright should not become Wilson's co-pastor, but would be sent down the coast to the new settlement at Mount Wollaston.

Keeping him far from Anne.

"Aye, they will have him form a new church there," he said. "We shall barely hear tell of him."

—

All summer, women gathered at "whangs"—work-bees to make dreary tasks less arduous. At Goody Pearl's house, they gathered a winter's worth of soiled clothing, pillowcases, sheets, dishcloths. Water steamed over the fire, the windows were thrown wide to the warble of blackbirds. Scrubbing, splashing, they spoke of childbirth and children, nostrums and illness; they pondered passages from the Bible, argued points of Mr. Cotton's lesson; then they lowered their voices to whispers, as if compelled to unburden themselves of the old country fairy stories or the folk customs once woven like ribbons into the season's tapestry—Maypoles, ash faggots, Devil's stones.

"Hush . . ."

They discussed Anne's ideas. Or they murmured of Roger Williams, who had surfaced after fourteen months of perilous wandering. He had been saved, in the dead of winter, by an Indian, who had kept him fed and warm. He had made his way to Narragansett Bay and had founded a new settlement, which he named Providence, on the Moshassuck River and proclaimed it a refuge for religious dissenters who suffered for conscience's sake. The women expressed their relief that his wife and children had finally joined him.

"Reverend Wilson did tell us we should spy on one another," a woman remarked. She was sitting cross-legged, a small bucket on her lap filled with soapy water. She scrubbed a baby's cap.

A burst of laughter, quickly hushed.

"I know all your secrets, Joan Croucher," another woman said. "Shall I go tell Mr. Wilson about the itch in your . . ."

"Shhhhhh."

"His mouth," one whispered, "doth look as if he sucked a lemon."

Soapy water, splashed across the kitchen. Little girls looked up from their wooden dolls, open-mouthed at the giggling.

"If he do speak so about us one more time. Saying we are weak and timorous. I should like to see *him* push a baby through . . ."

"We should stand at his outrages and leave the meeting house," Anne Hutchinson remarked.

The mood changed, swift as shadow.

"They would whip us."

"They would have us in the stocks."

"Nay," Anne said. She bent over a washboard, scrubbing a pocket. Its string wrapped around her soapy wrist and she paused to unwind it. "We may plead a woman's complaint."

The idea was too outrageous to contemplate.

They talked, instead, of beans and the white mould that grew around their stems, separating plant from root.

Reverend Wilson preached for an hour and a half. Empty bellies gurgled, rumbled. A dog began barking, close by. Men exchanged glances but no one rose to silence it. Mary felt sweat trickle down her back. She had ceased to listen; imagined, instead, the moors of Kettlesing with their cool, heathery winds.

"Women are incapable of reason," Reverend Wilson announced, changing topic. He leaned over, set his elbow upon the pulpit and turned his palm upwards, fixing his gaze on the men. His upper lip was so short as to appear swallowed by the lower. Large, hooded black eyes brooded beside a nose curved as a sparrowhawk's beak.

"Men, do you attend to your wives. They are credulous and easily led astray."

Anne, Mary and two other women caught each other's eyes. Anne's idea had taken root and bloomed into a plan. They rose to their feet. Wilson's hand went to his square bib collar. His mouth opened and a prune-dark flush spread over his cheeks.

Their skirts made soft brushings, their heels were as knuckles on a midnight door as they filed into the aisle.

They walked from the meeting house.

"Remember, we cannot be punished," Anne said, as the four women gathered by the well. And Mary saw that Anne, who would calmly argue doctrine with Reverend Cotton—a man of whom the pastor of Ipswich had said, "I am unfit to polish his slippers"—had evidenced, by trembling voice, the racing of her heart.

Samuel learned to crawl, then pulled himself onto a chair.

Sinnie made walking bands, attached them to his apron and took him to the dusty road where she held the bands like reins, calling out encouragement. It was a hot August day and Mary worked at a table near the open door, plucking a wild turkey—watching, smiling.

Down in the marsh, children moved randomly as hens, their white collars glinting as they gathered horsetails and huckleberries. Far away, out on the mud flats, people dug clams, plucked periwinkles.

And over them, clouds piled, golden edged.

She gazed at the sky, her hands resting on the carcass. *Surely 'tis a sign that the Lord doth bless our enterprise.*

William, now a freeman. And so he had been awarded land north of the peninsula at Rumney Marsh and he and Jurden had ferried cows across the Charles River. Corn, they had planted there, and salt-water hay. Last night, William had muttered over his accounts, pleased, placing a large order of Monmouth caps. Warm rain made elephant ears of her squash leaves.

The Holy Spirit is within you . . .

October.

The leaves of apple trees turned to yellow leather and the marsh was a red-brown quilt. Pigeons spread over the sky like oil, their wings making a deafening clatter.

Mary was pulling carrots in the garden, when Sinnie burst from the house.

"Indians," she panted. "They are passing, just now."

Mary swept up Samuel and they hurried to the corner of their street.

Twenty-four Narragansett men walked down Corn Hill Road. They strode steadily, straight-backed, and did not look from side to side. They wore leather mantles hung with furs. Fringed, beaded leggings. Wampum glinted in black braids; ash patterned their cheeks. Deerskin clad, their feet made no sound.

Before, and behind them—jingling and tramping, a regiment of musketeers.

Mary and Sinnie waited until the men were out of sight and then followed, fascinated, their leather soles silent as the Narragansett's deerskin. Other women came from doorways, stepped through gates. They did not speak to one another, as if the leaf-scented air was itself a flux binding peace and could be broken by the merest whisper. They gathered by the meeting house and watched the militia and the Narragansett milling beneath the tavern's sign, two carved bunches of grapes creaking in the shadow-cooled wind.

Governor Vane arrived, and the magistrates, and the ministers. English and Indians exchanged greetings—filed inside.

"'Twas Miantonomi," William told them, at supper. "The Narragansett sachem. We have made an alliance with them against the Pequots."

"Why?" Mary lowered her spoon.

"Last month, an English bark sighted a ship filled with Pequot. The English attacked and killed those Indians who did not throw themselves overboard. They did find an old Englishman below-decks . . ." He lowered his voice. "Stark naked with his head cleft and his arms and legs cut, as though in the process of removal."

Mary thought of the road leading to the mainland, a finger of land so thin that it was covered with water at high tide.

"For revenge, we burned two of their villages and spoiled their canoes," William said. "There will be more. And worse."

Darkness had fallen and the crickets throbbed—feebler, now, a silvery scraping.

SEVEN

Unravellings - 1637

✳

MARY HUDDLED BENEATH THREE QUILTS and a deerskin.

"What is it?" she said. William had been grim at supper, had muttered the prayer as if the words disgusted him. Now he lay on his back, arms crossed, not seeking sleep but watching the devilish dance of shadow on the walls. He had built a fire, for a late autumn storm swept down from the northeast.

"Mr. Wilson," he said. "That porridge-mouthed prick."

"*William.*"

"Nay, Mary. If you knew."

"What, then?"

"*Am I doing my duty. Why is my wife not producing babies. Am. I. Doing. My. Duty.* Pompous Cambridge ass. He would interfere in a man's very bed."

Sleet pattered against the oiled paper.

"Mr. Wilson will be seeking retribution for our actions," she said. "When we walked from his insufferable sermon. You know that Anne was queried and she said we had cramp."

She looked up at him but he would not meet her eyes. Samuel was now two years old. Her flowers continued to arrive—full moon, crescent moon, new moon.

"'Tis true, though," she reasoned. "Although Mr. Wilson has the wrong reason for it—in fact, we have no new babe."

She pushed herself up onto the bolster beside him. He rolled, gathered her, pressed his lips to her hair. She heard the yipping of foxes.

"They are hungry," she murmured. "Looking for hens."

She felt William's body relax as he slipped towards sleep but she had been quickened to wakefulness by his words.

Porridge-mouthed prick.

"Perhaps," she said. "Perhaps the Lord doth punish me."

She felt the steam of his breath.

So many confusing things. Loving too much, or not enough. Her agile hungry mind. Her questions. Her pride.

"Nay," William said, yawning. "I do not think so, Mary, for then he would have punished me too and he has not. Our crops did prosper. I am a freeman. We are in good health."

"He doth test us, perhaps."

"Because of the controversy and our part in it?"

"Aye."

But our reasons differ, she thought. Faith and politics. Both make a wedge that cleaves the colony.

Mary curled against William. She sought prayer but instead remembered finding a grass snake, last summer, trapped beneath a rock, lashing from side to side. From pity, she had lifted the stone. Underneath, lying on the cold soil, had been an enormous milk snake with the smaller serpent in its mouth—half-swallowed.

In January, a Fast Day was called to mourn, and mend, the colony's dissension. John Wheelwright had been invited up from Mount Wollaston to give the sermon.

We are like sheep, Mary thought, glancing up. Winter sheep, huddled upon the moor.

Woollen hoods, capes, greatcoats—grey, black, goldenrod yellow, pokeberry red, squared on men's shoulders, draped over women's heads. January light gleamed on the men's white collars; their garments exuded the tinge of pipe smoke. Women and girls set their feet on foot stoves, filled with hot coals; men's calves were thickened by heavy, gartered stockings.

She felt her ribs curve round the gnawing cave of her stomach. They had eaten nothing since last night's supper. She glimpsed Governor Henry Vane, seated near the front. He bent in prayer, blonde curls and gloved hands covering his face. He wore gloves like those William had sold in London—blue kid, with a pattern of seed-pearl lions and long gauntlets of brushed suede.

Wheelwright gathered his papers, mounted the steps and stood beneath the sounding board that overhung the pulpit. He laid his hands on either side of a cushioned Bible.

At least half of the people in the meeting house are Anne's follow-ers. They think to appease us. They hope her brother-in-law will calm the troubled waters.

Wheelwright waited until only the distant plaint of gulls could be heard.

"Christ did prove and show that it was not for disciples to fast," he began. The deacons glanced at one another, startled.

"Those that are the least acquainted with the Lord Jesus are given *most of all* to fasting. The papists are given much to fasting. If Christ be present with his people, then they have no cause to fast."

Mary glanced at Anne, who was watching her brother-in-law with an expression of amazed approbation. Mr. Wilson moved as if to rise and knock Wheelwright to the floor. The minister at his side caught his arm, forced him down. Mr. Cotton laid a shaking hand over his eyes and bent forward to stare at the floor.

From the inviolacy of the lectern, Wheelwright gave a lengthy sermon on the evils of fasting, on the spiritual barrenness of those who would so advise, and then asked: "What will be the end and issue, do you think, if people so set themselves against the ways of *grace* and the Lord Jesus Christ?"

He pointed at Reverend Wilson.

"Why do you resist the Holy Spirit?"

He savours his chance to preach in the place from whence he hath been shunned.

"Brethren, those under a covenant of works—the more holy they are, the greater enemies they are to Christ. If men do not know the work of grace and ways of God, they shall die, sayeth the Lord."

His voice rose, a flush swept up his neck and bloated his face.

"*Enemies of Christ!*" He swept his gaze along the front row. "We must kill them with the work of the Lord! We must prepare for a spiritual combat! We must put on the whole arms of God. We must be ready to fight. *We must all prepare for battle and come against our enemy!*"

He returned to his seat.

The deacons rose at once and strode down the aisle. The door opened.

Cold evening air blew in.

February 1637

My beloved Aunt Urith,
We pass our days in apprehension, since there is trouble afoot in our small colony. My friend Anne hath set the place buzzing, as when a foot is stept upon a ground-hive. She is a woman of great learning and hath cast aspersions upon the teachings of the ministers, save two, her brother-in-law John Wheelwright and her own teacher, the Reverend Cotton. Wheelwright gave a Fast Day sermon in which he did terribly admonish the ministers. The General Court did meet and judged him guilty of sedition and contempt. One man wrote a remonstrance, which seventy-five signed, including my William. They think him neither guilty, nor

seditious. Were I a man, I, too, would have signed. So far,
nothing has come of it, but I fear more repression will
come before long. When we arrived here, the place ran
smooth as a mill, every piece in place and perfectly work-
ing, and we received assurance of God's approval thereby.
Now I do not know what to think as it seems there are
many unravellings.

Too, there is trouble with the Pequot of Connecticut
which commenced last summer when a pinnace filled with
Indians was found to contain the body of an Englishman.
Our men went to the mouth of the Pequot River and
demanded a sachem, who did not come, and so they did
burn the Indian towns and spoiled their canoes. I pray
there will be no war, yet all are feared it will come to pass
and so we have made alliance with the Narragansett of
Rhode Island . . .

Strange words they would be to Aunt Urith, Mary thought, putting away her quill, tucking the paper back into the drawer. *Pequot,*
Narragansett, sachem, pinnace. These things were as familiar to her,
now, as walls pearled with frozen pitch; the raw smell of boiling
cornmeal; or the moan of wind.

On a cold day in January, Mary and Anne were returning from a
childbirth when they saw Governor Henry Vane outside the tavern.
He spotted them and seemed on the point of turning away but then
changed his bearing. They met under an icicle-speared overhang.

He was red-faced, puffy-eyed.

"I am coming from the General Court," he said. He looked past
the women, out over the harbour, brooding. "They blamed me for
the dissension. I . . ."

Burst into tears, Mary thought. Ah, dear. He is but a boy.

"I announced my resignation. I said I would go home to England on the next ship."

"And?" Anne said.

"They chided me and so I agreed to stay until the May election to . . ." He tugged at a long, curled lock.

"Keep the colony from utter chaos," she snapped.

He met her eye, miserable. "Aye."

January passed, and February, and once again a head-high drift built on the seaward side of the house, its lip teased by the wind into a fragile curl.

Report came from Connecticut that an Englishman had been set upon by Pequot. He had been tortured for three days, fingers, toes, hands and feet cut off, skin flayed, hot embers placed between flesh and skin.

In March, the people of Boston flocked to the gallows, set on a rise overlooking the isthmus.

A man had copulated with a cow. He stood on a ladder with a noose around his neck. Militia approached the gallows, leading the cow, a little heifer the colour of deerskin with large brown eyes, curved horns and a dished face. She shambled down the icy path, stepping delicately with a patient, hopeful expression.

The hangman swung a maul up over his head and brought it down between the heifer's horns. Her knees buckled, a bawl came deep and desperate. Again and again the maul landed—on the cow's head, her neck, her cheekbone.

Men, women and children stood in the snow, not daring to look away. The deacons held their Bibles.

When the snow bore a shawl of red blood and the cow was still, they knocked the ladder from beneath the man's feet.

Do I love God?

On the way home, Mary tried to erase the thought and the outrage that accompanied it; for although God was watching England, his wrath quivering at the transgressions so rampant in those desecrated churches, here in the New Jerusalem he loomed much closer. She felt his face behind the thin gauze that evolved across the charcoal clouds. She felt his mind in the fretful waves that broke upon ice-glazed rocks. His wrath—in the gales, the blizzards, the harsh light.

Whose will, whose rules, whose God?

She stumbled on a stone, pressed fist to mouth and whispered into it.

"I am sorry for my doubting thoughts, they do come unbidden, try as I do to banish them. I am sorry. I am grateful. I will obey."

Her mind filled with the little cow. Her hopeful eyes.

Mary went to the outhouse carrying a pail of ashes, chicken bones and a broken clay pipe. Afterwards, she stood with pail in mittened hand. Smoke rose from chimneys, white against a leaden sky. The path to the house was a tramped coil between diminishing snow banks. She stood, listening. No bird cried, no gate creaked.

Her flowers had not come. For a week or more, she had been expecting blood.

Another child? Have you sent me a child, my Lord?

She set down the ash pail and placed both hands on her belly. She looked at the clustered houses, their lisping chimneys. She thought of the women within, stirring pottage, sewing, scrubbing. The men— splitting wood at chopping blocks. Girls, stitching samplers. Boys, plaiting broom corn or sharpening knives.

She heard Wilson's pitiless voice.

God is watching. God is watching us.

Sinnie was washing clothes in a bucket outside the house. Before coming outside, she had opened all the windows and doors. The chime of frogs rose from the swamp, gurnippers swarmed from the heating soil. Blankets and linens made an exultant snapping, tied to a line. Samuel toddled away from her down the dirt lane with his arms wide.

I did teach him!

She watched, kneeling by the washtub. Dandelions, fuzzy-topped. She picked one, rubbed it on her cheeks. Mary, standing in the doorway, laughed.

"You should see yourself, Sinnie!"

Sinnie gazed at her mistress. Pregnant! And she did look so happy, now. Going off most days with Mistress Hutchinson, the two of them looking into their baskets, comparing. Tinctures, scissors, linens.

And I am peaceful, alone with house, hens, bairn. Ah, may they keep me after my indenture is over.

Sinnie sniffed at the dandelion. Bitter, the smell of life. She rose, shaking soap from her hands. Samuel had wandered off.

"I'll go," Mary offered.

"Nay, I'll be after the peevie bairn."

Happy, she be happy at last. She ran over the grassy track, leapt a pile of manure, heard Samuel's delighted squeal as he caught sight of her.

Anne Hutchinson persuaded Henry Vane to stay and run again for governor.

He was defeated by John Winthrop, as was every other Hutchinsonian on the General Court, since the vote was deliberately moved to Newtown, too far for some of Anne's Boston supporters to travel.

Quickly, Winthrop made a new law—no newcomer might remain in the colony for longer than three weeks without permission of the General Court. For it was the merchants who were arriving in greatest number and who were most likely to side with Anne.

They will silence us, Mary thought, hearing the news. Decree by decree. Or worse. As Laud did to their own, back home.

Governor Winthrop summoned the people of Boston to the meeting house. It was sultry, so humid that Mary felt sweat at the roots of her hair. Mary, Sinnie and Samuel passed the whipping post where bits of frayed rope lay in the new grass. Dandelions lined a path worn along the south side of the building. Mary joined the women. They walked quietly, with bent heads, and Mary, too, lowered her eyes, less with obedience than to hide her lack of it. She followed Anne into the building. The smell of childbirth came from Anne's clothing, a vinegar-blood brightness. Blue bags beneath her eyes—and her expression was acute, stern, as if examining a wound.

"Were you . . ."

"Aye," Anne whispered. There were fine hairs on her upper lip; her skin had begun its complex collapse. They were now inside the sanctified room. "A girl. A long labour."

Some knew why they had been gathered. Those who did not slid questioning eyes at others, fanning themselves with hats or turkey-feather fans. Governor Winthrop waited until the doors were shut. Then he rose and stood behind the lectern. He was silent until every stir, cough, or boy's wriggle had ceased.

"As you know," he began. "The salvages are instruments of the Devil. He is their commander. You have heard that he hath stirred the salvages up against us English."

He glanced at Reverend Cotton. "Our ministers tell us that God hath *allowed* the Devil to raise his forces in order to awaken us from our slide into sloth and sin. So it is particularly notable that in this time we have been sorely put to the test."

He paused.

"The Lord hath allowed our triumph."

Triumph. Mary's eyes went to her lap, rested upon her own hands, known since childhood, with their daily refinements. *Salvages*; but she could not picture the imps of Satan he would have them imagine. She remembered, rather, Miantonomi, the Narragansett sachem, accompanied by the son of Chief Canonicus and twenty sanaps, striding down Corn Hill Road, summoned to parley.

Clasped hands tightened. Her thumbnails flared red, then white.

". . . our English marched in the night to their fort at Mystic, Connecticut, and beset it at the break of day. After two hours' fight, they did set fire to it. They slew two chief sachems, and one hundred fifty fighting men. They slew one hundred and fifty . . . people . . ."

Her eyes flew up. Winthrop had slurred the words, like spreading softened butter. Her mind shouted them.

Old people. Sunken of chest, with spotted, gnarled hands.

Women. Firelight, terrified eyes. Arms around their . . .

Children.

Babies.

"We shall have a day of thanks kept in June for this victory."

At night, every window in the house was swung wide on its hinges to admit the sea air. By breakfast time, the catnip beside the stone doorstep wilted. Sun stretched across the sill and burned the scoured floor. Fire glimmered in the grey coals and Sinnie bent over the hearth, stirring them to life.

Mary sat by the door, eyes closed, holding to her nose a linen-wrapped package of toasted bread steeped in vinegar to assuage her morning sickness. Sweat slid down her temples as she fought waves of nausea. Sounds became sharp, sudden, senseless: the child's chatter, Sinnie's croon, a loud snap from the fire.

"Mistress."

"Yes."

"Shall I fetch the oven wood?"

Ah, 'tis bake day.

The fire, stoked to ferocity in the domed oven. Coals, scraped out. The table, covered with flour, molasses, vegetables, pans, spoons. Wash, dry, chop, sweat, feed Samuel, walk to the spring. While wanting to curl on her side with her eyes closed and her breathing spare, shallow.

"Aye."

William spent his days at his milliner's shop in the market. He had bought a share of the new town dock, which included a wharf crane and a warehouse. Jurden had proved as much a godsend to William as Sinnie was to Mary. Patient, uncomplaining, he anticipated William's needs like a foreman; and along with other men William had hired, made the long daily journey to fields and pastures on Pullen Point where William grew corn and kept cattle and pigs. They set forth before daybreak, rowing up through the inlets and marshes, landing on a sandy beach. Jurden attempted to describe the place; how, veiled in mist, were grasses looped by dewed spider's webs, and vine-draped fences, and pig pens, and fields of corn. How eagles soared overhead and the cows wandered amongst the trees, grazing in their shade, while the pigs rooted in pens built between the boles of girdled hardwoods.

Mary stood and went outside. She gazed out over the marshes, the glittering water, the islands. So peaceful, she thought, while those who looked upon it fought over the proper template for salvation.

—

Mary and Anne walked slowly, tired. A cool breeze threaded its welcome way through the July heat. It came up between the close-set houses to their left, smelling of the harbour—tarry wharves, tide wrack. In their baskets, they carried small crocks of goose-grease, knives, pennyroyal, rue, juniper berries. A baby boy had been born after a night of labour.

"I did not imagine that the New World would be so hot."

"Aye, as hot as it is cold," Anne said. "'Tis a place of extremes."

She is stretched, Mary thought, sliding her eyes at Anne's face. The meetings had grown unwieldy, volatile. Anne had become sharp, dismissive and the women were afraid to ask their questions. For they saw how she had no time for slow minds, and that in the cold art of debate she was without compassion, separating thought from thinker. Even men were careful to consider their words before offering them up for Anne's pronouncements.

"Reverend Cotton hath become . . ." Anne mused.

She spoke as if the thought had escaped, unwittingly, from fatigue. The sun beat down upon the dusty grass and the burning soil.

"What?"

Anne's footsteps made a *pat-pat*, her skirt dragged in the dust. Her pace increased.

"He is no longer so welcoming to me. He seeks excuses to avoid my visits. His child is sick and must have silence. He hath not the time, his sermon is not yet complete . . . And so on."

She shifted her basket to the other arm. An insect made a long trilling that increased in volume until it broke.

They came to the square. On one side was the market, with its long porch, women slipping into the shops. Across from it, the meeting house.

"Ah," Anne breathed. "Do you see, Mary. In this heat. No water, no shelter. No shade."

A woman was chained to a post. She wore a leather collar with an iron ring. Her dress was black with sweat. She leaned forward to ease the pain in her arms, bound behind her. Her eyes slid and rolled, the whites prominent, their expression shifting between rage and terror.

They hurried across the square. Anne sought a cloth in her basket, moistened it with a tincture. She pressed it to the woman's cracked lips.

"What was your transgression?" Anne asked.

"I did strike my husband. I did lift my hand to him."

A jingle of lifted muskets. The woman wrenched her head within her collar to spit at the approaching watchmen.

"There is nothing to be done, Mary," Anne murmured.

Henry Vane made his plans to return to England. He would leave in August. Until then, he picked through Boston's filthy streets with a distrait air, plucking at his lace cuffs.

"I am going to investigate the Narragansett Country," William said. He was carving the design of a stag on an axe helve, having broken the last. He probed with his gouge, forming the horns.

Samuel slept, Sinnie had climbed the ladder to her bed. From their chairs set before the open door, they could smell the smoke of Jurden's pipe. They listened to the crickets, the crying sea birds. They watched the clouds, smouldering over the islands, drifting, evolving from fire-red to cottony pink.

"'Salvation by works, salvation by grace.' On the ferry, Josiah and Hugh were nose to nose, the colour of beets. Roaring on the subject. And then there are those who name her . . .'"

He broke off, his lips worked over unspeakable words. Still nothing had been done about the remonstrance that he and the other men had filed with the court. Still John Wheelwright had not been sentenced. Yet the watchmen were vigilant and there were more public punishments in order that no bad deed should bring down God's wrath; whippings, hangings, placing cleft sticks on tongues, the imprisonment of both men and women in the stocks. Even children were brought to the elders or magistrates to be questioned about their own parents; and were threatened by the death penalty in case of their own "extraordinary sinfulness." Neighbours were wary of one another, watching, terrified, for signs and wonders. Boston hissed with hateful words: *sedition, contempt, slander.*

"Witch or whore," Mary said. Anger had grown in her, fitfully, over the summer. It ebbed and then bloomed larger at each recurrent outrage.

William set down his gouge, considered her. She saw the stubble on his cheeks, pricks of hair reddened by the light.

"Witch or whore," she repeated, coldly, her voice pitched so that neither Sinnie nor passing neighbour would hear.

She bundled her knitting, leaned to put it into a basket at her feet.

"They will destroy her. They will cast her out."

It neared the hour. Soon the watchmen would pass by the open door.

"Aye," William said. His hands clenched. Outside, the gulls carried the light's last dusting on their wings as they dove and wheeled. "There is no freedom here. Not that I would name as such. They say that we attain freedom by doing God's will. Then they tell me what I may charge for my goods. They make laws that would not stand in England."

"If they banish her, I will follow."

They considered the view framed by their door. The marshes with their bayberry bushes. Fiery clouds over the sea.

He lowered his voice, leaned towards her. The watchmen approached. "We should leave before that comes to pass."

He pointed southeast, beyond the dark hunch of Fort Hill.

"Providence. If you agree, I will go seek counsel of Roger Williams. I would go on my own volition rather than—"

"I *do* agree," she said. "Go. See if it be better over there, where a man doth govern who speaks of soul liberty."

September 1637

My dear Aunt Urith,

Terrible deeds have occurred. I must unburden myself of them and trust you may bear my abhorrence. Our English hath marched to a place in Connecticut named Mystic where they found a fort of the Pequot. Oh, my aunt, how could the Lord countenance the murder of 150 men, women, and children? Our governor Winthrop hath reported this to us with great satisfaction and we have sat in the meeting house with bowed heads, thanking the Lord for our victory. All this summer such things have continued. On one occasion forty-eight Pequot women and children were marched into Boston. They were branded and given to various for servants. I would not have one and was hard put to say why, but did so. On another occasion the Pequot men did hide in a swamp and sent away their women and children to be saved. After a battle wherein the Pequot men were killed, wounded or escaped, the English did find the women and children. They divided them as we do cattle or sheep, sending them hither and thither, to Bermuda, Massachusetts and Connecticut. Now they say that the Devil hath been defeated, eight or nine hundred of his army being killed dead and the rest dispersed. I came upon a child in the street following after her English mistress. Oh, my aunt, had we been home you and I would have taken her and searched high and low for the

mother for whom she wept. Yet I dare not speak my mind
for there is for the smallest offence the lash, the stocks and
the gallows. 'Tis a dark place despite the sun which blazeth
upon us and doth reflect off the sea like butterflies. What
would I do without my Sinnie, who hath taught our Samuel
to play the cat's cradle and hath made for him a doll of
stockings. Who laughs and feels not the horror . . .

She woke from a dream of grief. William slept beside her; he would
leave for the Narragansett Country next month on some pretext.
She stared up at the bed's canopy. She could not understand this
pregnancy. The child within did not stretch, urgent as a swelling
seed. Rather she felt jolts of change, a jagged momentum accompanied by dread. And although Sinnie was thrilled by the pregnancy,
and perceived her mistress to feel the same, Mary did not tell her
how her physical distress, oddly, had no commensurate and antici-
patory joy. Her morning sickness lasted far longer than normal. She
was continuously dizzy, rising from the washtub and reeling, snatch-
ing at chair backs or walls, standing with eyes closed against the
world's doubling. Her legs were seized by cramps that woke her,
shouting with agony, so that William would waken and knead at her
calves with his thumbs. Her belly was but a slight bulge and the
movements within her womb were furtive ripplings rather than the
bold shoves she remembered from Samuel's tenancy.

Her lips moved. She whispered into the cold darkness.

To thee, O Lord, I call; my rock, be not deaf to me . . .

EIGHT

Signs and Wonders — 1637

ALL DAY THEY HEARD THE screaming of pigs.

Slaughter season. William had killed theirs before sailing for Providence two weeks ago. Mary had received no word from him since.

She went to the garden to pick parsley. Samuel followed, carrying a basket. Mary saw how the pouched skin on his hands was sun-browned. He trotted ahead of her between the sunflower stalks. The carrot tops were feathery, turning pale, and the air bore the regretful spice of decay.

"Parsley," Samuel called, squatting. Milkweed seeds pinwheeled, landed on the child's head.

She stood stock-still, gazing at him. Love came as if from the drifting seeds, the sun-warmed tufts of goldenrod, the scent of mint. She wondered why it came pouring upon her just now. Perhaps because Samuel had himself chosen to leave Sinnie's side. Perhaps it was the way his deer-hide slippers had patted so confidently over the path. Or because he was a boy now, not a baby. His lips would not turn white.

She came up beside him, knelt. The green lacy leaves were crisp to the touch, as if already dried.

"Parsley," she agreed. She took a breath to tell him a story from her childhood—how once she had found a robin's egg in the midst of a parsley plant—and was struck with pain so intense that she fell forward, her face in the leaves.

Samuel screamed. "Sinnie! Sinnie! Sinnie!"

A crash, pan to floor. Sinnie came running, her voice jouncing with the thud of her shoes.

"Mistress! I'm coming."

Mary felt Sinnie's small body pressed close, arms circling her.

"Stand, you must stand."

Mary cried out as she came to her feet. The pain augered her belly, her back. "I am only seven months," she panted. "'Tis too soon. Too soon. William is away . . ."

Mary bent forward over Sinnie's arms, face in her hands. Everything rushed up and dwindled away into specks. Anne Hutchinson and her meetings. The Puritan ministers, pontificating. Pigs. Children picking bayberries in the autumn marshes. While she went down into a dark slippery place with translucent walls. Fire. Black flicker. The cadence of her heart pounding, blood so thick in her veins that hearing reduced, swooped away, became only a rushing. Now her feet were moving over the path, Sinnie was talking, a stream of words.

She was on her knees again, clasping the pain with both arms.

Ah. Hold it, appease it.

Swimming towards mahogany light.

Mary opened her eyes. Afternoon had faded into dusk. The familiar bedchamber—her bedchamber—was made strange by the presence of several bustling women; and by Sinnie at the doorway, peering in, Samuel at her skirts; by a kettle set over the coals; by Anne, at the hearth within a cloud of basil-scented steam.

Pain seized her womb, a spiralling craze. Despair swept over her. She squeezed the hand of the young woman at her side. Mercy Talford, mother of three. Nutmeg freckles on her nose, widely spaced brown eyes. She held a Bible in her lap.

"Read," said Anne, glancing up from the infusion. "Read to her, Mercy."

Pain.

"'Praise the name of the Lord . . . whatever the Lord pleases he does, in heaven and on earth . . .'"

Pain.

"'Sent signs and wonders / against Pharaoh and all his . . .'"

Pain.

"'Will vindicate his people . . . have compassion . . .'"

They had slid her from the bed, held her sitting upright. She felt sudden humiliation that she should be so reduced, she who often worked at Anne's side—swift, competent. Anne put an arm around her waist.

"Take her other arm, Mercy," Anne said.

She was standing.

"Walk, Mary," Anne said. "You must walk."

The pain came again and she crumpled forward. Anne's voice was like a rope, pulling.

"Walk, even in the pain, Mary. Walk."

"Will I die?"

"Nay, Mary, you will not die."

"But 'tis too soon. And if the baby comes, Anne, and should die, and should take me, too, I have not prepared. I have not prepared my soul."

"If it comes to such a pass, we will see that you are prepared. But you are young and strong, do not think that you shall die. *I will not let you die, Mary.*"

Mary paced.

Back and forth between bedstead and wall, chest and hearth, her eyes on the pine floor that she and Sinnie had scrubbed yesterday. Sand prickled her bare feet. The wind rose, a white mutter. Wind,

Mary thought, with sudden anger. Always wind, fretting the Shawmut Peninsula.

In the next room, Samuel began to cry.

Anne went to the door.

"Sinnie, take the child to my house for the night."

"Yes, Mistress."

"Do not return till I send for you."

"Yes, Mistress."

Mary arched backwards, hands to belly. Screamed.

The waters broke.

They tipped her onto the bed, soothed her until she could roll onto her back. Anne pressed Mary's knees apart, slid a lard-greased hand inside.

Mary heard a sharp intake of breath. She lifted her head, opened her eyes. She saw Anne's gaze become fixed as her fingers probed, her lips compressing into a grim line.

"What . . ." Mary began, but fell back, panting.

Anne withdrew her hand and gently pressed Mary's knees together as if closing a book upon learning its ending.

The women rubbed her belly with warm oil, held a mug of caudle to her lips. They spoke in low voices edged with panic.

"Hold her shoulders."

Aunt Urith, Aunt Urith. Dust spinning from red wheels. Mother.

"Mother!"

Her cries rose like flames, consuming walls, ceiling, house.

"Feet."

A hand inside her, working. Mary fought. Fought to rise from the bed, to leave her body, to tear herself from the women's hands. She twisted her spine, bit, panted, screamed. Her body was shaken with spasms. Froth at her mouth. Convulsions.

The neighbour women covered their faces. One ran from the room.

"Go then," Anne panted. Her voice rose to a shout. "Go. All of you. There is nothing you can do. Jane, stay by me."

Mary's last scream rose, split.

Darkness came upon her.

Anne stood in the centre of the room, fingers against ears, mouth pressed into the heels of her hands. Jane Hawkins knelt in a dark corner lifting a blanket with one hand. Down, the fabric. Around, up, down. Twisting. Swaddling.

Anne removed hands from face, drew a long breath. "We must wrap Mary against the child-bed fever."

"Aye," Jane said. She was an older woman, Cornish. Her coif had slipped over her forehead, drew a black slash above shrewd eyes. Finished, she pushed herself to her feet, hands to knees, crossed the room to a pile of linens.

"I should wash her," she said, glancing at Mary, who lay sleeping, blood-soaked shift tangled round her.

"Goody Hawkins. You saw."

"Aye."

Experienced midwives, they held one another's eyes. The fire had died to ashes and the pine splints flickered, at the point of extinction.

"What was it?" Anne whispered. Her hands rose, she gripped Jane's shoulders.

"The sex. I could see the sex. 'Twas a girl's."

"But. The rest. Have you ever . . ."

"Never. Never in all my days, Mistress Hutchinson."

"You know how . . . 'twill . . ."

"Aye."

"You must never tell. Never, never, Jane Hawkins. For her sake, as well as ours. Mine. And yours."

"Aye."

Mary stirred, her head rolled on the pillow. Even sleeping, her face was distressed.

They heard a scream, so distant they could not tell if it were wolf or wildcat.

"Jane, I must go . . . out. Do not let anyone come into this room."

Exhaustion, and what had come to pass, settled in Jane Hawkins' hips, face, hands. She turned towards the pile of linens, wavered, and then sank onto a chair. She glanced at the wrapped bundle. Then she looked at wine in a pipkin, steaming over the coals.

"I do not fancy being left alone with it," she whispered.

"Mary is here," Anne said. Her own voice had dropped and she stepped forward, shook Jane's shoulder, briskly. "Verily, Goody Hawkins. 'Tis *dead*."

Mary felt warmth on her face, knubbled cotton beneath her cheek.

Awake. Where am I.

There was no sound. No screaming. No pain.

Baby.

She opened her eyes. October light sleeked the ceiling joists, the oak mantel. She felt the low cramp in her womb, tried to bring knees to belly and found herself swaddled from the waist down, legs and belly wrapped tight.

Where is Sinnie? My dear . . .

Sinnie appeared in the doorway, began to speak and then disappeared. A murmur, in the next room. Anne came, her steps swift and sure. She carried a bowl of cornmeal mush, set it on the table, added a log to the fire, poked with the tongs until flames rose against the granite's blackened crust. She drew a chair close to the bed, took up the bowl.

"Where is my baby?" Mary said.

"Quiet," Anne said. Her voice was uneasy beneath its calm. "Eat and I will tell you."

The spoon pressed into the fine, moist meal, causing a pool of maple syrup. Anne lifted the mush to Mary's mouth.

"Girl or boy?" Mary whispered, frightened.

"Shhh, you must eat." She slipped the spoon into Mary's mouth, watched as she chewed and swallowed. "Mary." She whispered, laid a hand on Mary's cheek. "'Twas dead."

Mary's eyes stilled, as if life had left them, too. She stared at Anne, the question unspoken.

Anne raised her hand like a shield. "Nay, do not ask me, Mary." The skin of her forehead pulled back, tightened.

"Do not ask you . . . what? Where is my baby?"

Cold air came over the windowsill, stirred bunched herbs hanging from the summer beam. Sunlight revealed the room's plainness: wainscot, mud-daubed walls. Anne's hand shook, suddenly, violently. She put down the bowl.

"Mary. 'Twas a blessing the child was born lifeless. Truly, you must believe this. Only Jane Hawkins and I saw it—her. She was . . . disfigured."

"How so?"

They heard the slapping of Samuel's bare feet in the next room. Sinnie's shushing.

"Disfigured, you say," Mary repeated. "How so? Where is she?"

Anne looked away, and Mary saw her assurance falter, as if sapped by self-doubt, or, oddly, shame.

"There was . . ." Anne paused, looking at the counterpane. "Mary, the child had no . . . head. Barely a face. The eyes were oddly . . ."

She sighed and fell silent.

Mary lay back on the bolster, looked down at her hands. Curled and empty, like all the beautiful, finished vessels that rattled in the autumn wind: pods, husks. She looked through a blur of tears at the front window, saw waves upon the bay lifting the morning light as if no great change had come in the world; equally oblivious, the hillsides burned in the rising glow of morning, filtering sunshine through the red grasses.

William, in Providence. He had begun his day not knowing.

"The women could not bear your screams and I bade them leave," Anne said, her voice strengthening. "Only Jane Hawkins saw the poor thing come into my hands. When I saw it, I knew, then, that . . ."

Mary could barely speak for the thickening in her throat. Her words came in rushes, separated by struggles for breath. "Should the truth of my birth be spread about, the people will say that I have been punished by God. Or that you have been punished by God."

Anne seized Mary's hand, stroked it as she would stroke a child's head. Grey hair escaped from the confines of her coif. She laid Mary's hand back on the counterpane and clasped her own hands in her lap.

"I went to Mr. Cotton," she said. "I told him what had come to pass and asked his counsel. I begged his confidence. He thought upon it."

"But—"

Anne's eyes snapped to Mary's, shifty with repressed doubt. "Who else was I to ask?"

He avoids her, Anne told me. He is no longer welcoming, she said.

They listened to milling gulls, a confusion of sound.

"I will tell you what he said," Anne said, finally, drawing a breath. "He said God intended only the instruction of the parents."

Mary started up from the bolster. "No. No. Not William."

"Nay, listen. He spoke kindly, Mary. He said if it were his, he would bury it in secret. I protested. I reminded him that in England, midwives may bury a baby in private, but here the council hath forbidden it so that they may ascertain if the child was illegitimate, or murdered, or bore signs of witchcraft. He said: 'You shall register the birth and say that you came to me and that I gave you dispensation.' We are safe, then, as long as Jane Hawkins does not speak. And she will not, for as I reminded her, she hath been called a cunning woman, even a witch, more than once."

She leaned close to whisper in Mary's ear.

"I returned and bade Jane Hawkins fetch Sinnie to watch over you. Then she and I took the child. The child is buried where she shall not be found."

A daughter, Mary thought. Buried. Alone in the wind and the black night. Where the wolves might find her.

"So what should I . . . what does Mr. Cotton wish us to say?"

"Your labour came early, Mary, 'twill be seen as a simple miscarriage. You must tell no one. For it will . . ."

Give the men cause for triumph. Vilify both of us. Even Reverend Cotton wishes to hide the truth, for it will damage him, since Anne, still, is his acolyte.

"Oh, Anne," she said. She began to weep, a simpler weeping, a mother's grief. "Oh, Anne. The wolves will dig . . ."

"Nay," Anne said, quickly, positive. "She is buried deep." She leaned over Mary, busy with covers and bolster. "She is buried deep."

NINE

Sedition 1637–1638

✳

IN EARLY NOVEMBER, snowflakes fell, large as shillings, drifting from a white sky. Sinnie stopped to watch them.

Like those wee marks in books, she thought. Each one different, making words that Mary can read.

Sinnie was playing fox and geese with Samuel. The little red-capped fox came running down the path marked in the snow, and Sinnie shrieked and ran.

"A fox, a fox!"

She clapped hand to mouth, darted a glance up the street, but no one loomed from the snow to bid her cease such childishness.

'Tis a shame to be happy when Mary be sae pitiful sad. And William still away and not knowing.

Ever since the birth, Mary's silence had burdened the house. Sinnie sang under her breath, aiming the sound towards Samuel. Even Jurden spoke up at meals, for the sake of the child. He told of seeing steam holes in snow, "a sign of sleeping bears"; he told of giving chase to a wolf upon the sands.

Mary could not help her lips' sweet upward curl but her eyes were haggard and she did not eat.

Will make an apple pandowdy. Tempt her . . . poor thing.

She clapped her mittens at Samuel.

—

Mary stepped outside and stood holding a bucket in each hand. Sinnie and Samuel's red knitted caps were vivid against new shuttered houses with their dark timbers. Seeing their happy play, Mary wondered at her lack of jealousy.

I was not meant to be a mother.

Since the birth, Samuel had absorbed Mary's mood. He was querulous—wept and screamed until Sinnie bundled him up and took him into the frigid air. Mary watched Sinnie's small, quick fingers tying ribbons, tucking hair, lacing shoes; listened to her Nornish croon. She felt no ease with the child, since she could think of no songs or fairytales, could not smile or play silly games. At bedtime, when she said her prayers—on her knees, murmuring obedience and begging redemption—a furious whisper seeped into her mind, like air beneath a sill, saying that she and William did not deserve their punishment. She tried to stop it, knowing that the Lord was listening. Her hands went to her temples, she collapsed against the bed and pressed her face to the coverlet.

I shall go mad. I shall go mad. Oh, that I ever came to this accursed place.

Sinnie—kneeling, arms out for Samuel, eyelashes laden with snowflakes—looked up as Mary came down the path from the house.

"Mistress, I will fetch the water. You stay and play with the bairn."

"Nay, I will fetch it, Sinnie."

Mary needed to walk, smell the ordinary goodness of lobster pie on the metallic air. She hung the buckets on the yoke, picked her way over the street's hummocked detritus: half-frozen spoiled beets, peelings thrown out for pigs, a staved barrel. There was not a breath of wind, as if the snowflakes in their density had quieted the air.

In the square, women in hooded capes or broad-brimmed leather hats were gathered at the well.

If I avoid their eyes, they will see that I hide something. If I return their look, they will see my suffering. And become curious.

She knelt, pretended to disengage a bit of her cape that had caught in the bucket's bale. She attached her bucket to the rope and sent it plummeting downwards.

At the whipping post, a punishment was in progress—three armed men stood by, while another knotted a man's wrists and lifted his shirt. The whip whistled.

Out-of-doors, her despair did not rise, spread and diminish—she found herself containing it, with fear, like all the other goodwives. They drew closer at the man's cries and did not look at one another.

Returning with the water, Mary saw William turn the corner and come striding down Mylne Street. She knelt, set down the yoke and buckets, and ran to meet him. They threw their arms around one another, stood without speaking. Then his lips moved against her cap.

"I met Anne Hutchinson in the street. She told me."

Mary nodded, face on his shoulder.

"Are you well, Mary?"

"In body, yes, I am well. In mind, greatly disturbed."

Sinnie came to the door, Samuel at her skirts.

"Papa!" The little boy ran through the falling snow.

William shrugged from his pack as he went down on one knee, spreading his arms. Samuel went limp in his father's embrace and Mary, too, felt a crumpling within herself, a desire for safety and a place to hide.

"There are some islands in the bay where Roger Williams thinks we might settle," William said. "The land is good, with grazing grounds and trees."

He laid down his spoon, reached for the water jug.

About the baby, they held their words—all through supper, and prayers, and Samuel's nightly routines, and the household's settling. They waited until they had closed the door to their bedchamber.

Mary pulled the quilts to her chin. William sat at the fire with iron tongs, lifting and resetting the blazing logs.

"I do not remember the moment of birth," she said. She drew a long breath. "So terrible it was that I was rendered unconscious."

"Girl or boy? Anne did not tell me."

"William . . ." Hands covering her face.

He looked up at the sound of her voice. He set down the tongs, went to the bed and drew away her hands, but she would not meet his eyes.

"What?" he said. "Tell me."

Her eyes filled with tears.

"'Twas a girl. But Anne told me she was . . . disfigured."

"How disfigured?"

"She . . . she told me there was no . . . head."

"No head? How could there . . ."

"A face, yes, but no . . ." She drew a breath. "Head. She told me no more than that. Although something about . . . the eyes being . . ." She covered her face again, spoke into her hands. "But in any case, William . . ." Her voice broke. "The child was dead."

"My love."

He put his arms out, gathered her up. She spoke into his chest.

"She told me that Mr. Cotton said God intended it as an instruction for the parents."

His arms loosened, blood rushed to his face. He rose.

"Damn Mr. Cotton to hell."

"William. Remember . . ."

Her voice thickened, her tears fell.

"The Lord did take our first child. Then he gave us Samuel."

Her chest lifted with a sob. Her words were gasped, torn, choked.

"But now he doth send some . . . some warning. I do believe he hath . . . hath damned me. Or that I was damned at birth. Why, I know not. I have searched my heart."

He sat back on the bed but did not gather her. She pushed herself upright.

"'Tis *not you*, William. 'Tis me. Only me."

He lifted her hands.

"I do not believe any such thing," William said. "You have committed no sin. You do what is required of a wife and mother. You attend church, you work, you—"

"I attend Anne's meetings."

"As do many other people, Mary. Why would God punish only you?"

"I . . . we cannot know his reasons. I am filled with dread and darkness. I feel my punishment."

That night, Mary slipped from bed, lifted her cape from a hook, slid hands into mittens.

She eased open the front door.

Over the sea, slivers of cloud shimmered like minnows. The moon was full, and the house cast a black shadow. She heard the surf breaking on frozen sand.

A single wolf trotted across the marsh.

Purposeful, she thought, watching its steady progress. It went up a rise. It sat in the numinous light, its back to Boston.

A howl rose, its tremulous descent dying into silence.

Baby, marked. A sign. Come from her womb.

I try, I try, I try. I cannot understand.

—

He left the house before breakfast. When he returned, his eyes were puzzled, grim.

"What did she tell you?"

"No more than she told you."

He spoke with sudden vehemence, and she saw both his love for her and his rage at the men of higher education.

"You are not to blame, Mary. I do not believe God sent punishment to either you or me. *Do you understand?*"

She nodded, knowing acquiescence was her gift to him, for she did not believe his words, nor understood, nor thought that his own understanding was complete. Yet she would not say more, for he glanced at his musket.

He longs to be away from this.

"Go," she said. "The sky is filled with birds."

Men and women almost overwhelmed Anne's next meeting. All bore the dazed and frustrated mien of having left one kind of urgency for another. Men stamped snow from their boots, removed hats and gloves. William stood amongst them along the wall; Mary sat in her usual place by the fire, clutching her Bible like a wrapped, warmed stone. People cast assessing glances, gauging one another's anger.

Anne waited for silence and for the door to be shut tight. She glanced at the window where Governor Winthrop's house could be seen through the warped glass—icicles glittering, curtains drawn.

"As you know, they have come to me," Anne announced. "They have told me that I may no longer hold these meetings. They say . . ."

She broke off, searched not through the pages of her Bible but amongst her papers.

"Here, let me read it to you: 'Though women might meet (some few together) to pray and edify one another, yet such a set assembly (as is now in practice in Boston) where sixty or more do meet every week, and one woman (in a prophetical way, by resolving questions of doctrine and expounding Scripture) takes upon her the whole exercise, it is agreed to be disorderly and without rule.'"

An angry murmur rose from the room.

"They do choose to ignore that this is a gathering of women and men, and that we do all agree on many matters. Shall we continue these meetings?"

"Aye. Aye."

"What care we for their . . ."

"'Tis a campaign of persecution . . ."

Anne held up her hands for quiet but it was some time before the voices subsided.

I will follow her, Mary thought. Still she looked down when other women spoke kindly of her miscarriage, fearing what her eyes might reveal; but she had resumed her work with Anne, accompanying her to births and illnesses. They did not speak of what had occurred.

William returned home one evening carrying a dead grey goose. He dropped the goose onto the hearth, hung his musket on its pegs over the mantel and shrugged from his snow-laden greatcoat.

"Do you remember that remonstrance that I signed? About Wheelwright, stating our belief in his innocence?"

"Aye, I remember."

"Wheelwright hath been disenfranchised and banished. Aspinwall, he who drew the petition, is the same. Others are disenfranchised, including me."

Sinnie froze, laden trencher lifted. Her eyes touched Mary's.

"They have sent for Anne Hutchinson. We shall see what they do make of her case."

They assembled at the narrow trestle table as was their custom and ate in silence—William, Mary, Sinnie, Jurden—Samuel in his high-legged chair. There was no sound but the drag of spoons against wood. *Disenfranchised.* Mary's shock was offset by the room's settled peace. She left the last scrapings in their trencher for William and sat watching Sinnie and Jurden, seated side by side, each with a bowl. Jurden's kindness towards Samuel had won him a loosening of Sinnie's shoulders and the occasional nervous glance.

We are, truly, as a family. Knit together.

William, seeing that all spoons were still, began the prayer.

Knocking—loud, insistent. William broke off. His face darkened, he strode to the door. Two men stood on the step, carrying muskets.

"You did not turn in your weapons as ordered, William Dyer."

"Of course I did not. How am I to hunt? Protect my family?"

Mary dropped her napkin, stood.

He did not tell me of this.

The two men came in without being invited. One man walked to the hearth, kicking aside a basket of onions with his snowy boot. He lifted down William's musket.

"'Tis ordered. Where are the rest? Pistols, sword, knives."

Wax brimmed in the candle, reached its breaking point and poured onto the table. Jurden had half-risen from his chair.

"You have come to take them, then you will have to find them," William said.

Slowly, Jurden resumed his seat, fists set beside his bowl. Sinnie untied the sash holding Samuel in the highchair and carried him into the bedchamber.

Mary stood watching the obscene intimacy of William's unmanning. *London. The day he returned with musket, shot, wadding. His soft hands caressing the stock.*

The men rummaged through chests, pulling out clothing and linens, leaving them heaped on the floor. They went into the bedchamber. Sinnie screamed and ran out clutching the weeping child.

She stood trembling, Mary's arms around her, while the men returned and climbed the ladder into her attic. Mary heard the scrape and thud of skidding chamber pot, overturned pallet. They climbed down, kicked open the back door, went through to search the sheds. They returned, bearing a collection of two pistols, hunting knives, and three muskets. One paused to aim a kick at a long-legged trivet on the hearth. It flew, taking with it gridiron, bake kettle, broiler.

The door slammed shut.

William took one violent step, then turned back to the room. He looked at the dead goose, dusted in ash. His eyes were hard. Unrepentant. Seeking loopholes.

November 1637

My dear Aunt Urith,
My teacher Anne Hutchinson hath been gone this past week.
She is being held under house arrest at the home of Joseph
Weld, two miles away in Roxbury, on the mainland. There
she must stay without communication save with family and
clergy, till such time as she is tried by the church. She was
called up before the General Court and 'tis said the magis-
trates found no reason for banishment until she spoke of
direct revelation from God. Thereupon they found her guilty
of two crimes—the first being heresy, for the Puritans believe
the word of God may be revealed only through Scripture
and thus transmitted only by the clergy. The second is the
crime of sedition for her questioning of the ministers. It is
my belief that they fear her, although they say she is unfit for
our society. Such is their fear that they have today ordered a
college in a settlement near to Boston, the name of the settle-
ment to be changed to 'Cambridge' and the college to be

called "Harvard." 'Tis is for the education of young men to keep them from "corruption" by the likes of Anne. Today would have been the day for my dear friend's meeting, when I would go to her house. It is as if a light hath gone out which once graced the day's toil and tribulation, giving me balm of spirit. William, however, hath gone this day to the Hutchinson home, for he and other merchants plan our departure from this place. We shall leave in the spring, where to I do not yet know, perhaps the Narragansett Country, perhaps New Hampshire. I do miss Anne Hutchinson with whom I can talk as I could talk only to you, my aunt, or with uncle. I am forbidden visits to her.

I do grow tired of this barren peninsula. The wind here is worse even than the moors. We are living at the edge of wilderness whose terrors are unknown and thus magnified. One day, God willing, I will return to you, my aunt, and will see once again the gentler lands of home . . .

Another Christmas came and went, unmarked, save that Mary gave herself one gift. She took the letters she had received from Urith. She sat by the window and read them. One word—all she needed to evoke an entire epoch and the people she held in her heart.

Yorkshire.

Mary and William set out before dawn, trudging westwards out of Boston. There was no sunrise, only a gradual lightening that revealed storm-bearing clouds over a black January sea; meadows buried beneath drifts; and an Indian village, where rotting cattail mats hung from decayed wigwams and scavenged human skeletons lay exposed by the wind.

They stopped. Stared.

"Last summer . . . unspeakable," Mary said, hands to mouth.

In Connecticut, they had been told, the Pequot tribe "was no more."

William's eyes were grim. He nodded but said nothing in reply. He was friendly with many of the Englishmen who had gone with the militia. Only by chance had he not gone himself. In public he kept his counsel, although in the privacy of their home he had listened to Mary's diatribe against the violence; had agreed not to accept a slave into their home; and had voiced the opinion that he was unsure whether they were now safer or in greater danger.

At the narrowest point of Boston Neck, near the gallows, William swept snow from a stone and they sat to wait for low tide. They ate maize bread studded with dried huckleberries, sipped water from a leather bottle.

At noon, they crossed over the sand. The road wound up an incline to the mainland. In the distance, Roxbury broke grey from snowy fields, a cluster of buildings set around a meeting house. They kept to the road until they saw the house that they recognized by its situation as Joseph Weld's. The smoke of a banked fire was a desultory breath from the great chimney.

They made for a boulder surrounded by wild cherry trees. William squatted on one heel. A few snowflakes tipped from the sky.

"Be quick," William said. He had procured a musket from a friend, carried it slung over one shoulder.

Mary stepped out into the field, stumbling, since her toes were frozen within her shoes. She lifted her skirts, eyes on the window she had been told was Anne's. She carried a pack in which were letters from the silenced women.

Roger Williams's phrase burned like a beacon. *Soul liberty.* The reason they had left England—for the right to worship as they wished.

She thought of the Indian camp.

It was not for Winthrop's God that she began to run across the open ground, her heart racing.

As Mary crouched against the house, hands pushed the quarels and the window above her swung open. She fumbled the papers from her pack, pushed them over the sill. Anne slid her hand out, Mary pulled off her own icy mitten. Their flesh touched, a quick clasp.

Through the harsh winter of 1638, wolf heads nailed to the fence surrounding the meeting house bore tilted crowns of snow; inside the building, the cold was so intense that dogs were brought to lie on their masters' feet.

On an evening in early March, the disenfranchised men gathered at the Coddingtons' house. They had been given licence by the general court to remove themselves and their families from the Massachusetts Bay Colony before the next court, else they would be called to account. Anne herself was ordered to re-locate by the end of March, no matter the outcome of her church trial. Already, John Wheelwright and his family had fled to New Hampshire.

William had not returned for supper. Mary put the house to rights for the night, took her candle to the bedchamber, where Jurden had lit the fire. She lay watching the pulse of shadow, wondering what was transpiring in the Coddingtons' parlour. The logs had burned to embers by the time William returned. He eased the bedchamber door open.

"I am awake," Mary said.

She smelled tobacco and snow, sharp as the scent of newly turned soil.

"We have decided," he said. He unfastened his lace collar, slung it onto the chest of drawers. "Tonight we incorporated ourselves and drew up a compact. We have elected our town officers. Coddington is to be the judge, I am to be clerk."

He worked at his buttons with a haberdasher's efficiency, infused with new energy, empowered.

"Where are we to go?"

"Providence. Next week we will begin loading a vessel with building materials. A few of us will go overland to Roger Williams. We will determine where to settle—whether near by Providence, or on one of the islands."

"Will you go, William?"

"Aye. As clerk, I will be needed. And I would like to help choose where we shall live."

He slid into the bed, gathered her with icy hands. He wedged cold feet between her warm ones. They lay heart to heart.

"Tis you who began this, Mary," he said. "You and Anne."

He said it with neither gratitude, praise, nor belittlement, simply a statement of fact, and she accepted it in the same way. They were quiet, lying in the coarse sheets.

"They deserve it," he said. "They are as bad as was Archbishop Laud, back home, with his army of henchmen. I am not sure on which side of this works and grace controversy I stand, in truth. It does not seem such a grave thing to me. Rather I want to know my firewood is dry and my cattle are fat."

"They are not done with Anne," Mary said after a time. "Her church trial is to come."

"Aye, they will extract the last dregs. You will have to stand by her. Many of us will be gone."

"I will stand with her."

The delegation to Roger Williams left a week later.

Mary rose with William long before sunrise. She packed two deer-skin bags with travel food—nookick, dried apples, bacon, pickled fennel. She tucked in a small Bible, extra mittens and socks; paused with her hands on the bag's buckle, watching William, thinking how he had become the yeoman's son he would have been had he remained in Lincolnshire and not been apprenticed to a milliner—canny, capable; his torso bulky with wolf fur and greatcoat; his skin weathered by wind and cold; his fingernails permanently black.

William tightened the sinew strings of a pack, slung it over his shoulder. He strode to Mary, put his arms around her shoulders. His eyes searched hers and he began a few words which he could not bring to conclusion. She, too, could not speak but laid a hand on his cheek.

"Be well, my beloved," he said at last. "I will find us a place where we may live as we wish."

They heard the voices and the crunching footsteps of the other men. Mary followed William into the freezing air. Powdery snow sparkled in the lantern light. No horse would travel with them, for there were many rivers to traverse and they hoped to find Narragansett canoes along the way.

Mary watched from the doorstep until the swinging lanterns reached the corner and the street was empty. She gazed up at the moonless sky.

Beyond, in the celestial heavens—the brooding mind of God.

She went inside and latched the door. Sinnie, Jurden, and Samuel slept. There was no sound save for the crackle of flame and a loose clapboard clattering in the wind. She put fresh wood on the fire and sat reading her Bible by its light, looking up from the pages occasionally, as if listening for a voice she might trust.

TEN

Anathema Maranatha - 1638

✳

ANNE KNELT BY A CHEST, lifting out woollens.

They could take only what might be sent by shallop or be carried on their own backs; for, after the trial, no matter the outcome, they would begin the long walk to Providence, following the Pequot Trail, an old Indian path that wound through forests, bogs and valleys.

And I am pregnant. Forty-six years old and pregnant. How can they not see that the Lord doth bless me? Dear God, do not let it snow.

She considered the steamy room with its chests, tables and chairs, some brought from Lincolnshire, others built here in Massachusetts. The fire burned on the andirons, its light reflected by the copper warming pan. Rain lashed the windows.

Most of this will have to be left behind.

Her husband and many of the other men were still away seeking land. Perhaps they had begun felling trees and building houses. Down in the Narragansett Country, she'd been told, spring came earlier. When they arrived, they would dig a garden. *Seeds.* She must tip them from the crocks where they were stored, pack them where they could be easily found.

One of her daughters came into the room carrying a doll and a horse with wooden wheels. Anne felt the weariness of the days to come and the sufferings all would endure. She set down the woollens, held her arms out. The little girl came and leaned against her. Together they contemplated the fire.

I will not show only rectitude and sternness, even if 'tis for their own good.

Two days ago, she had been brought back from Roxbury to be with her family until her church trial. There would be two days of court—the first tomorrow and the second in a week's time. In between, she would be confined at the home of John Cotton.

So that he may make me recant.

He had said that he would not support her. In the cold Roxbury bedchamber, she had been told of his betrayal. He argued that her understanding of grace was different from his.

I could reveal that he colluded in the concealment of Mary's child. But I will not, for then I would betray her.

"One toy, Katherine." Her voice was calm, ignoring the agony of decision. "You must choose. And whichever you choose, you will have to carry, all through the forests and over the rivers. So be wise."

Mary sat at the edge of her pew, the back of her neck quivering with nervousness. The room was dank, chill, every seat filled, men and boys standing at the back.

"Anne Hutchinson, please stand."

Anne stood, unfastening the brass clasp of her cloak and letting it fall. She wore a white coif, white neckerchief, and a white smock. Her belly lifted the front of her skirt, exposing the toes of black boots.

Her best, Mary thought.

There was no sound save the spatter of rain on the oiled paper windows and the knock of Anne's heels as she walked to the front of the meeting house and stood before the pulpit. Beside it was a brass-bound hourglass, its white sand settled. The tithing man did not step forward to tip it. Mary saw how Anne held her shoulders back for greater ease of breath, slid a hand to her back.

She will suffer, this long day.

A ruling elder, Mr. Leverett, came to the pulpit. He stooped with the habit of a tall man accustomed to low ceilings. His face bore a pained, irritated expression.

"Sister Hutchinson, here are diverse opinions laid to your charge." He held up a sheaf of papers. "I must request you in the name of the church to declare whether you hold them or renounce them as they be read to you."

He read out the errors compiled by the ministers.

Anne listened intently, eyes fixed on the man's fastidious mouth.

She thinks of each word, Mary thought. Each word. And its weight and placement in the sentence, and the whole of the sentence's import and intent. And whether she did in fact say or intend it; or whether they twist her thoughts.

"That your revelations about future events were as infallible as the Scriptures . . . that we are not bound to the earthly law . . . that you . . ."

Coming to the end, he paused.

"It is desired by the church, sister Hutchinson, that you express whether these be your opinions or not."

Mr. Leverett glanced at the ministers, received their nods, and sat.

Mr. Cotton, Mr. Wilson, Mr. Peter, Mr. Shepard . . . They were sent to her in her Roxbury prison, with the express purpose of changing her opinions. Perhaps they sat beside her bedroom fire, sharing a pot of raspberry leaf tea. How she would have enjoyed their debates. Now, not one meets her gaze.

Exaggerated patience veiled the disdain behind Anne's words.

"These elders did come to me in private to desire satisfaction in some points of doctrine, professing in the sight of God that they did not come to entrap or ensnare me," she said. "And now they bring it publicly into the church. For them to come and inquire for light, and afterwards to bear witness against it, I think is a breach of church rule."

No one answered the charge. Rather, they stood, one by one, and explicated the doctrines they had argued with her.

Such anger! As if she personally insulted each one of them.

Anne parried their logic, expounding upon theological issues so abstruse that most of the congregation ceased to listen.

An hour passed. Then another. She staggered, took a slight step forward. Her son-in-law brought a stool.

"Thank you."

She sat, but lost no intensity.

"Yes," she agreed, once, after long thought. "Yes, in this instance I was, indeed, in error. I thank you for elucidating my mistake."

She answered another question with a long dissertation.

"May we have proof of your opinions?" Mr. Leverett asked, a sneer in his tone.

Exasperation swept over her.

"Who could interpret with *absolute certainty* individual passages of Scripture?" she demanded. Her voice sharpened and rose. "*Who* among you?"

Morning passed into afternoon. Reverend Cotton stood. He studied his papers. An image came, full-forced in colour and sound, so that Anne closed her eyes, attempting to expunge it. The baby, sliding into her hands. Her cry of horror. How she had nearly dropped it and Jane Hawkins had come to her side; her hands, too, had flown up, away, not wishing to touch it. *You must help me, Jane, please.* And together they had . . .

Stop.

Anne looked intently at John Cotton. His effort not to meet her eyes was betrayed by the set of his jaw.

He will say nothing. For he knows his danger. He played his part in the concealment. And after all, he did not see the creature. He can beg ignorance of the true facts.

"I shall now re-read all of the twenty-nine errors," he said. His voice was sorrowful, self-righteous. He described each in detail and then called, once more, for each theological issue to be debated.

For the first time, Anne felt grief—a sweet, savage ache, combining remembered passion with present loss. *Thy teachers shall not be removed in a corner anymore* ... Year upon year upon year, she had sat in this man's Lincolnshire study, meeting his pained kindly eyes, striving to understand his teachings. For him and for his wisdom, she had left the great timbered house, and the gentle wolds with their bluebells, and the parents and children who lay buried beneath English soil.

For my beloved teacher.

Mary sat, head bowed, surrounded by other silent women.

We have no part in this, save to watch.

In the large, bare room, the light lost whiteness and gained a film of grainy black.

The men on the front bench whispered amongst themselves. Reverend Wilson rose and spoke in his cold voice, announcing that the church was convinced of Anne's errors and that they would be considered as gross and damnable heresies.

Anne's oldest son rose.

"We shall refer further dealing with our sister until the next lecture day," Wilson continued.

"How can the church act without unanimity? I and my brother-in-law support our mother."

"You yourself, then, will need prove those opinions which you support," one of the ministers snapped.

Reverend Shepard stood, prominent nostrils flared, skin stretched tight over cheekbones. "If there be any of this congregation that do hold the same opinions, I advise them to take heed of it, for the hand of the Lord will find you out!" His chest laboured, mouth fixed in a peevish underbite. Then his voice rose. "She is likely, with her fluent tongue and forwardness in expression, to seduce and draw away many—especially simple people *of her own sex.*"

Simple. Mary longed to share a look with Anne. *Simple!*

Anne's son-in-law stood.

"The church hath throughout its history harboured those of unsound opinions. You do condemn my mother-in-law for nothing more heinous than opinion."

"She hath not been accused of anything in point of fact or practice, such as incest," John Cotton agreed. He spoke the words readily, as if they bore an equivalent value to what had gone before, ignoring the muted gasps. "Yet she holds errors, and as such must be admonished." He clasped his hands together, looked up and down the row of clergy. "Since only those tied to her by natural relation support her, I suppose that admonition may be agreed upon."

Reverend Wilson called a vote. The utter stillness in the meeting house was taken by the ministers as unanimous condemnation.

Anne sat straight-backed. In the fading light, her skin was pale as sun-dried linen. Mr. Cotton had risen to give the admonition, but he paused to point towards Anne's son and son-in-law.

"Instead of loving and natural children, you have proved *vipers to eat through the very bowels of your mother*—to her ruin, if God do not graciously prevent. Take heed how by your flattery or mourning over her, or your applauding of her when you come home, you do hinder the work of repentance." He turned to the women's side of the church. "To the sisters of our own congregation, I admonish you in the Lord to take heed that you receive nothing for truth which hath not the stamp of the word of God. She is *but* a woman . . ."

Then he turned to Anne. She stared back.

Her teacher. For whom she crossed an ocean.

"Your opinions fret like a gangrene and spread like a leprosy, and infect far and near, and will eat out the very bowels of religion. Therefore, I do *admonish* you and also *charge* you in the name of Christ Jesus, that you would sadly consider the just hand of God against you, the *great hurt* you have done to the churches, the *great dishonour* you have brought to Jesus Christ, and the *evil* that you have done to many a poor soul." He pointed to the women's side of the meeting house. "Take heed how you did leaven the hearts of young women with such unsound and dangerous principles, and labour to recover them out of the snares which you have drawn them to. And so the Lord carry home to your soul what I have spoken in his name."

Mary could no longer bear to watch Anne's brave face as exhaustion took its toll and injustice bore its weight upon her, relentless, like the tolling of funeral bells.

The ministers surrounded Anne. They walked her from the building, moved in a phalanx into the gathering dusk of late March.

As if I were a wild animal.

The air bore the seaweed stench of low tide. Beneath the cry of gulls came the *rat-a-tat* of drums. Couples moved away into the half-dark, women walking behind their men. They passed up along streets where icy puddles gave the only light. Anne caught sight of Mary standing alone.

Her eyes do see more than most.

She remembered what Mary had told her. How, in the first days of attending Anne's meetings, Mary had felt that the Holy Spirit dwelt within her—*and so, she told me, the world did seem lucid, rimmed with holy light* . . .

The men began to move and Anne was swept forward. In the set of their shoulders, she sensed their conviction that Cotton would succeed in his mission. *Six days*—for six weary days, Cotton would chivvy her to recant, to renounce her powers of prophecy, to admit that she had been in error. In the eyes of God, and for the good of the colony, she must become an example for the goodwives of the New Jerusalem—virtuous, submissive, humbled.

Cotton's words burned within her.

One week later, the meeting house was packed.

The magistrates and the ministers resumed their places. Again, Anne stood before them, hands folded beneath her belly, a mound of black wool.

Reverend Cotton held up a paper.

"She hath reviewed and recanted most of her errors."

A mingling of sighs and murmurs rose from the congregation.

"'I do acknowledge I was deeply deceived . . . my mistake . . . a hateful error . . . See that Christ is united to our fleshly bodies . . .'"

The long, isolated days in John Cotton's study, before and after which she had been given meals alone in her bedroom and been allowed no visits from her children or any other person, were revealed for what they had been: as rain upon a block of salt.

She looked along the row of ministers, realizing that the issue before her was none of the errors that Cotton had read out, but her own error in judgment, a misstep taken as in the ordinary parlours of the earth: she had offended their sense of mission. Yet how could they not see that they were not the only people to whom God spoke? *Surely they know this in their own hearts.*

She sought reparation, although her voice was sharp.

"It was never in my heart to slight any man."

Faces opened with surprise, there was a shuffle as people sat straighter to see the ministers' reactions.

"Only that man should be kept in his own place and not set in the room of God."

The ministers surged to their feet, furious.

"I would be glad to see any humiliation in Mistress Hutchinson . . ."

"Repentance is not in her countenance."

"Contrary to the truth . . . abuse of diverse Scriptures . . ."

Reverend Wilson pointed at her. His face was flushed, his voice was tear-filled.

". . . slighting of God's faithful ministers and crying them down as *nobodies*. It was to set up *yourself* in the room of God that you might be extolled and admired and followed after, that you might be a great *prophetess*, and undertake to expound Scripture and to interpret other men's saying and sermons after your mind . . ."

The white bands of Anne's smock drew taut as she straightened her shoulders.

"Remember the Fifth Commandment," shouted Reverend Peter. "You have been rather a husband than a wife, and a preacher than a hearer; and a magistrate than a subject—"

Mr. Leverett called for quiet. When the men had resumed their seats and the room was once again still, Reverend Cotton spoke. "I now perceive that Anne Hutchinson's confession hath been in vain, since it is clear that her pride of heart is still strong. Excommunication must follow—and it shall be of the most severe sort: *anathema maranatha*. She must be rejected from God and delivered to Satan."

Silence fell save for scratchings, clickings—time as measured by wind and branch. It stretched into a minute. Two minutes.

Anne had remained standing. She held her eyes on Mr. Cotton, sitting now with his fellow ministers, but again he would not return her gaze.

Hypocrite.

—

Reverend Wilson rose. He began to shout, his voice hoarse.

Mary felt her vision narrow, as it had during childbirth, when she had passed into oblivion. All known things grew small, blown as leaves before great wind, scattered. She saw only the stuffed wolfskin kneeling-bag on the floor, felt her knees, bending, the joints, the roar in her ears drowning out even Mr. Wilson's ranting voice, the words of Anne's excommunication, her own hands, touching, *excuse, please, excuse*, skirts, brown, purple, black, the empty space of the aisle.

Anne, coming towards her, her eyes wide and fatigued and clear.

Mary reached for Anne's hand. Language of bone, skin, tendon. *My friend.*

Space, around them, and the firm, swift rhythm of their steps, their skirts intermingled as they strode down the aisle towards a suddenly opened door from whence poured the day's light.

Just as they stepped through the door, loud whispers came from the last pew.

"Who is she who stands with Mistress Hutchinson?"

"The mother of the monster."

They did not falter, but passed into cold air smelling of horse manure and melting snow. They stood side by side, hands still gripped.

Their eyes met. Bewildered, Mary saw through Anne's exhaustion an expression of beseeching anguish.

"Monster?" Mary whispered. "Monster?"

"Goody Hawkins," Anne said, speaking hand to mouth. She looked away. "She must have . . ."

Mr. Cotton strode from the door, surrounded by men who would escort Anne home and see that she caused no more trouble until she had passed from their colony.

Mary watched them crossing the square. Brown hats, bobbing. One white coif.

ELEVEN

Wolves and Geese - 1638

GOVERNOR JOHN WINTHROP STOOD AT his window, watching the midwife coming up the street. He felt the lie, ripe in his mouth. Already, he had begged God's forgiveness for it.

Jane Hawkins entered, panting.

"'Tis a terrible wind," she said, glancing at his eyes, her own skewing.

The light of early spring filled the room, a remorseless brilliance, revealing cobwebs. Winthrop walked sombrely to his desk and passed his hand over a cedar box, clearing it of dust.

"Please sit, Goody Hawkins."

The smell of onions and cats rose from her clothing. She looked down—*right, left*—tugging at her sleeves, and Winthrop saw that her chapped red hands were an embarrassment to her. *Good. Better she be ill at ease.* He remained standing.

"An elder came to me and told me of Mistress Dyer's baby," he said. "Consequently, I have spoken with Reverend Cotton and Mistress Hutchinson."

Now the woman could not help but raise her eyes to his. She clenched her hands in her lap, skin drawn yellow over the knuckles.

It would be the best solution, he had thought, pondering, after Anne Hutchinson had left his study a day earlier. The end of this palavering nonsense. He would take the chance that the rumour was true in all its horror.

"She hath told me the child was like unto a monster."

Jane shook her head. "Nay," she breathed.

"Do not lie to me," he said. "God is listening." He lowered his voice. "Moreover, Goody Hawkins, 'tis widely known of your use of oil of mandrakes and the like." He pulled out his chair; its legs made a squealing scrape against the floorboards. He sat, slowly. "You have been called witch."

On the hearth, flames crackled, devouring dry wood.

"I am no witch."

He fingered his beard, felt the familiar, supportive ruffles of his lace collar. "Tell me what you saw."

"I did see . . ."

"Remember. Anne hath confessed, so if you lie, I shall know. Moreover, we shall this afternoon exhume the corpse."

He saw her eyes shift, widen, and become shrewd.

"Well, then." She took a long breath. "I will tell ye. When she be in labour, such a noisome savour rose from her body that t'other women were taken with violent vomitin'. They rushed from the room. The bed . . ."

"What of the bed?"

"Shaking. When the baby came. The bed shook up and down so the bedposts were a-thundering on the floorboards. The women said when they reached their homes, their children were in convulsions."

Governor Winthrop's hand closed over his beard and stroked down, closing into a fist at its tip.

"And what did the baby look like?"

He saw the woman's face slacken. Her lower lip was fattened, as from old bruises. It slid sideways, glistened. She pressed red hand to cheek.

"It had a face but . . ."

Her shoulders sagged.

She drew a breath, muttered.

"Your pardon?" he said, ironic. "I did not hear."

"I said, 'twould be best left in the ground."

"There you are mistaken, Jane Hawkins. God sent a sign. You and Mistress Hutchinson are saved only because you did as Reverend Cotton told you. He did truly believe 'twas sent only for the parents, but now he admits he was in error. To correct your part in the error, you will meet me at the tavern at one of the clock."

He gestured that the interview should proceed.

Jane Hawkins brushed her skirt with the flat of her hand, her lips turned downward.

Forgive me, he asked the Lord, again, as the midwife continued her terrible account. Anne Hutchinson had told him only that the baby was premature; that she had immediately wrapped it. "My care was for the mother," she had snapped.

My care is for this commonwealth.

Coming back along Corn Hill Road with her water buckets, Sinnie saw a group of men, Jane Hawkins and Anne Hutchinson in their midst. The men carried shovels, pickaxes.

Sinnie ran. The water spilled.

Mary stood on the hearthstone, feeding logs to the fire. Samuel was crawling beneath the table, following the cat.

"I saw a gaggle of men with Governor Winthrop and Mistress Hutchinson and Goody Hawkins. Shovels, they had. Heading up Corn Hill Road."

Mary watched the fire separate as she dropped the log—then knit, again, as flames wrapped round it in a sleek consuming caress.

She felt her womb gathering her into its emptiness, its power of corruption.

—

Evening light lingered, touching the Delft china teapot brought from England, and the cups and saucers, and the high-backed chairs that had once stood in Groton Manor. They ate supper early, for John Winthrop had returned in the late afternoon with twigs in his beard, his boots filthy, his eyes bearing an uncharacteristic wildness, and had demanded that they eat as soon as possible, and told his children to go to their bedchambers immediately after the meal, and bid his wife, Margaret, keep quiet—for he needed utter silence in the house.

After the children had gone upstairs and Margaret to the kitchen, the governor went to his desk. Sat, absorbed, making minute cuts with his penknife, sharpening the nib of a grey-goose quill.

The door opened, despite his edict. Margaret—dear and faithful wife—slipped into the room. She did not come immediately forward but left a beat, as in music, in which to study him.

Untainted, my beloved, in any way. No. I will not tell her.

He could not sound the unspeakable in this place where one thing was peaceably related to another. His father's inkstand, the carpet laid upon the table, books, papers. Order created in this wilderness he laboured to mould as God's kingdom, a place so savage that upon arrival many had died of starvation and his own son had drowned.

"John," she said. "Why do you ask for silence?"

"Things are awry in our commonwealth and I do endeavour to fix them. I will not sleep until I have done so, therefore I asked for silence the sooner to join you."

His smile bore only mollification. She bent her head—her habit, her wont. She slipped away quietly, as she had come.

He sat at his desk until two o'clock in the morning, writing in his journal. His quill scratched, scratched. His shoulders rose, energetic. His face was stern, eager.

. . . so monstrous and misshapen, as the like has scarce been heard of: it had no . . .

—

The following day, whispers spread about the town.

A fish, a bird, a beast, all woven together.

Sinnie heard women speaking of it at the well.

"No toes, but claws."

"Prickles, all over the back."

"Horrible. What could she have done to have been so punished?"

Seeing Sinnie, they fell silent.

Mary strode, agitated, to Anne's house. She found the rooms emptied of furniture, the family in the process of packing the food that they would take for the walk to Narragansett Bay. She and Anne sat in the parlour, where only two oak chairs remained and no fire burned on the hearth.

"Sinnie heard the women gossiping. She said they know more about my baby than I do."

Anne sat straight, hands in their customary position, overlapped on her belly atop another growing child. She spoke in her usual fashion, without hesitation.

"Ah, Mary. I thought to spare you the picture you would thereafter carry in your mind."

Mary's heart raced, her voice sharpened.

"'Twas *my* baby, Anne. You treat me like a child."

Anne faltered. She raised a hand, tipped the palm towards Mary. "Nay." Now her voice, too, wavered. "I would have done the same for . . . for the Queen of England."

"Tell me."

They heard the house make its settlings. Anne was silent.

"*Tell me,*" Mary repeated, more loudly.

Anne looked away.

"'Tis no use, Anne," Mary insisted. She heard her voice take on new tone, harsh. "*Part fowl, part fish, part beast.* This is what Sinnie told me the women were saying. Spread by the men who dug . . . it . . . up. I have heard these words and *they cannot be unheard*."

She crossed her arms, her eyes remorseless upon Anne's face.

"They do exaggerate," Anne said, at last. "'Twould have been greatly decomposed. But . . ." She sighed. "I will tell you."

She spoke rapidly, staring at the floor. "As I told you, there was no head."

Mary pressed hands to cheeks.

"The face was strangely distributed low on the torso. Atop the face were ridges and other fleshy bits, curved, so that one might interpret them as fish-like . . ."

Mary slid one hand down, clasped her mouth.

"The eyes were exaggerated . . ." She paused, glanced at Mary. "Set on either side and bulbous . . ."

"Enough," Mary murmured, raising her hand.

"But there were no horns, as he is saying, Mary. No pricks and scales. No claws, no talons."

Mary's heart had thickened, as if too large for her chest, sending the taste of blood to her mouth and a roaring in her ears.

"Winthrop uses it for his own ends, Mary. He doth gloat in the discredit this casts upon us both. Upon my doctrine. As we knew he would."

Why she tried to keep it secret . . . for all of our sakes . . .

They sat in silence. Mary's fingertips were cold.

"How was it discovered?" she said, finally.

"Goody Hawkins might have told only one person, Mary. Only one, who confided in the next . . . and so it goes, like fire to curtains."

She wishes for my forgiveness.

"I had no choice." Anne's voice had returned to its normal strength and clarity, as if she addressed the women at her meeting. "As I understand it, Mary, *I had no choice*."

She leaned forward and took Mary's hands. Mary met her gaze; saw that Anne was perplexed, grieving. Tender.

"I believe you to be a fragrant and pure flower in the sight of God," Anne whispered.

Ah, spoken with fervour, with fear.

For the first time, she did not believe her friend.

Three days later, William returned ahead of the others, walking through the night to bring his news of purchased land.

It came from her in a torrent.

Everywhere in the town, like the spring snow that had begun to fall, words hissed and expired and were replaced and repeated. All that William had brought to tell her shattered in the rage she could not contain.

"They dug up our child."

He took hold of her fists, removed them from her temples.

"Who?"

"Winthrop and his men. He hath been spreading a horrible description. He . . . hath . . . he hath called for a public day of humiliation. Tomorrow."

William could not speak. His lips quivered, he stroked her wet cheeks with the back of his hand. He pulled her to his chest, rocked her.

"They shun me," she said into his doublet. "They shun me. They shun . . ."

She heard a choking sob, felt a shudder. William turned away from her, face in hands. He lashed out, punched the wall.

He sat, then, nursing his fist. She put her arms around his shaking shoulders.

—

Sinnie lay on the floor, looking through the crack.

They wept.

Oh, help them. Help them.

She did not know to whom she sent her plea.

William's weapons were returned.

On an April morning, Mary stood at the railing of a pinnace. They were sailing towards the Hutchinsons' farm at Mount Wollaston, a few hours down the coast, where those leaving for Providence were to gather.

From the sea, Boston was reduced to a mere concretion upon the land. Mary turned her back upon the place, took Samuel by the hand and went to the ship's bow. Light snow fell, but the sky was like old cloth and sun broke through, rendering the flakes as particles of light. The sails filled and the small boat settled into a steady rise and fall, heading southwards.

She was reminded of the day they left England and of how she had taken a long, last look at Plymouth's stone houses. How she had felt she obeyed God's calling, going to Boston, the New Jerusalem.

That night, the snow continued to fall as they laid down pallet beds in the Hutchinsons' Wollaston house. Mary dreamt that the house was buried, only the chimney visible like a gravestone in a white waste. In the morning, the snow had ceased. They wrapped their legs and feet in leggings of wool or leather and set out in a long line: five banished families—parents, children, servants, dogs, pack-horses—like a bright moving quilt against the white landscape. A smudge of trees edged the meadow.

"No fear," Wil Hutchinson called out, sensing the group's unease as the trees grew closer. "These salvages are friendly. 'Tis a praying town."

They entered the forest. Snow slid from hemlock boughs with sudden wet thumps. Samuel rode on William's shoulders. Babies were slung to parents' backs, their fretful crying lulled into sleep by the sound of stretching leather and the crunch of footsteps. Roots and frozen puddles lay, treacherous, beneath the snow. They passed swamps whose bushes were tipped with the red buds of spring and came to streams too large to cross, where they struggled along banks, seeking fords.

Wil called a halt at a boulder the size of a small house. Trees sprouted from its crevices. Men gathered stones to make fire pits, women and children scavenged dead branches and twigs. They made nests of baggage and bedding against the boulder's rocky wall. They set iron pots over the flames, shook cornmeal into brook water.

Mary squatted beside a pot of bubbling porridge, stirring. She felt excluded from the people moving beyond the fire's glare who shared words with one another, for she could not hear what they said and could barely speak herself, even to Sinnie or Samuel or William. She had insisted, finally, upon knowing exactly what Winthrop was telling everyone. A neighbour woman had told every detail of what was being spread about. She could not—and would never—speak the words that had reached her ears. So terrible, Winthrop's lurid description, going so much further than what Anne had told her that she did not dare imagine the creature that he proudly proclaimed to have seen, a sign from the Lord sent to show displeasure to the Puritans of Massachusetts for allowing heretics in their midst. For the first moments after the words had poured into her ears like Shakespeare's *cursed hebenon*, she had considered how she might do away with a body that had created such a thing.

She glanced over to where Anne sat by another fire, instructing a child who poked the burning branches with a stick and knelt to blow the coals.

No. It was only meant for me, God's message. Only for me.

When prayers and the meal were ended, the company settled for sleep against the boulder. In the darkness, the patch of humped and twitching wool was broken by the firelit shine of child's hair or man's eye or woman's glistening teeth. A child's whimper, shushed, came again and broke into a wavering wail. It was a sound of such pure misery that Anne unwound herself from her blanket and stood before them like a preacher.

"Listen," she said. "The Lord is with us. Remember Psalm 71—'Be thou to me a rock of refuge, a strong fortress, to save me, for thou art my rock and my—'"

The words were cut short by a passionless animal shriek. She looked over her shoulder into the black night, cleared her throat, finished the verse.

Curled between William and Sinnie, Mary lay awake listening to random crepitations—an acorn's fall, shiver of twigs. The eerie shriek came closer; then she heard the first notes of the wolves' chorus.

Dear Lord, she began, and could not continue, as if forbidden. If she had not been pressed between husband and servant, she would have risen and walked into the darkness, towards the alluring, mournful song.

After seven days' march—filthy, irritable with fatigue—they straggled into Providence, a collection of houses wedged between a river and a high hill. Roger Williams answered their knock, stood with a broad smile, wiping food from his mouth with a cloth. Some stayed at his home, others were billeted with families or went to the tavern. They bathed their raw, calloused feet, ate mutton stew, and slept indoors between sheets smelling of lavender.

—

On a fine April day, they set sail down Narragansett Bay, travelling past wooded shores and small islands. At sunset, their boat drifted into a channel that snaked through tall, nest-rich grasses. They embarked on a soggy bank.

"Pocasset," William said. "As it is called by the Narragansett." The island had been purchased from the natives. The chief sachems, Canonicus and Miantonomi, had received forty fathom of white beads and the other inhabitants had been given ten coats and forty hoes—as part of the purchase, they had been required to leave.

There were no houses. Felled trees were strewn about burned stumps.

The women were silent. Mary had imagined it as a Yorkshire valley, with a village of thatched cottages.

They stood listening to the throb of tree frogs, the rustle of reeds.

In warm morning rain, Mary and Sinnie and the other women and their children gathered rocks. They lugged them in baskets, clattered them in heaps. Over the next days, hearths and chimneys sprouted from the muddy soil. The men cut green saplings and drove them into the earth, bent them around the hearths in the shape of bread loaves. They lashed bark or sailcloth over the frames.

Inside their English wigwam, Mary and Sinnie spread reeds on the ground, put their packs and bundles along the walls, set a cooking pot on the crude hearth.

Mary went to bed with aching back, her hands curled like an old woman's in the shape of stones.

All night long, the wolf howls rose, quavered, faded away into silence and then recommenced.

William sat, listened, lay back down. Mary buried her head in his armpit. Vinegar, damp wool.

"We shall destroy them," he murmured into her ear. "Sleep, you are safe."

III.
AQUIDNECK ISLAND

1638~1651

Vain hopes are cropt, all mouths are stopt,
sinners have naught to say . . .

"The Day of Doom"
MICHAEL WIGGLESWORTH

TWELVE

Pocasset - 1638–1639

✳

A FLOCK OF RED-WINGED BLACKBIRDS swept down like a wind-tossed shawl, bending the rushes with their slight weight.

Mary stood in the doorway of their new house. *Spring.* Its energy in the kindly light, its buds and birds; so simple, it seemed. The green slopes around the cove were cut and torn by the wheels of oxcarts; her eye was drawn less to the land than to the square shapes enforced upon it, where the village of Pocasset grew. The air rang with the thud of mallets, the creak of wheels and whinnying of horses. Behind her, the settled state of their own house—a fire on the hearth and a quilt-mounded bedstead—made her wish that it were not finished; its construction had crowded her daytime mind and graced her with the sleep of exhaustion. She had peeled bark, dug postholes, lugged water. And she had been wearied by the gruelling walk from Boston; the exigencies of their first crude hut; the wolf slaughter, when they had been so beset that the Narragansett had come to their assistance, hurling an injured doe into a pit, bidding the men corral the wolves and the women to cower in their hovels.

She leaned against the doorframe. An image filled her mind and she pressed palms to eyes. It hovered, always, sometimes sweeping over her with such force that she cried out, or dropped kettles—*part fowl part fish part beast, holes like mouths, horns, no toes but claws, talons, prickles . . .*

—

Feet, slapping the packed soil. Running.

Anne's serving girl bent in the doorway, hand to ribs.

"Prithee, Mistress Dyer," she said, gasping. "Anne's time has come."

A young preacher trained in medicine stood at the bedside, bloody hands hanging. Anne lay with bare legs spread, clutching her shift. Eyes closed, she cried out as a quivering, jelly-like mass slipped onto the bedding.

Gooseberries, Mary thought. Numb, she looked on without understanding.

"She hath lost consciousness," the young man said.

Several weeks later, Mary and Anne sat in a doorway, stripping pin-feathers from mallards. Northwards, they could see the bright timbers of new houses as the settlement grew. Behind them, in the single room of the Hutchinsons' new house, Anne's daughters worked at the hearth.

"I have heard," Anne said.

She had lain near death for days. Now colour bloomed in her cheeks and her prodigious energy had returned.

"They say that the young minister wrote to John Cotton of my miscarriage. Cotton did tell Governor Winthrop. Now, they say the news has spread far and wide. 'Anne Hutchinson, too, hath birthed a monster.' Ah, but mine was not *one*, like yours, Mary, but thirty! *'Each a different shape!'* Winthrop doth proclaim. As I brought forth thirty misshapen opinions, he says, so I must bring forth thirty 'deformed monsters.'"

She secured a feather between thumb and butterknife, gave a violent pull. Then she slapped down the knife.

"I *do not care*," she snapped.

Mary, startled, looked up. Anne had maintained her equanimity throughout her house arrest and trial; now, it seemed, this final outrage was as the flooding of spring tides.

"I feel the same for myself as I did for you," Anne said. "I am a lily in the sight of God. I do not feel sullied by what came forth from my womb. 'Tis only that I am too old to be bearing children."

Mary tugged at a stubborn feather.

"Of course, you are young," Anne said—considering, amending. "Your next babe will be perfect, I am certain. I do believe you are graced, Mary. Your baby was . . ." She broke off, brooded. "Perhaps 'twas a message for Mr. Cotton, warning him of his weaknesses. Or for Governor Winthrop himself. God chooses his methods, we cannot understand."

Mary did not answer. She heard in her teacher's voice a veiled impatience. With her. With her obdurate grief, darkness, despair. With the entire subject, which sapped time better spent on the building of Pocasset.

"Perhaps 'twas nothing more than a misstep of nature," Anne added, glancing at Mary. "Such as mine. Such as you see in a pig's litter."

Mary bent forward over a basket, shaking feathers from her hands, suddenly furious, thinking that Anne understood theology, but not friendship. She trampled upon the heart's seeded soil.

"Do you not remember?" Mary said. She heard the harshness that frequently, now, edged her own voice. "I did lose my first boy. In London. My first perfect boy, William, who lived but three days. Then Samuel came, another perfect boy. And then . . ." She threw up her hand, her mouth warped. "How can I not think that this was intended for me?"

Teach me, she wanted to cry. *Give me the answer.*

She looked away, out over the bay, where a shallop headed out to the fishing grounds. Anger towards Anne was an unwanted glimpse into vacancy, where once had been trust.

—

Spring yawned into hot summer.

At low tide, Mary and Sinnie picked periwinkles along the shores of the cove. Sinnie—blonde hair like thistledown, pumpkin-yellow petticoats and red stockings revealed in the breeze. Samuel—a pudding cap, quilted. He trailed Sinnie, holding her skirt, then letting it go in order to squat, his tiny fingers plucking. Mary watched them.

I should be happy.

She lifted a mat of bladderwrack. Beneath, clinging to the rock, were the innocent snails, their tender cream-coloured feet clinging.

William was busy, preoccupied. As clerk, he attended frequent meetings with Coddington, now *Judge* Coddington, and three elders. As surveyor, he allotted plots of land with strokes of his quill. He was appointed to deal with the Indians in the matter of venison procurement. He named men as sergeants or corporals of the train band; he disposed monies from the treasury, made laws and memoranda—all "according to God."

He feels a kind of exultation, she thought. Power, thinking to improve upon such laws as were imposed in Boston. Freedom.

She watched Sinnie and Samuel, who had moved farther out on the mudflats. Beyond them, small waves quivered, running under the sky, tossing the light. She lowered herself to a rock and sat with arms round her basket, pressing it to her belly.

"I say merely that a person may have direct communion with God. How doth that interfere with the 'running of this colony'?" Anne sat on a high-backed chair, hands clasped as if for restraint and her eyes hunting the men's.

Mary sat beside William on a bench beneath the Coddingtons' parlour window, which was open to the sound of rain on the pond across the road and the smell of autumn leaves. Across the stippled water, maples drifted in mist, a red cloud.

The men exchanged glances. Wil Hutchinson was no longer so proud of his Anne, Mary thought, seeing his eyes lower. She saw her own William's fingers drum his knee, knew he wished to be home on this wet day, for there was still work to be done before the coming of cold. Judge Coddington, however, held Anne's stare. He had been Boston's wealthiest merchant and had built its only brick house; yet from the time of Anne's arrival in the colony he had never stopped supporting her.

"We must needs have unity of purpose," Coddington said, exasperated. "As would any new enterprise, be it colony, business, or church."

"I am tired of the interference of government in the affairs of people and religion," Anne snapped. "I am *opposed* to magistrates."

"How would you have us keep order, then?" Coddington exclaimed. "Punish the riffraff? Control drunkenness, thievery, all the evils to which society is prone? You would set us one against the other."

Again. Again.

Anne set her jaw, held his eyes.

Without her, Mary thought, there would have been no rebellion. No diaspora. And thus, no Pocasset. She longed to be buoyed by such passion of conviction, as she had felt long ago in London when she had first beheld Anne's cool, intransigent eyes. She did not know, now, if she followed Anne from habit, envy, or fear.

"You exhibit arrogance, Mr. Coddington," Anne snapped. "You hold that you are of the aristocracy and that we are not. You wish for control over my spiritual as well as my temporal life. I have gathered a few families around me. Hereafter, I will hold my own church and will nevermore set foot in yours."

She rose, sought her work basket. She strode from the room without waiting for her husband.

Wil Hutchinson made a helpless gesture, as if appealing for leniency.

Mary saw Anne pass beneath the window. Into the silence came the voices of children, jumping from rock to rock laid out on the road, taunting when someone missed their footing: "Poison, poison!"

Sinnie curled on a pallet by the hearth. Moonlight cast shadows, the windows were opened to the shrilling of peepers.

They forget that I am here.

Murmurs, then hisses. Then—loud voices.

". . . my teacher."

". . . not to go. I am the Clerk, how would it . . ."

"And she is my friend. We followed her here, William."

". . . other reasons . . ."

Sinnie sat upright, pulled the blanket around her shoulders. The lazy-eyed embers warmed her face. Ashes were gritty beneath her bare heel.

Fighting over words. For they do both breathe the same air as one another, eat the same stew. Feel the same sunshine.

"I believe in direct communication."

"Do you? Have you received such?"

A crabbit tone. He gets above himself. He asked for me to slick-stone his ruff.

She waited for Mary's answer. She did not understand the question but realized it had brought the fight to a halt.

Be she weeping? I would go to her, oh, that I could go to her . . .

"I cannot come anymore."

They stood beside a rail fence. Cow pies in the lane were crisp, flaky. Corn hung on dried stalks and boys carried armloads of firewood into sheds.

Mary raised her eyes to Anne's sun-browned, wry face.

"William forbids it."

Their eyes met with a rebounding, as arrow striking steel.

William forbids it.

"Do I fail you, Mary?" Her tone was a plait of threat, sarcasm, wonder.

Yes, Mary wished to say, but did not.

The word had no place in the clarity of island autumn when each thing—falling apple, migrating birds, passing whales—had its truth and sequence.

William had called them outside, noticing a smudge on the full moon. He held his son, bundled in quilts. Mary put an arm around Sinnie, hugging her close for warmth. Crisp shadows lay across the snow.

The smudge grew, slowly veiling the bright face.

"Now 'tis like bloody egg yolk," Sinnie whispered.

Trees, houses, boulders faded into the maw of blackness as the snow ceased to shine.

"What does it mean, Mistress?" she whispered.

Mary had grown weary of signs and their interpretation. She turned to William. His eyebrows lifted, relief replacing a new and unpleasant shiftiness in his face, the mask of ambition.

"We will not stay here," he said. "'Tis clear enough even without this. Coddington has told me he wishes to leave. He has no interest in sharing rule with Anne and her people. He is sick of dissent. As am I."

In April, William returned from an exploratory trip down the western side of Aquidneck Island. He paced the hearth as he gave his report.

"There is a natural harbour, but around it the land is swampy. We will cut trees, and burn them, and dump the ash and wood on the swampy ground. Then we'll haul in sand and dirt. And gravel. The Narragansett have offered to help, for payment."

She sat at the table swirling fiddleheads in a bowl of water, skimming the dried, woolly scales floating on the surface. Although it was their second spring on Aquidneck Island, she did not plant peas, nor set Jurden to manure the gardens, nor bid Sinnie deep-spade the carrot patch.

She felt William's excitement but was not infected by it. He was invigorated by challenge, whereas she and Sinnie anguished over what to take and what, once again, to leave behind. And in any event, she did not care whether they stayed in Pocasset or moved down-island, and despaired over the fact that William was so intent upon his goals that if he thought of her state of mind, it was only to dismiss it as a phase, transitory as the moon's warning veil.

She wondered if she would ever again see Anne.

With whom will I share my thoughts? Discuss the Book of Martyrs or Latin grammar? Engage in theology or talk of communion with the Holy Spirit?

That night, William extinguished the candle and lay upright against the bolster.

He is not preparing for sleep.

He rolled towards her and found her face in the darkness, slid fingers into her hair.

"Many children, Mary," he whispered. "Sons and daughters. Samuel doth grow lonely."

Always, his hands described her to herself. Belly, waist, the insides of her thighs. His lips sought her nipples, unleashing need, need, so urgent. His pleasure, still, waited upon hers.

Afterwards, she lay with arms outflung, eyes open, legs spread, savouring the respite from sadness.

Love. So fierce. No words for it.
Beyond.

Mary and Sinnie sat on the hearth, knitting.

"You do not wish to go, Sinnie?"

Sinnie quirked her eyebrows at her tipping needles.

"I am tired of moving, mistress."

Mary laid down her work.

"I am, too," she said.

Samuel had turned three in December. Today he had a cold and had tired himself playing outside in the crisp air. He lay sleeping in the trundle bed.

"You be like mother to me," Sinnie observed. "Mother and sister both."

Mary looked up, acknowledged Sinnie's intention with a smile.

"My friendship with Anne hath faltered," she said. "So I feel lonely, for there were things we talked of that I cannot discuss with anyone else. And I do feel . . . I do feel as if there is no life inside of me. On the brightest day of sunlight, my spirits do not lift."

"Aye."

"I feel abandoned by God. If such is true, I see no reason for my life. I am like rock. Or dirt. Or dog."

"I love rocks and dirt and dogs," Sinnie protested, and then blushed. She set down her knitting to pluck a twig from the yarn.

"Oh, Sinnie." The wind rose. Mary looked out the window, saw a shudder run across the waters of the cove.

Sinnie spoke again. "Those that tell of your baby and say you are bad because of it . . . *they* are bad, *they* are the cruel ones. Winthrop and those ministers. And those gossiping women. I do believe . . ."

"What? I truly wish to know, Sinnie, for t'will help."

"I think you be the best person I know. If a bad thing was within you, it was not your badness." She lowered her voice. "Sometimes I feel sorry for the creature. It did not wish to be so formed."

"'Tis so confusing. So confusing."

"It will pass," Sinnie said. "Terrible things do fade away."

I forget. Her pain.

Mary studied Sinnie, whose needles moved more quickly.

And still she is a loving person.

Mary stood before the Hutchinsons' house. Anne was spreading linens on alder bushes. She straightened, hand to back. Her daughters, elbow-deep in a washtub, looked up. Wind lifted suds from the froth.

"I come to bid you farewell," Mary said. She clasped her hands to hide agitation. "We sail tomorrow."

They walked to a bench overlooking the cove. Beneath the hard blue sky, shadows defined each house, shed and barn—adding stripes to clapboards, edging each bundle of thatch.

"Much hath changed in one year." Anne spoke evenly, as if withholding different words.

Distance, Mary thought—fifteen miles—would preclude the small, necessary stitches to knit the torn edges of friendship.

"Despite this remove," Mary began. She gazed southwards at the haze where land bled into sky. "Despite the differences between us, Anne, I wish you to know that you opened me to many things and that I am grateful. You did teach me that I might have my own thoughts, my own understanding, my own . . . communion."

"With the Holy Spirit, do you mean?"

"Aye."

Anne turned on the bench and took Mary by the elbows.

"Which I see you have lost." She studied Mary, sternly, as if searching for unvoiced symptoms.

Mary smelled her odour of smoke and lavender; saw how her skin was dry, sunken in pockets, quilled with fine lines.

"If these are my last words to you, Mary Dyer, you must believe them to be true. You are a lily in the sight of God. You must pray, listen and wait." Her words came weighted, now, as Mary had heard her speak to dying women. "The Holy Spirit will return to you."

She put out her arms and Mary, yielding, leaned forward.

Heartbeat. And the body's warmth.

Anne stood, brushed down her skirts. Mary took a breath. What words she would say, she did not know, only felt that such tangled threads as had wrapped them should not be so easily broken; and then Anne turned and walked back towards her daughters and the steaming linens.

THIRTEEN

Massacre - 1643

THE GRAPES HUNG IN CLUSTERS, dusted, translucent. Mary extracted one and laid it on her blue-stained palm, the pearly seeds just visible.

"Is it not beautiful?"

"'Tis beautiful to me that you say so, Mistress," Sinnie said.

Faint, startling lines on Sinnie's face. Twenty-five, she must be. Her freckles, larger, no longer like pepper.

Yet still so tidy, so tender.

"I wonder if I will always be afraid during my pregnancies," Mary murmured, so that the children would not hear.

With every stirring in her womb, she had imagined horns, talons. The fight to dispel such imaginings had had an effect opposite to its intention. "A perfect baby," the midwife had said, handing over the new child; and Mary had begun to weep, and could neither hold nor behold the infant.

Her darkness remained for ten months.

William had grown frustrated.

"God hath blessed our enterprise," he had said. He'd stood before her down-turned face, hectoring. Had he not sent them a perfect baby boy? Samuel had suffered no childhood illnesses. The land bore incomparable fruits, vegetables, grains and grasses. His various businesses prospered. These remonstrances had burst from him when he could no longer suffer her silence, her slow movements, or the days when she would not leave the house.

Forsaken, she thought, gazing at the grape. Abandoned by God.

She looked southwestward over the water, towards what she pictured as infinite forest, amidst which was Dutch territory—where Anne and her family had gone. Before leaving, she had written Mary to say that she had had a revelation from God to take her family—servants, children, even animals—away from the reach of *the cursed English*. "Winthrop doth write me," Anne had written, "Telling me of his plans to annex Aquidneck: if he is successful, I am certain he will not tolerate me."

Mary planned a letter to Anne in her mind. *I see in those around me that they are destined for paradise. I have felt that I was not so destined, nor ever would be, since it seemed that God had so removed himself from me that I was filled with darkness. And yet lately the light hath returned to the world, in my eyes, and I dare to hope that* . . . Yet she would not write the letter, for she did not know where, or by what means, to send it.

"William wants a large family," she explained, seeing that Sinnie watched her. "To fill a big house."

Samuel followed one-year-old William along the vine-laden fence. Jurden and other men had built it the summer of their arrival, when William had decided to settle on these eighty-seven rich acres a mile north of Newport's harbour.

Nearby stood the new house with its massive stone chimney. Apple orchards and pastures filled with horses, cattle and sheep ran out into a broad point, surrounded by the waters of Narragansett Bay.

"William says he shall build a larger house out there," Mary said, studying the point.

Sinnie, kneeling before her basket, followed Mary's gaze.

"'Twill be a goodly place," she said.

Samuel, eight years old, raised hands to just under Sinnie's nose. He fanned them open and a cricket sprang into her face. Baby William, crawling in the summer-dried grass, paddled back at their laughter.

Samuel dropped onto hands and knees and he and the baby swarmed away into the meadow, seeking more crickets, other treasures. Sinnie reached up, snapped stems, set bunches of sweet-smelling grapes into her basket.

"I do think the next baby will be easier," she said.

Mary looked at her.

She speaks with too much reassurance.

Sinnie reddened. Neither spoke, conscious of the pause. Then Sinnie proffered her basket. "I think 'tis enough for our winter jam?"

Mary nodded. She acquiesced in this small matter, as in larger ones. Sinnie had begun to run the house, as Jurden, now married, ran the farm. William came home each night from his mounting civic and business duties, gathered the boys on his lap. He looked over their soft-haired heads at Mary, perplexed, as if she had ceased to speak or understand their common language.

Knocking. It was a rainy night in early October, and William set down his clay pipe, went to the door. Mary glimpsed a neighbour's long, cautious face, heard a mutter pass between the men.

". . . from me, first . . . news . . ."

Rain streamed from his greatcoat and wide-brimmed hat. William bid him enter.

"What news?" Mary said, as the man sat. He did not answer at once but rummaged for his pipe.

"I thought to tell you before you should hear it from anyone else, wrongly told in its particulars. You know that Anne Hutchinson took family, goods and servants and went to the Dutch territory."

"Aye, I did receive one letter from her."

He sipped at the pipe, breathed out the pungent smoke.

"The governor of New Netherland ordered a massacre of the Siwanoy Indians. Eighty men, women and children were killed."

Mary laid her hand flat against her chest.

"So the warriors set out for vengeance. A raiding party came to Anne's home. We surmise she did not hide, as did her neighbours who told us the tale."

"She is not Dutch," William said. "She would not have felt culpable."

"Indeed. Nor, knowing Anne Hutchinson, would she have had fear."

The man glanced at Mary.

"The family was murdered. Cattle, hens, dogs . . . every living thing was put into the house and the house was burned to the ground."

The moment froze, pipe smoke, the man's red hands.

"I have heard reports of what they are saying in Boston," he continued. "They say that the Indians of those parts have never committed the like outrage on any one family. They are saying that the Lord heard our groans to heaven—and so picked her and her family out to be an example of Indian cruelty. Above all others. They say 'twas her final punishment."

William made an exclamation of disgust. He stood, thrust a log into the fire. Sparks showered upwards.

Mary stared at the man.

"That makes no sense. You do not think such?" she said.

"Nay, this is more of their . . ." Disgust, like William's. And shock. He looked kindly at Mary. "I am sorry. I know you did love her."

Her forehead was pressed against the cold windowpane.

. . . a warm day, crickets feasting on fallen apples. Her neighbours, warning her and her family to beware, *nonsense,* she would have retorted, *I have always had friendly relations with the natives on Aquidneck. Besides, we are not Dutch. The Lord will provide.* Men in animal skins. Stepping up the path. *Tie up your dogs,* they would have said, and perhaps one of Anne's boys—Francis? Zuriel?—did so. Did she die first? Was she spared the sight of her family being butchered? Or did she see them pile the bloody bodies on the Turkey rug that had travelled from Alford? Watch them smash the glass-windowed sideboard, hurl the Chinese vase into the fireplace? Lie bleeding, scalped, when the fire kindled and raced up her skirt? Did she watch a warrior grasp her son's soft hair and slice a knife to . . .

William threw off the bedclothes. "Mary, Mary."

He rose and went to her. She turned, let him gather her like a child. She wept, gasped.

"Oh, Anne. Oh, Anne."

They stood holding each other, listening to the patter of rain.

FOURTEEN

Indian Summer - 1650

※

THE DOOR STOOD OPEN, framing a dirt path lined with mari-golds. At its end was a granite hitching post; beyond, the patchwork of fields and pastures running down to the sea.

Sinnie set down a bowl of mashed turnips on the table between Mary and William. Steam spiralled, blue in the dusty September sunshine.

Littlemary, five, retched. She slipped from the bench at the children's table and fell to her hands and knees, where she vomited violently. She took a breath and broke into a wail until choked by another paroxysm of retching.

The boys were on their feet.

"Samuel, ride for Dr. Clark," William rapped. He lifted the little girl in his arms, carried her up the stairs.

Mary stood by the table, one hand clutching a napkin. The other hand fell slowly to her side.

"Sit," she said to the boys—William, Maher and Henry. They returned to the long bench. Baby Charles sat in an arrow-back high chair. "Sinnie, will you see that the meal is served and eaten?"

Her heart raced.

Dr. Clark bade William tighten a tourniquet around Littlemary's fore-arm. He was a tall, sunken-chested man, spectacles perched on the bridge of his nose. The seams of his kersey doublet were filled with dust and crumbs.

"I am sorry," Littlemary whispered to her father. "I could not stop it." She stiffened, fixed her eyes on the ceiling. The child had been taught to stifle complaints, protests, fears.

They heard the patter of blood in the bowl.

The physician straightened, wiped the lancet. "Good lass," he said. "Now. Pain in the belly? Yes? Headache?"

To his questions, Littlemary whispered yes or no. Her eyes swivelled from the doctor to the ceiling.

"Now I will tell you how to treat this," the physician said, turning to Mary. "You must—"

"Wait," William said. He called down the stairs to Sinnie who was poised at the bottom, watching the boys while straining to hear the doctor's words.

"Ah, my poor bairn!" Sinnie entered, quick and dry as a sparrow. She knelt by the bed, stroking Littlemary's forehead.

When Sinnie's indenture date had come and gone and still she was unmarried, William had declared that she need never leave their care. "As long as she wishes, I will pay her wages and provide for her."

The doctor glanced between servant and mistress. He spoke to Mary, but his eyes returned to Sinnie.

"Have you a syringe? Yes? Good. Once a day, beet juice in each nostril." He squeezed his fist before his nose. "I want you to take an egg, prick it with a large needle. Pour salt and rum into the hole. Bake it in the ashes. Give her that egg to eat when 'tis hard. Follow it with mint and fennel tea, steeped strong."

"How much rum?" Sinnie asked.

The physician glanced at Mary. She saw that his respect was but a formality. She held out her hand, palm upward; fanned her fingers towards Sinnie.

"She hath a better mind for these things," she said.

—

For a week, Sinnie and Mary continued with daily chores and the fall harvest—drying herbs, braiding onions, hanging shell beans—while nursing the child.

William fretted, beside himself with worry over his little girl.

He had begun building the house on the point that he had been planning ever since coming to Newport. *The great house*, he called it. Mary looked out of Littlemary's window. Sea, sky—the wind pressed between them making clouds race, clipping the tips of waves, bending the grasses. She could see William, a blue-coated speck, his voice carrying as he directed the workers who sawed, swung mauls and pushed barrows amidst the stacks of yellow lumber.

Through the open window, the air bore the sweet, desiccated smell of spent goldenrod.

Indian summer.

Mary turned to the room. It bore the plainness of haste, built to endure a New England winter: white plaster walls, adzed timbers, brick fireplace. And on a roped oat-straw mattress, Littlemary, asleep beneath a quilt made by Aunt Urith, strips of gold and brown slanted around a central block of red, appliquéd with a silk bee. "To remember your mother's garden," Aunt Urith had said, giving it to Mary when she left for London. "You must tell your children of their Yorkshire grandmother."

This is what I have given the world.

Children, as it was commanded of us on the ship.

The women of Newport, like those in Boston, were continuously pregnant or nursing, bearing child after child after child—until most, by the age of thirty, were haggard and gap-toothed.

And I bear them in terror, no matter that each child since has been normal.

William, Maher, Littlemary, Henry, Charles.

With every birth, she fell more profoundly into despair. Sinnie had placed Charles, her sixth living child, to Mary's breast and held him there, crooning, as Mary stared at the infant. She had no feeling for the baby or for herself. She was like a mote of dust, so weightless as to find no landing place.

Soon afterwards, she had turned from William's caresses.

"Please," she'd said. It was not to William that she had begged, but to whom, she knew not. *Please.*

She listened to the thump of the mauls, the rasping of saws; and heard in the sound William's restless search for betterment.

In the meeting house, Mary closed her eyes. Littlemary sat beside her, bravely upright although she was white-faced and weak.

"We read in 2 Corinthians 3:6: 'Who also hath made us able ministers of the new testament; not of the letter, but of the Spirit: for the letter killeth, but the Spirit giveth life.'" The minister followed Anne Hutchinson's teachings.

Within ourselves, we may apprehend God.

So Anne had told her, in her strong voice. Thinking of Anne, Mary felt such a sickening as a child feels before punishment.

She looked at the bent heads of the Newport women. She worked side by side with them at whangs, spoke with them of pickles and radishes, of flax and thistles; they met her eyes with bland friendliness and she wondered what they said about her. They must respect her as the wife of a successful farmer, merchant and politician. Yet her education accorded only wariness, resentment. And since, after the birth of each child, she did not invite the women for ale and cakes but, rather, vanished from view, the other wives were affronted. They did not visit or send food.

She no longer prayed nor asked for forgiveness. God's silence was absolute and the light of the world was not hers, neither beauty nor joy nor peace—the baby's face beneath his pudding cap, wild roses in a pewter pitcher. She was restrained as if by a forbidding hand. *Feel no joy. This is not for you.*

She turned her eyes to the window and watched the silent, tossing leaves. She had become a vessel for bearing children, never knowing when God might see fit to send another monster or call home the tiny creatures.

"Let us now give thanks for the life of Littlemary Dyer," the minister said.

Only last week she had stood behind two men in Newport. They did not see her, and she had heard one tell the other of a newly published pamphlet. "New England Heretic, Mother of a Monster," he'd murmured.

Fury had pushed her past, shaken by the same violent impulse that had made her stand at the Boston meeting house and walk down the aisle with Anne.

August 1650

My beloved Mary,
I must needs report the death of your Uncle Colyn. He rose to withstand the raging of a client who was distraught over a settlement and did blame your uncle. I heard the shouts and ran from the surgery but my husband had fallen. 'Twas too late, there was naught to do. He lies in the churchyard with your parents and brother.

I would have you come home once more before I die, for depart I will, soon, called by my Lord. A dimness comes over my eyes and a doddering to my limbs. I know that I bear disease. 'Tis new and I despair, for I have many demands upon me, a child arrived this day with oak splinter in the eye . . .

The children came through the door carrying baskets of mottled yellow apples. They poured the overripe fruit into wooden basins with a knocking rumble, went out for more. Over the fire, a kettle of beans hung from its pothook, making quiet slaps. The smell of baking bread wafted from the oven as Sinnie swung open the iron door and thrust her arm into the heat to tap the crusts.

Mary shuffled the letter back into its envelope. She went to a chair set well back from the heat and began slicing apples. Baby Charles slept in his cradle, bathed in sunlight. Through the window she could see a hedgerow of wild roses running down to the cove, their hips like varnished cherries. Everywhere, seed vessels burst with the insistence of survival. Burrs hooked socks or the fetlocks of horses. Silk exploded from milkweed pods and spilled into the wind. Orange pumpions sprawled, crusty-leaved, their vines frail as abandoned rope.

Mother, Father, my brother, my babies, Anne, Uncle Colyn. Gone to Christ. And now Aunt Urith had written of her own impending death. *. . . a dimness comes over my eyes . . .*

On the wind came the sound of shouting. Geraniums on the windowsill, blurred by sun, framed the shapes of William and another man who came around the corner of the house.

"You'll not come into my house," William roared.

"I'll follow you wherever you go till you give me your promise."

"I'll promise you nothing. 'Twas your pig and you will pay. The suit stays before the court."

"You have no proof."

"No man in Newport will believe otherwise. Every other man's pigs are on the islands."

"Could be 'twas no pig but a wild creature."

"I am a Lincolnshire farmer's son. Dost think I cannot recognize the prints of a pig or the damage it can do? Now be gone with you, Nicholas Babcock. Else I will add to your charges the fire you let run at random. Or harassment. Or the time you did not complete your corn fence."

"I care not a fart for your charges."

"Take your pigs to the island or strengthen your fences, else you will find yourself worse than fined."

William stormed into the room, hurled his hat onto a chair stile where it whirled to stillness. He sat, working his scalp with his fingers.

"And last week my sheep killed by Marston's dog," he fumed.

And so many other things, Mary thought, that he found necessary to take before the court. Contumelious words from a neighbour. A copper kettle missing from the barn. These slights were as the small fires of a vast, inner conflagration.

Sinnie pushed the lug-pole from the fire, took up a basket of apple skins and slipped out.

Peelings curled from Mary's knife, tapped to the floor, writhed and settled. She glanced at him without moving her head.

Ah, my William. Her love for him was like a buried seed without the conditions for growth. She saw that he felt this and so channelled his own love into a passion of work, displaying pride to those who would condemn his wife, refuting the impugned "instruction of the parents." He thickened in body. Coarsened in mien. And ever since Winthrop's henchmen had taken away his arms, he had become outraged by the slightest infringement upon his, or another's, rights.

"Littlemary is well, William," Mary said, like a suggestion. "She is working with the boys. She carries a basket and hath a bloom in her cheeks."

His fingers relaxed. He dropped his head back against the chair.

He was my young man. My glove-seller. She wondered if he ever thought of the wealthy London merchant he might have become.

Truly, she knew, he loved his part in the creation of a new society, watching his children thrive, standing at the centre of a community as one of its governors. He sat on committees to establish laws: pro-hibition of tree-peeling or fire-starting by Indians; cash rewards for fox and wolf heads; compulsory fencing of corn fields, woods clear-ing, the marking of pigs' ears. He marched musketed militia in the fields. He began to practise law.

Loneliness, a cold rill.

"The letter you brought me from Aunt Urith." She held it up. "My Uncle Colyn hath died. I long to go to England, William."

"So did my mother die," William replied. "So does every person here in the New World lose family in the old country. We cannot go stand by their gravesides."

"I do not care to stand by his graveside," she said. "I care to see my living aunt before she, too, dies."

"You are the mother of six children."

Outside, a cat scurried by, mouse in mouth.

"The children do not need me. They have Sinnie."

"Sinnie is our servant."

"And I tell you, William. They have Sinnie."

Out the window, blurred by the swirled glass, she saw the chickens clustered round Sinnie and the yellow peelings falling from her hands.

"You cannot go to England. I forbid this, Mary. You must put it from your mind. The very thinking of it makes me . . . You cannot go alone to England! Where would . . . how . . . I . . ."

He rose from his chair, took up his hat. He rolled it on one finger, hand chopping the brim.

"Make an end to these thoughts, I beg of you."

"William," she said. "Please . . ."

She put her face in her hands, muffling her words. "I cannot imagine another winter. I cannot bear another pregnancy."

And he is sick unto death of hearing these words from me.

—

I long to go to England . . . Sinnie had lingered at the almost-closed door long enough to hear these words. Then she had eased it shut, hurried over the scythed grass.

The children, in the orchard. Contented chickens, pecking at the peelings. The big house, rising on the point.

May I never leave here.

Oh, may she not go.

A sheep trail.

Juniper bushes.

Outcroppings of granite.

Up the coast, a group of Narragansett were digging for clams, distant, bright figures—pausing, stooping.

The waves rolled with languorous potency. They crested, crashed. Spent, frothing water slid towards her bare feet.

No head. A face, but . . .

Monster. I am. Mother of a monster.

The children at the table. Speaking to William, to Sinnie. Their eyes meeting mine and then . . . then . . . shifting away.

She pulled Urith's letter from her pocket, pressed it to her cheek and slipped it back. She pulled her hood close around her face. Tears came to her eyes, slid into the corners of her mouth.

Neither to lie down nor to stand up. Neither to eat nor to starve. Neither to begin nor to cease.

She stepped into the shallows. Her feet were instantly numb. Watching—the gathering water, towering, sleek curve at its throat, the thunderous pound and rush, inevitable. She entered farther. Her cloak floated around her hips, swirling. The next wave struck her chest. She lost her footing, went down into froth and chaos.

Torture, howls, the fires of damnation.

No.

She staggered to her feet, turned back towards shore. A new wave buckled her knees. Again she fell, undertow dragged her over the hollowed shelf, she heard the sinister hiss, clutched at gelid pebbles.

Another underwater tossing. She gasped, clawed her way to the beach and crawled from the surf. Face down in the sand, she drew long, shuddering breaths.

Mary rolled onto her back and lay with her arms outspread.

No one watches.

FIFTEEN

Decision - 1650–51

✳

WILLIAM NUDGED THE TRENCHER closer to Mary.

"Eat," he ordered beneath his breath. She had taken a chill weeks ago and had only recently risen from her bed.

Every day, the wind rose at noon. Through the window, Mary saw November light slanting over the fields, glistening in the gone-to-seed meadowsweet. The children's wooden spoons—too big for their mouths—tapped the trenchers, a small, furtive sound, like mice.

Sinnie set down pewter platters heaped with baked pumpion, boiled cod, apple pandowdy. The lace on her cuffs was neatly folded and tucked under her sleeves.

Mary dipped her spoon into the hot, molasses-sweetened apple.

William had returned from his office in Newport, angry. He began to talk, looking at no one. Words that he could not keep inside, exploding from him.

"Coddington hath been in England for over a year." His nostrils were white at the edges. "Now I hear that he is beseeching Cromwell for a separate charter for Aquidneck Island."

The children, accustomed to his rantings, paid no attention. Sinnie was busy with an iron lid, wrestling it to the hearth.

Nor is he speaking to me.

He filled his mouth, chewed.

She glanced at him, repelled by the juicy sound. In Boston, it had been she who had returned from Anne's meetings, keen with new

ideas; and he who had queried her. Now, William spent his evenings at gatherings and returned home so roiled that her health, or
thoughts, were as an excess that strained his patience.

"Coddington doth indeed think himself of the aristocracy. He feels
himself the fit ruler of Aquidneck." He scraped at their shared trencher,
leaving nothing for Mary. His voice became argumentative. "We should
send Roger Williams back again this spring to reaffirm *his* charter. At
first we thought 'twas Roger's bid for authority over us all, but then . . .
well. We saw that 'tis good for Providence, Newport, Warwick and
Pocasset to make up one colony. Providence Plantations. There is no
need for Aquidneck to split away. For there are merits in unity and . . ."

At meals, the children were not allowed to speak, or meet each
other's eyes, or slouch, or ask for more food.

". . . now that Massachusetts hankers after our lands, 'twill behoove
us to reaffirm of ourselves as a patented colony."

"Would you go to England with Roger?" Mary asked. She spoke
with an edge in her voice.

Startled from his inner rooms, he looked up with habitual affront.
Relaxing, then, when he met her eyes.

A scuffle beneath the children's table—Samuel and young William
sent thoughts to one another through the sides of their boots. Maher
was holding apple in his mouth, not swallowing. He liked to taste
his food for as long as possible. Littlemary sat with her hands tight-
folded in her lap, watching a fly whose feet were trapped in a pool
of molasses.

"Perhaps. Nay, there is too much for me here. Although . . ."

He shrugged, folded his napkin, pushed back his chair. In the
kitchen shed, the workers were finishing their meal.

*Men sail to England. They go and then they return. And then go
again. It is not to them a place so remote as to be lost.*

The bay's sparkle livened the sunlight, illuminating crumbs on the
table, making silver cuticles on the apples.

The children have Sinnie.
William hath no need of me, in fact he . . .
Anger. A surge, like energy.

One bayberry candle flickered on the chest of drawers. Wearing only a linen shift, Mary shivered, putting away her coif. The floorboards creaked as William approached.

"I will have a fireplace in our new bedroom," William said. He slid his arms around her. "Ah, my lovely. Skin and bones. You are starved as a mongrel."

She slid from his arms and climbed into the high bedstead. She pulled the quilt up to her chin, set her feet on a flannel-wrapped brick.

"'Tis not an illness of the flesh," she said. She had seen him clasp his hands as if to hide the uselessness of palms that could apply neither knife nor potion to alleviate her pain.

He set his candle beside the Bible on the bedside table, slid in beside her, taking a breath at the linen's dank chill. Their feet tussled for the brick. She saw that this would make him laugh, then sigh and blow out the candle; and so, forestalling, she relinquished the lovely warmth.

All day long, she had planned how she would tell him what had recently clarified in her mind.

"You cannot know how it is to be ordered by men to 'eschew the sin of barrenness' and continuously produce children, even when they have told me my womb is as a malevolent pit, seeded with evil."

He began to speak but she held up her hand, conviction darkening her voice.

"I have only dread when nausea announces new life. I cry out in terror when my babes slither from my body. 'Do not cry,' they say, ''tis a perfect child.' But I am hollow as the vessel they have made me. It is not that I *do not* love them. I *cannot* love them."

He pushed himself upright against the headboard.

"How can you not love your children?"

"I *cannot*, William. I yearn for the feeling that I have for you, or for Aunt Urith. But it is as if there is a door closed between me and my children. I do not know if they notice. If they do, the boys no longer, nor ever, it seemed, care—but Littlemary . . . asks of me . . . and I needs must . . ."

There were no words for the emptiness where love should be but was not.

They would never be her children. Governor Winthrop, the black-frocked clergymen, the magistrates and their followers had taken them from her when they had dug up her baby and brushed the soil from its body. When they had handed it about, groaning with triumph and disgust.

"I feel myself unworthy to love or to be loved," she whispered.

He sat so still that she was afraid to glance up at him.

"I must go to England on the spring sailing. I must go see Urith. That, I do believe, is the only cure."

"Ah, Mary . . . I would that . . ."

"Children may have other mothers." The words came as if spoken without her volition. She was swept with sudden, profound regret and realized that until this moment, she had never truly understood this. "Sinnie knows their every thought. Her life is naught save for them."

"As you had your aunt," he said, slowly, surprised by the realization and its implications.

"Aye. Yes, my William. As I had my aunt. And now she is dying."

He drew a long breath. Then he reached for her hand, studied it. He rolled to his side.

"I remember the first gloves I gave you," he murmured. His fingers were delicate as the legs of a foraging bee. "They were of lamb skin, dressed flesh-side out. Silk-lined, silver-gilt thread. Your left hand slipped into the glove. A perfect fit . . . Will you miss us?"

She saw that he struggled against long-withheld grief. She could say *yes, my William, surely you know I will,* but did not, for she knew his question was a wedge and this but the first tap.

"I fear to lose you," he said.

"You will lose me if I stay, William. If I do not go to England on the spring sailing, I will surely die."

The quilt rose as he took a breath so deep he must sigh its release. She was touched by a wisp of memory, the essence of what had once been: Mary Barrett from Yorkshire, supple as a lily, seeing love in a young man's eyes.

November 16, 1650

My dear Aunt Urith,
May this find you well, for I shall come to you. William hath agreed that 'tis best I go in spring. William wearies of what he sees as my foolishness, for all my children have thrived. I strive to cast away my darkness but cannot. The children are happy in the care of Sinnie and do think of her more as mother than they do me and for this I am grateful, for I have been as a wraith all these past years. 'Tis now the beginning of New England's deepest cold. The great house is not yet finished but William shall take the family there next fall, when I shall be with you. We spend our days in reading of the Bible, spinning, baking, sewing and . . .

They left at dawn. Sinnie had been long awake, stoking the fire, preparing food. The children had been called from their beds and sat on the settle, stupefied with sleep. In the iron pot, cornmeal heaved, emitting puffs of steam.

The latch clanked, the door opened. April air chilled their ankles. Jurden leaned into the room, bearing the smell of barnyard; beyond him, two horses stood saddled, two others laden with packs. Mist ghosted the meadows.

"Ready," Jurden said. He eased the door shut.

Baby Charles had been carried down from his trundle bed but had not awakened. He lay, now, in the pine cradle that Sinnie had set just beyond the reach of sparks from the fire.

Mary's eyes burned, dry. She had lain awake all night. She turned to the cradle, knelt, reached to touch the baby's face. The children rose from the settle, gathered around her.

"Best not wake him," she whispered.

She stood and gazed at her children, leather travel mask pushed up onto her forehead. The children stood facing their mother—barefoot, wearing linen night-shirts—as if already an ocean separated them. Last November, William had told them of Mary's "trip." Her aunt, he'd said, who had been as a mother to her, was ill and had begged her to come. *Your mother has no choice.*

Their eyes winced into hers and slid away. William waited by the door in his greatcoat and boots, gloves in hand. His silence, Mary knew, was maintained with difficulty.

They know. They know. What child does not sense their parents' deepest inclinations?

She embraced the children, one by one.

"Goodbye, Samuel."

"Goodbye, mother." Fifteen. Conscious of his self-control.

"Goodbye, William. Maher. Henry. Littlemary."

A horse whickered. They heard the jingle of bit, Jurden's low command. Sinnie stood on the hearth, fists tight against her breast.

Littlemary burst into tears.

Mary knelt, arms spread. The little girl came to her, buried her face in Mary's shoulder.

"I will write. I will be back. I must go see my auntie before she dies."

The child's sobbing caused Henry, aged three, to burst into tears. Maher and William, seven and eight, looked towards their father, frightened. William stepped forward, went down on one knee to gather the little girl into his own arms.

"I am sorry," Mary said. She stood, stepped back. Her wide mouth crimped at the corners, she pressed hands to cheekbones, distorting her eyes. "I am sorry."

"Come," William said. "Say goodbye to Sinnie and then we must leave."

"Ah, Mistress."

Sinnie ran forward, Mary spread her arms.

"You are my dearest friend," Mary whispered into Sinnie's hair. "You are my dearest friend. Oh, my Sinnie."

The children and Sinnie clustered in the doorway. Littlemary put her arms around Sinnie's waist, face half-hidden, tear-wet.

William helped Mary to her saddle, then mounted his own horse. Mary took a breath, but only raised her hand in a wave.

I am led, she wished to say. *I have no choice.*

At the northern tip of Aquidneck Island, they crossed the narrows of the Sakonnet River on Howland's ferry and spent the night in Providence with Roger Williams and his family.

At supper, the men spoke of the charter, of the king's beheading, of England's civil war. The women compared their children's ages. No one spoke of Mary's departure or the reasons for it.

The next morning they rode north along the Great Salt River, passing farmsteads whose fields sloped up steep hillsides. Men walked behind ox-drawn ploughs. Others stood in carts shovelling rotten fish meal onto the soil. On the riverbanks, waterwheels turned, creaking, water spilling from bucket to bucket; and from the mills came a rhythmic pounding and the smoke of risen dust.

They entered the forest on the Pequot Path.

Mary watched William as he rode before her, gun jutting over his shoulder, shadows running and slipping over his buckskin jacket. Every so often, he leaned over his stirrup, calling her attention to fresh scat, or the prints of deer, moose, wildcat. The light was made tender by its passage through new leaves and the horses' hoofs fell silently on the red-tasselled catkins of beeches, butternut and hickory.

There were no other travellers on the narrow Indian path, so ancient that it had cut deep into the soil, winding like a watercourse around boulders and rocky outcroppings. The clergymen who had exhumed her child and proclaimed her *the mother of a monster* had preached that God had prepared this land for the English by ridding its forests of the bedevilled salvages. Mary thought of the native mat that had lain beside her bed. The smallpox, she had heard, broke and mattered, oozing, so that when a person rolled, skin would cleave to the rushes and flay away, leaving a mass of gore.

At noontime, they came to a river the colour of dark ale, paling to cinnamon where a sandbar corrugated the water. White pines grew on its banks. They dismounted, hobbled the horses, sat on a rock. They laid out beer, sausage, pickled radish.

The horses drowsed, their lower lips loose and foolish. Once Mary caught William's eyes on her—loving, worried—and yet she saw how, bit by bit, she had slipped from the centre of his concern.

She watched leaf-stippled shadows play upon a bed of violets. She had grown accustomed to the vast emptiness of this land and of her displacement within it; how it scraped her with its searching light.

So small, she had become. So insignificant.

He will not miss me for long.

—

They spent three days in Boston waiting for the ship to sail.

Mary did not venture forth from the tavern. She was sickened by the proximity of Governor Winthrop and the clergymen and the meeting house at the top of the street.

She sat at the window and watched men loading hogsheads and casks onto ships, horses standing patient before wagons of timber. Out beyond the harbour, amidst the winking, wave-crinkled water, she could see blue islands, dwindling away down the coast.

"Goodbye, William."

She felt numb with disbelief at the turnings of their life.

He wept and held her.

"My love," he said.

"I love you, William." Her whisper was half-choked. "I will return. Perhaps . . . healed."

He helped her into the rowboat. He stood at the edge of the wharf, waving.

Smaller, he grew. Smaller.

William? There . . . ? Or . . .

Mary stood on the foredeck next to a woman with whom she was to share a berth. She was travelling to England with two young daughters.

"There," the woman was saying, pointing. "*That* be your father. And there's your brother."

The little girls waved. "Papa, papa! Ezekial! Goodbye."

Mary could not discern William amongst the crowd, nor, she guessed, could this woman discern son and husband. She went below decks and sat on her bed, a narrow box with a flock mattress. Drained of the energy she had summoned to bring her here, she listened with little interest to the commotion of departure. She had no desire to watch New England become a molten speck upon the western sea.

IV.
ENGLAND
1652~1656

O thou North of England, who are counted as desolate and barren . . . out of thee did the branch spring and the star arise . . .

"Works"

EDWARD BURROUGH, QUAKER

SIXTEEN

Between Worlds - 1651–2

"DANGLING LIKE A TURKEY'S WATTLE," she said. "Not that I do mind. I could bear with some trimming." Broad-faced, wide-bodied, Ann Burden spoke with the accent of the English north. Over the weeks, she had lost flesh. She pinched the skin beneath her chin.

They sat cross-legged on their beds, facing one another. Ann had made blanket-nests for her daughters: Elizabeth, four years old, and Hannah, six. When the sea was calm, they were allowed to cook on a tiny brazier in the common area 'tween decks; when it was stormy, they ate what the cook sent from the fo'c's'le.

They could hear the dim shout of the navigator down the speaking tube; the helmsman's response; then the whipstaff's ponderous creak. And against the ship's planking, the rush and rustle of water, a cold boil.

They had lived in Boston at the same time, yet had not known one another well. They told one another the places of their births—Newcastle, Kettlesing—and discussed their husbands—Ann's was a shoemaker; and the similar reasons for their voyage, ailing relatives. Their fathers—*a shoemaker, a physician*—and their mothers, children, childbirths. Their lives were like freshets, arising from different springs in the same wood, converging.

"Lost my first. Thomas," Ann Burden said. She was knitting a sock.

"How long did he live?" Having no one to care for but herself, Mary neither knit nor sewed but sat with hands folded. No one waited for her. No child tugged at her.

Alone. For the first time in . . .

"Born and died the same day. The first of April, it was."

"Mine was named William. He did live three days."

"I lost three more baby sons: Elisha, and twins Joseph and Benjamin. I left my ten-year-old, Ezekial, in the care of my two fine servants—Francis and Johanna," she said. The girls looked up and Mary felt a stab of longing, seeing in their eyes her own Littlemary's sweetness. "Aye, my flitter-mice. You love your Johanna."

So calmly she speaks of her losses. Mary felt ashamed of her own anguish and resolved not to speak of it.

Mary was accustomed, if not to aloneness, to loneliness—and kept herself quiet, contained, thinking to allow Ann and her daughters unwalled privacy. Hands thickened by grey fingerless gloves, she bent over her Bible, absorbed.

"My father did teach me reading and numbers, just for to help in the business," Ann Burden remarked, watching Mary. "I am not otherwise learned. Not like you and Anne Hutchinson. I were there on that day you walked out with her. I was put in mind of it on the day I was myself excommunicated."

Mary laid down the hand-sized book. The woman's guileless blue eyes, rough-pored skin, and the odour of tannery in her clothing had caused Mary to assume that she was of easy and uneducated mind, taking life as it came.

"Excommunicated? Why?" She tugged her cloak close around her shoulders.

"'Twas me and Nicholas Upshall and a few other men," Ann Burden said. She considered the yarn she jerked, arm-length, from a ball. Drew her hand down its length, checking for weaknesses. "I withdrew from fellowship of the church. I could not abide with some practices. I did not think the church covenant was an ordinance of God. And other differences I had. Last month, it was."

Mary listened to the ship's sawing creaks. Candlelight made a tapestry of Ann Burden's faded red dress, grey wool, the pine boards.

"I do hate them," Mary said with sudden violence. "I hate those men."

"Which men?"

"The ones who dug up my baby."

"Ah, Winthrop and them."

"Aye." Mary's low voice rose, strained, and her eyes filled with tears. "Gloating over what they did find. Filled with vindication, saying 'twas proof of heresy. Anne stood up to them in two courts and fought them with words. But I . . ."

Ann looked up from her needles. The little girls broke off their dolls' whispered conversation.

"My husband did sign that petition," Ann Burden remarked, after a silence.

"As did mine."

"Aye, but mine did go two days later and apologize. He said he had been in error. He was fixing to buy a house on the water, with a wharf opposite. He was making a pit for soaking leather."

"They sent *men* to our house." Removed from the New World, Mary felt, now, the enormous injustice of this. The betrayal, the hypocrisy. "They *took away* my husband's weapons."

Ann knit and tugged extra-tight three stitches.

"And we left old England for our freedom," she muttered.

"Sometimes, it fears me that I shall find myself with the comforts of home, back in Yorkshire, and I will forget my children and my husband. They will become like unto a dream and I shall never go back."

Ann Burden narrowed her eyes. "Ah, well, but you haven't

forgotten your old aunt, have you? She still be real to you, real enough for you to step onto this tub? You'll not forget."

The ship, filled with sleeping creatures, plunged eastwards through the North Atlantic.

At first, Mary had dreaded hearing Ann's coarse whisper, coming as soon as the little girls' breathing grew steady. She had murmured, yawned, or feigned sleep. She was certain that Ann's interest in her would fade and be replaced by critical evaluation, yielding dislike. Or disgust. Or pity.

Night after night, however, Ann whispered, calmly. "Mary, be you sleeping? Mary? Mary?"

"No, I am awake," Mary said, on this night. She rolled to her back, lay listening to the ship's creaks, its long groans.

"Did you ever hear tell of Alice Tilley?" Ann Burden whispered. "Sentenced to die?"

"No," Mary whispered, watching a finger of light stroke the ceiling. "I have not heard of her."

"She is a midwife of Boston. Something did go awry in the delivery of a child and she was accused of witchcraft. The case was taken before the Court of Assistants. They did cast Alice Tilley into jail." Her voice dropped a notch, even though it was clear that the little girls were asleep. "Were you ever into that place?"

"No."

They had extinguished their candle-lantern. The hanging blanket that served as a door slid along its pole, bunched, then splayed out. The common room's candlelight, like another world, was glimpsed, hidden again.

"I did go to visit Alice. 'Tis a terrible, foul pit. She had a scrap of straw for a bed, 'twas black as night and chill as winter, although out-of-doors the sun was blazing."

"What did happen?"

"We women came together, from hither and yon. Some from Boston, some from Dorchester. We did know Alice Tilley to be an honest midwife and no witch. We drew up a petition. Around the country, six other petitions were drawn up. We took them to the court. Seven petitions, signed by two hundred and seventeen women."

Mary pictured the women walking to the court house, their capes wind-billowed, their broad-brimmed hats ribboned beneath their chins.

"They released her," Ann whispered.

"They released her?"

"They released her. They did not dare to hang her for a witch. She walked from the jail and returned to her practice and no word has ever again been spoken against her."

Mary lay with her hands crossed upon her belly.

She absorbed the story, like music from a foreign country. Parts of it were familiar, parts were entirely alien. It made her breath come quick and shallow. She remembered how she had been moved to rise at the moment of Anne Hutchinson's sentencing; how she had walked with her from the meeting house, shored by sureness of purpose.

And at the doorway had faltered, hearing the cruel epithet for the first time.

Mother of the monster.

Had Alice Tilley come to think of herself as a witch?

"You have no right to accuse Mary Dyer . . ." She imagined women writing such a petition. Then two hundred and seventeen of them, one by one, signing their names.

She felt a lightening, a release. Gladness? Something new, that she sought to identify.

—

They endured spring storms. The ship bucketed, rolled. Rain slashed the deck, wind shredded the sails. Women screamed, children wailed. The minister prayed for deliverance; afterwards, held prayers of thanksgiving.

Mary and Ann Burden and the girls became as a family in the cramped space. They read, told stories, reminisced, sang. Ann's blunt fingers scissored, her wrists turned: knitting, sewing, darning. Mary scratched words with a goose quill, the inky letters blotched and motion-skewed.

Dear William,
I do miss you. We count the days and are now nearer to
England by far than we are to you and the children . . .

But she felt the lack of warmth in these letters, for the William to whom she wrote was made abstract by distance, while her immediate affections had been kindled and now flamed for a new friend.

Friendship. Oh, friendship.

It was like being offered cinnamon cider when shuddering from cold. It was like returning home after travel, sinking into the shape of one's own body in a feather ticking. After Anne Hutchinson, she had had only William and Sinnie as friends. No other married woman; no other mother.

One day they discussed their time of bleeding. On another, how to avoid love-making. They compared their husbands' farms, business enterprises and vagaries. They laughed at shared annoyances, whispered intimate details.

They spoke again of their lost babies.

They debated baptism, the singing of psalms in church, the covenant.

It became their custom to whisper together, long into the night. Salvation, they spoke of. They recognized in one another the anguish of disaffection with the thing that had once been as a jewel in their hearts.

Ann Burden scrawled an address on a slip of paper.

"Here is my sister's house in Bristol."

Mary wrote Aunt Urith's name. *Kettlesing, Yorkshire.*

"Anyone will know her."

Land, they'd been told, would be sighted within the next four days.

The ship sailed up the Thames into London. The vast, sombre concretion of brick houses huddled beneath a pall of smoke. Garbage, offal, and water-logged timbers floated past.

Mary stood on deck beside Ann Burden and the little girls.

She felt power, danger. It pulsed from the muscling river, the distant neighing of horses, the barking of dogs; the rumble of wheels, the clang of hammers; the shrieks, sighs, and clatters that comprised the city's murmurous roar.

She thought how this was a different London. The persecuted were now the powerful. Puritans, led by Oliver Cromwell, ruled the country. These were the men who had beheaded King Charles, one winter morning in 1649. Their beliefs had been her own.

Are these Puritans my people?

She reached for Ann Burden's hand.

SEVENTEEN

The Man in Leathern Breeches - 1652

✳

MARY LIFTED HER WOOL CLOAK from its hook, chose a flat-brimmed beaver hat. She left Urith's house. Late autumn, a dark sky. The stone walls exuded a dank, mossy smell; her shoes slipped on the cobblestones.

In the churchyard, sheep grazed; they lifted their heads, wary, and watched her with rectangular pupils. She went to her parents' headstone, stood with her hand on its rough surface. *Tiny William. Apple blossom cheeks, lonely headstone in London.* She sought, then, her brother's stone, and Uncle Colyn's, with Aunt Urith's name freshly inscribed. The soil still bore the marks of spade and boots. She pictured her aunt as she had last seen her, laid in her coffin, a fragile husk surrounded with tansy.

"Aunt Urith," she whispered. "Canst hear me?" Wisps of mist clung to slate roofs. She left the churchyard, followed a path behind a row of houses. Past the sheep dip, she climbed a stile and slipped like a fugitive through the walled field-garths, heading for a small lake in the hills, "the tarn" they had called it when she was a child.

She turned from the road, followed a footpath that rose and twisted beneath rocky escarpments. Like a beacon, she saw the tarn's solitary, stunted oak. Rain began as she approached and she stood beneath the scant protection of its branches, watching the blinking silver of rain-struck water.

The insidious thoughts began. They had started once Urith was gone and she had remained, alone, in the house.

Massachusetts. Chill air rising from the spaded soil. The bundle coming towards me, a hand moving to pull the shroud from its face. Would I see, then, not a monster but a perfect infant girl? "No, Mary, 'twas true, 'tis a blessing the creature did not live."

She looked up towards the fells. She could simply continue walking. Until she succumbed to starvation. She pictured it—a stagger, a fall. Too weak to rise. Palms clasping the earth. Sleep. A scroll of snow between her lips. In spring, rabbits, heedless upon the bones of her fingers.

Then she remembered the Boston meeting house. Sermons detailing the fates of the damned. *Extreme torment. Racking torture. Dreadful grief, groaning and shrieking. For ever and ever.*

Movement, high on the moor, dark in the veiling rain. People. Emerging from the mist.

They carried long cloth-wrapped bundles by ropes tied at each end. Two women came first, wending their way down a slope. The bundle swung heavily, throwing off their balance. The rope gave a jolt.

"Sorry, love."

The words carried across the emptiness, small and clear.

Corpses.

Two men trudged behind them, lugging a second body. Three others, two women and a man, carried packs. All seven wore broad-brimmed hats and sad-coloured clothing.

"Tarn, dost thee see?" she heard one call.

They worked their way down the switchbacks until the young woman in the lead tripped, flung out her arms, fell. Her companion lost hold of the rope and the wrapped corpse flew forward. Mary saw it sprawl on the young woman, watched her struggle from beneath it, saw her sit, rocking, holding her ankle. Someone took her place and they continued picking their way down the hillside.

As they neared the tarn, one of them noticed Mary and waved. She raised her hand.

The people came up to the tree, laid their burdens onto the grass. The woman who had fallen limped forward. She peered at Mary from beneath hair multi-coloured as a hen's feathers—rust-red, orange, scarlet, ochre.

"Be thee unwell?" she said. "Be thee lost?"

The men and women gathered around. Their faces were calm, inquiring. They rubbed their hands, kneaded bruised shoulders.

Mary looked from face to face.

Something, different. In the way they regard me.

"I am not lost. I have walked from Kettlesing." She heard in her own voice the flattened accent of the colonies.

"But surely thee be in sore distress."

Mary began to shake her head in disavowal. Then she hesitated. Words came, surprising her.

"I did come to this tarn as a child to gather rushes. When I lived with my aunt and uncle. Recently my aunt hath died. Now I am alone. I am . . . I feel . . ."

They listen, patiently, they care to know. They seek my eyes.

"I am as a dead woman amongst the living . . ." She checked herself, glancing at the rain-tapped bundles.

"We will wait upon the Lord with thee, if thou hast a mind for it. We are Friends," a young man said. "Our brethren were imprisoned in York Castle for many months. They died there, within a day of one another. The authorities would not give us leave to bury them in their churchyard so we bear them to our meeting place."

"Quakers?" she said. Hand flew to mouth. "I am sorry . . ."

"Nay, we do not mind the name, though it be spoken by some in misunderstanding."

The rain intensified, made runnels down the men's leather doublets.

"My aunt's house is large," Mary said. "Kettlesing is but a twenty-minutes walk. And one of you is injured. I would have you come and stay the night."

A man gestured toward the bodies. "We have, as thee sees . . ."

"I have stables," she said. "Sheds."

They looked at one another. Then they hoisted their packs, lifted the rope-bound corpses.

Mary turned to the red-haired woman. "Please, do you lean on me."

They stepped from the sheltering tree into the rain. The young woman gasped as she put weight to her ankle.

"Ah, 'twill be good to sleep beneath a roof tonight. My name be Dafeny Hardcastle."

"Mine is Mary Dyer."

By the time they reached Kettlesing, their lanterns illuminated handfuls of rain falling like coins through darkness. They carried the bodies past half-timbered houses, over the humpback bridge. Aunt Urith's stone house was halfway up the hillside. They took the bodies to an outbuilding, laid them in an empty stall.

Mary served mutton pottage, made with oatmeal and the garden's last greens—parsley, thyme and strawberry leaves. They ate at a table in the great hall. Wet clothing steamed on the hearth.

No one spoke, so fatigued they could say no more than "thank thee" before following Mary upstairs.

After the others had gone to bed, Dafeny and Mary pulled chairs close to the fire.

Dafeny removed her cap; her hair fell to her shoulders. Her face was a map of cinnamon freckles, some placed so densely as to be a continent. She was goat-thin, green-eyed. She raised long-fingered hands to the flames.

"A year ago, 'twas a blizzard, and all the family was a-bed. My husband, Dougald, did go to the barn to check an ailing cow. He did find a man sitting in the hay loft and brought him to the house. 'Twas a young man, round Dougald's own age, twenty-eight. His hair . . . long . . ."

She passed her hands over her shoulders. She drew a quick breath as with the acceleration of her heart and Mary saw that she relived the excitement of the moment, the door of the tiny cottage opening with a flurry of snow, and a stranger, come from the night.

". . . and he had no beard. Too tall, he were, to stand straight. Dressed all in leather—pack, breeches, doublet. He had a big hat. Wide-brimmed. We did pull forth our chair. Dougald's mother and our wee ones, they sat up in their beds."

Box beds, with curtains. Mary had seen them long ago in hill cottages, on visits of mercy with Aunt Urith. And the beams, so low that cobwebs caught in one's hair.

"He did sit and tell us his name. 'George Fox,' he said." She paused, her lips parted, gazing at the flames. "'My name is George Fox.' Ah, we did not know! Who 'twas 'neath our roof. I took him my good turf cake and he ate like a starved person, smiling the while. 'I am walking over moors and dales spreading the word of the Lord,' he did say."

Dafeny pulled her cloak close around her neck. "I am walking over the moors and dales spreading the word of the Lord," she repeated, hushed, as if to secretly inhabit the young man's mind. Mary did not take her eyes from the young woman, nor blinked.

"Dougald did ask what was the word."

"Canst remember?" Mary said.

"Aye." The young woman straightened. "Now that I travel to spread his words, I do know them by heart. But 'twas the first time I had heard them."

"Tell me."

Dafeny laid her long fingers upon her temples, closed her eyes. "'I have been opened to the Lord. I desire to pierce the husks in which people are wrapped and bring them into the light of day. I am sent to direct thee to the Spirit that gave forth the Scriptures, by which thee may be led into truth. Truth is in the heart, in thine own hearts. The manifestation of the Spirit of God is given to every one of us to profit withal.'"

A rapt stillness entered the room.

"'All the world's religions are in vain. Those ministers who have been taught in Cambridge and Oxford preach form without power. Their dogma, prayers and singing be . . .'" Dafeny corrected herself. "'. . . are unneeded by those who stand directly in the rays of God's unspeakable love for the world.'" She paused. Then, nodded. In a rush—"'We need no images and crosses, no sprinklings, no holy days, no sacraments.'"

She drew breath, opened her eyes.

"And then he did jump to his feet, and I went to the children, who were . . ." She made an excited flurry with her hand, rushed ahead. "'I declare against them all,' he did say. 'I declare against the steeple houses. We need pay no tithes to maintain church or minister. God is at home in house, meadow, barn or fireside.' And I did think, 'Our house?'"

Mary imagined it. Smell of cows and peat-reek. Stone floor with worn rugs, bulging plaster walls and manure-crusted boots by the door.

"Like an angel," Dafeny whispered. "Come from the dark. He said he had been cast into prison and dragged before the magistrates, only because he did use 'thee' and 'thou' to all, whether they be squire or magistrate. Because he would not doff his hat before any man. Nor take oaths, as being an artifice to ensure truth. And he said: 'I carry no arms.'"

Mary made no move to replenish the fire, nor to stir the metheglin that steamed over the flames. Her hands lay open, palms upward. She felt a fine tingling around the edges of her lips.

"How?" she said, after a long silence. "How would he worship?"

"Anywhere," Dafeny said. "Beneath tree or cliff. In parlour or stable. Men and women sit together in silence and if the Lord doth move within them, they stand and speak. Together, he would have us listen and wait for God, who lives in every second, in every hour, in each house and in every heart. He doth call us Children of the Light, or Friends."

"Did he sleep in your house?"

"Nay," Dafeny smiled. "Dougald's mum came from her bed. She did take her stick and make her way across the floor to George Fox. She laid a hand on his cheek. 'My son,' she said, 'I will sleep the rest of my days in peace if thee rests in my bed.'"

Mary half-smiled, guessing the conclusion.

"'Thank thee. But I go back to my good nest in the hay.' He opened the door and he pointed a finger and said: 'Stir up that which is pure in one another . . .'"

"Did you see him again?"

"He was gone in the morning. Awhile after, when the snow was gone, Dougald went down into the village and he did hear that George Fox had opened many people and that a meeting had been settled. 'Twould be held at a neighbouring farm on every First Day, as Friends name the Sabbath. So we did ride over the moor to attend. 'Twas only a cold room and we did sit in silence and 'twas as if had come a presence. 'The Lord doth appear to us daily,' the farmer's wife did tell us, when we sat on our ponies, after. ''Tis to our astonishment, amazement and great admiration. We are but people of small parts and little abilities but we will take this honour and carry it to all corners of the earth.' Her own husband had promised George Fox that come spring, he would take to the roads and publish the truth."

"How do you yourself come to be travelling?" Mary asked.

"Ah, we both wished to follow, but when lambing began, the old cow died and the walls of the laithe house needed repairing, and we

knew that if one of us went, it must be me. I waited to plant my
garden. Dougald's mother said she would care for it. 'Could be my
travels will bring me round this way anyhow, sometime durin' the
summer,' I said to her."

Mary pictured the exchange. Hill folk were silent people, for they
saw few others besides themselves. The quiver of a mouth's corner
was happiness, thanks or gratitude; an eye's darkening might be
either anger or a decision taken. She imagined the children, silent,
worried, as hers had been on the morning of her departure. Perhaps:
a little boy and girl, in the lee of the garden wall, scratching at dirt
with slate shards. Dafeny—hands at waist, sober glances at the old
woman and then at the children, hair playing over her freckled face.

"Thee be sad," Dafeny said, glancing at Mary.

"I left my own children," Mary answered. They held each other's
eyes.

"'The Lord will see to the children,' Dougald's mother did say to
me, 'since he doth send for thee.' I went to the house and packed." She
laughed. "Only a chicken, come to the door to watch me. My heart . . ."

No words for it, Mary saw. How someone could take your heart
and make it lift and then thud down again, as if askew. So George
Fox had disarranged Dafeny.

Dafeny sat back. Tired, now, as her tale came to an end.

"And your children?" Mary asked. "Do they understand? Do
they miss you?"

"My two be safe with my husband and with their granny." She
yawned and stretched, arms over head, feet to the fire. "I did tell
them that they needn't be feared, for the Spirit of God lives in their
own hearts. I did hold them tight and said I did love them and that I
had no choice in my leaving."

They sat listening to the rain. There was no other sound, save the
crackle of the fire and the purring bubble of metheglin, smelling of
honey and ginger.

"In Boston, you can hear the howling of wolves," Mary said. She spoke slowly, spaces between each phrase, like drips from thawing ice. "There is another world, there, the world of the wild, so strange and frightful that it takes hold of our own people and makes them cruel. The ministers say they have brought the New Jerusalem and that they will raise up God's kingdom. Those who disobey their rules are as if knocking holes in a wall. There is much talk of sin." Her voice hardened. "They told us that some are born sinful. Some will have no redemption. I am such a one."

"Why?"

Mary skimmed the metheglin. The spoon, forgotten in her hand, dripped onto the hearthstone. "I had a child," she said. "I never saw it, 'twas born two months early. It was dead at birth. They did not wake me to see it, the two midwives. They took it away and buried it."

"Why?" Dafeny repeated. Her voice was truly innocent, her green eyes fixed on Mary.

"'Twas rumoured that it was a monster. The ministers and magistrates heard of it and dug it up. It was a thing, they said, part beast, part fish, part fowl."

Dafeny stilled, alert as a cat.

"At first I did not believe it but my friend who had seen it said 'twas in part true. Then I felt it, as if 'twere still in my womb. A scratching, a horror. I prayed for release and found that God had left me. I was dark, within. Damned. Punished for my sin."

"*Sin.* Dost know why George Fox was jailed in Derby and thrown into the dungeon?"

Mary shook her head.

"The magistrate asked him if he dared avow he had no sin. And George Fox, he did say, 'Sin? I have no sin.' George Fox doth say that every man or woman hath received from the Lord a measure of light. He tells that if we hearken to that light we shall come into the state Adam was before he fell. Then we do be innocent. Pure."

Mary sat back and folded her hands. She considered the flames for a long time.

"I wonder," she said. "I went to the tarn to . . . I wonder."

Dafeny ran her fingers over a scar on her cheek. Her clothing smelled of pig manure. Her lips were so chapped that she could not smile.

Mary leaned forward, tugged at a burr on Dafeny's sleeve. The barbs released reluctantly, with tiny rippings.

"Why?" Mary said. "What maketh you to go abroad in rain and snow, to suffer such violence, to be so scorned? I was sorely abused by those who were my teachers. Now I do not know if I would ever again be disposed to follow any teacher." She half-turned to the great hall, firelight playing upon the carved dishboard with its wooden trenchers and copper pans. She lifted her hand to include the house beyond. "I have no joy in this place of my childhood. I care not for the smell of mutton, or anticipation of the assuaging of my hunger. I wait not for the arrival of friends, nor for the dawn of spring and the bursting of green leaves. My heart is dry and black as a bat's wing."

Dafeny watched the fire and listened without evidencing judgment. Then she turned toward Mary, elbows on knees, hands parallel as if she held a box and all that she wished to say were contained within.

"I go because I do believe that once all have known the inner light, then men and women, servants and kings, priests and drovers will be as equals, and such will put an end to strife, cruelty and suffering. George Fox's father was a weaver; as a youth, George were put out to a cattle-dealer who was a shoemaker by trade. The Lord's word hath been revealed to us humble people of the north. We have no choice but to go forth and tell it."

Her face lit with a sudden thought.

"He is in this region. May be that thee will see him for thyself."

"I see you are tender," Mary said. "I see that you and the others do love one another."

"We are as a family," Dafeny said. "As much family as our own blood kith and kin."

She yawned, closed her eyes, dragged them open with difficulty. Mary smiled and took up a candle.

"Come."

EIGHTEEN

Travelling - 1652–1653

THAT NIGHT, MARY COULD NOT SLEEP, aware of the Friends in the adjacent bedchambers.

Do you miss your children? she had wished to ask Dafeny, rather than if the children missed their mother. But she had not dared, for fear the question would be turned.

She tried to pick apart the memory of each child's birth. The first, she remembered best. Little William, luminous as a new rose, peaceful in his cradle within London's racket. The next child, Samuel, Boston-born, adored by Sinnie while Mary herself was haunted by dread of his loss and weekly reminders of God's jealous purview. Then. Pains in the garden. Screams. Anne's voice.

Move ahead to Aquidneck.

Babies, babies. Like following waves, one subsuming the next, all clouded by unending grief. Clouts, fevers, squalling, the day's other duties, her own darkness of mind so heavy that she sought her bed and pulled the coverlet over her head.

In memory, she could not set each child out upon a table like a row of apples.

I should not have fled. For if I had stayed, I would have come to love them.

She pulled knees to chest, clasped cold hands between her knees. She recalled how, earlier this evening, Dafeny had deepened her voice to imitate a man's.

Sin? I have no sin.

Who was this George Fox, who could say such things?

Every man or woman hath received from the Lord a measure of light. He says that if we follow the light we shall come into the state Adam was before he fell. We shall be innocent. Pure.

She opened her eyes in the darkness. She saw herself parting from Ann Burden in a London inn. She saw herself boarding a stage-coach, arriving in Yorkshire. There was Aunt Urith, arms wide in the doorway, wrinkles riding slack skin. Months passed. Pessaries, ointments, tinctures. In the cooling autumn, she knelt at Urith's bed-side, watching the long departure; collapsed, at the last breath, and flung her arms round the porcelain-still body.

Then, the empty house. No simplers' feet hurried down the narrow halls nor caused the stair treads to creak. No cooks and maids worked red-armed in the great hall, nor groans came from the sur-gery, nor clatter in the stables. From Uncle Colyn's study, she had stared through the rain into the courtyard, where once women had laboured over the copper washing vats, their reed-paddled flails rising and falling, their arms mottled with steam and cold. Her fin-gers had caused the room's only sound, lifting books from shelves, settling them back. Herodotus, Livy, Procopius. Froissart. Sir Walter Raleigh's *History of the World.* Camden's *Britannia. Purchas His Pilgrims. Antichrist the Pope of Rome.*

And she had begun to hear the whisperings.

You, too, should have been buried with the baby.

The inheritance went to the oldest son. He had come to review his property. Before leaving, he had bid his cousin Mary stay as long as necessary. Then, a letter from William, asking when she would return. She had written back—*I must delay. There is much still to be settled.* She had prevaricated, and it gnawed at her.

She rolled over and lay face down on her bedstead. Then she thrashed back up, pulled her covers to her shoulders. Mixed with the patter of rain came a sound like the faint, irregular creaking of timbers.

Ah. Snoring!

The next morning, Dafeny's ankle was swollen, purple and throbbing.

"Fat as a suckling pig," she said, sitting in the bedstead, rueful.

Mary provided the others with bundles of cold meat and cheat rye bread. She stood in the doorway watching as they made their way down the street, encumbered by the swaying corpses. Then she helped Dafeny down the stairs and to a chair by the fire; plastered the ankle with a paste of vinegar, bread crumbs, honey and figs.

"My aunt taught me many things," Mary said, kneeling to tuck up the ends of the cloth.

"Tell me of her," Dafeny said. "Tell me of thy life."

Two weeks later, Dafeny's ankle was healed, but still she stayed with Mary.

At the hiring market in Kettlesing, smoke rose from braziers, carrying the smell of mutton through the cold air. Scarlet pennants snapping in the moorland wind, the green wheels of a gypsy's wagon—their colours were so bold in the clarity that they appeared less objects than strokes of light.

Dafeny clutched Mary's arm. "That be him."

"Who? Where?"

"George Fox. There, by the market cross."

They stood shoulder to shoulder with tradespeople and servants, who clustered, waiting their turn to step up onto the auction block to offer their services and skills. Thatchers held tufts of golden reeds;

dairy-maids clutched stools. Sun made a pocket of warmth, releasing the smell of unwashed clothing, smoke-befouled hair.

Fox rose over the crowd, sturdy in a leather doublet. Unlike the close-cropped Puritans, hair spread from beneath a broad-brimmed hat, lay across his shoulders. His hands were large as a labourer's, and scarred, like his leather trousers.

He called out suddenly, as if announcing a matter of extreme urgency.

"I declare that the Lord has come with the Word of Life!"

The auctioneer glared and then continued his bawling cries. Fox paid no attention. He held up one arm. He was flushed with health, face ruddied from days spent out-of-doors.

"The Lord God hath sent me to preach the everlasting gospel and Word of Life, and to bring you from all these temples . . ." He pointed at the church tower. ". . . tithes, priests and rudiments of the word. They have been instituted since the apostles' days, and have been set up by such as hath erred from the Spirit. I come to save the church from deadness and formalism."

Mary put a hand to Dafeny's shoulder in order to rise up on her toes. The young man's eyes were stern, compassionate.

"Quench not the Spirit . . ." he called out.

"Shut yer cakehole!"

The crowd milled. Some turned towards the auctioneer, others to Fox. Those who shouted were shouted at by those who wished to hear one or the other. Fox's voice soared over the discord.

". . . and live that ye may feel and see to the beginning, before the world and its foundation was; and that nothing may reign but the life and power amongst you. And live that ye may answer that of God in every man . . ."

"Out of me way."

Mary was pushed from her toes as a goose herder shoved past, leading hooded birds attached to one another by a rope. The herder flailed with her stick, hissed.

Fox's words unfurled upon the fatty scent of roasting mutton, the jingling of farthing boxes, the bawling of cattle. Mary was dimly aware that Dafeny had asked her a question, but Fox's words were such that she felt if she did not attend them, a gulf would yawn and all would slither to perdition, the world rendered into nonsense and rubble.

He is so young! His lips had not yet acquired the bitter down-turn of age. She pulled herself up, again, hand on Dafeny's shoulder. He turned away. Broken phrases came and those around Mary also craned to see, shushing one another, seizing the words like grains spewed from a passing cart.

". . . go forth . . . in the sun of God's power . . . you will see where the lost sheep are. And such as have been driven away . . ."

She lost his next words as cattle filled the street, their driver shouting, cracking his whip. She cupped hands behind her ears, straining to hear. *Such as have been driven away.*

A man roared, rushed towards Fox and knocked him down. Fox rose, calm, and placed one hand against the man's chest, keeping him at arm's length. Still he preached, although now his words were intensified by intimacy, as if he addressed the man alone and thus, by implication, each separate listener.

". . . you will see the bright morning star appear, which will expel the night of darkness that hath been in your hearts . . ."

My heart.

". . . by which—"

He wavered again as he was seized by two men. Mary could hear his voice. ". . . by which morning star you will come to the everlasting day, which was before night was. So everyone feel this bright morning star in your hearts, there to expel the darkness . . ."

"Where did he go?"

"Like an angel, he were . . ."

The crowd surged to follow. Mary put out her arm to keep herself from falling, heard a shriek, felt a blow on the side of her head. Her hat slid over one eye as she struggled amidst legs, shoulders, baskets and dogs.

"Come," Dafeny said, pulling her up by the arm. "He will make for the church."

They were jostled along a street, past the tavern, up a lane. At its end was a lych-gate; beyond, the square-sided church tower. Two men dressed like Fox were setting a wooden placard in front of the roofed gateway.

Dafeny brushed red curls from her face, stood on tiptoe, squinting at the scrawled letters. "What do it say?"

"'God is not worshipped here,'" Mary read, raising her voice as people gathered round her. "'This is a temple made with hands: neither is this a church, for the church is in God. This building is not in God, neither are you in Him, who meet here.'"

A woman carrying a basket of onions clapped hand to mouth, too horrified for speech. Mary saw a farmer repress a smile, eyes bearing sly delight. A small man ripped cap from head, waved it in a frenzy of outrage.

"Call the constables!" he shrieked.

Other men picked up the placard and began to hustle it away but were restrained by officers wearing the yellow-cuffed red wool coats, grey breeches and felt hats of the New Model Army.

"Put it down," one of the officers snapped. "Let others see what it do say."

People pushed through the lych gate and entered the church to see if Fox had invaded the sanctuary. Mary and Dafeny followed those who went around to the churchyard.

Fox stood on a carved bible box beneath an oak tree. Sunlight sparked on the tree's yellow leaves and on the alchemy buttons of his doublet. He stood with fingers spread, as if holding a nest of sticks.

"You will think it strange to see a man preach under the sky; yet the fell side is as holy as any other ground . . ."

The heathery wind snatched at his words.

"Ye may come to see that which was in the beginning, before the word was, where there is no shadow or darkness . . ."

He spoke for over an hour. He described "the tender thing" that was in them all. He told of his spiritual journey, how he had left his apprenticeship and wandered in despair.

"Then hope underneath held me, as an anchor on the bottom of the sea . . ."

As Mary listened, she forgot that the words came from the lips of a young man with black fingernails and sunburned face. They were thoughts like her own, released from long immersion. She did not so much remember as become the earnest young woman she had been in London when she had listened to John Everard, the Puritan preacher; or the young mother she had been in those first days in Boston, hearing Anne Hutchinson speak of "grace"—and in both instances had felt the vitality of hope.

This time, the constables themselves came.

A short, walnut-faced man, one eye squinted by a thick scar, wended his way through the crowd, walking like a sailor on a tipping deck. He was followed by a younger constable whose skin was pitted by smallpox. Both held carriage whips. Fox stepped down from the bible box. The constables shoved his shoulders while kicking his feet from under him. One snatched his hat and sent it flying.

The nut-faced constable mounted the box. "How is it that you have stood by and allowed this filth on our sacred grounds?"

People stirred, recovered themselves.

Some began to shout at George Fox, as if their entranced listening had been not of their own volition.

"Aye, off with you, foul face."

"Be gone, puddinghead! . . . blockish grutnol . . . doddi-pol-jolt-head!"

They shouted at each other.

"You did not call him such earlier! Listened to him, you did. He hath spoken sense . . ."

Fox and the two young men who had placed the placard began to make their way to the gate. One of the constables cracked his whip. It fell across Fox's cheek, raising a line of blood. Mary was jostled to the ground, felt a boot tread upon the back of her hand, saw her basket fly away. She struggled up in time to see village men seize Fox by the shoulders and force him to his knees. They dragged him face-downwards from the churchyard and up the street, the young Friends following close, and the two constables in the rear.

People turned away—shame-faced or satisfied.

Mary and Dafeny hurried up the street; saw, at the top of the village, the men clustered in a field garth. Fox was rising from his knees, brushing off his coat. He began walking towards the moor, the young men at his side. The village men turned back, but the constables toiled behind, shouting, their whips slashing Fox.

The five men became as flies, dwarfed by the hills.

"I know that path," Mary said.

They stepped onto the hoof-hardened trail. On the breeze came the scent of furze—fresh, wild.

The constables, coming down, passed Mary and Dafeny. They trudged with whips against their shoulders, tilt-faced, like children who have broken some essential tool.

"Where are you going, women?"

Neither woman spoke.

"Keep away from them crazy folk. See there, the sky's gone grouty."

Clouds had come up from the west. The constables paused, as if to dissuade them, but Mary quickened her pace, hand to a stitch in her side. Rounding a boulder, they encountered the Friends. George Fox sat, slouched forward, head in his hands, blood oozing between his fingers.

"The final time they struck him, he fell unconscious," one of the young men told them. "He hath just now revived."

The other kneeled, arm around Fox's shoulders.

"*George,*" he urged. "Can thee speak?"

"Aye." Fox tried to stand, stumbled and sat back again. He sat brushing soil from his sleeves, looking at the sky. "Storm."

"Are thee thyself, George?"

The big man sighed. Then he smiled.

"Aye. 'Tis of no account, just a smash."

"You may come to my house," Mary offered. "I can make a poultice."

She held herself still and did not look away, even as his eyes lingered upon hers, travelling through her closed doors, her wrapped secrets. He gathered her into himself, like a pebble that he might lift, and think beautiful, and tuck into a pocket.

"Thank thee," he said. "But I must needs travel onward to York."

His voice was firm, as if what had occurred needed no contemplation. He tipped his head to probe the wound, examined his bloody hand.

"Hast thee a rag, Richard Farnsworth?"

He scrambled onto his feet and stood looking down at the church bell rising over the village on its tower, like the eye of a snail.

"But I'll pass once again through Kettlesing. I must find my hat. 'Tis in the yard of that steeple house."

Mary knelt by the bedstead and pressed her face to the prickly wool. She did not pray, but saw George Fox's eyes. They became the world—houses, trees, fire, lavender, birds, water—and yet held something more, as wondrous and searing as the pressure in her heart.

Mary wrote to her cousin, advising him that she would be shutting up the house. She and Dafeny rolled carpets, sheeted furniture, gave away cellared cheese, ale and apples. They baked a quantity of biscuit bread, filling the house with the scents of aniseed and coriander. In the evenings, they stitched wool petticoats or lined their cloaks with heavy blanketing. They knit mittens, darned socks. Mary wrote to William:

November 1652

My dearest William,
I booked passage on the Chapman for the spring sailing but find I must advise you not to expect me, for I shall not be able to come.

She laid her quill down for so long that Dafeny looked up from her knitting.

"What shall I tell him?" Mary said, glancing at her friend.

"The truth," Dafeny said, surprised.

Mary turned her eyes to the fire. Within her was all that the truth entailed and she did not see how she could distill it. Her friend's resolute green eyes. The tender, fierce, stalwart Friends. England like a finely detailed tapestry, its red-coated army, the looted churches, Royalists in hiding, Oliver Cromwell the Protector. George Fox, who had sprung from this, his message a thread of the tapestry, a part of the mind like the ticking of Uncle Colyn's clock or the wisps of smoke sent sideways by the draughts of Aunt Urith's ancient house.

Nor did she see how she could convey to William the truth of her heart—that within it lived still the young man who had run up the stairs, bringing gifts. He and she sat in the little house by the Thames, alert and happy, waiting for a different future.

I have become a Friend or what they do call a Quaker. It has brought me comfort. I have a companion, a married woman named Dafeny Hardcastle, and we set forth this day week to publish the truth. Please tell the children that I do think of them every day, as I do you, my love,

Your,
Mary Dyer

They set out in grey cloaks that anticipated colder days to come. Their packs were laden with biscuit bread, dried meat, flagons of cider. Buried at the bottom of Mary's was a drawstring bag filled with coins.

They crossed the humpback bridge and walked away from the village, heading north.

They did not know where they would arrive at nightfall, nor whether they would sleep in tavern, barn, house or propped against one another at the roadside.

"I do not care," Mary said, when Dafeny pointed this out to her. She felt buoyant, eager. They strode side by side, their ankles wrenched by frozen mud. Wind chased clouds over the dale heads, the moors pulsed with waves of light and shadow. Nothing lay ahead but the narrow track, cutting deep into the soil, glinting beneath the mid-December sky.

—

All winter, and the following spring, summer and autumn, they passed from village to village, telling of George Fox and repeating his message to whoever would listen. *We do not remove our hats to those of superior status, for we believe all are equal before God, rich and poor, male and female . . . nor use "you" but equally address all with "thee" or "thou" . . . nor need ministers to intercede on our behalf . . . nor need churches with their appurtenances . . . for there is that of God within us and all have within the inner light . . .*

They posted papers on church doors, advising of the time and place where they would hold their meetings—on street corners, in haylofts, parlours, farm kitchens, commons.

By word of mouth or letters sent to other Friends, they heard of the persecutions of Fox's followers, called by other Friends "The Valiant Sixty." Many were run out of towns. Others had been thrown in jail—for vagrancy, or for blasphemy, or for disturbing the peace. Women had preached to the students at Cambridge and been stripped to the waist and whipped. One excessively fat man, who wandered the streets dressed in sackcloth, barefoot and barelegged, holding sweet flowers in his right hand and stinking weeds in his left, had been forced into a hole in the Chester prison named "Little Ease," so tight that blood came from his mouth and nose. Two women passed a winter imprisoned in a dank cell infested with frogs and toads. Meetings for worship were disrupted, doors broken down, hogs released into rooms, beards cut half-off, windows shattered. Friends were called whores, bitches, toads, dogs, rebels.

George Fox was hauled before magistrates, and thrown into prison, and then released, and then thrown in again. He wrote a letter, which was copied and found its way to those who were abroad. Mary read it aloud to Dafeny.

. . . spare no tongue or pen, but be obedient to the Lord
God . . . be valiant for the Truth upon earth; be a pattern to
others . . . that your carriage and life may preach among all
sorts of people . . . walk cheerfully over the world, answering
that of God in every one . . .

Mary slept on floors strewn with rye straw. Her stomach churned with hunger. Her clothing was greasy, lice tickled her scalp, her body itched, her lips were chapped, her hands bore the white spots of frostbite. She lay, at night, with knees drawn, hands cradling her chilblained feet.

She had no fear of those who might mock her, suffering pain and humiliation with gladness, since they had been reduced in proportion to her joy and became as the prick of brambles or the sting of an insect.

In Underbarrow, they were directed to the home of a woman whose husband was travelling with the Valiant Sixty. Her house was a way station where food, rest and mail might be obtained. They arrived at the long, white-washed house in late afternoon. At their knock, the woman came to the door—small, bright-faced.

"I heard you were coming. And I am glad, for I have been holding a letter for thee, Mary Dyer."

She showed them to a bedroom, with the promise of bath and supper.

From William. Dated . . . but how can this be? Last week.

Mary found her way to a chair by the window, eyes on the familiar handwriting.

October 1653

My dearest Mary,
I am in London. My brother hath died. He had no children
so all his estate has come to me, a considerable amount. The
other reason for my trip was the grouthead Coddington,
who did make secret parlay in England and then came back
to us like a peacock with a legal charter declaring himself
governor-for-life over all of Aquidneck Island. John Clark,
Roger Williams and I did travel over together and took that
charter to the Council of State, where it rests now. God
knows what will happen if 'tis not revoked, for they are all
in an outrage about it. In Providence, they say . . .

She paused to take breath.

Dafeny looked up. She was eagerly divesting herself of her dirt-flecked cloak, her kerchief, stockings and stays. *Come down in your shifts,* the woman had said. *You may bathe straight away.*

"The children?" she said. "All be well with them?"

"I . . . he has not yet said."

. . . there will be outright revolt. But of that, enough. My
more urgent mission was to find you and bring you back
with me. Indeed I have booked passage for two, and the ship
sails in a fortnight. I have had a time to find you, but upon
vigorous questioning amongst London Friends, this address
was provided and it was thought that you might be . . .

She sat, then, with the letter on her lap. In the distance, she could see Underbarrow Scar, dark against the sky; closer, the yellow leaves of an apple tree.

"Good tidings?" Dafeny watched her, fingers working strings.

I will not tell her.

"Aye, all is well."

The smell of cooking caused her stomach to growl. Dafeny laughed.

"Ah, such a savoury scent. When did we last fill our bellies, Mary?"

Mary folded the letter and tucked it into the travel-worn envelope. She sat for a minute, holding it in her lap—his crisp tone and his assumptions were like a plunge into frigid sea water. She pictured him, vigorous, canny, striding the streets of London. *My wife? My wife?* She stood, dropped the letter onto a table and set to work on her own stiff ribbons.

"Do thee go ahead, Dafeny."

"I be the filthier. Thee will have mud in which to bathe."

"Nay, thee go."

She listened to the loud-soft, loud-soft of her friend's shoes on the stairs.

She stepped forward and laid her hand on the letter.

Asking for me. Oh, my William. I will return, but not yet, oh, not yet.

In November, Mary and Dafeny arrived in the vales of Worcestershire. They were welcomed into the home of an army captain, who had been convinced by George Fox. He hosted a large meeting for worship; afterwards, people stayed to tell them of Friends who had been kept imprisoned in the local jail for several months.

"Why?" Mary asked. "What was their offence?"

The man beside her turned, spoke quietly.

"The Friends would not pay the fine for coming into court with their hats on and for setting their hands to a paper against the magistrates."

Something of George Fox, Mary reflected, already characterized Friends, for in this white-haired man's face was sweetness, patience.

"The jailor hath used them cruelly. He withholds their food and if they ask for water will offer a bowl of piss."

His wife leaned forward, earnest. "He did say he would hang them all if he could. So we watch day and night and smuggle what food we can."

"Sometimes we hear them singing," the man said. "Then a cracking and a pounding and we do fear for them but the singing will come again and so we do stand in silence without."

"We will go to the jail and visit them," said Dafeny.

"Aye," Mary said. "We can bring them comfort in the tales of those we have opened. We can read them our copy of a letter George Fox hath sent to all who spread the truth."

Mary and Dafeny and many of the Friends stood in the street before the jail, surrounded by jeering men, women, children.

"Quakers!"

"Ye ranting sluts."

"Come to visit yer proud friends?"

A clot of dirt flew. The sound of singing drifted from an open window in the jail. Another missile—frozen horseshit.

"We want no more of you northern vermin in this town!"

The crowd shoved the Friends, tore the men's hats from their heads, pulled the women's hair. Mary and Dafeny stood together, slightly apart. A constable arrived, accompanied by a man who identified himself as the town's mayor.

"Ye'll not be from here," the constable said, pointing at Mary and Dafeny. "We have laws about vagrants."

Dafeny stepped towards the man.

"Aye, we are travellers. But we do come in peace and will pass away soon. We come to spread the truth of the Lord, as we were taught by George Fox. We believe that there is rising a new and living way out of the north, from whence we come." She drew a breath, so deep that her chest rose. Her eyes were wide, unblinking. "The days of virtue, love and peace are coming. So doth our founder tell us. We believe that there is that of God in every one. We live in peace one with another, and dwell in the seed of—"

"I'll give you seed," a man called out. Laughter.

Snow began to sift from the sky. The singing continued in the jail.

"Come away," the mayor said, taking Mary's arm. He spoke in a low voice, glancing at the constable. "'Tis not safe for you here."

He led her down the street. The constable followed, leading Dafeny.

Behind them, Friends began to sing along with the voices in the prison. The mayor turned.

"Stop that singing!" he roared. "Stop that singing!"

The Friends pressed close, still singing. Mary pulled against the man's grasp.

"Calm yourself," he said, tightening his grip. He lowered his voice, spoke kindly. "We do wish to hear your message. I have heard much of George Fox. A good man, they say, a good man."

They came out in the town square.

"Ye'll stand up there, they can gather round and better hear," the mayor said, pointing to a platform with stocks. He turned to the people who had crowded up behind. "Come along, these good women are going to speak."

Dafeny went first, led by the constable. The mayor turned to give Mary a hand up the steps. She slipped on the frosty wood, went down on one knee. She rose to see a confusion of skirts, the soles of Dafeny's shoes, the constable bending, clamping her ankles into the stocks. Then the mayor's hands, hard on her own wrists as she tried to stand, shoving her, too, into a seated position.

Dafeny began to sing.

"Ye'll stay here all night. If you don't shut that singing, your hands will be put in as well as your feet. Tomorrow you'll be whipped for vagrants and sent with a pass to your own countryside."

I will sing, I will sing.

Mary lifted her voice along with Dafeny's. She kept her eyes on the falling snow as the men forced her to lean forward and clamped her wrists. She sank into the peace of acceptance, like the snowflakes, wending their way, sent this way and that by the wandering air.

The next morning, Mary and Dafeny were so cold they could not move when released but tumbled sideways. The constable nudged them with the toe of his boot.

"Be gone with no more jabber and jangle, and I'll not whip ye."

They lay still—exhausted, shivering. The sun rose, touching the branches of ice-silvered oaks.

They walked southwards, towards London.

NINETEEN

London - 1654–1656

✳

MARY AND DAFENY RAN THROUGH the streets. Weaving, stumbling. Skirts in hand, faces wrapped in scarves. Snow coated horses' backs, lined the sills of shop windows.

Bridewell Prison dominated the surrounding houses. Four storeys high, flags flying from towers, it had been the palace of Henry VIII. *All the people of Kettlesing could live here with room left over.*

They passed beneath a vaulted stone doorway and showed their loaf of bread to a guard, satisfying him that they carried only sustenance.

"We are going to Elizabeth Swale," Mary said.

They followed a matron. Tall and broad-shouldered, she walked rapidly despite a limp, manacles jingling from one hand. They passed a high-ceilinged, pillared room where women stood row on row, positioned before tree stumps, swinging short-handled wooden mallets against slabs of hemp. Children sat at their mother's skirts or roamed, distraught, in the dusty air. A man wearing a white apron prowled the room, prodding rumps with a cane. The women talked, sang, shrieked.

"Harlots, they be," the matron remarked, moving on. "Vagabonds, thieves and murderers."

She led them farther—up stone stairs lit by draught-flared charcoal braziers, past rooms lit only by snow's shadowless light. Inside the rooms, women sat slumped against walls, sewing; or huddled on flock beds.

"They are starving," Mary breathed into Dafeny's hair. "Twenty did die here last month."

The matron left them at a low door and limped away, manacles clanking.

They stepped into a room that stank of ripening piss. Its floor was strewn with clots of hemp, half-chewed cabbage leaves, rat droppings. Beneath a small window overlooking the River Fleet, a pallet lay on the floor—a spill of blonde hair, a motionless body face down. Three men in greatcoats and high leather boots clustered around it.

Mary and Dafeny paused until a short man with a swollen, bruised lip and close-cropped hair nodded; they slipped between the men and knelt by the pallet.

"The jailor will be reprimanded," he said, slurring from the injury. "I told him to stop, the punishment did not meet the crime. But I see that he continued."

"She provoked him," one of the men murmured into his fist.

"She *sang*," the first man snapped. "She sang while he whipped her."

The young woman was half-naked, her back a jelly. She cried out, suddenly, and threw out her arms as if fleeing sleep-terror. Mary and Dafeny soothed her, rearranged the thin blanket.

"We will take her," Mary said. "Provide us a carriage. Else thee shall have the costs of burial."

"You are family?"

"Friends," Mary answered. She looked into the eyes of the short man. "We are Children of Light, as is she."

Into his face came the expression—disdain, scorn, alarm—to which Mary had become accustomed.

"We will take her," she insisted.

"Take her, then." The man turned away, speaking as he stepped into the hall. "I will order a conveyance."

—

At the gates of Whitehall, they helped the young woman down from the hackney coach. The day was darkening to dusk, torch-light quivering in the swirling snow.

"We came to stay with my cousin Dyota," Mary explained. "She did once live here, but her husband hath died and now she hides in a stable with others who once served the king."

The palace was quiet, its courtyards strewn with rubbish. They turned into the dunghill yard, a cobbled square surrounded by long, low buildings. Smoke wisped from crumbling chimneys. One window was propped open; behind another, they glimpsed a hand pulling a curtain shut. Inside, no horses drowsed or paced in the stalls; no saddles or harnesses filled rooms where once had been a frenzy of polishing.

They supported Elizabeth up a staircase and manoeuvred her down a listing hallway, passing a room in which women gathered around a hearth. Steam rose from a kettle, stoneware pipkins stood in the coals. Hunger scooped the women's cheeks and evidenced itself in the children's listlessness.

Elizabeth's knees buckled, she staggered. They shuffled down the hall to Dyota's room, once a groom's lodging. Candlelight gathered the dried-blood red of a Turkey carpet, the black wood of an oak chest. Dyota lay on a curtained bedstead. Her eyes were closed, her breath was halting, raspy.

They helped Elizabeth to a pallet, eased her onto her belly.

"I felt the Lord's hands," she murmured into the pillow. "So vast they were. So warm. As if I were a kitten and he did lift me from harm."

"Aye," Mary said. Women clustered at the door, whispering, but did not enter. "Almost, Elizabeth, thee entered the Kingdom. But he did send thee back."

Dafeny went out through the group of women, who took her leaving as an excuse to enter and ask after Elizabeth's misfortune.

They clucked, stroked her hair. After a long while, Dafeny returned with a bowl of paste and strips of linen.

"Walkmill powder," she muttered, kneeling. "Had to go to the apothecary's."

She knelt, worked a strip of linen into the paste, handed it to Mary. They worked until half the girl's back was bandaged.

"Prithee, more linen," Mary said. Two of the women left. The others made way; coalesced, like duckweed. There was a sound of tearing.

Mary pressed a strip against the last seeping welt. Hands passed her a sheet, clean and folded, and she draped it over the plastered back.

Might have been her shroud.

She pictured the jailor who had whipped this young woman. How, afterwards, he would have gone to his home and sat before a fire, eating savoury pie. How he would have turned into a warm bed, feeling he had done his duty.

"They turned us from our home," Dyota moaned.

Two months had passed. The dregs of winter hovered over the city, their breath smoked on the air.

"'Twas a bitter cold day in January. My Ralf and I knelt in prayer."

In her palm, Dyota held a blood-stained chip of wood. It was a relic from the king's beheading, a remnant of scaffold the size of a banty egg, worn from handling.

She was propped against a bolster, shivering, sweat dripping from her temples. She suffered pain in her joints, faintness, fever, night sweats. Weekly, a physician came to administer bloodlettings and emetics. Her condition did not improve. On sunny days, Mary bundled the sweat-soaked bedding and hung it out the window.

"They took the king to his own bedchamber therein to await his death. Oh, and the groan that went up when the blow fell and severed his lovely head. The great groan! 'Twas the end of my Ralf. His heart brake asunder. Not three days later the Puritans turned us out. Into the snow. 'Take what you can carry,' they said. 'Take what you can carry.' We went from pillar to post until Ralf died. Then I crept back here like a rat. 'Oh, England!' my Ralf would cry out. In his great agony of mind. 'Oh, England!'"

She held the piece of wood to her cheek. Her voice lowered.

"That great beast and murderer." She turned fever-glazed eyes in the direction of the Cockpit Lodgings where Cromwell lived with his wife and children. "And now he is king in all but name."

Mary nodded. Only that morning, she had seen graffiti, crude portrayals of Cromwell and his cronies, scrawled on walls by those weary of the Puritan reign.

Cromwell and his wife and children were in the process of moving into the sumptuous apartments once inhabited by the royal family. The royal possessions had been salvaged—bedsteads, crates of silver, rolls of tapestries, retrieved artwork. And in the past two days, carpenters had begun refurbishing these stables. When discovered, the squatters had been granted time to find new accommodation. Some had already left to seek family amidst ruined country estates, but Dyota was too ill to move. And despite the grace period, Mary feared taking her into the armed camp London had become—twelve hundred troops recalled from Ireland, the Tower garrison increased, even a cannon placed before the palace walls.

"Oh, and we are to call him *Your Highness*," Dyota murmured. "May our dear king come back soon and cast out the beast."

Mary, Dafeny and Elizabeth listened to Dyota's complaints and said nothing. No cool cloth, no soothing words could ease her distress. After a time, their own silence spread like lulling music and stopped the parched, fevered lips.

Quiet.

Mary leaned against the wall, sewing. Tenderness loosened her palms. Ah, should she spread her fingers as George Fox had done in the Kettlesing churchyard—*life would quiver there, distilled to a single drop.*

Mary lived as if cloistered, caring for Dyota and Elizabeth, writing personal letters on behalf of those Friends who could neither read nor write, sending news to the north telling of the many in London who had embraced Fox's message—"convincements," they were called. She seldom left the stableyard garret, moving from room to room along the tilted hallway, eviscerating the chickens and chopping onions that Dafeny brought from the market, bending over hearths, emptying chamber pots, lugging water from the courtyard well, scrubbing clothes, sleeping at her cousin's side, exhausted. She did not see beyond each day to her own future and yet awakened, every morning, surprised by how her heart no longer weighted her chest but was as if floating, shining—*as if, as Anne Hutchinson once promised, the Holy Spirit did dwell there.* The room's window faced south. Sunlight warmed Mary's Bible as she read aloud to Dyota or told her of the reports that came from the countryside.

"A young woman Friend hath gone to a judge and asked to substitute herself in jail for an old man."

"What hath he done to be thrown in jail?"

"He travelled, spreading the truth. He fell afoul of the law against vagrants. He was searched and they did take away everything—money, Bible, inkhorns, paper. They did whip him and fastened irons upon him. He lies amongst common felons on straw upon damp earth. He is old and weak and like to die. She begged to take his place but the judge sent her away."

Mary wore no whalebone stays, only a collared dress over her shift. Her diminished face bore lines, scribbles across her forehead like the marks of bird's wings in sand; etched more deeply beside her mouth. Her hair, unwashed, was stiffened by grey.

The boys dimmed in her mind. She struggled to picture them in Aquidneck—tiny, vague figures running beneath the apple trees.

William, however, she saw clearly. And Littlemary, who had cried at her departure, and whose girlhood would be passing. She saw, too, the boulders glinting with mica and the shore's bursting, falling spray.

When Dyota dies . . .

A noisome fret began, a finger upon her heart.

Once her wounds had healed, Elizabeth Swale and another young woman left for Bristol, where they heard convincements had begun.

Dyota died in August, on a day of insufferable heat. Mary sent for an Anglican priest to administer the Holy Sacrament, for her cousin had remained steadfast to the Church of England.

In the stables, they heard less the sounds of the remaining squatters, and more the shouts of workers, with their saws and hammers.

One evening, Dafeny stood at the window, watching birds flying across the reddening sky. She brought the back of her hand to her cheek, ducking her head, and then paused, bent, forgetting to wipe away the tears, which came faster.

Mary came swiftly, put an arm around her shoulders.

"My babes," Dafeny said. "All my dear ones."

Mary wrote to William, and sent him the address of a London Friend, to which he could reply.

August 1655, Aquidneck

Dear Mary,
'Twas a great disappointment to find your letter rather than
your person on board Trerise's vessel and still my heart doth
ache. You say that there are those who require your presence
and for whom you bear love but sad it is to tell that the chil-
dren do forget you and it breaketh my heart to tell them of
you only in order that they remember that a mother was
once theirs. I beg of you that as soon as your cousin dies
return to me and to them . . .

Mary stood at the window of a small room overlooking the Thames. She and Dafeny had left the stable a year ago.

The sun rose, a fiery radiance softened by spring mist. Below, in the courtyard, cart horses drowsed, nose-to-nose. Gulls flew low, heading up-river.

She saw the birds, the mist and the horses as separating particles, vaporizing from the dream that had wakened her. In the dream, a young man put arms around her and she had felt drawn not against a man's body but into a love so sweet and vast that even in the dream her waking thoughts protested against its loss. He had placed her upon the back of a black goose. Stretching away on all sides were other people on dark-feathered geese. She had lain forward and clasped the bird's neck as its wings lifted.

She heard the rustle of Dafeny's awakening.

"Ah, such a dream I had," Mary said, turning from the window. Dafeny rolled to her side; her red hair burned in the light like marigolds. Mary thought of the moment she had first seen Dafeny and the other Friends—how they had loomed in the rain, blurred, indistinct.

Dafeny sat, leaned against the wall. She shuffled her hair from her face.

"I have decided," she said. "I mus' take to the roads again. I mus' make my way back north. I am going to go home."

She took a long breath.

"My children, my dear Dougald, my Sibilla. 'Tis too long. I have done my part."

Mary said nothing.

"Will thee come with me? Or . . ."

Dafeny's face. More familiar, now, than any other. The fingers, tracing letters on a page as Mary taught her to read. Chapped lips, murmuring prayer.

Her dream had forewarned her and now she could not tell it to her friend for the aching of her throat.

"Could thee not, Mary?"

She shook her head, pressed her lips tight. She turned back to the window. The carters had arrived to harness their horses. Horses and men moved, thickened and wavery as behind a fall of water.

V.

NEW ENGLAND

1657-1660

And in the shadow of thy wings I sing for joy . . .

PSALM 63

TWENTY

The House on the Point - 1657

SINNIE STOOD IN THE CHICKEN house door, eggs in a basket. The evening air bore the scent of turned soil.

She heard the slow clopping of hoofs.

Two horses turned in at the gate and came up the long laneway. A man rode one horse and a woman the other. Both lifted hand to forehead, shielding eyes as sunset cast long rays.

She ran to the house, heart skittering.

"They are come," she called into the entryway, glancing up the stairs. She went into the great hall, set down the round basket. Littlemary was knitting by the fireside.

"They are come!"

Sinnie ran back to the entryway, wiping her hands on her apron. Littlemary, she thought. She be terrified.

She harried the four boys, who came down the stairs, nervous as their sister. *Where is she now?* they would always ask their father when he received a letter from their mother. Sinnie heard the jeering sarcasm that hid their hurt. Last autumn, they had received word that Mary had left England with another Quaker, Ann Burden; and then that their ship had been blown off course and landed in Barbados, where they had stayed at a plantation owned by Quakers, lingering to do their "work," whatever that might be.

Ah, Mistress, you will lose them for sure now, Sinnie had thought, when William had raised angry eyes to announce this further delay.

And now. William had told them at supper, eyes communing only with his biscuit as he tore it in two. A letter had come from Massachusetts. "Come and get your wife," the magistrates had written to him. A new law forbade Quakers to enter Boston. Mary and her companion had been searched, arrested and jailed as soon as their ship arrived.

The children gathered around Sinnie.

Like chicks. Sensing danger.

She smoothed hair, straightened collars.

"There, now, 'tis your own mother who bore you, 'tis your own mother, my loves."

They went out onto the granite doorstep. Peepers pulsed and the winnowing of snipes shivered like the sky's lament. Stars appeared behind the chimney. The new house rose behind them, candlelight feathering tiny windowpanes.

The sun had set and the horses came dusk darkened past the fenceposts, hugely alive with their blowing breath, steaming flanks, jingling bits. Jurden heard the hoofs and strode from the barn. He took the reins as the horses came to a standstill, champing at their bits, tossing their heads.

William helped Mary dismount, since her legs were encumbered by stirrup stockings. Her first steps were hitching, stiff.

Aged, Sinnie thought. Stern.

Mary wore a grey cloak and a hat with a cock-eyed brim. Her face was weathered. Half-moon bags sorrowed her eyes and she bore a fretted, blind expression, as someone who has recently dwelt in darkness.

She turned from William, took Jurden's hand.

"Jurden, thee has not changed a jot."

She be half-starved. Her mouth, even yet so wide and beautiful.

William came around from behind the horses.

"This is your mother," he announced to the children, abruptly, as if abandoning intended words. Sinnie saw that he was baffled and would blunder.

Not like this, Master. Take care, or . . .

Mary turned towards the children. They stood in a line as on the night of her leaving. She spoke to the tallest. "Is this . . . are thee . . . young William?"

She truly does not know. My poor dear Willie, not known by his own mother. Fifteen, he was. Taller than Mary. Like his father, his face was narrow, his eyes predatory. Mary took the boy's hand and did not shake it but only held it, formally. He chewed a lip, looked down.

"Maher," William said, pushing the boy forward. Maher was a year younger, round-faced, with a spray of freckles. He, too, took his mother's hand, but glanced at his older brother.

Mary looked at the remaining children.

"Not Henry?" she said. Ten years old, Henry was sharp-eyed, lithe.

"Hello, Mother," he said. He tipped back his head to appraise her.

"Charlie, now," said William gently. Charlie had been a baby when she left. Now he was seven. Round-eyed, full-lipped. His hand was soft, sticky.

"Hello, Mother." A front tooth was missing; his voice wavered.

Sinnie nudged Littlemary, who stepped forward with a twisted smile. Black hair wisped around a broad, open forehead; she wore a white cap tied at the chin. Twelve, she was as tall as her mother.

"My dear Littlemary," Mary said. Her eyes filled with tears and she held out her arms. "My dear Little—" She drew a breath.

The one she did love the best.

"Hello, Mother." Littlemary's eyes met her mother's and slid sideways. She stood stiff within Mary's embrace and had not lifted her own arms by the time Mary released her.

"Samuel says he will come visit on the morrow," William said. Twenty-two, Samuel no longer lived at home.

William went down on one knee. The children crowded round him. He rummaged in the pocket of his greatcoat, drew out a fistful of chestnut-wood whistles.

Sinnie stepped forward, uncertain whether to hold out a hand or spread her arms, but Mary came swiftly and caught her up, pressing her against the cold, horsey cloak. Sinnie breathed the stink of prison, felt Mary's fierce energy.

"How I missed thee!" Mary whispered.

William and Mary's first meeting after five years had been at the door of a cell, under the eyes of a jailor. They had stared at one another, stunned by time's transformation; their embrace had been perfunctory. During the ride home, they had spoken carefully, feeling their way towards ease. The subject of Mary's long absence remained unbroached. Her words—*George Fox, Dafeny, the stable-yard dwelling*—had fallen like notes of music in a dead space. William had spoken, ramblingly, of political events incomprehensible to her; and of the children, whose names pierced her with guilt and fear.

In the bedroom, they undressed, backs to one another. They slid between the sheets.

Neither extinguished their bedside candle.

"I came to find you," William said. "I sent you a letter telling you I was in London. Did you never receive it?"

Underbarrow. I did not tell Dafeny.

In the long silence, she knew that he understood the answer to his question.

"The letter reached me, yes," she said. "But 'twas too late."

"I had already left England?"

Silence.

"William." Her voice hardened. "It was not in truth for me that thee came. It was for the charter. It was a scheme between thee and Clark and Williams, for the sake of Aquidneck."

He did not answer, and Mary knew that neither of them had been wholly truthful with the other.

Air passed over the windowsill, bent the candle flames. He reached for her hand, and she turned her palm upwards. Their fingers closed. Suddenly, it was as if no years had intervened: London, the red-curtained bedstead, their young bodies. Tears sprang to her eyes. She saw that his eyes, too, glimmered in the candlelight.

He touched her neck, pulled her lips to his. She tasted the salt of his tears, felt the dimension of his hurt.

Sinnie slept in a four-poster bedstead in a small room on the second floor, across the hall from the master bedchamber.

She made certain never to go upstairs before William.

She would tarry, banking the fire, setting sourdough, putting beans to soak; then would slip up the back staircase. She stood by his door, listening for his snores, hand shielding candle flame. Sometimes she could not keep herself from laying a hand on the door, stroking the adzed pine panel with the tips of her fingers.

A mirror hung on the wall over her dresser, too high. Ten-year-old Henry could stretch to his full height and press his nose against hers. On this night of Mary's return, she rose to her toes, held the edge of the dresser, peered into the glass. Her job was to teach them to love their mother.

Sinnie, Sinnie. Where is my hornbook? My buckle? Sinnie, I have cut myself. I am hungry, I am tired, I am . . .

She studied her own troubled, blue eyes, wondering how she was to do it.

—

The next day, Sinnie watched from her post at the hearth, pained, wishing that work and school had been set aside and the day made one of celebration.

They show how they do not need her.

After breakfast, William and young William rode to the Newport office. Charlie, Henry and Maher walked to dame school.

Mary sat by a window, hands laid palms upward, a random nesting, like fallen leaves. One side of her face was hazed with sunshine. She watched Littlemary, who was busy at the fire, avoiding her mother's eyes.

Twelve years old.

Sinnie set a wooden tub on the hearth, filled it, brought a cake of bayberry soap. Mary undressed and eased herself into the water.

"Canst tell us of the prison?" Sinnie said, running a cloth over the knobby curve of Mary's spine.

Mary ducked face in hands, splashed water, dragged fingers through her scalp. She drew a long breath.

She has hardly spoken.

"'Twas dark. Dark, cold, silent. I could hear rats chewing, especially in the night. Yet 'twas nothing as bad as some are enduring now in England."

Her voice was low, stark, with no attendant shades to enfold her listeners.

Littlemary left the room with a bucket. Sinnie watched her cross the yard, heading for the well—saw that her steps were confused, neither going quickly nor turning back, and that her shoulders drooped.

May on Aquidneck was the loveliest time of year.

The cows grazed hock-deep in dandelions and star grass. The sheep wandered on the hillsides where junipers exuded the scent of gin and milk-snakes coiled on boulders.

Sinnie threw open the windows of the big house, let the salt air blow through. She spread linens on the greening grass. She worked in the vegetable garden, watching flocks of birds coming up over the sea, so many that the sky was reduced to a crumpled blue between their fanning wings. She knelt, planting seeds saved in twists of paper. She stood at the trestle table, kneading dough, laughing at the sight of Littlemary who stood outside in a whirling, prickly cloud, stripping feathers from chickens. She scrubbed. Clothes, stone floors, wood floors. Her mind sifted the contents of pantry, root cellar, buttery—scrambled the findings into imagined meals. She proceeded steadily as the migrating birds, knowing by the soil in her fist when to plant, by palm's memory how to knead or knit, by heart's instinct how and when to soothe. Aquidneck, finally, was as familiar as Shetland.

She straightened from planting carrots and gazed at the house. Like a ship, it was—solitary on the point of land, the sea beyond, the fields like smoothed blankets. Beneath its eaves, swallows hovered, shoring up last year's nests.

William's great house, bigger than William Coddington's or anyone else's.

Sinnie loved its shelves of folded quilts, pillowbeers, sheets, linen drawers and stockings, silk caps and dimity waistcoats. She loved the hall and pantry, with its pewter platters, salt cellars, kettles; its store of cheeses and cured hams, its crocks of pickled cabbage and nasturtium buds, applesauce, grape juice.

Sinnie watched Mary come from the house and stand in the herb garden. She wore sad-coloured clothing without lace. She had politely bidden William return a bolt of pink-flowered dimity and exchange it for plain brown wool.

"Give me the herb garden to care for," she had said to Sinnie, on the first morning.

"But Mistress, the whole household is yours."

"Sinnie, for now I am content to leave the running of the house in thy hands. But I do know my herbs, from my aunt's teachings."

Often, on these glorious days, Mary sat in the parlour, studying her Bible, writing letters—to London, she told Sinnie, who asked. To Yorkshire, to Barbados, or to the Boston magistrates, since her friend, Ann Burden, remained in jail. "I seek my friend's release," she said. "She hath no husband to rescue her."

She studied letters that came to her from other "Friends," as she called them.

She does not love the house, Sinnie thought, sorry on William's behalf.

"Will she like this valance, these curtains, dost think, Sinnie?" he had asked her, preparing for Mary's return. The elaborately patterned copper warming pan, brought home from Boston. He showed it to the children, smiling. "'Twill warm her sheets nicely." In the bedchamber dresser, one day, Sinnie had found a pair of gloves. Lambskin, dressed flesh-side out. They were lined with peach-coloured silk and embroidered with silver thread. Sinnie had slid them onto her hands, remembering the nobleman who had taken her from Fetlar as his serving girl and how proud her parents had been the day she had ridden away on her shaggy pony. *Gone into service in London!* Sinnie had removed the gloves and closed the drawer, thinking of how she had come to Mary and William, filthed. How she could meet no man's eye and felt that the sun would never again be as her friend, nor the wind stroke her hair, nor the flowers nod.

Sinnie dropped back to her knees, scrabbled carrot seeds from the paper and resumed sprinkling the drill. The seeds slithered from her palm, a pile that she nursed into line with a fingertip.

We be true friends. The poor thing, how she do suffer.

—

Sand glinted on the scoured floor. Sinnie offered the women cider, gingersnaps. The windows were open and in the spaces of their conversation came the creaking of a wheeled ox-drawn plough and the screaming of the gulls that followed it.

"There are two churches in Newport, one Baptist, one independent."

"Your husband has not made up his mind? For we *glimpse* him at both."

Three Newport women, visiting Mary.

Friends for you, Sinnie's eyes implored. Mary looked at each woman, pondering. A smile quivered at the corners of her mouth but did not spread.

"Has he not?" Mary inquired. She turned to Sinnie. "Does he not take the children to church?"

Sinnie started and the gingersnaps slithered on the plate.

"Sometimes, Mistress. Not always."

"Ah." Mary's voice, closing the subject.

So thin. Her eyes, like torches in the dark. She frightens them. She waits for them to speak. Oh, Mistress, talk of . . .

Sinnie stood stock still, so distressed that her urgings found voice.

"My mistress hath skill in herbs." She felt the burn of a blush, saw the women lower their mugs and look between Sinnie and Mary.

"Sinnie, Sinnie!"

Sinnie set down the plate, ran to the door. Charlie burst into the house holding his wrist, hand in a fist. She put an arm around his shoulders, eased open his bloody palm.

"Ah, not so bad, my pet."

Mary had risen from her chair, came swiftly, put out her hand.

"Go to your mother," Sinnie whispered. "She is a healer."

Charlie buried fist and face in Sinnie's apron. Forehead, hard against her breastbone.

I am sorry, Mistress, oh, I am sorry.

Mary stepped back, stood watching them—eyes tender, the smile that had quivered finding focus: acceptance. She turned back to the women.

Sinnie took Charlie to the kitchen and knelt on the hearth, dipping a cloth in the kettle. She murmured to the boy, while her mind apologized, explained. *You see, Mistress* . . . Still the boys and Littlemary turned to her with their questions, complaints, requests— and behind their masked eyes were the tear-swollen faces that Sinnie had seen. And Mary had not.

It was a sweltering evening. Sinnie's door was cracked open to encourage the passage of air from her window. Mary and William's door, too, stood half-open, and she heard their voices across the hall, a familiar night sound from all the small houses they had inhabited. Mary's. Agitated. Not bothering to whisper.

"She had no one to post bond for her, William. She had no husband nor influential friends."

"I did enough, Mary. It would not have reflected well on me if I had intervened."

Outside Sinnie's window, teeming of insects; surf, with its regular accents—roar and sigh of a vast wave.

"Well. 'Tis done." Mary's voice, again. Harsh. "I received word that they compelled the master of the ship that brought us from Barbados to take her directly back to England. She was allowed nothing, *nothing*. No goods, no money. Only sixpence did she have. 'Twas the *hangman* who rowed her out to the ship. They are not subtle."

Baby swallows chattered. In the crepuscular light, shadows were slowly absorbing the knobs of Sinnie's chest of drawers, six chestnut circles.

William, whispering. She could not hear the words.

Mary, pleading, her voice lower, dark.

". . . never again," Mary said. "I could not bear it."

"No more children," William said. "I will . . ." A lower voice. ". . . my pull-back . . ."

Sinnie clapped hands to ears, slid from her bedstead. Her shift fell down one shoulder, her hair was twisted and pinned, sweat beaded along her collarbones. She held her breath and raised a hand to her door.

Will it creak.

The voices in the next room fell silent. She heard the slight squeal of wood, the groan of a mattress rope. She eased her door shut.

Littlemary sat in a low chair by the door, bent over a bowl of wild strawberries. Shoulders raised, drawn into herself.

Sinnie glanced at Mary, gutting a fresh-plucked chicken at the table. *She is still a good worker.* Only she would rather let Sinnie or William organize, supervise. Most days, before William rode to Newport, he allotted the day's work, murmuring to Mary that she might help Sinnie should she desire. *He treats her like the sick lady she was before she went away.*

Mary caught Sinnie's eyes.

"Three more," she said. "Then I shall cut them." Pimpled pink carcasses sprawled beside a plate of viscera. She waved a hand—flies rose, a spinning iridescence. Deftly, she disengaged the crop.

"I would have thought this a feast beyond imagining when I was on the road with Dafeny." She worked her hand wrist-deep into the next carcass. "We were accustomed to walk miles on empty stomachs. To ask food of strangers and passers-by. To break ice from ponds, kneel to drink." She pulled out her hand, flicked kidneys onto a plate. Her voice sharpened, as if she realized her words were unwelcome and sullied the summer day. "Strange to say, but after a time I did not hanker after food, nor sleep, nor a soft bed. 'Tis good to strip away worldly possessions and walk in the light of the Lord."

Sinnie glanced at Littlemary, who bent lower over her bowl. Mary resumed her work—tugging, scooping, flicking. She wished to say more, Sinnie saw, but a muted insularity had come over her when neither she nor Littlemary had questioned or encouraged.

Silence, the ticking fire and the calls of men in the field.

Littlemary looked up.

Her chin crept forward, her eyes darkened. Sinnie remembered the angry thoughts that Littlemary had whispered to her. *Why* had her mother undertaken such hardships? *Why* had she bothered to return, if she did care so for her new friends?

Sinnie turned back to the fire, wool apron protecting her from the flames, sweat staining her cap and collar. She stirred the strawberries, boiling them down into a thick preserve. Charlie and Henry arrived at the door, mosquito-bitten, fingers stained red. They emptied their baskets into the one on Littlemary's lap. They went to the water butt, drank from the ladle, and were gone.

Littlemary sighed, pausing to contemplate the fresh supply of bleeding berries with their minuscule hulls.

No one was idle, ever. Maher was in a shed making a broom with last summer's broom corn, for Sinnie's old one was worn to a point. She could see Willie out in the fields working along with the hired men. They hoed weeds from long rows of cabbages, corn, beans.

She tries to love the children, especially Littlemary, but . . .

Sinnie paused, wiping sweat from her forehead. Mary stood with one hand resting on the last carcass. She gazed out the door, watching the travelling clouds, her mouth bent in a slight smile.

What do she think of? Who?

The children were afraid of her, this woman who had been in prison for an outlawed belief.

Perhaps, Sinnie thought, turning back to the strawberries. Perhaps William, too, is afraid, but for different reasons.

In August, William set men to scything the grass. A day later, when clouds covered the sun and the smell of coming rain sweetened the house, every person, from Charlie to Mary, was called to the fields to rake. Sinnie, Mary and Littlemary left twists of green wool hanging over a steaming kettle of indigo, goldenrod and alum. They pulled the iron spider, filled with biscuits, onto spent ashes; swung forward the simmering stew.

The sea was wind-scudded and shore birds flew low, skimming the beach. Sinnie worked beside Mary, shaking grass from the wooden tines onto a pile. The meadow was dotted with tall green hillocks, like beaver lodges.

"Look," Sinnie said.

Two horses and riders were coming up the lane. The men dismounted, rushed to take up rakes.

The first drops came. Men continued flinging hay onto a cart but then the skies opened and William signalled to desist. Sinnie saw Mary hurry over the stubble, animation in her shoulders as she took the men's hands. She watched as they walked together, crossed the lane and were dwarfed by the great house with its rain-darkened clapboards. The cart moved past them, mounded with rain-jewelled hay.

Sinnie slippered around the table, pouring cider, setting down trenchers of stew. The young men, Friends, were newly arrived from England. They had survived a stormy crossing on a small ship, the *Woodhouse;* they had stopped briefly in New Amsterdam, then had sailed up Narragansett Bay to Providence. They were sunburned, ecstatic.

"'Twas by divine leading, for not one of us knew any navigation," Christopher Holder said. He spoke with a high-born accent. He held his spoon delicately, as if it were silver rather than pewter and he gazed around the table with enthusiasm, then turned his attention to the stew poised before his lips. His hair, cut short over the forehead, fell thick and blond over his shoulders.

"Aye, and a dear leaky little vessel she was, too," remarked the other young man. He was shorter, with a strong jaw and gentle mouth, equally well-spoken.

"Where are the other Friends?" Mary asked. She had not picked up her spoon nor sipped her cider.

"Providence. At the home of Catherine and Richard Scott."

"Catherine! Has she become a Friend? She is the sister of my old friend Anne Hutchinson."

Sinnie set a plate of biscuits on the table. William sat with downturned mouth, annoyed by the visitors and the ruined hay. The children, silent, were seated at their own smaller table. Mary asked questions, gave opinions. She was eager, flushed from the heat of the fire and the room's summer damp.

After supper, William shook the men's hands and excused himself. He offered them all the hospitality Dyer Farm had to offer and smiled at Mary, eyebrows raised so slightly that only wife, or servant, might notice.

Mary rose from the table, bid the children good night and went into the parlour with the men. The door closed behind them.

Sinnie stood for a moment, absorbing the changed character of the day. The wool twists still hung, dripping, over the kettle. Darkness came early and the night was filled with the patter of rain and the shrilling frogs.

She took a pot of catnip tea to the parlour.

"Thank thee, Sinnie," Mary said. Sinnie lingered, setting down the pot, pretending a need to adjust the table rug, for they were reminiscing of gatherings held out-of-doors on Yorkshire's fells. *Langstrothdale, Pardshaw Crag*—the wild, northern words came so fervently and with such longing that Sinnie, too, was caught by the illusion that should she look out the windows she would see bracken-backed moors.

As she closed the door, she heard Mary's voice.

"Once I did meet George Fox. I followed him into the moors after . . ."

Ah, she be happy. Happy.

TWENTY-ONE

Persecution - 1657–1659

✳

"BOSTON," MARY SAID. She sat on a ladder-backed chair, furious. William stood at the parlour window, hands clasped behind his back, looking out over fields of stooked corn.

"The same men who excommunicated Anne. They do think it is their God-given duty to extirpate blasphemy. They have made more laws against us whom they call Quakers. Fines, imprisonments, mutilations, whippings. For no more than holding beliefs with which they do not agree."

He turned, opened his mouth.

"They fear us because we do not defer to temporal authority." Her voice was thick with anger. "Because we oppose oath-taking. Because we believe that men and women are equal and so women, too, may publish the truth."

Mary did not notice his intention to speak but continued the diatribe that had poured from her ever since she had returned from the new Friends Meeting in Newport.

"It maddens me to think that they remember perfectly well their own persecution, yet are content to visit a reign of terror upon us. Do attend to this, William. One of the Woodhouse Friends is a young woman from London—who came away from husband and children."

She allowed one heartbeat of silence.

"She was given thirty lashes with a three-cord knotted rope and then imprisoned. For some slight offence, I am not certain what it was. Speaking to the minister after a meeting, perhaps, questioning him on some point of doctrine. Christopher Holder—does thee remember that young man who came here last summer, the day it rained on the hay? He was nearly killed when a church-member gagged him with his own gloves and handkerchief. And the Boston jailor, oh, my old friend, William, thee remembers him from when thee fetched me. He hath become infamous for the severity of his punishments. He fetches his strokes with such cruelty that 'tis said women, watching, fall in dead faints."

The windows were open and the warm air carried birdsong and the faint roar of surf. Mary's pulse was racing; she breathed rapidly, fists pressing her knees.

"I do not love you any less," William said. "But I wonder if you do still love me."

Of the children, and her feelings towards them, they had had many discussions. But not this. She spoke without reflection, to dispel the question's import.

"We are both as drops of water in the sea," she said. "I feel I am but one drop, as thee is but one drop, and we are all of the One."

"That is not an answer."

He is right.

No single thing in her life was as it had been before. She dreamed of light, sheeting, shimmering; she dissipated into the shining motes. She did not wonder or worry about the children's future nor imagined herself growing old at William's side. Her only desire was to be with the Friends, in whose eyes she saw the same light of which she dreamed.

"Thee is right. My love is changed. Yes, it is changed."

He picked a dead fly from the window sill, examining it before crushing it to powder.

"Well," he said. His voice shook, his mouth warped. "Well."

"William. I do not love thee less, I love thee differently."

"I love you, Mary. I fear for you. I bid you take care."

She could have arrested the moment in which he rose and stepped towards her. She could have attempted to smooth the edges of her explanation, but she took too long—hands folded, watching the play of light and shadow on the plaster wall—and so he turned, violently, and strode from the house into the calm of the First Day afternoon. He did not see her come to the doorway. She did not call him back, for she thought it best to let the gulf widen.

He was gone when they arrived—Humphrey Norton, who had had a large iron key bound over his mouth to stop his words while a minister read out his sentence. He had been judged, publicly whipped, branded in the hand with the letter 'H' for heretic and sent from the town.

It was a cold week in March, and Mary had ridden to New Haven with three other Friends—another woman, two young men—to bear witness, since one of the Woodhouse travellers had been arrested. It had been a long journey through wind, rain and sleet and they arrived too late.

They put up in a tavern. A storm had come up the coast and rain drummed the windows. Mary huddled in a threadbare blanket, shivering with chills, her face flaming.

"We must go to Salem," the woman said. "I hear there are great troubles there."

"First we must see Mary safely home." One of the men laid a hand on Mary's forehead.

They determined to ride together as far as Providence but the next morning they found Mary's horse standing with lowered head and cocked hoof, lame. The constables came to the inn, insisting they leave the town, and would yield neither to Mary's illness nor her horse's condition. They fetched a bony mare with burrs in her tail.

"I cannot leave my husband's horse here," Mary said.

"Shall we pick you up, then, and set you upon this nag?"

The constables waited, mounted, until the Friends were ready. They escorted them to the town limits, a crossroads on a hilltop. As far as eye could see was a misty landscape of low, wooded hills, black-branched. Two crows flew overhead.

Mary leaned from her saddle.

"Woe be unto you, for Humphrey Norton's sake." She spoke in a low voice looking the nearest man in the eyes. "Woe be unto you, because of the cruelty done to him."

"Witch," the man breathed, stepping back. Then he roared. "Be gone from here!"

The Friends heeled their horses. On the bony mare, Mary rode towards Rhode Island.

Fever turned to pneumonia. Mary lay between flaxen sheets in a canopy bed, comparing this room to the dark bedchamber on the Shawmut Peninsula with its hanging herbs, its oiled paper windows.

Oh, William. Her eyes touched one thing, and then another, and she thought of his studied choices and her heart ached. Light silvered the canopy's silk fringe, sleeked the fine white curtains, and lay bright upon the mantelpiece with its imported clock, silver bowl, framed map.

And other things. She lay propped half-upright, breath crackling in her lungs. Red bedclothes. An imported Turkey carpet. The six-board chest ordered from Newport's best cabinetmaker. She had seen Sinnie gazing at the clock, fascinated.

Farther back, then, her mind went. London. William, running up the stairs. Hands on her face, his perfumed gloves. *You were not hurt?* What had it been. Ah. The men, the stocks. Ears, sliced from their heads.

She heard Sinnie and Littlemary's steps as they came up the stairs, lugging hot water, a tray of food. Mary had asked to be moved downstairs into the parlour for their sakes, but William would not hear of it.

"You need quiet," he had said. "I will have the children come up every evening to tell you of the day's doings."

Sinnie poured hot water into a bowl. Littlemary set down the tray.

"Thank you," Mary said but her voice caught on phlegm and she saw that Littlemary was thinking of some other project—butter, perhaps, left in the churn—and did not answer but turned to lay a log on the fire. Sinnie, on tiptoe, adjusted the curtains to keep sunlight from Mary's face.

Celia Grymston came to visit. Small, tidy, she was a Friend from Newport.

"What dost thee hear, Celia Grymston?" Mary asked. She sat straight up against her bolster; her breath was clearing. "I see by thy face that thee bears bad news. Thee fears to disturb me but 'tis . . ." She gestured toward her bedside table, where lay her Bible and a slew of letters, pamphlets, and epistles. "My work. My life."

Although William would call it otherwise.

"'Tis about doings in Salem," Celia said. "Despite the fines, their gatherings have been growing. Last week, eight people were taken from Salem to the Boston jail. They were whipped in the public square, men and women alike. One man of forty years was deprived of food for five days and locked in neck-to-foot irons for sixteen hours."

She went to the window, looked out at the day of watery April sunshine.

"And there is more, Mary. Terrible sufferings. Hored Gardner travelled to Boston to bear witness, with her suckling baby and a girl to help care for it. They were dragged before Governor Endicott, who spoke to them abusively and sent them to jail. They, too, were whipped and afterwards travelled sixty miles through the wilderness. Arrived home, half-dead . . ."

Her voice began to shake. She did not turn to look at Mary but spoke to the clouds.

"Thee knows they do not take the ears of women. Only the ears of men, for the first offence. For the second offence, the other ear. We women are only to be whipped. But both, man or woman, shall have our tongues bored through with a hot iron for a third offence."

Celia turned from the window.

"In what way do we harm them? How can they be so cruel, Mary?"

Mary pressed her hands together, palm to palm, cupped them over nose and mouth and closed her eyes. Faint, the twitter of birdsong. She drew breath.

"'Tis fear, the fear of weak men. They do not wish for the ministers to be usurped—for just as men rule the home, so, in effect, do the ministers rule the government."

Celia gazed at the floor, pondering, her own hands tightly clasped.

"I will not go to Massachusetts," she said finally. "I am not such a person as could bear to be whipped. But I will do what I can in the service of the truth."

Mary spread her hands on the counterpane. It was a quilt Sinnie had made from bits of the children's clothing. Blue wool, green tabby, white holland. Ribbed, burred, soft. Scraps, gathered together to serve a purpose.

"We needs must wait upon the Lord," she said. "Listen for his bidding."

"Would thee go to Boston if thee were to be called?"

Mary did not answer.

Elizabeth Swale's back. The swish before the whip lands. Pain, worse with each stripe. George Fox. "Just a smash . . ."

"Yes," she said. "I would go."

After her friend had left, Mary took up a pamphlet of Fox's sermons.

"We must have the patience to bear all manner of evil done or spoken against us for Christ's sake, and rejoice at it."

She pressed the pamphlet to her breast, thinking how the light within must burn so brightly, when refuted, that it became as a cushion to the most savage blows.

Spring, summer, fall. The skies darkened with migrating birds. The air smelled of apples.

Mary received a letter from Catherine Scott.

October 1658

My dear Mary,
Christopher Holder speaks often of his visit to Dyer Farm so
I know thee will wish to receive news of him. (Did I tell thee
he is to be married to my daughter Mary?) Many Friends do
come to our house here in Providence to plan how we are to
help our brethren in Massachusetts. He and two others
agreed to go to Boston to protest, and there they were
imprisoned. All of them suffered the loss of an ear, sliced off
in the secrecy of their cell so that the townspeople could not
witness the outrage. I did ride to Boston to protest. My
youngest, Patience, had to be constrained, so earnestly did
she wish to accompany me. I was whipped and they did tell
me if I came again, there would be a law to hang me. I did
say to them, "If God calls us, woe be to us if we come not." I
remembered my dear sister Anne Hutchinson and how they
did torment her. I wish thee to know that I am well, despite

what thee may hear, and that Christopher Holder and the
others have returned from Massachusetts, and that we have
written to George Fox, and do gather here in Providence to
plan what we may do next . . .

Winter.

At supper, William brought news.

"Oliver Cromwell hath died," he said. "He is to be succeeded by his son."

Mary thought of Cousin Dyota, clutching the chip of wood stained with king's blood. Cousin Ralf—"England, oh, England," he had cried, at news of the king's murder.

Another letter came from Catherine Scott:

January 1659

Dear Mary,
Our Meetings here in Providence do grow. We have truly a
live centre here, and many who long for the arising of the
Day Star in their hearts come here to our home. The
Power of God hath taken place in our children, most espe-
cially in my daughter Patience, who at such a tender age—
eleven—doth faithfully attend our Meetings and is privy to
the plans set forth as many gather here to plan our resis-
tance to the Bloody Laws. I write to thee as a mother and
healer, for my heart saddens for what this child has seen,
stripes upon my own back and Christopher Holder's
ghastly scar where they did cut off his ear. Thee knows
that she is the child of rebels, my own father was held

under house arrest in England, and her Aunt Anne was
outcast and murdered. But despite or because of her heri-
tage, the child does not eat, her body fails, and I fear she
lives on faith and ardour, and wonder if thee might suggest
any posset or herb . . .

Mary thought of Littlemary, who read her Bible not from passion but duty—and by preference went to Newport, returning with buttons or ribbon.

Patience, Mary thought, would have listened to the young Woodhouse Friends telling of how the Lord shepherded them across the Atlantic; would have helped soak her mother's bloody shift from her back; and sat, on every First Day, surrounded by silent adults, waiting upon the Lord.

She wrote to Catherine, advising daily walks and peppermint tea.

Spring. Peepers, and the first shad. William stripped a spine from the tiny, steamed fish, laid the bones on the trencher and lifted the flesh to his mouth.

"Cromwell's son abdicated," he announced, licking his fingers. "They say the king will return."

"And the Boston charter?" Mary asked. "Dost remember, William, once thee did think they were clever, to take it from England."

He glanced at her, a twisted expression, as if this memory evoked the way they had once been to one another.

"Aye, and so they felt they could make up their own laws."

If the king returns . . .

William reached for the next fish.

"The Puritan reign is over," he said. He laid another spine along the side of his trencher, nudged it until it was aligned with the pewter's curve. "England is in chaos."

The children, at their table, paid little attention but Sinnie paused for an instant before setting down the serving bowl, glancing at Mary, who sat with hands folded in her lap, head bowed as if in meditation but eyes alight with thought.

In the pre-dawn darkness, Mary rode through the gates of Dyer Farm. The gelding's long-reaching stride was a sudden, fearsome intimacy; she slid her hand beneath his mane for reassurance, felt the silky warmth. Her knees pressed leather saddlebags filled with secreted provisions.

As she rode up the island, sunrise glittered on the waters of the bay; against its coppery script, shallops set out for the fishing grounds. Smoke juddered from chimneys and women thrust doors and windows wide against the July heat. Already, the horse's withers slickened and Mary cast back the hood of her summer cape.

Too young for this. Her parents would not have allowed it. Perhaps she crept from the house.

Eleven years old, Patience Scott had ridden to Boston with three young men to protest the new laws. Catherine Scott had written to Mary, telling of how, upon arrival in Boston, the magistrates had taken the child to the House of Correction. How Patience had astounded them with her composure and knowledge of Scripture. How, nonetheless, she had been thrown in jail along with her companions.

Mary stuffed her cloak into a saddlebag. To her left, a pasture ran down to the shore. Sheep nibbled the grass, their spines lined with light.

I will not let them harm her.

Mary kicked her horse into a canter, heard the jingle of bit, watched between the horse's ears as the dirt track unfurled. Anger settled in the bones of her jaws.

—

To the keeper of the Prison:

You are by virtue hereof required to take into your cus-
tody the person of Mary Dyer, who on her examination
before Authority, professeth her coming into these parts was
to visit the prisoners, the Quakers now in hold, and that she
was of the same religion . . .

. . . and refusing to give a direct answer unto what was
proposed unto her, she came hither for affirming the Light
within her . . .

. . . keep her safely in prison until the next Court of
Assistants, according to the Law Titled, "Quakers."

Dated: July 21, 1659, at Boston

They bade her wait in the rain for an hour, under guard, while they conferred with the jailor inside.

Papers signed, the jailor led her to the cell.

Five flock beds lay on the floor, wool tufting from torn seams. In one corner, a blanket was suspended to make privacy for the chamber pot. The air was heavy with the reek of urine, tempered slightly by an open window, whence came the sounds of rain—splatter against cobblestones, steady river-splash from eaves.

Surrounded by men, the girl was a forlorn, grey bundle, huddled by the window, face hidden against knees.

"Patience," Mary said. She tried to keep her voice steady. "Thy mother wrote to me."

The girl scrambled to her feet, rushed to her. Mary opened her sodden cloak, pulled the girl to her breast.

William Robinson looked up from where he sat hunched over his Bible, long legs splayed across the floor. He was fair, sunken-cheeked, with thin, veined hands. Marmaduke Stephenson turned from the window. Mary had heard it said that he had left his plough at the

Lord's calling and walked away from his hill farm, leaving wife and children. He smiled at her, round lively eyes beneath a fringe of black hair. Nicholas Davis lay on his side, half-asleep, beard askew in a full-lipped, solemn face.

The jailor pulled back the blanket, reached in for the chamber pot.

"We need water," Marmaduke said to him.

The jailor tossed the contents of the pot, drenching the young man with urine. "As ye wish, so ye get. Makes my job easier." He returned the pot, wiped his hands on his breeches, and strode from the cell. The key turned in the lock.

No one spoke.

"I had to come," Mary said. Her voice shook yet strove for calm. She pressed her cheek on the child's head. "I heard they had jailed Patience. I said I wished to visit the prisoners and offer them succour."

William Robinson lifted the cloak from her shoulders. "And for such kindness, thee were cast in with such as us."

"Welcome, Mary Dyer," said Marmaduke, voice muffled from the shirt halfway over his head. "We will wait on the Lord."

The jailor had allowed Mary her Bible, writing paper, quill and ink horn. She set them beside the pallet and sat, untying her soaked shoes, peeling away her stockings. Nicholas Davis rose and settled his blanket over Mary to ease her shivering. Patience curled against her.

Mary closed her eyes. Marmaduke and William resumed their places on the floor and then a vibrant quietude grew such as she had known in a Yorkshire farmhouse. In a Whitehall stable. In a goldsmith's parlour. In a ship's berth.

Patience pressed her eye to the pine planks nailed over the window and could see nothing between them but the colour of the sky. She and Mary were in a smaller cell now, alone.

"I shall take thee to my mother's garden," Mary said. She had tied her coif low and tight over her forehead to hold back her greasy hair. Her grey petticoat was soft, sour. She described the walled garden and her father's glass apiaries shaped like castles. She closed her eyes and told Patience how she envisioned light like a cobweb of silver threads in which were woven a tapestry of poppies, pansies and lavender.

They sang. It steadied them, like the thought of the men in the next cell or the meetings they knew were being held by Friends in Newport and Providence, planning further assaults on the laws.

God is near as the beating of my own heart.

"What does thee wish for?" Mary murmured. Patience lay on her side. Her breasts were like mushroom caps, two perfect mounds beneath the grimy shift. They knew it was a fine summer day, since the cracks were blue.

"A husband. And a house in Providence near to Mother and Father. And children. And a nice riding horse and a flock of hens. And we will all go to Meeting together, all the family, and then I shall have them to my house and we shall eat all together. I will serve them apple pie and . . ."

She talked of food, enumerating puddings and pastries, steaming drinks, fruit tarts.

And for myself, what do I wish for.

Mary lay on her back, arms folded over her chest, hands tucked into armpits to keep them from tearing at her scalp where lice crept like trickling water.

She closed her eyes.

She thought of her children as if they were someone else's, glimpses gathered in the two years she had been home—hopeful, argumentative, restless with forward momentum. She sensed their frustration, wondered if perhaps they themselves did not know how deference, drilled from infancy into all Puritan children, was like the sound of a wheel turning upon an axle, a monotony whose variation was minimal and forced.

She glimpsed, then, the answer to her own question—*what do you wish?*—and knew she would never reveal it to Patience. Should the girl think to ask, she would tell her—"I wish to wander the world, spreading the Truth." For when she had been in Barbados, she had heard of women Friends who had visited the Sultan of Turkey; who had spoken to Catholics in Venice, Jews in Rome; who had been held by the Inquisition on Malta.

She remembered the dream she had had in London. A young man had lifted her onto a black goose. He had dissolved from man into love itself—wondrous and vast. And she had lain forward and clasped the neck of the bird, while all around her, others, too, rode birds. And the black wings lifted.

Do I wish to give my life in the cause of Truth?

She received a letter from William.

August 1659

The children are well, as am I, but anxious for your return and well-being. I wonder if word has reached you of the new law. All visiting Quakers in Massachusetts Bay Colony are to be banished <u>on pain of death</u>. You will surely be returned to me soon, never again to set foot in that cursed place, my dearest wife, for I trust you will be banished . . . We are busy with the harvest, the hay is heavy and there is a crop of apples beyond my expectations, I cannot get away at present, do you keep quiet and patient, I have written the Court of

Assistants, I do all I can with what influence I can wield.
You will be released soon, I am certain . . .

The jailor held the door open.

"Court of Assistants," he said. "You are bidden to hear your charge."

Walking the hallway with Patience at her side, Mary's legs trembled and her knees had scant strength. Sunlight blazed in the jailor's office, making her squint, and as they passed through, ordinary things struck her with their intricate strangeness: a pewter candlestick, the jailor's cloak, the cracked leather of a bellows.

Marmaduke, William and Nicholas joined them in the street. It was a day of morning-glory blue, with vast cloud pillows and light so brilliant that birds rode the wind like sparks of a bonfire. The air was crisp, the leaves had turned. They followed six officers up the street and into the square. They mounted the outside stairs of the new two-storey market, Keayne's Town House, and were prodded into a large room where the courts were held. Windows stood half-open on their iron hinges, shadows stretched across the floorboards. The room smelled of lumber. They were made to stand facing a row of magistrates.

Their eyes. Filled with hatred.

"I shall heckle," William had told them, back when they were still confined in one cell. "I shall argue, rail, speak without cessation."

Governor Endicott held his pointed beard with one hand. He wore a black silk cap with purple braiding.

"You have interrupted our meetings," he began. "You have caused disturbances." He spoke at length, detailing their offences.

When he finished, William Robinson stepped forward.

All summer he nurtured this plan.

"Is this thy converting of others?" he began. "By compelling of people to come to your meetings? By imprisoning, whipping, putting in stocks, burning in the hand, and cutting off the ears of those that come to bear witness against your cruelty and idolatry?"

His blue eyes widened, a vein pulsed beneath blanched skin.

"By fining people and taking away their goods? Hath thee no other way nor word to convince those you call heretics and deceivers but to take away their lives?"

"You will BE SILENT or you shall be gagged!" Endicott roared, jumping to his feet. "The child will be sent from here under custody of her uncle. She is under no banishment. However, you and the others are hereby banished from Massachusetts. Should you return, you are under pain of death."

"Know this," William Robinson said. "If thee puts us to death when we return, thee will bring innocent blood upon thyself. And this thee will certainly know one day, that the Lord God of heaven and earth, whom we serve, sent us among you—"

Men closed on him, took his arms. The others were seized as well, their shoulders held, their ribs poked with musket stocks. They were hustled through the door, out into the sounds of gull-cry and snapping flags, and marched down the stairs. At the bottom, William Robinson lurched wildly as a man thrust a foot to trip him. He was dragged to the whipping post. Men hauled his hands up, began to bind them. Others stripped away his shirt.

"Look there," Mary said to Patience. She stepped between the whipping post and the girl, pointed to the piling clouds. "Surely 'twill thunder later on."

She did not repress a knife edge from sharpening her words, knowing how it would startle the girl and keep her tears from falling.

The following day, Mary returned to the tavern, where her belongings and her horse had been kept safe by the sympathetic owner.

Two nights later, she arrived back at the farm, took her horse to the barn, and walked wearily to the house. She let herself in, for they had not heard her arrival. Sinnie was putting linens in the hall dresser. She turned as the door opened.

"So thin, Mistress!" She reached for Mary's cloak with both hands.

"Nay," Mary said, staying Sinnie's efforts, making her way into the parlour, where the family sat by the fireside. William looked up and his face opened, like a sleeper suddenly wakened. He was teaching the boys how to carve; Littlemary was sewing a quilt piece. "I am only thin, Sinnie. I am strong as trees, my heart feels delight."

She untied the strings of her riding hat. Her hands shook. William rose to his feet, his mouth working to shape words, not finding them.

"My heart feels delight, in truth," she repeated in a hard voice, hurling her hat onto the settle.

Sinnie and Littlemary exchanged a glance.

Mary went to her bed, too tired to eat. She slept without dreaming.

The next morning, she sat up and at first could not comprehend the puzzle that surrounded her.

At breakfast, word arrived that Christopher Holder had passed into Boston on the same day that Mary had left. His intention had been to set sail for England. He had been seized, arrested as a Quaker and thrown into jail.

Mary insisted on riding to Newport in order to consult with other Friends. William protested.

"You need rest, Mary, you are . . ."

She took up her riding hat that still lay on the settle where she had tossed it. She tied the strings beneath her chin.

Sinnie folded corn cakes into a cloth, fumbling in her haste and not daring to meet Mary's eyes. William stood on the hearth, slapping the side of his boot with a poker.

"This time, they will kill him," Mary Scott said. She was Christopher's fiancée, the older sister of Patience. Her voice, Mary noticed, carried her aunt Anne Hutchinson's cadence—assured, urgent. Her hair made two black slashes on either side of her forehead, like wings. "He was nearly dead after his torment in Barnstable. Three hundred and fifty-seven lashes. He lay for days near death. They have already had his ear. Nay, this time, they will surely kill him."

Mary, Hope Clifton and Mary Scott sat in the parlour of the Cliftons' house overlooking Newport Harbour. Sunlight spooled in dimity curtains. They could hear the slap and creak of ships rocking in their moorings and the voices of men passing beneath the window.

"They will not dare. He is too well known, his family is too highly placed."

In the hall, they heard the African serving girl humming a tune and the splash of a dipper. Hope went to the hearth, took the fire tongs and pushed back a smouldering stick.

"In old England, Christopher Holder was known to Cromwell and to many others. 'Twould be the undoing of the Boston magistrates if they would kill him. For their laws are unjust. He has done nothing but profess his beliefs."

"We must leave this afternoon," Mary answered. She felt her heart lift.

"Thee cannot go to Boston, Mary Dyer," Mary Scott exclaimed. "Thee is banished under pain of death."

"Remember thy mother's words," Mary said. "'If the Lord asks it, woe be unto us if we do not come.'"

The women sat in silence.

If the Lord asks it . . .

TWENTY-TWO

Anguish and Wrath - 1659

✳

CHRISTOPHER LEANED OUT A PRISON WINDOW.

"Praises be to the Lord," he called down. "The jailor returns soon with hammer and nails to shut out the light, but 'twill not matter. In this cell is the sweet smiling savour of glory."

"Aye," Mary Scott called back. "But doth thee wish food or any other thing?"

Frost crunched beneath their feet and the women kept their hands fisted beneath their cloaks.

"I would wish thee to be gone from this dark place," he said. "And especially thee, Mary Dyer."

"The Lord hath called us," she said. She stood back from the younger women, watching their fearful faces. She felt alert, neither calm nor afraid. Her eyes quickened to the flick of a rat, scurrying behind a barrel.

I am where I belong. Assured of the grace of God, I will wait.

Their hands were not gentle. They came upon them at the door of the tavern, six men carrying knob-tipped staves.

"Be you Mary Dyer?"

"She is not," Hope Clifton cried out at the same instant that Mary said yes.

The tavern's sign swung, creaking.

Wind, the smell of the sea.

They turned her away from the other women, pushed her up the street.

"I wish to say goodbye," Mary said. She turned, but the man placed a hand on the side of her head, forced her forward. She watched the cobblestones as her feet came forward. Wave-rounded. From the sea, from the beach. She saw how each was divided, light on one side and on the other a caul of shadow.

So fast, it happened. The morning after their arrival.

On pain of death.

Outside the jail, Mary turned her face to the sky, took her last breath of salty air.

The jailor's eye was swollen, suppurating. The constables handed him a mittimus and he read it, then squinted at Mary.

"Ye come back, did ye. They told you they'd have yer life. Your lookout's but a poor one." He seemed satisfied, as if seeing a wager won.

She stumbled as one of the men yanked her closer to the jailor's desk; she caught herself, straightened.

"Please to bring me a candle and a tinder box," she said. "And scorched linen. What you gave me in the summer would not catch."

No one deigned answer. They bent around the mittimus, watching the jailor's laborious signature. His hands were stained with oak gall ink. The goose-feather quill bent in his fingers.

"And a quill," she continued. "And ink. And paper. I must write to my husband."

She observed the sunlight sprawled across the desk. It paled the wide boards of the table, the pages of a book, a pewter ladle. It sank into the fibre of a worn rug, caressed the jailor's pitted skin. She followed the slant upwards to the window, whose wooden shutter was half-folded. Dust shone upon the glassblower's ponty swirl.

—

The prison's air bore the scent of damp, as in a root cellar. Only candlelight, now, flickered on the long, scrolled hinges and iron spikes that covered every door. The jailor put his key in a lock. The door creaked, opened upon darkness. Mary put up a forbidding arm.

"Do not touch me. I will go forward. I will walk into the light of the Lord."

Reverend Symmes. Reverend Norton. Reverend Wilson. Governor Winthrop. Governor Endicott.

Names tossed like wrecked boats.

When she awoke in the darkness, her dreams faded like ink in water. She pulled them back into the light of consciousness, read them, listened to them, gazed at them. In the long, empty days—broken only by the exchange of food for chamber pot—she studied.

Back, she went, walking the roadway the Lord had set her upon. She saw how it led, step by step, to this place.

Here. In this place of glory.

Some days, she prepared a room filled with light and then allowed William and the children to enter it. She took their hands as they stepped through the door.

Why did you go to Boston? they asked.

I came to be in the Lord's house.

What if you are put to death?

I will come to this place of peace and light.

Some days she became as analytical as her Uncle Colyn had taught her to be. She wondered if other Friends had heard of her incarceration. They would themselves come to Boston, then. Surely. And if the magistrates were to fulfill their threat and execute them? The Massachusetts Bay Colony's new laws had no standing in the British courts. Perhaps there would be swift retribution from London. Possibly there would be an end to these heinous laws. Or the weight of the magistrates' desperate measures would tilt, like a poorly built dung heap, and crush them.

Morning paled the spaces between the window's boards, making four threads in the darkness. She plucked a piece of straw from her mattress and worked it into a crack in the wall, counted the other straws with her fingertip. Ten.

October 18th.

When the door opened, she sensed a change. The jailor thrust it wider than usual and stood squarely in the middle with no bowl in his hands. His torch cast shadows like black tulips.

"You'll be coming out today. Going to court with them other two."

"What other two?"

"Them as were here before. Git up."

She waited with her hands folded so that her rising would be of her own volition.

She followed him down the hall, down the stairs. The door opened to daylight so brilliant that she levelled hand over eyes, squinting. She was startled to see the same arrangement of things in the room, as if the change in her circumstances should be mirrored by the jailor's office but was not—there, before her, was the same ink horn, pounce pot and quill stand, the same dusty mantelpiece over the same hearth, and the same small, smouldering fire, casting little heat.

Another door opened. William Robinson and Marmaduke Stephenson stepped into the light, wrists shackled, chins lifted.

Their faces registered alarm at the sight of her.

I have changed? Thin?

"Dearly beloved," William Robinson said. His skin was translucent, his temples coiled with blue veins, the pouches under his eyes purple-black.

"I have met with true peace," Mary said. Her own voice made unaccustomed vibrations in her ears and she dropped it to a whisper. "And you, my friends?"

"Also, he hath been with us," Marmaduke said. His face was haggard. He closed his eyes as if to recall the strength sent to him in the cell—lost, it seemed, in the fearful glare of daylight. Mary remembered what he had told her, how he had been filled with the love and presence of the living God and had been told by a clear inner voice that he had been ordained a prophet.

Constables crowded into the room and Mary found herself next to William Robinson as the prisoners were swept from the prison into the bright day. Word had preceded their passage and people were gathered on street corners or clustered behind windows. Mary saw a hand drawing a curtain, a woman's eye, mouth, cap.

"What hath been happening?" she murmured. Her breath came fast from the pace that was set. She staggered, her legs weak.

"Marmaduke and I were in Salem, but we came to Boston as soon as we heard of thy plight. Eight other Friends came with us. All are imprisoned."

"What of Mary Scott and Hope Clifton?"

"They, too, are being held in the jail."

"Nicholas Davis?"

"He stays in Barnstable. He fears the bloody laws and will not return to Boston."

"Christopher Holder?"

"Still in prison."

They reached the Town House. The constable herded them up the staircase, ushered them into the court. The room echoed with the scrape of chair legs, the din of voices as dozens of deputies took their seats.

Mary sank onto a bench between the two young men. She glanced behind her. Lace collars, wool socks, boot buckles; the ugliness of the men's faces with their rotting teeth and fleshy noses; resin-bleeding knots in the walls and the oily scent of grain coming from the storeroom on the floor below.

William and Marmaduke refused to remove their hats. A constable snatched them from their heads, sailed them into a corner.

Governor Endicott and the other magistrates took their seats at a table. Endicott's goatish face, elongated by a narrow beard, was barren of expression save for disdainful eyebrows. Moisture glistened along the sagging lower lid of one eye.

He laid a hand on his square collar.

"Why did you come again into our jurisdiction, being banished upon pain of death?"

"My coming was at the bidding of the Lord and in obedience to him," Marmaduke answered. William answered the same.

Mary heard her own voice next, so low that it caused an intensified hush.

"I did come at the bidding of my Lord and in obedience to his command."

Endicott looked at a paper on the table before him. He pushed it with the tips of his fingers. He opened his mouth and then shut it. When finally he spoke, his voice had changed. It was faint and urgent.

"We have tried and endeavoured by several ways to keep you from among us. And neither whipping, nor imprisoning, nor cutting off ears, nor banishing upon pain of death hath kept you away."

There was a silence into which came the distant creak of a swinging sign.

"I do not desire the death of any of you." His voice was barely audible.

The room stirred as the deputies leaned forward. Marmaduke's chest rose with a sudden breath. William's hands clenched. Mary's heart beat—thick, buttery.

"Give ear," Endicott said. Then he stopped. His words were almost a whisper. "Give ear and hearken now to your sentence of death."

William Robinson rose to his feet before the reverberation of the words had had their desired effect.

"I desire to read a paper," he said. His voice was firm, matter-of-fact. "'Tis a declaration of my call, wherein is declared the reason and causes of my staying in thy jurisdiction after banishment upon death."

He waved the document, which he had pulled from his sleeve.

His words were to Endicott as a dash of water in the face.

"You will not read it," the governor snapped, his voice returning to his former strength. He stood, both hands on the table, eyes wide and wild. A flush burned his cheeks.

"'Tis my right to read it before sentence of death be pronounced."

"You will not read it. It *shall not* be read!"

William Robinson remained standing. "If I cannot read it, nor have it be read, then I shall leave it with thee."

He stepped forward. The constable started up, but William only tossed his document onto the table where it slid into the hands of one of the magistrates. Endicott sat, slowly, and reached for the papers with shaking hands. He glanced at one page. His mouth worked and then he stood again and pointed at Robinson. His words rapped, without pause or reflection.

"William Robinson, hearken unto your sentence of death. You shall be had back from the place from whence you came, and from thence to the place of execution, to be hanged on the gallows till you are dead."

Mary's vision narrowed and was filled with Endicott's face. She saw that his fear had been replaced with injudicious recklessness.

The jailor came and took William from the room. The same sentence was passed on Marmaduke. Then he, too, was led away.

She sat alone on the bench, facing Endicott—behind her, a roomful of silent men.

Endicott looked at her and she saw that he was aware of her advanced age and the man to whom she was married and the circles in which he moved.

"Mary Dyer," he began. "Please to stand."

The rustle of her skirt and knock of her heels sounded as she stood.

His voice quivered, then settled. "You shall go to the place whence you came, and from thence to the place of execution, and be hanged there until you are dead."

There was not a sound in the courtroom. She looked directly at the governor.

"The will of the Lord be done," she said.

"Take her away, Marshal," he said. Blood had drained from Endicott's face. He was spent, beyond exasperation. He lifted his pen, looked blindly at his papers.

The marshal came but she did not move. She stood straight-backed, facing the row of men.

Look at me.

Endicott raised his eyes. She stared at him, so fiercely focused that her gaze might slice his flesh, should she desire it. Her lips barely moved.

"And joyfully I go."

The jailor lingered. He was enjoying the attention centred upon his prison and seemed more interested in Mary now that she was sentenced to death.

He told her the news:

Thomas Temple, governor of Acadia and Nova Scotia, had written to Governor Endicott. He had pleaded that the three Quakers be spared. He offered to pay for their passage out of Massachusetts. He promised to give them homes and land.

Governor John Winthrop, Junior, of Connecticut, too, had written, asking for the prisoners.

"He would crawl on his bare knees, he did say. He would crawl all the way from New Haven, if need be, to plead for your lives. What do you think of that?"

All across New England, the jailor said, they were being talked about. "Three Quakers, and one a woman. To be hanged in Boston. Big news."

He squinted at her in the candlelight.

"They put twelve men on the night watch. They be marching round the jail. Just for you and them others . . ."

"I thank thee," Mary said, quietly, respecting every glimpse into the man's humanity, even if she saw only pride, hate.

Mary was given candles, paper, a board and writing materials.

She was not told the date of the execution. Since her conviction, she had added five straws to the wall.

Sunlight slanting through a barn door, warming the neck feathers of a rooster and the red-tasselled broom corn. Her mother's needle, glinting silver, silken strands composing grasshoppers on satin. Candle-lanterns swinging from the hands of villagers, casting their patterned lights. The moors beneath a star-sprinkled sky.

A blueberry pie cooling on the windowsill. The smell of lilies.

The children's skin with its flush of blood. Hunger, in their bellies, in their hearts.

Life.

Oh, life.

She took up her pen but could not begin to write of the particulars of the world she must leave behind. She wept for the first and only time.

October 1659

My dear William,
My children,
 The Lord has asked of me to come home to him and so I
go. I beg that you hearken to your hearts therein to find him,
for there, too, I shall be with you.
 George Fox hath said: "We are not against any man, but
desire that the blessing of the Lord may come upon all men,
and that which brings the curse may be destroyed; and in
patience do we wait for that, and with spiritual weapons
against it do we wrestle."
 So do I go, as I am bidden. I commit my body and soul
unto the Lord. Live in peace one with another and keep in
the seed of God that you come to know the living truth in
your hearts.
 Your loving wife and mother,
 Mary Dyer

He came with a bowl of hotchpot and a chunk of salted cod. He grunted, placing them on the floor. The cell filled with the smell of hot vegetables: carrots, kale, turnip.

"I do not know whether 'tis worth the effort to eat," she said. "Yet my body bids me take comfort."

He paused in the doorway, watching her.

"Thine eye," she said. "'Tis healed."

"Aye. 'Twas a syrup made of sow bugs drowned in white wine."

I must tell Sinnie. Then her mind tipped, dizzy. Sinnie. Lilting voice, hands reaching for hers. She would never see her again. The soil vanished from beneath her, she swung by the neck. Her hands were bound to her sides so she could not reach up.

Keep close to the light.

"The other prisoners. Please tell me of them."

He looked at her, considering. She took up her bowl and tasted the hotchpot. It was flavoured with savory and she wondered who had cooked it and whether kindness was in her heart.

"All the women are together."

"Good."

"They moved them two men that is to die. One of them was a-shouting out of his window so we put 'em down deep, in irons. There's a few other men. They be just there." He jerked a thumb over his shoulder.

"I heard hammering," she said.

"They called for a fence to be built. Too many people are coming round."

"Jailor," she said. "Will thee tell me? Will thee tell me the night before I am to die? I needs must have a night to prepare my soul."

He did not answer. The door shut behind him and she was in darkness.

Eight straws, now.

She held the candle close to the tiny letters of her Bible.

O God, whose might is over all, hear the voice of the despairing, and save us from the hands of evildoers. And save me from my fear!

"Save me from my fear," she said aloud, her eyes fixed on the four lines of light high in the wall.

The tiny spring which became a river, and there was light and sun and abundant water—the river is Esther.

"The river is Esther," she murmured. "The river is Esther."

—

Nine days had passed.

The door cracked open.

The jailor lifted a fist, tipped it towards her.

"Tomorrow."

Her heart leapt.

"What is the time now?"

"'Tis just past five in the afternoon." He closed the door.

They rose before her, all the men. The night in the vale of Worcester when she and Dafeny had sat in the stocks. Bent double, freezing. Men, warm in their houses, laughing, talking of the foolish Quaker women as they ate stew, drank beer, went to their feather ticks. She imagined the Boston magistrates, bringing up the dirt-caked bundle. Groaning, peeling back the cloth. She thought of how they had looked at her—the English constables, the Boston magistrates—and did not see Kettlesing, nor her soft childhood hair, nor her mother's fingers on the strings of a harp, nor bees and moors, nor London streets and a young husband's caress.

No. They saw a creation of their own making, to serve their own ends.

She remembered the moment on the moor when George Fox had looked into her eyes.

She prayed to still the rage in her heart but it remained, and grew, and so she supposed the Lord had left it to her as a gift.

One night.

One night left here on earth.

She would not regret the minutes as they passed.

She would think, rather, of the future that unfolded before her.

It lay on the other side of her suffering.

Rage would be with her even when they thrust her from the ladder. Rage, like light, increasing in proportion to her passion. Without it, she could not continue. Rage was neither anger nor hate, and this, she thought, the magistrates did not understand.

She struck the tinder, held spark to linen, flame to wick. She set the candle next to her, leaned against the wall with the board on her lap. She dipped her quill into the ink and began to write.

Her letters were square and even.

> ... *greetings of grace, mercy and peace to every soul that doth well: tribulation, anguish and wrath to all that doth evil . . .whereas it is said by many of you that I am guilty of mine own death by my coming as you call it voluntarily to Boston . . .*

She wrote all night, until she saw the lines of light and knew the day of death had come.

She finished, hastily:

> ... *I desireth that the people called Quakers in prison or out of prison that are in the town of Boston at the time of our execution may accompany us to that place and see the bodies buried.*

A knock at her door.

The jailor never knocked.

"Come," she said. She laid down her board, clambered stiffly to her feet.

The door opened wider than the meagre gap the jailor allowed himself; torchlight revealed the stone floor, the lidded chamber pot, her straw-flecked skirt. The jailor stood back to admit the Reverends John Norton and Zachariah Simmes.

"I do not wish to speak to you," Mary said.

Both had preached incendiary sermons concerning the Quakers. John Norton had spoken out firmly for the passage of the laws inflicting the death penalty. Zachariah Simmes had come over on the *Griffin* with the Hutchinsons and had been one of Anne Hutchinson's most bitter accusers.

"Mrs. Dyer," said Reverend Norton. His accent was of Cambridgeshire; his words key-holed his nostrils. He held a hand up to forestall her speech. "There is no need for your death. I say this to you with every hope that you will believe me and trust me. There is no need for your death, I repeat—and indeed, if you will depart from this city quietly and promptly, never to return without prior permission, we shall grant you your freedom."

Mary watched the man closely. His eyes met hers and then shied away to the straw on her skirt.

"Thee hath said the same to Marmaduke Stephenson and William Robinson," she said. "I see by thine eyes that thee had from them the same answer I shall give."

"How shall you answer?" Norton said.

"That I *scorn* thy offer unless 'tis proved to me that the General Court hath repealed its bloody laws and shall release all 'Quakers,' as thee calls us, now in this prison. And that thee never more shall cut ears, whip, trammel, murder or otherwise persecute those who do no evil but to come amongst you."

She took a step towards the men—cramped, unsteady.

"Can thee give me a paper or some other way to prove such to be the case?"

Symmes opened his mouth but she raised a hand, pointed at him.

"Can thee promise me such? For if not, I wish to be left in peace to prepare myself for the dreadful hour to come."

She knelt, gathered up the letter she had written. She handed it to John Norton.

"Take this," she said. "Do not destroy it."

She held his eyes, took a breath.

"For my husband will know whether or not thee hath delivered it to the court."

She turned her back on the men.

A diminishing slice of light; then—blackness.

An hour later, she was slumped on the pallet, head on her knees. She had fallen asleep.

The jailor put out a hand and touched her shoulder.

"Come wi' me, now," he said. "I've a treat for ye."

For the first time, he took her hand and helped her to her feet. She followed him from the cell. They went along the hallway, down a flight of stairs. He opened a door and stepped back. She saw a large room filled with men and women. *Friends.*

"You've an hour," he said. "They be having their execution sermon. Then they'll come for ye."

She spread her arms, not knowing whom to embrace first.

Mary Scott, Hope Clifton.

"Mary, Mary. Oh, Mary."

An older couple. John Copeland, Samuel Shattuck. Two other young women. Two men. And an old woman who held out her arms to show Mary the linen shrouds she had prepared.

Mary could not speak. The Friends gathered close around her, clasped her tightly.

The door. Opening.

Hope Clifton fell to her knees. Mary turned, turned. Quieting, hushing, stroking a cheek, a man's tear, sunlight in their eyes, the parting words, hands. *Goodbye, Mary, goodbye, God be with . . .*

Drums.

She stepped outside.

A coif on her head. The same cape she had worn on the day that she and Hope and Mary Scott had left from Newport.

The two young men were led forward and placed beside her. They were unbound.

William, Marmaduke.

She reached for their hands. One on either side. Bright-faced young men, smiling at her. They called out to the crowd.

"This is the day of your visitation, wherein the Lord hath—"

The captain of the guards shouted. Drummers began their work of drowning out the prisoners' words. They were marched down Prison Lane; taken by a back way to avoid the largest crowd.

One hundred guards. Before them, after them. Filling the streets.

Sun on the men's white collars. Glinting on muskets, pikes.

"Mary! Mary!"

A woman's cry, a face in a window, waving a handkerchief.

A chill coming from the shadows beneath the jettied upper storeys. Sun glancing on window glass. A feather, drifting down.

William. What is he doing now. Does he know.

The rattling drums were the size of barrels, bound with red leather, brilliant against the drummers' blue frock coats. Their rhythm drowned out even the tramp of boots.

The children.

Sinnie.

She pictured her mother. And her father, and her brother. They stood in a meadow where bluebells had sprung from the winter soil. There, too, was her first baby, William—and the "monster," a perfect tiny girl. They looked in her direction, not quite seeing her but realizing the imminence of her arrival. The air smelled of the flowers' sweet spice, and the air thrummed with the drone of bees.

They turned onto Corn Hill Road. Over the rooftops she could see the hills of the tri-mountain. People pushed forward to get a better view of the prisoners. The guards raised the butts of their muskets.

"Keep back."

The drums fell silent for a time. Marching boots, the jingle of musketry. A whinny, from ahead. The clatter of hoofs.

A man shouted out.

"Are ye not ashamed to be walking hand in hand with two men?"

Mary turned to search the faces, found the speaker. It was the marshal. She remembering having seen the man when the world was normal—standing on the docks, papers in hand, conferring with a ship's master.

"Nay," she called back. Marmaduke and William turned their heads towards the man. "'Tis the hour of the greatest joy I ever had in this world."

"This is your hour—" Robinson began.

"Drummers!"

The tattoo began again, silencing Robinson.

It was a mile. The cobbles gave way to packed dirt.

Just in front of Mary was a scratched leather jerkin. She remembered the Kettlesing Market, George Fox's face above the crowd. Moors, swallows, the church tower. Mother, Father. Bluebells.

Wings. Legs, marching. *Wings*.

They arrived at the gallows. Low tide; the October grasses were red-silver, sleek, rising from the glistening mud. Across the isthmus maples and birches tossed—all the colours of a fire's heart. Ducks, flushed up, headed southwards with clapping thunder. People in boats. Men on horseback. Glinting muskets and pikes. Helmets. Drums.

Wings.

The scaffold stood on a small hillock. One of the uprights was fresh-milled. The ministers gathered at its foot. Two ladders leaned against the cross-post, one for the hangman.

The drums made a long rolling. An official stood forward and the crowd fell silent. He read the warrant for the execution. Every word could be heard, yet the voice was thin in the expanse of sky and light.

Marmaduke, William and Mary turned to one another.

Arms, chests, breath. Alive, in this moment.

Alive.

"We will meet in the everlasting day," she murmured.

Lips against her ear, strong arms, quick and fervent. Marmaduke, then William.

William was pushed forward towards the gallows. He did not resist, yet looked up at the sky as he stumbled over a clump of sod and Mary wondered, suddenly, if he had changed his mind, if he had decided that by remaining—to preach, to convince, with his powers of persuasion—he might better serve the Lord.

He will recant.

He will pause, and turn to Wilson, and recant.

He climbed the ladder, rung after rung, hand over hand.

He stopped when his hands reached the ladder's last rung. His voice rang out. "We suffer not as evildoers, but as those who testified and manifested the truth . . ."

The executioner tied William's neck cloth over his face, knotted it at the back of his head, and still the young man shouted. Mary straightened her shoulders. Her heart was hammering and she tasted blood in her mouth. His voice. Other voices, haranguing him. Her vision narrowed, dark at the edges, so that she saw only William's blonde hair, the rope sliding over his head, adjusted, his tall figure against the sky, the ladder pulled from under his feet, the fall, the drop, a great roar from the crowd. The birds, flying up.

William, struggling.

Struggling.

Swinging.

Marmaduke. Red-cheeked despite having been weeks in darkness. Marmaduke, climbing the ladder next to the body of his friend. Neck cloth over his own face now. Shouting out, over the crowd, over the isthmus, his words small and silver like the light on the leaves. "We suffer not for evil but for conscience's sake. This day shall we be at rest with the Lord."

The drop. His body, twisting, twitching.

Swinging.

Joy. He is there.

Mary felt the eyes of a thousand people. Watching her.

I will not look away.

The blood in her mouth.

I will speak before I fly.

She walked to the ladder. A man knelt beside her. He bound a rope around her skirt, not so tightly that she could not climb. Reverend Wilson stepped forward and handed the man his handkerchief. The man bound it over Mary's face. The cloth smelled of cedar and bayberry. Hands, placing hers on the rungs.

Joyfully I come.

The light filtering through the handkerchief was not the light of an October day but warmer, more golden. Filling her head, her mind, her heart.

She placed hand over hand. Felt in the air. Nothing. She had reached the top. Air beneath her, only air. Her arms were bound to her sides.

The heavy halter settled around her neck.

She took a breath to speak into the surrounding silence and heard the percussion of hoofs, galloping along the road, the shouts of its rider.

"Stop! Stop!"

The ladder had stirred beneath her feet.

"Stop!"

Men's voices. A disturbance. Beside her, she heard the hangman climbing down. A different man's voice, coming closer as he climbed up the hangman's ladder, panting. She heard a rustle of paper. He shouted out the words.

"*Hereby, I read an order of the court.* Mary Dyer hath been reprieved by the order of the governor and by the petition of her son, William. She shall return to the prison for forty-eight hours and then shall depart the Massachusetts Bay Colony. After which time, if she be found within the colony, she shall be forthwith executed."

She felt the ladder bounce as a man climbed up behind her. The halter was lifted from her neck. Her hands were unbound, the handkerchief removed.

"Nay," she said. Bewildered, wild. "Nay! I disown this order! I utterly disown it."

Below her, a man stood with the halter in his hand.

"Put it back," she ordered. "Put it back on my neck and let me fall beside my brethren."

People ran towards the gallows. Women screamed. She heard her name called by many voices.

"Mary! Mary!"

"Mary, come down!"

The man backed away down the ladder. Others rushed forward. Two men crowded up the ladder to seize her at the waist.

Cold. She was freezing, shuddering. A roaring in her ears.

The ladder slipped, slid sideways. Hands caught them. She walked through a press of faces. Reverend Wilson, taking back his handkerchief. A smile, a leer.

She was lifted up and set on a horse. The horse threw its head up violently, she gripped the saddle. Someone settled her feet in the stirrups.

The drums, the drums. Horses and riders close on either side.

The light is gone and I am freezing.

"I disown the reprieve!" she screamed, but her words were only as a beat in the vast din.

—

She stumbled into the jailor's office, stunned. Afternoon sunshine. A healthy fire on the hearth, warming the room. The space was crowded with two men and two women, friends from Aquidneck. And her son. Young William bent over the fire with the tongs, settling a log. Far taller than she, now, a man.

"They tell me the letter was from thee and not from thy father," she said. Her voice was harsh, as if her vocal cords had been damaged. "Why?"

"It was . . . thought . . ."

For the people, for England, for the world to see. The compassion of magistrates, to spare a mother for her children's sake.

A woman stepped forward.

"You may come home with us, Mary, when you are free to leave," she said.

The woman's collar lay against a yellow dress, draping her shoulders. It was edged with a neat roll, every stitch perfect. It was ironed and sun-whitened.

Mary was in the same clothes she had worn for weeks. She had slept in these clothes, used the chamber pot in them, spilled food upon them.

There was emptiness where once had been William and Marmaduke.

"Where is the jailor?"

She wished only to see his pocked, familiar face and to be back in the darkness with a candle and a sheet of paper.

My life doth not avail me if it be given by you.

The words formed in her mind and they included her son. She wished to write them down so they would never go unsaid or be forgotten.

"Come, Mary," the woman urged. "Only forty-eight more hours in this place, and then—"

"Take hands from me."

My voice? They step back, frightened.

"I wish neither food, nor warmth, nor sleep. Give me quill and paper."

No one moved.

"Mother . . ."

She pointed at her son, finger shaking. "Fetch me ink, paper, quill." She took a step towards him and he clutched the tongs to his chest. "They shed their innocent blood and I will not be silenced. I will not be silenced. *I will not be silenced . . .*"

October 28 1659

*. . . my life not availeth me in comparison to the liberty of
the truth . . .*

*. . . I rather choose to die than to live: . . . therefore, seeing
my request is hindered, I leave you to the righteous judge
and searcher of all hearts . . .*

. . . verily the Night cometh on you apace . . .

She laid down her pen. It was as if an earthquake rocked the stone walls of the prison. She put both hands to the pallet to stop the shuddering.

TWENTY-THREE

Deerskin Bags - 1659

✳

MARY AND WILLIAM WENT STRAIGHT to the parlour. In the lengthening shadows of late afternoon, she had arrived from Boston— alone, as she had been fierce in her refusal of accompaniment.

"I saw no other way," William said. He had closed the door behind them. He did not sit but stood with one hand on a chair's back, addressing Mary, who stood in the middle of the room. "They could not deny a son's plea."

"Before leaving Boston, I wrote to them," Mary answered. Her words came swift upon his, dismissively. Her clothing reeked of sweat and horse. "I told them my life availeth me not as a gift from the murderers of innocents."

"You are the mother of children."

"Aye, and they are the same men who did ruin me for a mother. The same who sent pamphlets to England so that even in Yorkshire they did name me *mother of a monster*. Now they show their magnanimity in releasing me back to the yearning arms of my children."

She stood so rigidly that she put a hand on the table for balance.

"Do you not see this house, Mary? Do you not see all that I have . . ." He threw up a hand. His face was drawn tight with hurt.

"Tables, yes, I see. Bedsteads, draperies, porcelain, silver."

Suddenly she bent forward, hands across her stomach. She pulled back a chair, slid into it. He stepped towards her, hand hovering.

"Oh, William. I am sorry. Oh, I am sorry." She rocked, cradling pain. "Oh, that I were there with them. With Marmaduke and William Robinson and my dear ones. Oh, William. I was almost there and 'twas more beautiful than thee could imagine. A meadow of light. I did not wish to return. I did not wish to return."

He straightened.

"I am sorry, as well," he said.

She looked up at his harsh tone.

"But I will say to you, Mary, whether you care or not. I have been in agony of spirits, fearing your death. I am sorry you do not care to be here with me. I am sorry you will not suffer my touch. I am sorry that my comfort is as an insult."

She closed her eyes.

Layer upon layer of words, flooding.

Yes, love. Yes, suffering. Yes, life. Yes, death.

William's neck cloth was pressed with salt and slickstone, imported waistcoat embroidered with a pattern of vines and flowers. His red stockings matched the heels of his shoes.

"Did she eat?" he asked Sinnie, a week after Mary's return.

"A bit more than yesterday, sir."

The boys glanced at one another. Charles cleaned his bowl with the side of his finger.

"Your mother has been ill," William snapped, noticing the boys' exchange. *Ill.* It was as he chose to see it, Sinnie thought, and he had told her to explain it to the children as such—*an inconvenient madness*—from which Mary would recover if well fed and housed.

After breakfast, William and the boys collected their satchels.

Their horses stood against the breaking sky. Before them, mist wreathed the fields. Clouds like loosening rolls of wool became golden in the sunrise. William sat easy on his horse, the young boys rode together on a pony.

Sinnie shut the door and turned back to the great hall where Littlemary was clearing away the breakfast bowls. Still the two youngest boys went to grammar school; Maher had gone to sea, and young William, too, had returned to sea immediately after attending the hanging. Littlemary had finished her book learning. She studied, now, how to boil the heads of pigs, make cheese, hackle flax, set a warp, pluck geese. Every day, she walked miles at her spinning wheel—one step forwards, one step back—and waited for a husband.

"What is she doing?" Littlemary murmured, looking at the ceiling. There was no sound from above, save the creak of Mary's rocking chair.

"She be sitting with her hands on her Bible. She does naught but stare at tree or sky. She watches the branches when they do bend and the clouds as they sail past. 'Tis all her eyes can bear to see."

Sickle-blades of frost on the windowpanes shimmered, their edges dissolving in sunshine.

"Does she read, Sinnie?"

"Nay, Littlemary. Sometimes I wonder if she even thinks."

"'Tis as if . . ." Littlemary began, and then bit back the words.

As if her mother wished for death. Cared only about the dead. Be what the child is thinking.

Sinnie sighed. "Your father did say wait, Littlemary. She will recover from this . . . illness."

Littlemary took a sudden step and dropped the crock she was holding. It smashed on the hearth, splattering oatmeal. She hissed with fury, her hands flinging as if to shed work, house, crazed mother. She flew to the wall and pressed her forehead against it. Sinnie knelt and began picking up the pieces.

—

Ah, a friend. May be she will be comforted . . .

Celia Grymston had come to visit, bringing a basket of apples—Rhode Island Greenings—and a geranium in a pot. For several hours, Littlemary and Sinnie could hear the sound of voices coming from Mary's room, a music whose cadence rose, quickened and then fell to a minor key. Then there was no sound of footstep or rocking chair, only a stillness so profound that both Sinnie and Littlemary paused.

"Should I stop?" Littlemary whispered, staying the spinning wheel with her right hand, the left holding high the drawn yarn.

Sinnie resumed kneading. "They be listening for the Lord. If he do come here, he will not mind our purposeful noise."

On First Day, Mary came downstairs. She had scrubbed her face with cold water and soap. The family were seated at table in the great hall. A servant had just brought in the morning's milk and the bright smell of frozen soil lingered.

"I am going to Meeting in Newport," Mary said. She spoke to William, did not look at the children. Her voice was so empty as to be crystalline, unbearable.

There be nothing betwix' them but fear, Sinnie thought, lifting a steaming bowl.

"You should eat," William said. He looked at her, shifty, his words more suggestion than order. "Sinnie has oatmeal ready."

Mary's voice warmed, a trace. "Thank thee, William, but I am not hungry. I shall take the mare. I do not know at what hour I shall return. I will have much to discuss with the other Friends."

That evening, Mary joined the family at the supper table. The November sun had set. Sinnie worked at the hearth, making busy sounds—the nick of ladle against iron kettle, the shuffle of peel over stone as she slid corn bread from the oven. Mary, she observed, was as an interruption in the family's flow, like a tree fallen across a stream—she scooped succotash onto her spoon and then did not carry it to her mouth; she attempted to converse with William but her words trailed away.

Littlemary raised reluctant eyes, made rapid pattings at her stew with the back of her spoon. *They need one another.* So many burdens mother and daughter should share: caring for the men, running the household, bearing babies, instructing the children. Henry and Charles seemed easier in Mary's presence, in the way of people who suffer a stranger knowing that they themselves are soon to leave.

After the meal, Mary asked the boys to tell her of their day. She complimented Littlemary on her embroidery and the skeins of wool she had spun. Sinnie watched from the corners of her eyes. Unassuaged emotion tightened the skin around Mary's eyes and warped her mouth even as it curved into a smile.

My bonnie mistress. How they have ruined you.

The house was quiet; even William had gone to bed. Mary and Sinnie heard no creak of branch nor wind's moan, since winter's first, tentative flakes fell from the darkness.

Mary held a wooden darning egg beneath the frayed edges of a sock heel; a needle, threaded with yarn.

"I cannot find my tenderness. It hath gone from me." Her voice faltered. "As, too, hath my closeness to paradise. I see it, still, but it hath faded, like a buttercup laid in the sun."

Sinnie's hands worked wooden knitting needles. On the firedogs, a birch log was burned to a gridwork of pulsing squares. Yarn rolled from Sinnie's lap and disappeared under a blanket chest.

"I should stay here and learn to love my children," Mary whispered. She put down her work.

Sinnie's fingers fell still on the needles. "Mistress," she said. She cast a brave look at Mary, and then looked back, quickly, at the half-knit mitten. "I do not know how to help you."

They listened to the shift and crumble of the fire.

"Last night I dreamt of George Fox. He drew open my curtains and the light of a summer's morning flooded in. Then he directed my gaze to a line of people who crossed the moors carrying dead bodies. He told me to return to my work, what I did do in England."

She picked up her needle but did not prick the sock. "Ah, if only I had my friend Dafeny here now. We travelled together, spreading the truth."

So dangerous, Sinnie thought, watching Mary's face, drawn and inward, the firelight warming her face yet settling shadows into the pouches beneath her eyes. Wolves, Indians, blizzards. But she will go, there be no stopping her.

"Where would you go?"

"Sylvester Manor where Grizzell Sylvester and her husband, Nathaniel, provide haven to Friends arriving from Barbados or England; and nursing, for those who have been brutalized. 'Tis at the tip of Long Island, on a place called Shelter Island. I will make my way there. I will preach as I go. They do tell me that there have been many convincements on Long Island and that many there are as dry seed in drought, waiting for rain."

"*How* will you go?" Sinnie set aside her needles. She leaned forward and reached for Mary's hands.

"On foot. I cannot deprive William of another horse. I have told a few people at the Newport meeting, begging secrecy. They have supplied me with money and I have accepted it, for it doth come from a common treasury supporting the Ministers of the Truth."

"And when, Mistress? When shall you go?" Sinnie fought to keep anguish from her voice.

"Soon, my Sinnie. Soon, before the winter storms. Do not tell William. I will depart in the night and shall leave a letter for him."

Long after Mary had tiptoed upstairs Sinnie remained by the fire, her needles sliding as her finger lifted the yarn: looped, linked, looped. Tears fattened, fell. Were absorbed by the grey wool.

In the hall dresser, below the racks of pewter, Sinnie began to hide food—a leather bag filled with nookick, maize bread studded with dried huckleberries, rusk biscuits, johnny-cakes, salted cod. Together, they prepared clothing. They sewed new larger pockets to tie around Mary's waist. She would need five petticoats and an extra pair of woollen stockings. A kerchief for her head and a wool scarf to pull over nose and mouth. Two pairs of mittens. A belt. A long, hooded cape. A basket, a pack.

"I deceive him," Mary said, once, glancing at Sinnie.

She hears my thoughts, clear as if I spoke them.

Mary's eyebrows drew into an anguished warp. She stared at the floor, the snippets of cloth.

Two in the morning.

Sinnie listened at the bottom of the stairs, holding a candle. The door-latch rattled; a snick as its pin dropped. Mary appeared at the top of the stairs. She floated down soundlessly on stockinged feet.

"I did leave the letter on the bed," she whispered as they went into the great hall.

—

"Cloak, basket, the deerskin bag, mittens. Sinnie, dost remember the night long ago when we packed bags with nookick and bacon?"

Mary tied her hat strings.

"'Twas a snowy night in Boston and Samuel was but a tiny babe. I stood in the door and watched the men trudging away to find a new life in Rhode Island. 'I will find us a place where we will live as we wish,' William said."

Sinnie turned and picked up the lantern. She lit the candle and handed it to Mary. She adjusted the straps of Mary's packs, fussed at her cloak.

They stood facing one another, overwhelmed by the succession of memories that flooded between them.

TWENTY-FOUR

Shelter Island - 1659–1660

※

SHE CROSSED THE PETTAQUAMSCOTT RIVER in a dugout canoe paddled by a Narragansett Indian. She sat loose and balanced, holding the sides of the tippy boat, watching as snowflakes starred and dissolved against his deerskin cloak.

On the bank, she dug in her bag for coins, laid them in the man's palm. The weathered skin of his face was furrowed, folds running downward beside his mouth; his eyes held hers, so acute that she was reminded of the moment she had met Anne Hutchinson and had felt a sear of fright. He said nothing, but pointed in the direction she was to go and turned back to his canoe.

She followed a track that ran uphill through close-set beeches, hickories and maples. The snow came more heavily. At the top of the hill, the sky opened before her and she could see that the track wound downwards into a valley of cleared land, where cows clustered by a barn and smoke drifted from the chimney of a farmhouse. She made her way down the rutted track, knocked at the door. A woman opened it; her features were puddled in a chinless face, her eyes pale and puzzled. Mary held out coins.

"I am travelling to visit friends," she said.

"Aye, you may come in," the woman said. "'Tis coming on for snow so you'd perish otherwise."

She showed Mary to an attic room. Cobwebs looped the timbers of a slanted ceiling, on the floor were baskets of dried beans, and in a corner was a flock bed covered with wolfskins.

Darkness fell early and the wind rose.

In the kitchen, the woman set out hare pie, pumpkin bread and applesauce. A candle guttered on the trestle table. Mary was given the only pewter plate. Their hired man, a young Irishman, sat at the table's end. The children—three boys, two girls—waited silently behind their father. After the blessing, the children took their trenchers and filed to a tall-backed settle by the fire.

As they ate, no one spoke. Mary felt their curiosity, yet to her surprise, no questions were asked.

"I can tell you my business since I am still in Rhode Island," she said. "I am a Quaker bound for Long Island."

The woman slid her eyes to her husband, who looked up sharply.

"Ye'll not be going into New Haven Colony, then," he said. "No Quakers allowed in the colony unless you can prove you're on lawful business."

Mary saw the children's shoulders stiffen in the effort not to look at her.

"They'll brand you with an 'H.' Or throw you in jail. You'd not like that, hey? Being in jail? They'll fine you just for having pamphlets. Nay, you'd best stay here where people are civil."

"I thank thee for thy advice," Mary said. Her grave voice fell into the room's scant comfort. The man looked at her. He resumed eating more quickly and without seeing his food.

In the light of her candle, she read Psalm 63:

> *O God, thou are my god, I seek thee,*
> *my soul thirsts for thee . . .*
> *I think of thee upon my bed,*

and meditate on thee in the
watches of the night;
for thou hast been my help,
and in the shadow of thy wings I
sing for joy . . .

She lay beneath the wolfskins listening to the storm.

Wind, snow, branches. God's thought at the end of the stars. She lay on her back with her arms spread to the cold, apple-scented air.

The next morning, there was a foot of snow on the ground and the road stretched as a white stream between the fields.

"I will go on," she said at breakfast. "Can I find passage from Rhode Island so that I need not step into New Haven Colony? A boat, to take me?"

She listened carefully as the man gave her directions. She thanked the couple, slid a coin onto the table, and stepped outside. The sky had cleared and the snow glittered.

Sylvester Manor was like a palace, with eight large rooms, a red-tiled roof, cobblestones laid in a diamond pattern before a two-storey vestibule. Built in the shape of a cross, it stood alone on its own island, surrounded by oaks.

Mary was given a sleeping chamber filled with three bedsteads, trunks, baskets. She would be obliged to share both room and bedstead with whoever might be passing through—newly arrived Friends from England or Barbados, or ill and injured refugees from Massachusetts, but for now the room was hers alone.

On the first morning, she woke to a sighing roar. She went to the window, breath smoking, hands tucked in her armpits.

Heavy oak boughs lifted and fell in a gale-force wind. She watched a brown leaf twirling on its frail stem.

By day's end, it will be gone.

Below, a group of Manhanset Indians clustered around Nathaniel Sylvester—he made arm gestures, drew lines in the blowing snow with a stick. Beyond the cobblestone yard was a sloping hill on which sheds ran down to the water. She glimpsed the masts of a ship anchored in deep water, saw two rowing boats bucking over waves, falling into troughs, approaching the cove.

Shivering, she lifted her chamber pot and carried it down the stairs.

In the great hall, the stink of unwashed bodies lay sharp and sour beneath the smell of Indian bannock, browning on a sloping board. Firelight quivered on the floor's red tiles. Three African slave women worked at a vast fireplace hung with hams and bacon. They spoke to one another in Creole, and the soft rhythm swept her to Barbados and the hilltop plantation owned by Quakers where she and Anne Burden had stayed. Whistling frogs, in the hot nights, and woodsmoke from the sugar factory. Rattle of palmetto leaves. A slave who had dug an insect from beneath her toenail, where it had laid eggs. Drums from the slave quarters. Barbados—the "nursery of the truth," Friends called it, for so many had been convinced there.

And become wealthy, as had the Sylvesters, from sugar.

She set down her chamber pot to thaw by the others.

Grizzell put a hand to her spinning wheel, stopping its roll. She stepped light-footed across the crowded room, skirting chairs, baskets, chests. She was Mary's height, her eyes serene. Motherly, Mary thought, taking Grizzell's strong hands.

As if she is amazed and delighted at the very sight of me. Ah, that Littlemary could look at me so.

"Didst sleep well?"

"I did, thank thee. Though I fear I did oversleep."

Two children played on the bedstead—Giles gnawed the coral stem of a teething toy; Little Grizzell played with a wooden doll.

"Aye, we ate long ago. Thee must be hungry. Hannah?"

Mary sat at the table. Hannah set a bowl of porridge before her. Her arms were thick, purple-black. She smelled of ginger, smiled wryly at Mary's murmured thanks.

Grizzell returned to her spinning wheel. She gave it an absent stroke, setting it in motion, still gazing at Mary as if reluctant to return to her work.

"Where are you . . . ?" She broke off, looked down as if distracted by a larger tuft of wool that she must coax onto her spindle.

Where am I going to go next, she doth wonder. What shall I say?

For the moment, she was content to be here, in the home of Friends, waiting for news brought by travellers. She blew on her spoonful of steaming samp.

Grizzell spoke quickly. "It is our hope that thee will stay as long as thee wishes, Mary. 'Tis a joy to me to have thee here. Someone who remembers London!"

Yes, Mary thought, looking at the young woman, whose belly showed the slight swelling of another pregnancy. Grizzell would be happy to have another Englishwoman here, for it was clear that Nathaniel Sylvester was busy; and when there were no visiting Friends, this young woman who had grown up in the court of Charles I would have no like-minded companion: only the children, and the slave families sleeping in corners, and the Shinnecock, Manhansets and Montauks arriving in canoes, through veils of snow.

Every day, Mary dressed in many layers—long wool stockings secured around her thighs, neck cloth, mittens, hooded cape. She stepped out into snow-refracted light.

Wolves had been exterminated on the island, and cattle, horses and pigs wandered unfenced; the land was riddled with their trails, crisscrossing meadows, ribboning down to the shore. She followed a trail into the woods where branches stirred with dry creaks, shifting the prisms within ice-coated twigs. She walked slowly, dazed by the brilliance and by her own tenuous presence within it.

Sometimes she could not bear the sound of voice or tool. Crying, laughter, the creak of spinning wheel; raw, excruciating, it was the sound of time—slow, so slow.

All of life's minutes . . .

At the edge of the cove, she stood watching the sea birds. She remembered the scaffold's threshold, the moment when her foot had lifted to step forward. Still she could feel that brush of tissuey sweetness, like a poppy's heart. And the joy she had glimpsed of which earthly happiness was but a remnant.

An elderly couple arrived from Salem—Lawrence and Cassandra Southwick, recently released from prison and driven from Massachusetts under pain of death.

They were given chairs close to the fire. Cassandra's lips were blue; Lawrence bore yellowing bruises beneath his eyes.

"Mary Dyer!" Cassandra exclaimed. Mary took the mouse-boned hand. *The cruelty, the savagery.* Cassandra was small, soft, her cheeks pouched like pudding-bags within a square face whose eyes bore the wrinkles of kindness. Men had stripped her to the waist and whipped her for carrying Quaker pamphlets.

Lawrence bent forward, face in hands.

"'Tis Provided and Daniel we fear for," he said into his hands. "Our youngest children. We heard that they have been imprisoned for not attending church."

His woollen mittens were unravelling at the cuffs. Melting ice dripped from his beard.

Nathaniel and Grizzell stood together, the children half-hidden within Grizzell's skirts. Low afternoon light rubied bunches of seed corn dangling from the beams.

An African girl came with a bowl of soup. She handed it to Cassandra; returned with another bowl for Lawrence. He sat upright to take the bowl and held it so loosely that it tipped forward, slopped onto his boots. He looked around the room, his face clearing.

"The Lord is here," he said.

"He is wherever a heart welcomes him," said Cassandra.

More Friends arrived on a ship, seven weeks out from England, men or women who had been called to leave home and family.

They wore plain clothing and were spare of language. Out-of-doors they walked in silence, engaged in sober reflection.

Sometimes Mary accompanied them as they travelled through the forests on foot, guided by Indians, crossing streams and coves in dugouts, seeking those who might be glad to receive the "blessed truth." In villages, they stayed at the homes of those who would receive them kindly. They held their meetings in houses whose unpainted lintels oozed sap, whose walls smelled of plaster, whose windows framed the stumps of cleared fields. The air in such rooms was as the air of forest or sea, unpeopled by history. Into such clarity, the Friends' message crept—kindled, blazed.

After one such expedition, Mary returned to Sylvester Manor to find Lawrence Southwick lying in the hall bedstead where the children played. The curtains were drawn back so that firelight would touch his face. He had died on the previous night.

Three days later, Cassandra lay in the same bed.

Mary, at her side, slit open a letter from William. It had been delivered to the Manor by an Indian runner.

> ... I must tell you that the Court hath published this statement in the Bay and sent another copy for publishing in England. It hath been published both here and abroad. It reads thus: "The sparing of Mary Dyer upon an inconsiderable intercession will manifestly evince that we desire their lives absent, rather than their deaths present."

Inconsiderable. Her heart raced. However manipulated, was the request of a son to spare the life of his mother *inconsiderable*?

She could hear distant shouting as men ferried lighters filled with barrels of salted meat out to a Barbados-bound ship lying at anchor in the deep water.

We desire their lives absent.

Again, they used her. *Mary Dyer, mother of a monster.* Read by mariners, at sea. By purveyors of meat, in Southwick Market. *Mary Dyer, cursed by the devil.* By milliners, cobblers, and powdered London ladies. *Mary Dyer, irresponsible mother, heretic.* Read by innkeepers, farmers, wheelwrights, teachers. And now: *See our graciousness. We have been so kind as to spare her.*

She felt violent energy lift her scalp. Her thoughts honed.

He says—this is thy path, walk it and thee shall find me.

She laid the letter on her lap. Rather than Cassandra's pouched, pale cheeks, she saw the Massachusetts General Court, with its magistrates and elders, its pine walls and dusty air. Court met twice yearly, once in autumn and once in spring.

They had promised to hang her if she returned.

She would offer Governor Endicott two choices.

Repeal the bloody laws, or hang me.

If they repealed the laws, she would live and the prisoners would go free. But Endicott and his government would appear to have lost their war against the Quakers.

If they hanged her. Already, people were sickened by the brutality. If they executed an innocent woman—fifty years old, wife of a prominent Rhode Island merchant, mother of six children—the news would be taken to London, would spread to the continent. It was rumoured that soon, within months, Charles II would ascend to the throne. He would take note of the brutality, carried out by the same Puritans who had murdered his father.

She smoothed her hand over Cassandra's forehead, bony and box-like as a turtle's shell, thinking of the dream that came night after night. The bluebell meadow. Where they sat; Mother, Father—

Cassandra Southwick jolted from sleep. She sat with sudden strength, arms reaching. She cried out, full-throated.

"Lawrence? Josiah? Provided! My Daniel!"

Grizzell dropped her spindle; toys startled from the children's hands. Hurrying footsteps sounded from the stairwell.

Mary ran her hand up Cassandra's back, her fingers rising and falling over the scars of the jailor's whip. Cassandra fell back on the pillow. Her face cleared as breath left her body and did not return.

In April, a group of Friends sat in the Sylvesters' parlour. A woman read out the names of thirteen people now held in the Boston jail.

Mary Trask. Margaret and John Smith. Edward Wharton. Robert and Deborah Harper. Wenlock Christison. William King. Martha Standley. Mary Wright. William Leddra. Joseph and Jane Nicholson.

One need, only. It was less need than impetus. One step forward into the heart of time.

—

Sinnie was in the great hall, stirring laundry in a wooden tub. William stood rigid in the front door, silhouetted against the spring sunshine, reading a letter.

She laid the stick against the side of the bucket, carefully, so as not to make a sound. She heard the tick-tock of hoofs as the messenger rode back down the lane.

He came into the room.

"Mary hath been sighted riding to Boston."

Littlemary came up the path carrying a basket filled with chives and dandelion greens. She stepped into a patch of light.

"Father?"

"Do you tell her, Sinnie," he said. His voice was hoarse. "I am going to the parlour to write a letter. Tell Jurden to be ready to ride for Boston within the hour."

He sat at his desk, quill poised.

The last time, he had appealed to their consciences. They had struck a deal—they would take her to the gallows, with no intention of hanging her. It would frighten her so terribly that she would change her ways. They had insisted that it be son, not husband, who begged for her life.

He tossed down his quill and went to the window. He did not see the orchard's pink-blossomed rows but watched his life unreeling, all his decisions reversed until he arrived at his pew in St. Martin-in-the-Fields and saw a young woman sitting across the stone-flagged aisle.

And lost his heart to her grave, luminous eyes.

His throat tightened.

This time, I will appeal to their hearts.

He resumed his seat, began to write rapidly, with shaking hand.

. . . I only say this, yourselves have been and are or may be husbands to wife or wives, so am I: yea to one most dearly

beloved, oh do not you deprive me of her, but I pray give her
me once again and I shall be so much obliged forever, that I
shall endeavour continually to utter my thanks and render
your love and honour most renowned: pity me, I beg it with
tears, and rest your

most humbly suppliant
W Dyer

Sinnie saw dried tears on William's face. She stood in the lane before the house. Jurden was running from the barn, dragging an alarmed gelding by the reins.

"Ride with all haste, Jurden, and if you do sight someone who can get there faster, send word that this letter is on its way."

"Aye."

"And deliver it straight into Endicott's hands. See that you do so, Jurden, I pray you."

The grey's restrained energy exploded. Pebbles cracked against the house. Horse and rider dwindled down the lane and turned northwards at the gate, Jurden's whip a streak of silver.

William and Sinnie stood by the hitching post. Hens bustled around the corner of the house, stopping to scratch beneath a catnip plant.

"I can only think that she is mad, Sinnie."

Sinnie looked down. Her shoes had been wet from the washing and had attracted a layer of dust. She glanced at the house, where Littlemary stood in the door holding a forked stick, her sleeves rolled.

So much work to do. Sunshine, a good day for drying. And the garden to plant.

"If only I had not allowed her to go to England. If I had . . ."

Sinnie put a hand to William's sleeve and he collected himself. He laid his hand over hers, his eyes reddened by tears.

TWENTY-FIVE

Blowing Grasses - 1660

EVERYTHING WAS THE SAME in shape and substance, yet seemed profoundly changed. The same four-poster bedstead at Fairbanks, in the same room. The same view overlooking the harbour. She sat on a chair.

She stared.

Out the window at the swaying mastheads.

At a shoe, held in her hand.

She remembered Anne's voice. *Only God's grace can bring salvation.*

Listened. The watchman, calling out the all's well. Gulls.

At night, she could not sleep but lay watching the dim square of the window, feeling as if she were a fish swimming through waters in whose shafts of light she drifted and lingered, fluid and free.

Although she had been sighted, she remained in Boston, undetained, for a few days.

They hope I will lose my nerve. They do not wish to hang me.

Then they came for her.

She was put in a cell with other Quaker women. They said little to one another. They had no energy for one another's earthly needs. They did not hug, weep or speak of their fears.

Mary did not tell them how she looked forward rather than back. How she felt steady in her faith, certain of the glory to come. How she pictured the fear on Endicott's face rather than her own. How she was grim, eager for her day.

Darkness. Silence. Five days, six.

The General Court sat. The following day, the marshal came for Mary. He escorted her through the streets of Boston, up the staircase over the market and into the courtroom. He seated her on the same bench where she had sat before with William and Marmaduke. She imagined them at her side. Pictured their faces when she saw them next.

Soon.

The same Court, smelling of resin and grain dust.

The same men, only with different expressions. Uneasy, solemn. Luminous with terror, as if the presence of death curtailed each of their breaths.

Endicott seemed diminished—thinner, distraught.

"Are you the same Mary Dyer who was here before?" He pretended to be in doubt and she saw that he hoped she would say "no" in order to release him from the conundrum of her arrest.

"I am the same Mary Dyer who was here at the last General Court." She spoke robustly, remembering William Robinson's voice—how, at his sentence, he had spoken with such firmness.

"You will own yourself a Quaker?"

"I own myself to be reproachfully so called." She smiled, her chin crept forward, and she narrowed her eyes at Endicott.

Look at me, man. Remember your deeds.

Endicott rose, agitated. He motioned for the magistrates to follow him into the consulting chamber.

Mary watched the sunshine on the wall. No leaf or wing interrupted the light's passage and yet it quivered. The men's voices were a rumble behind the door. A fly landed on the back of her hand and she made no move to flick it away but felt the padded tickle of its feet, observed the purple-green sheen of its wings.

"*. . . he who loses his life for my sake will find it . . .*"

The door opened.

The men filed back to their seats, not looking at her.

Endicott remained standing. His face was whey-coloured. Shadows lay in the deep lines running from his nose to the corners of his mouth. She saw that his neck trembled, shivering the tassels at the corners of his white bib collar.

"You must return to the prison and there remain till tomorrow at nine o'clock; then from there you must go to the gallows and there be hanged until you are dead."

"This is no more than thee said before." She allowed her contempt its full voice.

"Aye, aye," he said. He made a dismissing gesture, looked away from her eyes. "But now it is to be executed. Therefore, prepare yourself for nine o'clock tomorrow."

No one spoke.

Suddenly, Endicott leaned forward and put both hands on the table.

"Why do you think this sentence should not be executed?" he asked. He peered at her, squinting, as if he could not quite make her out, though she sat so close.

"I came in obedience to the will of God to the last General Court, praying thee to repeal thy laws; and that is my same work now, and earnest request, although I told thee that if thee refused to repeal them, the Lord would send others of his servants to witness against them."

"Are you a prophetess, then?" Endicott mocked.

"I spoke the words which the Lord spoke to me," she said, evenly. Her eyes did not leave his, and he looked down. She felt them in the room—all the brutalized Friends, robust and warm-hearted—and imagined it was their presence that caused the men to shrink back in their seats and made Endicott look sideways. "And now the thing has come to pass."

She paused and took a breath to speak again, but Endicott had begun gathering his papers, fumbling, sending some across the table, others flying to the floor.

"Away with her," he snapped to the marshal. "Away with her."

—

This time, she was placed in a solitary cell. She watched as the familiar lines of light in the window's pine planks slowly passed from yellow to grey, and then vanished.

She sat upright against the dank wall, hands on her Bible, not seeking sleep.

Muted by the thick walls, a wolf's quavering call.

Then, far off, a reply.

The marshal came for her at seven-thirty the next morning.

"Wait one moment," she said. She sought his eyes. "I shall be ready presently."

"I'll not wait upon you, you shall wait upon me. *Get up with ye.*"

She pushed herself to her feet. He propelled her before him. Down the hall, through the door.

She stepped out into the spring morning. Salt air.

A phalanx of drummers and soldiers waited, closed around her.

As before, people lined the streets.

One mile, the walk to Boston Neck.

Drums. Hands, important on wooden sticks. Faces, pressing. Cries. *Up. Look. Up.*

The clouds, silvery, wisping. Pulling apart and drawing together again.

Her hands, clasped before her and the cobbles beneath her shoes. *Up. Look. Up.*

The cobbles turned to dirt, they left behind the houses and came out onto the ridge. The town fell back and below. Beyond, to the east, was the sea. Before her, the marshes where birds burst from nests, soaring.

She stood where she had stood with William Robinson and Marmaduke Stephenson. People called out to her. Some voices were derisive, others were kind. Reverend Wilson asked her to repent. She searched his eyes. *That of God in every man . . .* She turned from him without speaking, settled in the moment, a perfect balance. Her rage, disseminated, was in the soil, on the sea wind, in the smell of spring grass.

She mounted the ladder. The executioner climbed the second ladder beside her. She saw the marshes darken with cloud shadow, then brighten again.

One, grip. Another, grip. The rungs were sun-warmed.

The executioner tied a rope around her skirt. She watched the grasses blowing, blowing. A white handkerchief came over her eyes and still she kept them open. Then nothing more happened. No hands on her skirts, no adjustment of the halter around her neck. No sound from the crowd. Only the sweet, oblivious birdcall.

And in her head, her own voice steadily whispering George Fox's words.

Walk in the light, walk in the truth, with which light, that never changeth, come to see that which was in the beginning, before the world was, where there is not shadow or . . .

TWENTY-SIX

New Day - 1660

✳

ON THE MORNING OF JUNE SECOND, William did not go to his office but dressed in his working clothes and left the house at dawn. Sinnie could see him speaking with the men by the barn; behind them, fenceposts loomed in the white mist, like flotsam. Sun broke over the sea. She turned from the window and went through the room where every tankard and bowl and silver spoon bore a flush of red. She opened the back door. Blackbirds, robins and song sparrows trilled, whistled.

Such wee things, to be so proud. Proud of a new day.

The house rose around and above her, like her own ribcage and beating heart: in the bedsteads, the sleeping boys and Littlemary; in the chests of drawers, shirts and caps and breeches and William's trousers and garters and stockings and waistcoats; in the cupboards, candles, soap, linen; in the buttery and pantry, cheeses and hams; and all of it her purview, even if Mary should come home.

Still Jurden had not returned.

Sinnie walked down a gravel path towards the garden. Onion sets sprouted grassy stems in neat rows, rhubarb bore flowering stalks, and asparagus thrust up fat, scaled spears. She stopped at the herb garden, walled with fieldstones. The grey-green leaves of last-year's plants were half-buried in dead leaves. *Let me care for the herb garden.*

She stopped at the wrought-iron gate.

Where is she now?

She was accustomed to holding Mary in her mind's eye. She saw her small and cape-swirled on the English moors, or making purchases in London's markets, or sitting in darkness in a jail cell, or walking through the forests, or knocking on the doors of taverns. She had pictured her sailing across Long Island Sound.

Where is she now? Oh, my Mary.

The sun began its swift climb. The bird chorus reached its peak, notes colliding and streaming into one sustained exuberance of sound.

They were not little children anymore. The baby, Charles, was ten. Henry was thirteen. Littlemary had her flowers and her shifts were too tight across the bosom.

Their mother had been gone most of their lives and their forbearance had been summoned so often that it had become less resentment than habitual irritation. On this evening, when they knew that Mary had ridden into the jaws of death but had not heard whether or not she would return, William did not say a word after the prayer but snapped open his napkin, took a bite of his food and sat chewing, staring over their heads. Then he set down his spoon. A muscle shifted in his cheek.

"It would do no good for me to go," he said, refuting an accusation that had not been made. "Better that my words reach them by a rider speedier than myself."

"Father?"

"Yes, Henry."

"George Gawler walked all the way from his house to the schoolyard on stilts."

Sinnie leaned between the boys to set down a rhubarb cobbler.

"Mind, it be hot," she said.

With William's permission to speak, Henry and Charles began a debate as to the height of George Gawler's stilts. Littlemary was not listening. She bent her head slightly sideways, a smile touching her eyes, and ran a fingertip along the rim of her bowl. Yesterday, she had confided in Sinnie. He was sixteen.

William's face relaxed. He told them of the stilts that had carried him over East Anglian fields.

The peepers started up in the marsh. One frog's shrill, then another, more and then more, insistent as tiny hands on the blanket of darkness, pulling it up, rolling the day into oblivion.

They heard the sound of horse hoofs, coming up the lane. William went to the door. The chime of peepers augmented as he opened it. Sinnie ran up behind him, peered out. It was Jurden Cooth, riding slowly.

EPILOGUE

MARY DYER WAS HANGED on the morning of June first, 1660. It is commonly believed that her family was allowed to collect her body and that she was buried at Dyer Farm.

After the death of Oliver Cromwell, support for the return of the monarchy gained strength. On May 8, 1660, Charles II was acknowledged rightful king and invited to return from his exile in France. Three days before Mary's execution, May 29th, 1660, Charles II returned to London amidst wild rejoicing. Peaceably, the Puritan era ended.

News of William's, Marmaduke's and Mary's executions spread across the Atlantic. George Fox wrote in his journal: "When those were put to death I was in prison in Lancaster, and had a perfect sense of their sufferings as though it had been myself, and as though the halter had been put about my own neck, though we had not at that time heard of it . . ." ("The Journal of George Fox," Friends United Press, 1976.)

—

In March 1661, a fourth Friend was hanged in Boston—William Leddra, formerly of Cornwall. Others awaited execution.

In England, the young king declared his support for religious tolerance. Alarmed, the Massachusetts authorities sent a letter justifying their actions. New England Friends countered with a letter of their own, detailing the punishments. Their letter was delivered to the king by the English Friend Edward Burrough. The king, appalled by the report of atrocities and hangings, responded with a mandamus requiring the authorities to forbear to proceed any further against those Quakers now already imprisoned and condemned to suffer death or other corporeal punishment; such persons, he wrote, must be sent to England, where they could be tried by English laws. He gave the mandamus to Burrough, who arranged for it to be delivered.

In Boston, two Friends, one himself banished from Massachusetts, delivered the king's Order to Governor Endicott.

After reading it, Endicott removed his hat before the Quakers as representatives of the king, even though they retained their own hats upon their heads. He immediately sent a letter to the jailor.

> To William Salter, keeper of the prison at Boston,
> You are required, by authority and order of the General
> Court, to release and discharge the Quakers, who at present
> are in your custody. See that you do not neglect this.

In 1686, the Royal Charter was withdrawn from the Massachusetts Bay Colony. The settlers lost their title to the land and the colony was ruled by a British governor. In the once-Puritan stronghold, an Anglican church was built.

William Dyer remarried four years after Mary's death.

In 1677, members of the Society of Friends were free to hold regular meetings in Massachusetts.

In 1959, a bronze statue of Mary Dyer by Quaker sculptor Sylvia Shaw Judson was placed on the west lawn of the Massachusetts State House, with the inscription: *My life not availeth me in comparison to the liberty of the truth.*

These Things Are True

✳

A Measure of Light is based on a true story; but there is much that I have invented.

Mary Barrett did, indeed, marry William Dyer in the church of St. Martin-in-the-Fields in 1633, and she did have a brother. William and Mary did lose their first son, and they did travel to Boston. Mary did bear a severely deformed stillborn child, delivered by Anne Hutchinson; and she did rise and walk from the trial at Anne's side. Mary and William did establish a farm in Newport, and Mary did go to England by herself; as did William, to dispute the charter, during the time that Mary was there. Whether or not he encountered her, while in England, is unknown. But Mary did, in fact, stop in Barbados, on her way home; and it is true that she returned to New England as a newly converted Quaker and was incarcerated for her belief on numerous occasions (including the incident with Patience Scott). It is true that she stayed at Sylvester Manor; and she did, famously, travel alone to Boston, one last time.

Nothing is known of Mary's childhood: nor why she left Newport to go to England, leaving her children behind; nor why she stayed away for so long; nor what she did there. Thus I was free to create Mary's early life in Yorkshire, as well as her married years in London. Sinnie stepped into my mind and onto the page. I invented everything that happened to Mary when she returned to England, including her companion, Dafeny.

Of course, throughout the book, my imaginings of Mary's life, both outer and inner, are lifted and eased through the warp threads of history. George Fox is real, as are his companions and many of the other Quakers I mention during Mary's time in England. Fox's sermons, too, are real, as are the atrocities visited upon those early English Friends. As well, the two letters that Mary wrote to the Boston Court of Assistants on pages 272 and 281 are real, as is William's letter on pages 299-300 to the same magistrates. Mary's writ of incarceration on page 252, beginning "To the Keeper of the Prison," is also real, as is the letter to the jailor on page 312. These are in the public domain. I invented all the others.

Here are some facts and incidents that are either based on reality, or slightly altered, as well as definitions of some words that may be difficult for the reader to find.

– The incident with the martyrs in the opening scene is inspired by an historical account. On June 30, 1637, Puritans William Prynne, Henry Burton and John Bastwick were put in a pillory and had their ears sliced off. I have changed a few details, setting the scene in winter, adding the slit nostrils, and not describing the fact that William Prynne also had the letters "S" and "L" (seditious libeller) branded on his cheeks. www.historytoday.com/richard-hughes/ears-william-prynne

– Page 8, "quintain"—an object hung or mounted on a pole used as a target during jousting training.

– The descriptions of the New World on pages 6 and 30 are based on *Wood's New England's Prospect*, by William Wood, published 1634, written to inform prospective English colonists (on-line e-book); and *John Josselyn, Colonial Traveler,* an account of two voyages to New England in 1638 and 1663 (published 1675—I used the University Press of New England edition, 1988, ed. Paul J. Lindholt).

– "The lecturer" referred to on pages 7, 49 and 52 is the real John Everard, reader at St. Martin-in-the-Fields during the years Mary Dyer lived in London, and these words were taken from a collection of his sermons which can be found on-line ("Some Gospel Treasures Opened," published 1653). archive.org/details/somegospeltreasuooever

– I found the hymn on page 45 in the Bay Psalm Book. archive.org/stream/baypsalmbookbeinooeame#page/n277/mode/2up

– Many of Reverend Cotton's comments (including about how babies are born "sprawling in wickedness") came from his writings, which can be found on-line. www.digitalpuritan.net/johncotton.html

– Page 85, "gurnipper"—from *John Josselyn, Colonial Traveler,* p. 88: "There is another sort of fly called a Gurnipper that are like our horse-flyes, and will bite desperately, making the bloud to spurt out in great quantity . . ."

– Page 30, "eft"—a small lizard.

– Wheelwright's famous sermon, with his admonitions to the Boston clergymen, makes fascinating reading and is far, far longer than the bits I quote on pages 80 and 81. See Google Books, "John Wheelwright: His Writings, Including His Fast-Day Sermon, Volume 9."

– The admonition to Anne Hutchinson on page 109, determining her meetings to be "disorderly," is taken verbatim from "The Journal of John Winthrop" (ed. Dunn and Yeandle), page 130, in which Winthrop tells about "questions debated and resolved" at the General Assembly.

– Pages 115, 288, 289—"Nookick" is corn, baked and ground to powder.

– Anne Hutchinson's trial came from my perusal of various sources, both Eve LaPlante's *American Jezebel* and David D. Hall's *The Antinomian Controversy, 1636-1638: A Documentary History*. (see below)

– Page 158—"kersey" is a coarse, woollen cloth.

– Although it seems probable that large wolf packs would have been kept from the Shawmut Peninsula by guards at Boston Neck, I have taken the liberty of imagining that a few may have slipped through.

– Alice Tilly was a prominent Boston midwife. The story that Ann Burden (also a real person) tells Mary is true.

– Page 191, "metheglin"—"A strong, sweet drink made from fermented honey and water, and flavoured with aromatic herbs." Glossary, p. 304, *The English Housewife*, originally published in 1615, Gervase Markham. (see below)

– The library books in Uncle Colyn's study were such as would have been found in a gentleman's library. My source was *Fire from Heaven: Life in an English Town in the Seventeenth Century*, David Underdown. (see below)

– Somewhere in my readings I came across a description of early Friends crossing a moor, carrying bodies. It stuck in my mind, although I can no longer find the source.

– Here's where I found George Fox's sermons. www.sermonindex. net/modules/articles/index.php?view=category&cid=410

– Page 199, "cheat rye bread." "Bread of middle grade, made of sour dough." Again, from *The English Housewife*, page 210, with detailed instructions.

– Dyota's life in the stable is based on a true story, which I found in Alison Plowden's *In a Free Republic; Life in Cromwell's England*, page 91, describing the "squatter problem" at Whitehall, when it was discovered that aged grooms and widows of former royal servants of Charles I were living over the stables.

– Page 218, "walkmill powder." A walkmill was a fulling mill where cloth was thickened by beating with mallets. The resulting powder was mixed with egg white and wheat flour; the paste was laid on cloth, and applied to stanch blood.

– Page 252, "To the keeper of the Prison"—I am indebted to Johan Winsser for this letter. In his manuscript, he states: "Dyer's writ of incarceration survives," footnoted "Copeland, *Secret Works*, 1659, 19-20."

– William Robinson's words to the court and Endicott's response exist in many of the records of the period, as do Mary's words to the court at both of her trials.

– Some Quakers owned slaves until as late as 1784, when Quaker opinion turned decisively against slavery, and Quaker reformers united in condemning it (*The Quakers in America*, Thomas D. Hamm, Columbia University Press, 2003, p. 34). Slave ownership is a dark and shameful irony in the history of Quakerism, deserving of further exploration (see Linda Spalding's 2012 novel, *The Purchase*). I decided to include the presence of slaves in Mary's world without exploring the moral dilemma they may (or may not) have caused over a century before the condemnation, leaving the stage clear for Mary's own considerable personal struggles. However, I believe that Mary would have been opposed to slavery on principle, no matter how well a slave may have been treated, as reflected in the letter that I imagined her writing to Aunt Urith about the Pequot slaves brought into Boston.

Here are some of the books and resources I used (a complete bibliography can be found on my website, www.powning.com/beth).

Mary Dyer:
Manuscript biography of Mary Dyer by Johan Winsser, unpublished; *Mary Dyer*, Ruth Talbot Plimpton, Brandon Publishing, 1994; *Mary Dyer of Rhode Island*, Horatio Rogers, General Books, compiled, original pub. date various 17th century

England:
English Costume of the Seventeenth Century, Iris Brooke, A & C Black, 1934; *English Society, 1580-1680*, Keith Wrightson, Rutgers University Press, 1995; *English Women's Voices, 1540-1700*, ed. Charlotte F. Otten, Florida International University Press, 1992; *Fire from Heaven: Life in an English Town in the Seventeenth Century*, David Underdown, Fontana Press, 1993; *In a Free Republic, Life*

in Cromwell's England, Alison Plowden, Sutton Publishing, 2006; *John Evelyn's Diary, 1620-1706*, ed. Philip Francis, Folio Society, London, 1963; *Stuart England*, ed. Blair Worden, Phaidon Press Ltd., 1986; *The English Housewife*, by Gervase Markham, ed. Michael R. Best, McGill-Queen's University Press, first publication 1615, this edition 2008; *The Letters of Dorothy Osborne*, J. M. Dent and Sons, 1914; *The Seven Deadly Sinnes of London*, Thomas Dekker 1606, ed. H. F. B. Brett-Smith, Houghton Mifflin Co., 1922; *The World Turned Upside Down: Radical Ideas During the English Revolution*, Christopher Hill, Peregrine Books, 1988; *Women in England, 1500-1760: A Social History*, Anne Laurence, Weidenfeld and Nicolson, 1995

New England and Puritans:
American Jezebel: The Uncommon Life of Anne Hutchinson, Eve LaPlante, HarperSanFrancisco, 2004; *Child Life in Colonial Times*, Alice Morse Earle, Dover Publications, 2009, originally pub. 1899; *Documentary History of Rhode Island*, Howard M. Chapin, Preston and Rounds Co, 1919; *Everyday Life in the Massachusetts Bay Colony*, George Francis Dow, The Society for the Preservation of New England Antiquities, Boston, 1935; *Home Life in Colonial Days*, Alice Morse Earle, Jonathan Davis Publishers, Inc., 1975, original publication 1898; *John Josselyn, Colonial Traveller*, ed. Paul Lindholdt, University Press of New England, 1988 (original pub 1674); *Puritanism and the Wilderness*, Peter N. Carroll, Columbia University Press,1969; *Saints and Strangers: New England in British North America*, Joseph A. Conforti, Johns Hopkins University Press, 2006; *Slumps, Grunts and Snickerdoodles*, Lila Perl, Clarion Books, 1975; *The Antinomian Controversy, 1636-1638: A Documentary History*, ed., introduction and notes David D. Hall, Wesleyan University Press, 1968; *The Healer's Calling: Women and Medicine in Early New England*, Rebecca S. Tannenbaum, Cornell University

Press, 2002; *The Journal of John Winthrop 1630-1649*, ed. Dunn and Yeandle, Belknap Harvard, 1996; *The Puritan Dilemma: The Story of John Winthrop*, Edmund S. Morgan, Little, Brown, and Co., 1958; *The Puritan Family*, Edmund S. Morgan, Harper and Row, 1966; *Wood's New England's Prospect*, William Wood, Boston: John Wilson and Son, 1865

Sinnie:

Shetland Life Under Earl Patrick, Gordon Donaldson, Oliver and Boyd, 1958

Quakers:

A Call from Death to Life, Marmaduke Stephenson, 1659; *Narrative of the Martyrdom, At Boston: Of William Robinson, Marmaduke Stevenson (sic), Mary Dyer, and William Leddra, in the Year 1659*, taken from Besse's account, 1841, reprint Kessinger Publishing; *New England Judged, by the Spirit of the Lord*, George Bishop, General Books, original pub. date 1703; *Quakers and Baptists in Colonial Massachusetts*, Carla Gardina Pestana, Cambridge University Press, 1991; *The Beginnings of Quakerism*, William C. Braithwaite, Macmillan and Co., 1923; *The Journal of George Fox*, ed. Rufus Jones, Friends United Press, 1976; *The Quakers in the American Colonies*, Rufus Jones, Norton Library, 1966

Other:

The Oxford Annotated Bible, Oxford University Press, 1977

ACKNOWLEDGEMENTS

✳

Thanks to Mac Griswold, Director of Archival Research, Sylvester Manor Project, for generous sharing of her own research, for answering questions, and for giving me ideas for materials and sources.

Although Mary Dyer's visit to Barbados did not make it into the novel, I spent fascinating time there. Thanks to author Larry Gragg ("The Quaker Community on Barbados") for answering questions; to Pedro Welch at the University of the West Indies; and to archivists at the Barbados National Archives for pulling and photocopying files.

Thanks to Brian Smith, archivist, Shetland Museum Archives; to Liz Francis, Library Assistant, Massachusetts Historical Society; and to Christopher Densmore, Friends Historical Library, Swarthmore College.

Most of my questions about this period were answered by historians who have spent lifetimes making sense of the past's leavings. I am grateful to the authors of the many books and on-line materials I used, too many to list here.

Huge thanks to the Canada Council for the Arts; a Creative Writing Grant from its Professional Writers Program facilitated the writing of this novel. Thanks to ArtsNB for a generous travel grant. And thanks to the Banff Centre for the Arts and the Leighton Artist's Colony—the first draft of this novel was completed in the Cardinal Studio.

Heartfelt thanks to all those readers who wrote to me during the years I was researching and creating this novel, telling me they were eagerly awaiting my next book. Their faith and enthusiasm kept me going.

Thanks to Ann Patty for her perceptive reading and keen editorial eye.

Thanks to all those at Knopf Canada who worked on *A Measure of Light*: Anne Collins, Marion Garner, Deirdre Molina, Nicola Makoway, Lindsey Reeder, Leah Springate and Five Seventeen.

Thanks to copy editor Angelika Glover and proofreader Doris Cowan for their careful work.

To my most wonderful agent, Jackie Kaiser, thanks for believing in the story from the beginning, for insightful critiques, for endless encouragement, for friendship, advice and tireless advocacy.

To my editor, Craig Pyette, who paid meticulous attention to the smallest detail as well as the largest concept and understood the book in all its facets. Deepest thanks and gratitude for making me a better writer and for being the best possible companion on this voyage.

My most profound gratitude goes to Johan Winsser, whom I discovered online at the very beginning of this project. I found a man with a passion for Mary Dyer, who, in writing her biography, has swept the crannies of history for any gleanings about this mysterious woman. He shared his research, his sources and his insights. He answered every question with deep attention and sent me fascinating ancillary tidbits. For his gracious sharing, his generosity, his fact-checking, his dedication to the truth, and his belief in my novel, I am profoundly grateful.

Thanks to my astonishing mother, Alison Davis, for letting me ransack her shelves for books on Quakers and Quakerism, for having the wisdom not to allow me to attend Friends Meeting until I was eight years old, and for a lifetime of love and support.

Thanks to my beloved family: Jake and Sara, Maeve and Bridget.

Thanks to my father, Wendell Davis, who didn't live to see this finished, but who always asked lovingly about my work, even when he couldn't speak.

And to Peter, my husband and best friend. Thanks and love, always.

BETH POWNING'S previous novels are the bestsellers *The Hatbox Letters* and *The Sea Captain's Wife*. Her works of memoir include *Seeds of Another Summer: Finding the Spirit of Home in Nature*, a collection of lyrical prose and photographs that celebrates the natural beauty of her New Brunswick home; *Shadow Child*, her story of coming to terms with the stillbirth of her first son, which was shortlisted for the Edna Staebler Award for Creative Non-Fiction; and the *Globe and Mail* Best Book *Edge Seasons*, about seasonal change within the natural world around her and in her life. She is a recipient of the New Brunswick Lieutenant-Governor's Award for High Achievement in English-Language Literary Arts. Beth Powning lives near Sussex, New Brunswick, with her husband, the sculptor Peter Powning.